the guy on the left

AN UNDERDOG LOVE STORY
BOOK TWO

KATE STEWART

1st Line Editor: Donna Cooksley Sanderson
2nd Line Editor: Grey Ditto
Cover by Amy Queau of Qdesign
Formatting by Champagne Book Design

For the little people in my life. When you're old enough to read my books, I hope you see how your big little lives inspire me. And how beautiful I think all of your colors are.

Your loving Aunt Katy

prologue

CLARISSA

FLIPPING DOWN MY VISOR MIRROR, I APPLY ONE LAST COAT OF gloss and then tousle my hair for a little volume. I spent hours this morning picking out the perfect dress, before bronzing some of the morning sickness out of my complexion. Somewhat satisfied, I smooth my hand over my dress, caressing my bump.

"Here we go, Peanut. Do me a favor, and let me keep that granola parfait down. Okay? Just give me half an hour. But if you can swing it, a full day would be greatly appreciated."

Nerves firing, I gather my purse and lock my car, darting my eyes around the parking lot before making my way toward the building.

The next twenty minutes will be life-altering. Mustering up my courage, I send up a last-minute prayer as I enter the school with a belly full of butterflies, the culprit responsible for this champagne buzz hard to pinpoint today.

And though some of the details are still fuzzy, I can't credit the baby for all this nervous excitement. It's a memory that has some of this anticipation thrumming. Those eyes, those lips, that night. It would've been hard to forget, even if I didn't have a constant and growing daily reminder.

I'm romanticizing and have been for the last few days.

While I'm sure it has a lot to do with the hormones, I can't credit it all to the pregnancy. It's the memory of him and the hours we spent—eyes locked, skin slick, hearts pounding. It was easily the hottest night of my life. But the truth is, no matter how often I fantasize about it, it was a no strings attached hook up.

Well, it was supposed to be, until the faulty condom listened to that feisty little sperm and staged a coup, which will result in his or her arrival in a little under five months. The first month I'd been oblivious, too caught up in the start of my career as a teacher. The next month, I'd spent in denial, though I'm not the type to avoid any situation. I take pride in the fact that I'm a planner, though my best friend, Parker, would say I'm an organizational freak, which I think is a plus considering my profession. But once I'd dealt with steps one and two—denial and shock—I decided confrontation could wait until I'd successfully completed my first trimester.

Before confrontation was acceptance and that's when the wooing started, a sure sign that he or she takes after their father. Because I'm already in love.

With the baby, not the father.

No, when it comes to him, the reality is I'm mortified. But today, I decided to let hope reign. And my hope is that maybe we can get some of the spark back from that night, form a connection of some sort, even if it isn't romantic, for the baby's sake. At least that's what I told myself this morning when I'd polished my body and painted my lips. It's a real possibility that I've waited too long. Because here it is over four months into the pregnancy, and I haven't worked up the courage to tell him yet. But that ends today. I know guys like him don't often stay single, and if my memory serves me correctly, he was a rarity. The idea this news may ruin something personal for him sinks in as I guilt myself for waiting too long. I bat that worry away, determined to see this through.

"No matter what, we'll be okay," I murmur, running my fingers along my belly before gripping the glass door and pushing my way into the reception area.

"I'm here to see Troy Jenner. Can you tell me what classroom he's in?"

The receptionist looks me over skeptically. "Are you on his emergency contact list?"

"I'm sorry?"

"That kind of information is only for those listed on his emergency contacts. Even so, I'd have to call him to the office."

"I'm sorry, I'm a little confused. Mr. Jenner is on staff here, correct?"

The woman snorts before taking a bite of her apple, speaking around a mouthful. "Troy Jenner, teaching here? Now *that* would be something."

I physically jerk back, and she sees it.

No. No. No. No. No. No. No. No. Please God, no!

Swallowing, I unintentionally palm my stomach, and her eyes follow. Suspicions raised, she leans in for closer inspection.

"And who are you again?"

I haven't said who I am in relation to Troy, and we both know it.

Think, Clarissa.

"I'm h-his stepsister."

She doesn't believe me. I wouldn't either. Because it's a lie. A lie that could cost me everything.

"Ah," she says skeptically. "Well, I'm really not supposed to, but," she glances at my baby bump, "if this is an emergency?"

"I'm afraid it is," I reply gravely. Her eyes fill with pity as my mind races back to that night at the bar.

"I just started teaching high school at Round Tree, first year."

He grins before taking a sip of his beer. "What a coincidence, I'm in my fourth at Burns."

From then on, it was all smiles, suggestive looks, followed by moans, grunts, and thrusts, inducing the best orgasm I've had in years. All of that bliss gave way to a hellacious morning after, though I had no regrets, until this very moment.

Because the man I've been fantasizing about is no man. Troy is a student. A high school student.

All of my hopes, along with any idiotic and romantic notions, disintegrate as I grip the counter to keep my knees from buckling.

I'd taken a half-day to deliver the news knowing this was my only way to get it to him. We didn't exchange numbers, our clothes the only thing we'd swapped when re-dressing in his back seat. Ironically, this is a detail I could never forget. Throwing caution to the wind for just one night to get some much-needed vitamin D had led to an alcohol-induced pregnancy in the back seat of a vehicle.

And *this* is the cherry on top? I'd procreated with a fucking high school student?!

Reeling, I swallow back the bile climbing my throat as the receptionist summons Troy to the office.

I could walk out of this school right now, and he would be none the wiser. But the sin he's committed, his blatant lie, has forever altered three lives, one of which he helped create. That can't go unaddressed.

It's too late to turn around. No part of this can be undone, and I'll forever hate him for putting me and his unborn child in this position.

Anger, like I've never felt, fills me as I stand in wait for the man who has betrayed me in a way I can never forgive. Surely, he's seen enough headlines for these types of scandals to know what consequences I would face if our tryst were ever discovered. And now, I'm walking evidence of said union.

He'd deliberately deceived me, so purposefully, that my imminent need to feel his flesh against my palm and sub his balls for a sparring partner is all-consuming. I could blame it on the hormones, but the truth is, I'm livid, disgusted, mortified, and a thousand other emotions I have no choice but to conceal, so I don't implode in front of the school secretary. My hopes for some semblance of a relationship with the father of my child has just gone from maybe to never. He looked like a man, fucked like a man, but was, in fact, a teenager.

I will face him today with the intent of never laying eyes on him again. If he has even the smallest amount of conscience, this news will turn his world upside down and instill in him some of the terror racing through me.

Reading my hostile posture, the receptionist, whose nameplate reads Mrs. Garrison, speaks up from where she sits in front of a group of incoming students. "Mr. Brown's office is empty today, if you'd like some privacy."

"Thank you."

She nods, again eyeing me with sympathy as I try to mask my fury. I'm too pissed off to feel any sort of comfort.

Once inside the small office, I sit behind the desk, nerves firing off at random. I only have a few minutes to grapple with what I'm going to say. But what is there to say? My reason for being here has completely changed. Realization hits me fully that I already have my answer without even discussing it with Troy. I'm going to do this alone—as a single mother.

I lift my phone to text Parker so she can give me the go-ahead to slice and dice some accordion-textured flesh to make new earrings, but it's then I hear his voice call out to the lady at the desk. The timbre only slightly familiar, but it's the distinct voice of a *man*. Even so, there should have been other hints. How, how could I have not known?

Vodka. Too much vodka.

"Stepsister?" He asks, clearly confused as he opens the door, his curious eyes meeting mine before widening in recognition. He pauses halfway inside the small office before lowering his gaze to the floor. "Thanks, Mrs. G." He shuts the door putting his weight against it, head hung, his hands on the knob behind him. I hide the bulk of my belly beneath the desk as I glare at him. Letting out a steady breath, his eyes again lift to mine.

"How old are you?"

He ambles toward me, looking very much the same as he did months ago, though my perception of him has definitely changed.

He's beauty and deception.

Tall, incredibly built, biceps bulging beneath his T-shirt with corded muscles gathered at his shoulders. Rusty blond hair, glacier blue eyes, slightly-wide prominent nose, square granite jaw, full lips—the features of a man and he's anything but.

"What I did—"

"You didn't regret nor feel an ounce of guilt for, until this moment. How old are you?"

He swallows. "Clarissa—"

"Oh, good, you remember my name. Because you were completely clear with yours, *Troy Jenner*. And, apparently, that's the only truth you spoke that night."

He hangs his head. "That night, I was so—"

"Buzzed? Me too. Yet, I still knew my numbers. Especially my age, and I could recite my alphabet and put the letters together to form the truth. How. Old. Are. You?"

He blows out a defeated breath. "Nineteen, in November. I failed sixth grade."

Pressing my lips together, it's all I can do to keep from screaming. I've never been so angry in my life. I give myself a few seconds to get it together but can still hear the shake in my voice when I'm able to speak.

"I should be relieved." Furious tears gather in my eyes. "But I'm not. And do you know why?"

He slowly nods, his eyes roaming over my face, neck, and chest, which has me recoiling.

The kicker of it is, that night, I felt an attraction to him I rarely have for other men. A connection, even though our common bond for those few hours was mostly physical need, or in my case, to ease the ache of loneliness after a breakup. I'd felt alive with him in a way I hadn't in years. I wasn't about to use the pregnancy as an excuse, but I hoped maybe he'd seek me out. When that didn't happen, I resigned to use that night in my future fantasies. Problem is that now I have been imagining him for *months*. Our easy conversation, the way we clicked, the way he kissed me, covered me, consumed me, made an impression that lasted. And now, as water gathers in my mouth, I fight the urge to be sick at the idea of just how often I replayed that night in my head.

It's all too obvious it was a foolish pipe dream as I sit in the middle of my worst nightmare. Troy runs a hand through his hair as his Adam's apple bobs, those blue orbs scouring me in inappropriate appreciation.

My stomach rolls as my anger boils over.

"I went to college for five years, Troy. *Five*. To make a difference. To mentor young minds. To help promote growth, so that one day those young people can become what they dream they can be and you—"

"Clarissa, I'm sorry—," he says, his hands up. "I've thought about you, but I knew—"

"I'm not a bad person," I bat my tears away, looking up at him with incredulous eyes. "But you know damn well what we did will make me look like a predator."

"We didn't do anything wrong, not legally."

"You're a teenager, a fucking student." I stand abruptly while his gaze follows the path of the hand used to accentuate my baby bump. "What did you do?"

His expression goes from remorse to disbelief as I round the desk and confront him face to face.

"Tell me, did you laugh to yourself the whole way home? Did you check some fucking sick fantasy off your list? Carve a T for teach in your bedpost?"

His eyes are still fixed on my stomach. "You're—"

I reach back and slap him as hard as I can. Palm burning, I barely recognize the indignation in my own voice. "Don't ever, *ever*, contact me. Don't come looking for me, for us, ever. You will have nothing to do with this baby. *This*," I emphasize, rubbing my belly, "is solely mine to *love* and a secret for you. A *secret* you will take to your grave and live with for the rest of your life."

He palms his jaw, his face reddening from my slap. "I deserved that, but please—"

"Don't even think about pleading your case. You don't have one."

He reaches out a hand to stop me when I attempt to step around him.

"This is not up for discussion. You're a fucking child. Don't touch me," I jerk away from his grip. Tilting up to meet his watery gaze, I glare at him. "I mean it with every fiber of my being. I never want to see you again." Opening the door, so he knows the discussion is over, I meet the stare of one Mrs. Garrison. She'll be one of four that will ever know who the father of my baby is. I say a silent prayer, tears I'm unable to stop streaming from my eyes as she looks on at me with a slow nod. If she knew who I was, if she, for one second, knew the real reason for my outrage, I have zero doubts my life would be over. But she doesn't, her eyes telling me that woman to woman, my secret is safe.

"Clarissa," Troy calls to me weakly, standing where I left him in the office behind me. I glance back to see a thousand emotions swimming in his eyes, but my anger outweighs anything he may feel. "Please let me talk to you."

"Stay away from us," I hiss before walking out.

1ST QUARTER

SUMMER

one

TROY

I SAW MY SON FOR THE FIRST TIME ON SOCIAL MEDIA BECAUSE Clarissa changed her profile pic. Her account was set to private, and I dare not think she would ever accept me as a friend. But I thanked God for mother's pride when she updated her picture with his birth announcement.

Dante Oliver Arden was born October fifth, eight pounds two ounces, twenty-two inches long. If I had any doubts about her claim that I fathered him, which I didn't, they would've been dismissed the minute I saw him. He had my hair color, my nose and chin, and *her* last name. But he was mine, and after laying eyes on him, I was his. After a stellar game where I scored three touchdowns, which earned me a visit from a scout, I found out I was a father. Once I'd returned from the out of town game, I'd visited every hospital within a ten-mile radius of the school she worked at and found she'd checked out the day before. At eighteen, I'd become a dad, which was both elating and devastating—because my son entered the world fatherless.

At the time, I was unprepared for all the responsibilities that title entailed. I had nothing to offer, but something inside me was dying to try and fill those shoes, at least in the sense of being present. In my eyes, any father who tried was better than none at all, which was the hand I got dealt. My dad is as deadbeat as they come. Something happened inside me with every promise he broke. I didn't want to be that father to my own son, but I knew, without a doubt, Clarissa had meant what she'd said to me in that office. And because of the position I put her in, I had no choice but to sit back and watch.

Well, I always had a choice, but none that didn't include jeopardizing her career or didn't put her in a situation of defending herself and causing her more harm. Not only that, I had shit in the way of supporting them both. I figured Clarissa didn't make much on a teacher's salary, especially in the first few years, and I knew if I worked my ass off, I'd get a scholarship for ball putting me in a better position to help her financially. That I managed to do but was red-shirted my whole first year of college due to player ineligibility. They had no space for me to start, leaving me on the sidelines. The upside was I got to keep my full ride and without school and ball, I could concentrate on supporting them both. I'd managed to find a gig working for a shit load of cash. I'd saved a few thousand, bought a new truck, and was finally ready to approach her, to approach them both, when my Mom lost her job, putting me back at square one.

A few times over the years, and selfishly I'd give up for a while, justifying it with the thought they might be better off. And then I would study my son's picture, watch his videos, and all notions would leave me.

So, I watched.

For years, I watched.

I'd follow her home from her school and watch Dante play in the little park across the street from her apartment. I stalked her on social media, which paid off because I got to see him take his first steps on Instagram. When he began talking on one of her videos, I was filled with a father's pride but had no one to share it with. Not even my own mother, who I know without a doubt, will never forgive me once I finally reveal the truth.

Clarissa shared so many milestones on social media that I'd foolishly convinced myself she was throwing me a bone. So one night when he was three, after a little liquid courage, I finally made a move by leaving a new car seat on her porch along with some cash hidden between the pages of my favorite children's book, *A Light in the Attic*. After that night, I'd catch her scanning the parking lot every so often when she carried him from the house, but when she spotted me, I was never acknowledged. Not once.

I felt like I was on trial every agonizing minute I watched but endured the punishment because I deserved it. In hindsight, it was the most selfish thing I've ever done, boldly deceiving Clarissa the way I did that night.

But now I long to hold my son, more than I fear her wrath. I long to tell him the good things I know about life. To give him his first football.

I know, without a doubt, now's the time to take action, or I'll regret it for the rest of my life.

I'm done watching.

Today's the day I meet my son.

I'm between places due to my old roommate moving in with his girl. And with Mom shacking up with her long-time boyfriend, I no longer have a room at the house I grew up in. So, the minute I spotted the ad for a vacant room in the house next to hers, I saw it as a sort of sign.

Dialing the number, I say a silent prayer.

"This is Theo."

In the locker room, I stuff my gear into my duffle. "I'm calling about the room for rent on Ohara drive. Is it still available?"

"Yes. I've gotten a few calls, but it's still up for grabs. Are you a Grand student?"

"Yeah," I mutter low as Kevin shoulders his bag and draws his brows in confusion at my conversation. "I play on the team."

"Ah, well, I'm the half-time show."

"In the band?"

"Yep."

"Nice."

"Thanks. So, the room is five hundred a month, including utilities. I've already rented the other out, so you'll get the smaller of the two."

"I don't have much anyway. When can I see it?"

"When are you free?"

Glancing at my watch, I see Clarissa won't pick up Dante for at least another hour.

"How about now?"

"Now's good for me."

"Give me fifteen."

"See you then. What's your name, man?"

"I guess that would be a good place to start, Troy Jenner."

"Ah, Jenner." His pause has me tensing. "Well, I mean no offense, but this may not be the house you're looking for."

I keep the indignation out of my reply. "I'm looking for peace, quiet. No bullshit."

Kevin chooses that exact moment to try and get my attention by dropping trou and presenting me with his nut-sack. Eye level with his balls, I rise from the bench and deliver him a bitch slap that would make a pimp jealous. He has the audacity to act offended, screeching when I grip him in a headlock.

"Get your dick beaters off of me, Jenner!"

Theo sounds up on the other end of the line, hearing the commotion. "Are you sure about that?"

"Positive," I grunt out, pushing Kevin away from me after gifting him a quick knee to the jugular. I have about thirty seconds until he regains motor function, maybe less. Kevin gasps on the floor, ass out, holding his neck as I step over him and cover the mouthpiece of the phone.

"Lance Prescott is the other who just rented out a room. Do you two get along?"

"Sure." I glance at Lance a few lockers down where he's packing his duffle, his usual 'fuck off' air surrounding him. He's known as the team mute and keeps mostly to himself, but he's a beast on the field, which has earned him mad respect from me. He's the only other Texas Grand Ranger with enough talent and attention to get drafted, which in a way, makes him my main competition for the draft, but I don't hold it against him. He defended his way into his spot, just as much as I ran my way into mine, and it's my hope we both get a contract come draft day.

"I mean, we're not exactly tight. He's not much for words."

"There's your peace and quiet. See you in fifteen."

"See you then. Thanks, man."

I end the call and nudge Kevin on the floor. "Dude, what the hell is wrong with you? That call was important. Get a ride home. I have shit to do."

He grunts as he lifts himself from the floor. "Why are you still looking for a place? I told you, Harris has room for you in his apartment and won't charge you shit."

I look over to where Harris stands airing out his junk while smelling his socks.

"Yeah, well, I'm over all the clowning for the moment. Including yours, dumbass. Later." I head out of the room, passing coach's office door, thankful he's on the phone. He doesn't bother glancing up.

Making my way to the parking lot, I weigh the cost of living next door to my son. It will be tight, but I should be able to make it. Though it would be more money smart for me to live with Harris and take the free ride, it's time I make a stand where Dante is concerned. Clarissa still refuses to cash the checks I mail, though I know she needs them, but teaching must be paying off because the house she rented is a pay grade above her last two places.

Now might be the time to finally stake my claim for a place in his life, but the fear is real. I don't want to make her life any harder, but Dante's passed the point of recalling his first memories, and I'm determined that from this day forward, I want as many of his memories as possible to include me.

"Dude, where's your head at?" Kevin asks, nudging me.

"Huh?" I ask distractedly pulling out my keys.

"You constipated, man?"

"What?" Kevin keeps up beside me as I head toward my truck.

"I've been talking to you for like, five minutes, and the whole time you've had this 'need to shit' look on your face. What in the hell are you thinking about?"

"Nothing...coach. He seems off. You know what's going on with him?"

"No clue. But God help us." Kevin does the sign of the cross as I unlock my truck, and he jumps in the passenger side.

"I told you to find a ride."

He shoots me a devilish grin. "Just drop me at the library."

"When are you going to take the hint? She's not feeling you, like at all."

"Nah, she loves me, she just doesn't know it yet."

"Fine, and I hate to say it, bro, but you're setting yourself up for failure." It occurs to me then that the statement might be just as true for me as it is for him.

Tracey's Incredible Breakfast Bake
Wildlife Photographer, California

Makes 8 servings
45 minutes

1 Can Flaky Grands Biscuits
8 Ounces Shredded Cheddar Cheese
½ Cup Milk
5 Eggs – Beaten
1 Cup Cubed Ham or Cooked Ground Sausage

Cut each biscuit into quarters. Mix all ingredients together saving biscuits for last. Pour into a greased 9x13 casserole dish.

Bake at 350 degrees for 25-30 minutes.

two

CLARISSA

After a quick stop at the market, I pull up to Dante's daycare, and his teacher greets me as he climbs in the back. "Hey, Peanut, have a good day?"

He wrinkles his nose. "It was a five at most."

His teacher and I share a smile. "Hi, Tammy."

"How are you, Clarissa?"

"Hanging in there. A few more days of mental prep and I think I'll be ready for another year of teaching teenagers."

"I don't envy you," she chuckles. "I like them much younger. Especially this little stinker."

"I'm fond of him too," I say, glancing back at Dante as he buckles in. "Most days."

"He got in trouble for trying to record on his phone during naptime." She hands me his cell.

"Sorry about that. He knows to leave it at home." I direct my sharp tone back his way, so he knows I mean business.

"I've seen his videos, they're pretty awesome, and my son loves them too. You've got a budding star on your hands."

"Don't I know it," I grin. "But I'll have another talk with him."

She ruffles his hair. "This one is bound for great things, and we had a talk today, no worries."

"Okay, thanks."

"Have a good one."

"You too." She shuts the door, and I glance back in my rearview.

Dante sinks into his seat, ready with an excuse. "It was only a minute."

"Son, we've gone over this."

"But I'm too old to nap."

"Uh uh. You're getting to be a big boy, but I need a few workdays before school starts. Just hang in there. Big school in *two* sleeps."

"I'm sorry, Mommy. I'll do better."

"You are better. You're the best."

"I know," he deadpans. I laugh, and he nods toward the dash. "Old Town Road."

I'm already shaking my head. "No. No way."

"PLEAAAAASE," Dante orders in the same tone I use when I'm at my wit's end.

"Motown?"

"No Motown! *Old* Town."

"Is there any other song?" I implore for mercy. "Like anything? I'll listen to tribal music, French rap, I'll even try bluegrass. Anything but that song."

"Mommmmmy," he whines impatiently.

I lift my head to the heavens. "Why, Lord, why? You gave him "Achy Breaky Heart," wasn't that enough? Couldn't you have just stopped there? Did he have to make another hit that was so annoying it makes you want to chum up and feed yourself to the sharks?"

Dante giggles behind me. "What is "Achy Breaky Heart"?"

"It's just as ridiculous as "Old Town Road" is, but for you, I'll play it. If it will keep me from hearing that song one more—"

"Fine, "Baby Shark" then!"

"God, no! "Old Town Road" it is, you little diva!"

My cell rings just as I hit play.

"HA!" I say as Parker's name flashes on my screen, and I show it to Dante. "Saved by Auntie Parker."

Dante kicks the back of my seat. "Fine. I guess you can answer it."

"Well, thank you very much for your permission, son." I hit answer and cradle the phone into the mount on my air vent. "You just saved my life by calling."

"Oh?" She says sweetly. "Why is that?"

"Your nephew wants to hear that song again, and this time, I may have driven us off the road. What is it about that song?"

"What song?"

"Old Town Road," Dante pipes up behind me, making sure Parker knows he's present. There's only one person on earth he loves more than her, and I'm the lucky one.

"Oh, I love that song. Hey, Duckie!"

"Hi, Auntie Parker!"

"What's wrong with "Old Town Road" anyway?"

"Never mind. You suck. Worst best friend ever," I grumble.

"Mommy, that's not nice!" Dante scolds. "It's my *favorite* song."

"Mine too," Parker giggles when I let out a miserable groan.

"It is not. You are so fired. Seriously, why can't you agree with me, just once?"

"Sorry." I can hear the smile in her voice.

"No, you're not. And in order to make it up to me, you have to stay on the phone for fifteen minutes, so I don't have to listen to it."

"I've got time to kill."

"Heeey," Dante protests behind me.

"Quiet, son, adults speaking."

"Yes, ma'am." He pulls out his tablet from the lip of my seat and puts on his headphones. When I hear one of his downloaded videos start, I know I'm in the clear.

"How's London?"

"London is fine."

"And the other part of London?"

"Not fine. Horrible. It was the worst blind date in the history of ever. He didn't know I was supersized, and I didn't know he had skin scalp. We both exaggerated the truth, and not only that, we were both too picky to live with it. Isn't that sad? I'm going to be the old lady in the home who talks to her shoes."

I can't help my laugh. "You are not."

"I am. I'm going to be that woman who wears the same sweatsuit and has in-depth conversations with her bunion cradling loafers. Just promise me something?"

"You're ridiculous, but what?"

"Promise you'll wax me."

"Wax you?"

"The only thing worse than being the old lady who talks to her shoes is the old lady with a unibrow and a mustache that talks to her shoes. Don't let that be me, buddy. Please, don't. I'll set up a fund specifically for waxing. Promise me."

"First," I say taking a right that leads us toward home, "you won't end up in a home because you've got me."

"You'll be married."

"I'll outlive him."

"Great. You'll be mopey, and I'll be hairy."

"Hush. When are you coming home?"

"Not for another three weeks at the least."

"Gah, this sucks. I miss you."

"Same here."

"Sorry about your date."

"I have a chest full of tartar sauce to clean up. I swear these tits are a shelf."

"You're nuts," I giggle.

"Well, dinner was on him, so I went bananas with the fish and chips. It was the least he could do for orgasm denial."

"Agreed."

"Clarissa?"

Her tone turns serious, and instantly, I wish she were in front of me. I hate that her job requires so much travel. We've been inseparable since our freshman year at Grand, more so after I gave birth to the love of her life.

"Yeah, babe?"

"He's out there, right?"

"Yes, and he'll love you like crazy."

"Swear?"

"Swear."

"Sorry to be needy."

"It was a bad date. You're not needy. And starting something there would be pointless anyway, your home is here."

"True. Kiss that kid for me."

"Will do. Love you."

"Love you, too."

"Now, chin up and go clean that tartar off those hooters."

"On it."

"Night, buddy."

"Pip, pip. Cheerio."

I take the streets that lead toward home thinking of how long it's been since I've been on a date. A year? Longer? I tell Parker all the time to take a chance and put herself out there, all the while not taking my own advice. It's a lot harder to simply date around with sensitive ears and an impressionable boy to keep in mind. For years it's been just the two of us, and I've been content with that. But I'm not getting any younger and with Dante's next birthday drawing near, I hear the biological tick getting louder. He's asked me for a brother or sister on several occasions, and on those, I've always been thankful I've been able to distract him from the conversation. But my kid's no pushover, and he's starting to prod, becoming more demanding. Soon enough, he'll have real questions that deserve real answers.

The first and one I fear most being, 'where is my father?'

three

TROY

FTER DROPPING KEVIN OFF, I TAKE THE FIFTEEN-MINUTE drive to the house and pull up, relieved when I don't see Clarissa's SUV. The rental house is a pale-blue, two-story sitting on a quiet, residential street. It's a nice spot for a budding family. When Clarissa moved Dante here, my stalking became a lot harder. I've had to drive by in the later hours of the night, parking on the opposite side of the street to catch glimpses of them here and there. After long, stressful days on the field, and before work, I take comfort in watching her read to Dante in an old recliner she's used to rock him to sleep since he was a baby.

Relieved about the delayed confrontation, I take the steps up the porch and glance around. The house is a well-kept duplicate of the one next door. A few rough knocks later, I'm greeted by Theo, who ushers me in while I welcome the burst of cool air wiping my brow. He looks fresh out of high school, a little wet behind the ears. Shaggy, but well dressed.

"AC works fantastic, but the plumbing is slow. I'm Theo," he says by way of greeting, extending his hand. I offer him mine.

"Troy. Nice to meet you, man." Stepping into the living room, I scan the furnishings. It's not anything I'd expect. The furniture is old, the walls mostly bare.

"I haven't had time to put much up," he says, closing the door and heading across a decent-sized living room toward an adjacent kitchen. "Something to drink?"

"Yeah, thanks."

Opening the fridge, he scans the contents briefly as I join him in the kitchen. He grabs two bottles of Gatorade, twists off the tops, and hands one to me.

Theo seems to have a decent disposition and a chill attitude. I can already tell we'll get along well. I dwarf him in size, which is ironic because he exudes an air of authority with the way he carries himself. He reads my mind about our physical differences and commands my attention, drawing a line in the sand. "I may have misled you a little on the peace and quiet. I play a lot of different instruments. I practice in the basement and mostly at night. I'll work on getting it soundproofed when I can afford it. Needless to say, the basement is off-limits. But the rest of the house is common area."

"Not a problem, I work nights and sleep like a rock no matter what goes on around me."

He eyes me curiously. "How do you manage graveyard, school, and ball?"

I've been doing it for years to help support my mother, and I'm used to running on little to no sleep, but I spare him the details and shrug. "It's the only way for me to work a full forty."

"That's rough," Theo says, cupping the back of his neck while silently assessing me.

I shrug. "That's life, right?"

"Hustler on and off the field, huh?"

"Yep."

"I can respect that. I am too."

He gives me a quick tour of the upstairs. Inwardly, I celebrate the fact that from my room I'll have a bird's eye view of Dante's. It couldn't be more perfect. Theo watches me as I stand in my would-be bedroom, staring out the window. "So, if you don't mind me asking, why your interest in this place?"

"My last roommate is about to marry up, and I don't want to move in with any of my friends, too much traffic. Just want to get away from all the bullshit, concentrate on school and ball. I'm always up for a good party, but on my own terms, ya know?"

"I get it. But I warn you now if you change your stance, this isn't a frat house."

I nod. "Cool with me. I'll have some friends over to watch the games from time to time, if that's all right?"

"That's cool. Lance is quiet. Like a ghost, so it's pretty uneventful around here. I don't expect much. Just a few rules. No keggers, pay rent on time, and clean your own shit up."

I can't help my grin at his stern tone. I already like him. "I can handle that."

He smiles back. "Well, other than that, mi casa es su casa."

"Sounds good. If it's okay, I'll take it." I cringe as I pull out my wallet. "I, uh, shit, this is embarrassing. I don't exactly have the first month's yet. This move was sudden, but I'll have it next week."

He shrugs as he pulls a key off his chain. "I'll take half now, half next week."

"Sure?"

"Yeah, man, I'm not hurting for it at the moment."

"Hey, thanks." I take the key and pull out a couple bills from my wallet.

"Neighbors are pretty cool. Mrs. Abbot is a widow and travels nine months out of the year to see her kids, and to the right, we have Clarissa and Dante. She's a single mom."

Hiding my cringe, I nod.

"Dante is five. He's a cool kid."

Father's pride runs through me at his statement. "Oh yeah?"

"Yeah, hilarious but a handful. She's a teacher, so we need to be mindful of them both. But she's pretty laid back." He turns to me. "Easy on the eyes. But don't go there." He's only half-joking, and it's apparent my reputation precedes me. I make no move to correct him because there's no point. I take advantage of my position on and off the field when it suits me, which is too often to play innocent. I'm no saint.

"I think I can handle it."

"I'm not much for yard work…" he trails off as we head downstairs. "But I cook a mean pancake."

"I've got the yard," I offer. "And I've been known to fuck up some pancakes."

"This'll work out perfect." He pulls an instrument case from the floor. "I'm off. Make sure you lock up when you leave every time. Non-negotiable. I have a shit load of expensive equipment downstairs."

"Got it."

"Welcome to casa de la Houseman."

"Thanks, man."

He leaves me to my own devices, and I spend a few minutes looking around. I have little in the way of possessions, a few in my truck due to the demand of my old roommate and his girlfriend for some immediate space. He all but threw me on my ass the minute she accepted his proposal under the Era Tree and gave me until the weekend to get the rest of my shit out. I make quick work of unloading the few boxes I have when Clarissa pulls up. Nerves of the unknown shoot straight up my spine. Bracing myself for impact, I set my box on the porch steps as she hops out of her SUV in a sundress, her auburn hair catching the light as Dante bursts from the back door. She grabs him by his backpack just as he runs past the hood of the car.

"Dante, I've told you a thousand times not to do that. You need to look before you leap. You never know what's going on around you."

"Gah, Mom, we're home. Duh."

"I've got your duh," she grumbles before circling her SUV and pulling a bag of groceries from the floorboard. "I said, don't do it, so don't do it."

"Yes, ma'am." He runs up the porch steps and opens the screen door. "I'll get the door for you, m'lady."

Shaking my head, I watch from the yard as she shakes her own head in amusement while trailing behind him. I've been waiting for this moment for almost six years, but fear paralyzes me where I stand openly gaping at them both. I'm so close in distance but so very far away. It's surreal to have dreamt of this day for so long and have it here. It's a bold move, but the only one to take. I'm about to meet my son for the first time. And ironically, Dante is the first to notice me when he gets the door open for her.

"Who are you?"

Clarissa follows his line of sight over to me, the smile disappearing from her face as the bag slips from her hands.

"MOM! You broke my sunny-sides!" Dante says in a huff, before bending over to gawk at the open carton of eggs.

"Dante," she chokes out. "G-g-get in the house."

She grips his shoulders in protective mode, eyes widening when I begin to cross the lawn. I need to play it cool, but years of pent-up longing pound against my chest as I make my way toward my son.

"Hey, little man. I'm your new neighbor," I introduce myself as I slowly approach the house. Dante moves to greet me stopped short by the iron grip of his mother. "I said, get in the house *now*."

"Mom, he's not a bad guy. He doesn't even have tattoos."

"Now, Dante!"

"Fine." He turns back to look at me with his hand on the doorknob. "What's your name?"

Dad. Daddy? What would he call me if given a choice? I've been waiting for this moment for so long, emotions are running rampant inside me. It's all I can do to even my voice when I answer.

"Troy."

"See ya, Troy." I look after him as he shuts the door, aching to bridge the distance and study him up close. A gnawing in my gut keeps me from taking a single step because I know I'll be denied that privilege as I have been for the whole of his life.

When I'm sure he's at a safe distance away from the door, I take the few steps up the porch toward Clarissa, who's glaring at me with tears in her eyes.

"What are you doing?"

I hold my hands up with a, 'please, just hear me out.' I bend down and start gathering her scattered groceries. The acid in her voice above me is exactly what I expected.

"I told you never to come near us. I meant it. You know I meant it."

I lift the tattered sack once I've gathered everything salvageable. "I just want him to know me. I just want to know *him*."

She gapes at the box I left on the steps behind me at the neighboring house. "You moved in next door?"

"I just want to keep an eye on him. He's my—"

"Don't," she hisses, "don't you dare say it. You can't just show up and claim parental rights."

"That's not the truth of it, though, is it? I know you've seen me. I've seen you see me. I'm done pretending, Clarissa. If you move again, I'll follow. You move then, I'll do the same. I'm not going anywhere. It's time we met. Past time. And I have to know him," I choke on my words because it's hard enough looking at her knowing she hates me and my chances of making this work are slim to none, but I have to try. "For him, please," I ask, looking up, my eyes pleading with hers.

She crosses her arms and shakes her head. "He's missed nothing."

"You don't know that."

She rips the bag from my grip. "No."

I shove my hands in my pockets and toe a loose wood board on the porch. "I've been doing more than watching, and you know it. You won't take my money, why?" I look up to see she's still got tears in her eyes and hate the sight of it. It's understandable she's scared. At the moment, I feel every part the villain her stare accuses me of being.

"I don't need your money."

"You have needed it, plenty."

"I don't want to have anything to do with you, Troy. Dante doesn't need an adolescent and conniving liar for a father."

"I'm almost twenty-four, Clarissa. I'm not that kid anymore."

Her eyes rake me up and down, and I can't help my smirk when they pause at my crotch before lifting back to mine. She's nowhere near as amused.

"Move out."

"No."

"You can't just do this."

"Then tell me how. Tell me how to get through to him.

Because I want to be a part of his life. You can't keep me from him forever."

"The hell I can't."

"I have rights."

Her face visibly pales. "You lost any rights you had when you lied and put both of us in jeopardy, and when I say us, I mean him and me, not you."

"*Legally,* that's not true. I have rights."

Panic flits over her features before her back straightens. I've triggered mama bear, and all I can do is admire her for it. I shake my head. "Don't even think it. I would never dream of pulling you into something messy like that. First of all, neither of us can afford it, and I don't want to do that to you, but I need you to let this happen. I'm not making excuses for what I did. I just want to do right by him. I know where you stand and how you feel about me. I just want to know him. Please, just let me know him."

Strangled by emotion, I think back to the night I spent listening outside her living room window when he had colic, and they both cried. Watching as she decorated a Christmas tree alone that she could barely afford. And the next morning when she celebrated alone, no family to ever come around, just a friend that pops up every so often who never fails to put smiles on both their faces. I caught Clarissa mid-breakdown once when I'd pulled up. She sat in her SUV and just cried because life had stressed her to that point, and all I could do was helplessly watch. I might not know the particular ins and outs of all that's gone on, but just by observation alone, I know it hasn't been easy and that she's done it all on her own. That guilt I'll never overcome.

"I've watched you struggle all this time just to be able to take care of him. I know what you're going through."

"You have no idea what it's been like."

"But I do. My mother's name is Pamela."

She draws her brows. "Okay, so?"

"My father's name is also Pamela."

Her tears fall, but she lifts her chin, her expression stern as she tries not to show the weakness, the vulnerability I've seen glimpses of over the years. Years she thinks I've spent carefree, but my frustration in the knowledge that my son exists without a father has far outweighed any adolescent highlights. Even when I'd selfishly tried to turn a blind eye, tried to move on, since the day she showed up to my school, I've never been free.

It's been crazy just how much I've wanted to know him since the announcement of his arrival. While everyone in school was scrambling around for a way to pay for a limo at prom, I was trying to figure out a way to chip in with Mom to keep the lights on *and* stalk my son's Easter egg hunt.

"I can't change what I did, but maybe I can change your opinion of me in the responsible sense. Please. I *am* his father, and I can *be* a father to him. Please just let me try."

She chews her full bottom lip as I patiently wait for her to mull it over. I don't think this woman has an impulsive bone in her body. Matter of fact, the words "I never do this," poured from her the night we hooked up. She sighs heavily as she scrutinizes me.

"There is no *trying*, Troy. If it doesn't work out, you don't get to go on your merry way. That's not how this works."

I nod. "I know. It…just, fuck," I sigh, palming the back of my neck, "came out the wrong way."

"Yeah, but you have a penchant for twisting words when it suits you, don't you now, *Mr. Jenner*?"

"There's no way to tell you how much I regret lying to you in that way."

I can't even bring myself to regret the rest of it. Often, I wonder if at times, she remembers just how fucking spectacular that night was. Instead, I'm browbeaten by just how much she wishes it had never happened. I want to regret it, but no real part of me ever has. Not even when I felt at my lowest.

"Why are you doing this? You have football and college. You're telling me you can handle this *now?*"

"You been keeping tabs on me?" My playful grin is met by a scowl. I clear my throat. "Look, all those things considered, I've been in your parking lot every spare minute for almost six fucking years, Clarissa. I think I've proven he's a priority without even having met him, despite the ways you've thrown my offerings away. You want more proof? I'm offering it, right here, right now. You make the rules, I'll follow. I'm just asking for a chance."

Studying me carefully, I see the war waging in her mind, in her clear-blue eyes. I can still remember the jolt I felt when I got my first glimpse of her up close. Fiery dark hair, bee-stung lips, and perfect features. At twenty-three, she was a stunner when we met. At twenty-nine, she's a fucking knock out. She seems to read my mind and her eyes narrow. "Don't ever let what you're thinking past those lips."

"You're even more beautiful than you were the night I met you."

Her eyes narrow to slits. "If you're that bad at following simple directions, how do I know this will work?"

"Sorry, couldn't be helped. It's just...good to see you from less than ten feet away."

"You're not helping your case at all."

Sinking where I stand, the idea of being so close, coming this far just to get the door shut again is too much to handle. I reach in deep and speak straight from the heart.

"I can't stop myself from being here anymore. This is tearing me apart and has been for years. I need to know him. I have to know him. I can't live with myself any longer, and I can't live another minute without him knowing me. All I'm asking for is a chance to prove myself a worthy father. I'm not discrediting anything you've done. I just..." I close my eyes, willing myself to stay strong, my words coming out in a ragged plea. "Please, just give me a chance." Opening my eyes, I take a step forward, my hands covering my chest, imploring her. "I'm not here to hurt you. And I would end myself before hurting him. Please."

After the longest minute of my life, she sets the bag down on the porch and holds out her hand. "Give me your phone."

Heart singing, I hand it over as she programs her number in and slaps it back in my hand. "You are the *neighbor*. You can start that way, and we'll see how it goes from there. Don't you dare come around unannounced. You have no say in his life until I decide otherwise. All decisions concerning him are up to *me*."

"You've done an amazing job with him."

"I had no choice."

Anger flaring, I push that to the side and try to reason with her. "I'm telling you now that you do. I want this job more than I want to play pro ball. But I'll respect your wishes. You call the shots, *neighbor*."

"Neighbor first," she props open the screen door with her hip, and I hold it for her while she palms the door handle. "Then we'll see."

"Thank you."

"Don't thank me. I don't want to give this to you, but you've given me no choice."

"And you've done the same. Does I'm sorry matter?"

"No."

I exhale a heavy breath. "Didn't think so."

The pulse point at her neck jumps as I crowd her a little at the door. "Eventually, maybe, we could be friends? It wouldn't hurt to try."

She snorts out her disgust. "You can't be serious."

"Right," I nod and take a step back. "I'll go."

With the door open an inch, she pauses, seeming to run through her thoughts. Hopeful, I step back into her space as she leans over in a whisper. "He could use some new shoes. Boys size seven and a half."

I chuckle. "Big feet, huh?"

She glares at me.

"Sorry. Okay, what else?"

She bites her lips, and I know it's her pride keeping her silent. "Nothing."

"Clarissa, please."

Her shoulders drop. "I wasn't able to get him many new school clothes. I'll text you his sizes."

"Thank you."

"I should have known better." She seems lost in her thoughts. "Speak, or even think of the devil, and he shows up at your door."

"So, you've been thinking about me?"

My comment snaps her back into the present. "Get over yourself, Troy. This is for *him*."

"I know."

I have no fucking idea how I'm going to dress my son because I just gave the last few hundreds I had to my new roommate. Her voice cuts through my rambling thoughts.

"I'll never forgive you."

Lifting my eyes to hers, I see the hurt there. It's residual. And it's then I know she does remember that night, and exactly how good it was, and it strikes me hard just how badly I fumbled with her.

"I don't expect you to."

She hesitates briefly before she opens the door and shuts it soundly behind her.

The ball lodged in my throat as I cross the grass is nothing compared to the voice screaming inside my head.

Don't fuck this up.

ERICA'S CROCKPOT FIESTA CHICKEN
Forensic Scientist, Indiana

Makes 6 servings
45 minutes

4 Boneless, Skinless Chicken Breasts
1 Packet Fiesta Ranch Mix
1 Can Black or Pinto Beans
1 Can Rotel
1 Can Corn (not drained)
1 8 oz. Block Cream Cheese

Place chicken in crockpot and pour Fiesta Ranch Mix evenly over chicken. Pour beans, Rotel, and corn into the crockpot but do not stir them together. Lay block of cream cheese on top of mixture.

Cover and cook on low for 4 to 5 hours or until chicken is tender. Remove and shred chicken. Add chicken back into the crockpot and stir well to mix all other ingredients together.

Great served over rice or may be eaten with tortillas.

four

CLARISSA

TOWELING DANTE OFF, I PEEK OUT THE BATHROOM WINDOW for the umpteenth time as he tells me about his day. The first day of kindergarten is a breeze, according to my little man.

"Jase is not as smart as me. Neither is ugly Carly."

"Not nice," I remind him as he puts his hands on my shoulders, and I pull up his underwear, studying his profile. After seeing Troy up close a few days ago, I realized just how much he favored his father. It had been so long that I'd almost forgotten how striking, fuck that, how ridiculously hot Troy is. Even more so now. My baby's wet lashes are as thick and long as his. His eyes the same brilliant blue.

"Mommmmy," Dante draws out, "did you hear me?"

"No, buddy, what did you say?"

"I said that Carly is ugly."

"Even if that's your opinion, you keep it to yourself. Do you hear me? She could turn out to be a good friend one day." He shakes his head beneath the towel in protest as I scrub off the excess moisture. Once he's dry, I study Dante carefully to try and distinguish which of his features are mine.

Noticing my scrutiny, he widens his eyes and leans in with his nose pressed to mine, drawing out my laugh.

"Why are you looking at me like that?"

"Just looking, Peanut."

"I'm not a peanut. I'm getting *bigger*." He flexes, and I end up on my butt in hysterics as he exaggeratedly shows off his muscles while pinching his hands making twin beaks and animatedly moving them back and forth. "These swans are legit."

I agree through my laugh. "*So* big."

"Don't say it like that. I know you're just playing when you say it like that."

"You may be getting big, but you'll always be my baby," I say, gathering his dirty clothes as he struggles with his shirt before poking his head through the hole. "I'm going to be as big as Troy one day."

I bite my lip, doing my best to hide my reaction. Hearing Troy's name from his lips is earth-shattering. "There's a really good chance you will be."

"I'll be so big. You'll see. Then I can tell Carly she's ugly."

"No, son. You can never ever tell Carly she's ugly. Ever. Being bigger doesn't mean you can pop off at the mouth and hurt people's feelings."

"I heard you tell Parker that Mr. Brown was destined for shit city."

"BOY!" I turn him to face me, eyes bulging.

"Sorry, just saying it the way you said it."

"Do as I say, not as I do. I wasn't insulting him, and I said he was destined to float shit creek. If you're going to quote someone, do it correctly."

"K." He looks up at me, confused. "Mommy, what's a shit creek?"

"Dante, let's breathe for a second here. It's been a long day. Let's save the rest of the questions for later. Don't you have a video to make?"

His face lights up. "Yes! I'm doing a review today!"

"Awesome. Go ahead and make it while I get your dinner ready, and I'll approve it after."

"K." He runs off just after I get his sock on. In the kitchen, I unwrap some leftover Fiesta Chicken and slide it in the oven. Moving to the living room, I take my syllabus out from my leather brief and grab my red pen before getting cozy in my recliner. Teaching high school is challenging. Finding a way to keep kids interested in more than Instagram or Snapchat these days is damn near impossible.

Last year was by far the hardest of my career, and I'm determined to turn things around this year and find new and creative ways to get them to interact during class. I'm a few days into my lesson plans when voices outside my window grab my attention. At the blinds, I curse my curiosity. Troy admitted he watched, and that he saw *me* watch. I did know he was watching. Of course I knew. I'd been aware of him since he left the present on my porch along with the envelope full of cash. Truth be told, I'd spotted him before that but refused to acknowledge it. When he left the gift, he gave me no choice but to recognize his lingering presence. But, no matter how many times our eyes met over the crown of his son's head while I walked him into my apartment, or how remorseful or pitiful his expression, especially in my weakest moments, I'd always slammed the door behind us. And still, he'd refused to stay away. His truck parked facing my apartment, on guard.

My disgust and contempt for what he did was by far the easiest grudge I've ever held. Living through labor alone had sealed my anger. He'd robbed me of the chance to experience it with someone capable of feeling the same type of emotion. Not a kid who had a curfew and a prom date waiting. I had no intention of letting him back into my headspace. But one long look at him on my doorstep had made it impossible not to. Of the words he spoke, he seemed so sincere in his apology, in his eagerness to prove himself, at least concerning Dante. But he'd also seemed sincere the night he talked my panties off. Years ago, with anger being my motivator, I swore what I said was true. I would never get over what he did. The way he manipulated his way between my legs.

I could never trust him for myself, but for Dante?

He's been more persistent in the last few years with his gentle stalking. He'd respected my wishes from afar trying to be a silent support. I'd torn up his checks and, even in the most desperate of times, refused to cash one.

Over the years, I've tried to rationalize what he did, tempted at times to open the door and wave him in to get temporary relief from the hellacious days, but I never did. Because deep down there was still that voice of pre-baby Clarissa, who held too much resentment for his disrespect for my life, my career, for my plans.

And what would happen if he got a pro ball contract? Was his son a hobby?

Still, if he took measures to move so close just for the chance, who am I to deny him a relationship he could very well legally fight for? He's given me all the power, though I was forced to make the decision on the spot. Troy might not be able to afford an attorney now, but the minute he signs a pro contract, he will be able to afford the best. An unethical decision is not illegal. Lying doesn't make him an unfit parent. He does have rights.

"Damn you," I whimper as I watch Troy and a few of his friends unload his king cab. "Must be nice," I stare at his truck with longing before darting my gaze to my ancient SUV, which only has one AC setting. Freezing. Which is helpful on sweaty ass-to-leather days, which Texas is notorious for. Still, I can't deny my little man and I have come a long way from the one-bedroom apartment with the broken dishwasher. Admiring Troy's physique as he lifts a table from the bed of the truck, I sigh, resting my temple against the window. I've got an annoyingly clear view of him due to the last of the sun setting behind him.

"Why can't you be ugly like Carly?" Bright blue eyes blaze my way and pin me where I stand. He knows. He knows I'm watching him. His intrusive, penetrating stare followed by the twist of his lips and flash of teeth are enough to have me jumping back.

Busted.

"Shit," I mumble, mortified, just as my table lamp goes down. I know, without a doubt, he saw the room go dark.

"Mommy?! What did you break?" Dante shouts from his bedroom like he's scolding a child. Thanking God for my son's laziness in seeing for himself, I move to grab the broom and dustpan.

"Just a light bulb. It was hot."

"You owe me three dollars for today! Five dollars from last week! Curse monster!"

"Yes, son. But you said shit twice today, so we're even!"

"Give me a dollar and we're even. Now be quiet, I'm recording!"

Yeah, well, your 'hot as hell athlete daddy' just moved in next door, and your 'haven't had a proper penis in ages' mommy is hard up. How about a little grace?

"Don't talk to me like that, buddy, or I'll soap your tongue!"

"Mommmmy. I'm on take three now because you can't be quiet!"

"Sorry!"

"Gah, now take four!"

I sigh and try my best to keep my laugh quiet. The boy is serious about his videos on his YouTube channel, which he titled The Legit Life. In a way, it scares me, but he has enough personality for the two of us, it keeps him busy, and none of his info—including his name—is public, which gives me a little relief. I'm letting him have his outlet while monitoring it like a hawk. There's a whole hell of a lot more he could be discovering instead of reviewing games, and other vlogger's videos. So, like the old married couple we are, I've compromised. My son, though not quite six, is very much the man of the house.

Due to his arrival and unbelievably early skill set, I've never been in much need of a handyman. And I have no idea where he got it, but the boy is my own personal superhero. He can hook up anything with the word 'smart' attached to it in a matter of minutes. He's taught me more in his near six short years than any other human I've ever met. He's smart in a way that scares me and far more advanced than I can grapple with.

Once I've swept up my lamp, I resume my seat in the chair just as a soft tap sounds on my front door. I know exactly who it is.

I open it with my hip hitched and both hands on my side.

"Troy." My greeting is anything but friendly.

Towering over me, his 'I just ate the canary' smile is dazzling, and I want nothing more than to wipe it off his face. "Just wanted to make sure you were okay. I saw your spill from the street."

"I'm fine, *unannounced* neighbor."

He leans in, all six-foot-four inches of man steel, his coppery blond hair soaked in sweat, his T-shirt riding high on his bicep.

"Haven't had a girl fall for me that fast in some time. I'm flatt—"

The door is shut and locked before he can finish his sentence, but I hear his muted chuckle on the other side just as Dante comes out from his bedroom. "Who was that?"

Satan? My arch-nemesis? The living, breathing reason women stereotype?

"Just the mailman."

"No, it wasn't. It was Troy."

"Fine, it was Troy. He heard the lamp break, and he was checking on me. Ready to eat?"

Dante walks past me and opens the door.

"Hey, Troy!"

"Dante, no!"

Troy turns back, amused by the address of his son and jogs over to where Dante stands, his arms crossed. Out of breath, Troy leans in close, his hands on his knees to lessen the difference in height. "Yeah, buddy, what's up?"

"I'm the man of this house. If you want to know if my Mommy's okay, you ask me." Troy's smile slips, just as Dante slams the door in his face for the second time.

I widen my eyes, mortified. "Dante!"

"You always whisper to Parker, 'monkey see, monkey do.' Well, I'm your monkey."

Shit. Round one million, point Dante.

five

TROY

S CRUBBING MY JAW, I STEP BACK FROM THE FRONT DOOR AS
Kevin howls with laughter behind me.

"Damn, dude! That kid is off the chain!"

"Tell me 'bout it," I mutter as I take the steps down from
the porch, defeated.

"Is she as hot up close as she looked standing from here?"

I glare at him as he lifts the bulk of my mattress from
the yard.

"Don't even think about it."

"That has to be the hottest fucking MILF in the state
of Texas."

Kevin drops my mattress choking just as I withdraw my
hand from a swift blow to his throat.

I'm an impulsive man by nature, but that nature has to
change if I'm going to stick in the mind and heart of my
son. It's my first order of business as a new father to keep
those impulses in check. Kevin is my first fail.

Oops.

"What the," he coughs out, trying to regain his breath
as I lift my mattress and leave him kneeling on the grass.

I know I don't have a chance in hell of a repeat of the
night my son was conceived, but I have to admit it's been

hard watching her over the years and wondering *what if* I hadn't fucked up. The truth is, she was out of my league then, and even if I hadn't lied, I wouldn't have had a shot due to her job and the age difference. She was a teacher, and I was a teenager. If I'd started with the truth, she would have laughed me out of the bar, not to mention blown my cover. I'd been tossing back suds after hard days for a year at that place. I had the calloused hands of a hard-working man and the bills and responsibilities to go with it, so I had absolutely no issues bending the law or the rules to take the edge off. The edge of a life my mother had so tirelessly tried to pave smooth for the both of us.

My looks were deceiving then, and I'd used them to my advantage. Life never really had been fair to the Jenners, so my 'fuck it' mentality was par for the course. It seemed a harmless lie that night. Clarissa had been on the prowl. It'd been easy to tell the minute she stepped up to the bar and ordered a martini in her little black skirt. Once our eyes met and she took the seat next to me with a knowing smirk, there was no turning back, at least not for me. We were both clear it was a hookup. Never in a million years did I think it would bring us to this point, and neither did she. But the truth is, 'all in good fun' sometimes comes with serious consequences, and I've been careful since not to let any of my hookups go too far without making myself crystal fucking clear.

I know that my verbiage at times may be a bit harsh with the ladies, I can see it in the faces of the women I bed. That, in and of itself, has given me my reputation. But I live with my guilt, and my regret daily, so the words tend to come easy when it's time to speak up.

I fuck like there is no tomorrow because there isn't. My plans are ball and making a connection with my boy. That's my future. That and making sure my mother never has to work again. Pamela Jenner gave me a life, the best life she could having had me at age seventeen, and marrying my piece of shit father on a whim a few years later to make her family seem legitimate. The only relief she got out of that union was the day Dad slammed the door shut with his departure.

So far, the love of my life has been an inanimate object, a pigskin ball, and the feel of it in my hands as I fly toward the end zone. Clarissa is right to be leery of me for what I've done, though I'm capable of more. But since that day at school, I've been hard-pressed to aim for more than playing pro ball.

That day changed my life in more ways than one. It was my wake-up call. The first lesson that Clarissa unknowingly taught me was that no one with a hard life has a free pass to be reckless, careless, or heartless in any situation.

And even though I'm here by the skin of my teeth, I can't resist egging her on. She'd been watching me for a good five minutes before I called her on it. That's been our game for six years. Old habits die hard, and the only reason I caught her is because I'd been looking her way myself. I can't think, for one second, this is a mistake. I won't. But every move I make has to be the right one.

After lugging the mattress up to my bedroom, Kevin and I stick it on the frame before he leaves me to unpack. After sorting half my shit, I sneak a look through my blinds to see Dante playing in his room. In about five minutes, Clarissa is going to walk in and have him read her a story. Last year it was just the opposite. My son reads now. I'm not sure on what level, but he's getting pretty good at it because he finishes the books in record time compared to how long it used to take him. He's so smart, my son.

My son.

He wasn't a mistake. I refuse to believe it. I will be whatever he needs.

For my son.

It's time to be a father.

THERESA'S PULLED PORK
Legal Assistant, Dallas

Makes 6 servings
6-8 hours (in slow cooker)

2 Lb. Pork Roast
1 12 Oz. Bottle Root Beer or Dr Pepper
1 Bottle Barbecue Sauce (I like Sweet Baby Ray's sauce)

Place the pork roast in a slow cooker and pour the Root Beer or Dr Pepper over the meat.

Cover and cook on low until well cooked and the pork shreds easily (usually 6-7 hours but may vary depending on the slow cooker and size of roast).

Drain well. Shred and return to slow cooker. Stir in the barbecue sauce and continue to cook on low until sauce is heated.

Serve on hamburger buns.

Hawaiian buns are great with this. Also, a side of coleslaw and Southern Style potato salad make a really great meal.

six

CLARISSA

TOSSING MY FAVORITE LUSH 'SLEEPY' BATH BOMB IN, I MENTALLY unplug from another week of teaching youths about ancient books the world has mostly forgotten about. Students are a lot more outspoken and opinionated than they used to be in my school years. The web has given them false confidence that theirs is the only opinion that matters. I catch hell from the girls who I can see openly scrutinizing the way I dress and apply my makeup, and the guys, well, the guys are still guys. Some of them little Troys, great genetic makeup but infuriatingly cocky. It seems to be a daily pissing contest amongst the little Troys I teach on who can get the biggest reaction from me. I like my men bold, but the operative word is *men*, not little jockstraps with a recurring Proactiv monthly charge who have barely hit their second growth spurt.

I cringe at the thought that only years ago, I'd taken one of those at that inexperienced age between my legs and enjoyed every second of it.

Troy had acted like no boy. But was he really so different? The only conclusion I can draw is no. He was not. During my morning coffee on the porch yesterday, I'd caught him escorting a girl out on her walk of shame. She looked melancholy as he bid her goodbye. He might be capable of fathering as he claims, but he's still a wildly sought-after college senior, apparently still getting where the getting is good. And I can't exactly blame those women, Troy is ridiculously appealing, with his athletic build and natural swagger. I'm sure to women of all ages and types, Troy's that guy. The guy others want to be, and the one women fawn over. He had wooed me after all, and I'd been raised by a womanizer. Even with my grudge, I must admit there's definitely a sort of charm, a charisma about him.

Too bad I hate his guts.

I'm about ten minutes into my soak when Dante's conversational voice distracts me from my read, so I gather myself from the tub and unplug the water. It's when I hear the gruff voice in reply that my whole body goes on high alert. Troy is in my house. I angrily towel off, dressing with my hair still soaked.

How dare he go back on our agreement so soon?!

I can already tell this arrangement isn't going to work. Throwing open the door, hair dripping, I march into the kitchen where Dante stands dictating his day off to Troy while he washes his hands in my sink.

Troy's gaze trails up my frame, his eyes resting briefly on my pert nipples through my tank, before his smile fades as he sees my repulsion to his attention.

"Troy cut our grass, Mommy," Dante says uneasily, reading my temperament. "I wanted to give him some of the lemonade I made. He told me you wouldn't like it if he came in unannounced, but he did something nice," Dante explains as if I'm a four-year-old while I have a silent standoff with his father.

In response, I glare at our intruder, unable to hide my aversion to our new neighbor. I've been able to keep him away for nearly six years, and suddenly he's everywhere.

"Mom-*my*, he's not in trouble. He did the yard. It was nice of him." Troy's hair is disheveled and in need of a cut. Sweat runs down his throat, his skin darker from his stint in the sun. He's shirtless, his rippling muscles jarringly defined from the light workout. He stands satisfied with his son's protection as his neon blue eyes burn into mine.

I once read if you stare down a dog long enough, you prove your dominance if the dog is the first to look away.

I lift a brow in challenge, refusing to blink.

Troy's thick lips turn up before he drops his gaze to the floor.

That's right, Fido. Now, go lick your ass.

"He, uh, insisted," Troy says as Dante tugs me into the kitchen by my hand.

"Don't be mad. I'll make some for you too, Mommy."

Because my son is nervous, guilt wins, and I try to reel in my anger. "Okay, baby. That was nice of you to offer."

"Mommy, you're supposed to say thank you," Dante scolds, widening his eyes in expectancy. He's trying to impress Troy, and nothing about that sits well with me. Troy turns, arms crossed accentuating his broad chest, weighing me carefully. He's so imposing in our kitchen, the space too intimate.

I pull my hand from Dante and excuse myself. "I'm going to finish getting dressed. Can't wait to taste it. Thank you for cutting the grass, Troy."

He slowly nods, unsure if I'm plotting his death. I am.

"You're welcome."

I walk away knowing revenge is a dish best served cold and chuckle when I hear Troy's sputtering after he takes a drink of Dante's lemonade.

"This…is," cough, cough, "well, this tastes great, little man."

"I know. Mommy, yours is on the counter!"

Checkmate, Fido.

"Thank you," I shout through my grin. Point Mom, thanks to little man.

The next morning I'm scrambling around the house as my son watches me at a standstill from the door.

"Don't just stand there, son, we're late!"

"I'm not late," he taunts from the front door. "You're late!"

"I'm not late, we're behind!"

"Behind is late!"

"Uh," I scan the living room. "Where's your bookbag?"

"Got it," he says, lifting it up as I frantically load my purse.

"Oh, no! Your lunch!"

"Got it," he says, patting his backpack.

"No, you don't got it."

"Bread, jelly, crunchy peanut butter, and an apple. I didn't cut it because I'm not allowed to use a knife. It's *so hard* to make peanut jelly with a spoon. For snack time I put a bag of Sun Chips and *one* cookie not two."

I stand, stunned. "You made your own lunch?"

"You're late!" He reminds me.

"Right. And no, you can't use a knife."

He rolls his eyes. "I could put your seat belt on for you too, Mommy." The look I give him scares him into backpedaling. "I went too far?"

I can't help my laugh. "Yes. And even if I'm laughing, I'm not happy. Let's go."

We both burst through the front door and nearly trip over the bags of clothes and shoes on the porch.

Dante rummages through the boxes, his face lighting up. "Size seven and a half! Are these for me?!"

Eyes bulging, I look through the bags briefly before I put

them into the entryway and attempt to lock the door, but Dante stalls me, tossing his shoes to the side of the porch and pulling one of the bags into his lap.

"Can I put these on? Puh-lease?"

Hiding, I turn to lock the door, wiping a stray tear away. Troy had to have dropped these off after his shift, leaving them at the door to avoid waking us and blowing his cover. Thoughtful.

You hate him, Clarissa.

"Mommy, can I try these?"

"Of course."

"Where did they come from?"

"Just something I ordered," I say as he ties them, admiration clear in his features before we make our way down the porch steps.

Dante looks up at me skeptically. "They weren't in a package."

"New service."

He doesn't believe me. I wouldn't either. I'm a horrible liar. I climb in behind the wheel as Dante buckles in. "These are the kind I wanted for school, like Austin's!" I had assumed Troy forgot or ignored my request for help with the clothes, but clearly, I was wrong because Dante now has hundreds of dollars' worth of new gear. I look back at him, marveling at his animated face while trying not to burst into tears.

"They're so awesome."

Whoever said money can't buy happiness, forgot what misery is like on piss-poor days. Unable to help myself, I glance at the house next door and see it's lifeless from the outside. I want my anger back. I want it back so much. But gratitude is all I feel as we pull out of the drive.

A large part of me does hate Troy, but for Dante, I'll try.

seven

TROY

I T'S BEEN THREE WEEKS SINCE I'VE MOVED IN NEXT TO DANTE AND I've made a little progress. Between my shifts at UPS, practice, school, and our first away game, I've had little time to do much more than catch Dante a few hours after school. I'm still the neighbor, so I can't see him every day, but in doing what I can, I've made enough headway that my presence is no longer questionable but more routine. I'm hoping it's a start. Clarissa has yet to look at me like I'm not shit on her shoe, but she's no longer watching our every move. Dante comes over once in a while with permission to play Xbox with me. I make good with the time, careful with my words. "Take that, sucker," Dante utters from his seat next to me, working the controls like a pro as I study him. We look so much alike it's uncanny, and I take pride in that.

Mom will never forgive you for this.

I've never told anyone that I'm a father, not even my mother, who I'm closest to. I have a few reasons. The first is because I'm ashamed of what I've done. The second is that she very well would have reprimanded Clarissa for something that was entirely my fault. Pamela Jenner invented the phrase 'mama bear,' and in her eyes, her golden boy can do no wrong. But the most important reason is that if I told her, I know she would make it her mission to be a part of Dante's life, and I have yet to earn that privilege for myself. I don't want Clarissa to hate me more due to a confrontation with my mom because she is a force to be reckoned with. She's my best friend, and when I finally do confess, I know it will irreparably break her heart. She's missed nearly six years of her grandson's life. But to be fair, so have I. Still, she won't understand, and there's no way she'll ever fully forgive me.

As with Clarissa, there will be no redemption, but I'll try my damnedest to make amends with them both.

"Did you know?"

Dante eyes me from where he sits on the couch, his feet swinging.

"Know what, little man?"

He rolls his eyes. My eyes. His mother's eyes. We both have the tricked-out blue. Clarissa's are lighter. Maybe they're hers. "The trick I just showed you."

"No, I didn't. Good one."

"You weren't even listening," he grumbles.

"Sorry. I was just wondering if you're hungry?"

He shrugs, his attention back on his game. "I could eat."

I shake my head. How does a five-year old speak like such an adult? His mother, that's how. And I love that about her. She's no bullshit. She wasn't the night I met her. She's brutally honest, and though she would never believe it now, aside from my lie and the fact that I lived for ball, I was myself with her. Dante commands respect, much like her, and much like my roommate who walks in the room, dumping his backpack on the floor.

"Sup, guys?" Theo asks, making his way toward the couch.

Dante's eyes light up. "I showed Troy the trick you taught me."

"Yeah?" Theo asks, taking a seat next to him. I pass him my controller.

"Grilled cheese?" I ask Dante.

His eyes light up. "Yes, *please!*"

Pride fills me. Dante has manners in abundance, though I can't take any credit. Making my way to the kitchen, I hear Dante rambling to Theo.

"Cup your balls, you're going down."

Theo cracks up, and I do too. But I know Clarissa wouldn't appreciate that language. Is this where I begin to parent? And if I do, will it break our new connection and embarrass him? His mother hasn't given me any privileges yet, so I say nothing. That's on her. Knowing what I do about Dante already, he wouldn't take too kindly to discipline from a neighbor.

Dante devours his first grilled cheese and damned near begs for another, so I make myself busy catering to him as he slides into easy conversation with Theo. I think on some level, it's easier for Theo because he grew up with siblings. I'd been more of a loner up until high school when I started running and hit a growth spurt. High school was easy for me because ball paved the way. It'd been an avenue of wealth after I got my braces off and discovered my talent for catching and running with that pigskin in my hands. I developed then too, along with my taste for pussy and it was a whole different world. I ran with the sudden attention and popularity, especially with the ladies, like every other red-blooded male would, but I wasn't as privileged as my friends. Always driving my mother's beat-up Dodge around on the weekends rather than getting my own, so I took and took until I choked on greed. All of that ended the day that fiery redhead slapped it out of me.

I deserved what I got. Karma and all of her friends, especially humility, came and made it known, a man is only as worthy as his last act.

As much as I want to admit I've grown up, I do still partake when the pressure gets to be too much. But that's got its own set of problems.

The front door sounds and I glance at the clock knowing exactly who it is. She doesn't let Dante hang for more than an hour or two without checking in. Opening the door, I see Clarissa waiting a few feet away as if she's afraid to approach it. She might be a mama bear by nature, but she's wary of me. I take note of her form-fitting blue sundress and pink painted toes.

"Hey, you look beautiful."

She ignores my compliment, her eyes darting past my shoulder. "I, uh, was wondering if Dante could stay a little bit longer tonight?"

"Of course. My shift doesn't start until two."

"In the morning?"

I nod.

"You work nights?" She's looking anywhere but at me.

"I'm sorry, are we having a conversation?"

Reluctantly her eyes meet mine, and I can't help my smirk. I'm rewarded with a scowl. "You know how hard this is for me to ask."

"Sorry, but I'm just wondering why you're having such a hard time looking at me."

"I have a date." She swallows. "Well, not a date, kind of a date. An old friend from college. He wants to have a drink and catch up."

"Good for you. Go. I'll take good care of him."

She hesitates, glancing over my shoulder. "Just forget it. I can do this another time."

"What changed your mind in the five seconds since I agreed?"

"I just…he hasn't eaten dinner."

"I fed him already."

She gapes at me. "What?"

"Grilled cheese."

She palms her forehead. "He's lactose intolerant."

"Shit," I glance back at Dante, who's still mouthing off to Theo on the couch. "Do I need to take him to the doctor?"

"No," she sighs. "He knows better. You've been suckered."

"That's my boy."

Her glare has me swallowing.

"And there's my hesitation. He's probably going to run over you."

I lift my hand, "I think I can handle him."

"Do you?" The smile she's sporting scares the hell out of me. She bites her lip and looks up at me through her lashes. "Good luck with that, neighbor."

"Have a good time on your date, not a date, old friend get together."

She rolls her eyes and sighs. "I'll be back in a few hours."

"Sounds good."

I shut the door and mentally roll up my sleeves. This is my shot.

"TROY!"

I close my eyes and scrub my face with my hand as Theo chuckles from where he sits on the couch.

"Bet you're wishing you didn't offer your child sitting services up so fast."

"How much shit can a five-year old have inside of them?" Grumbling, I take the steps back up to the bathroom and double tap on the door. "Sup, little man?"

"I pooped again."

"Good on ya."

"I need you to wipe me."

"What? You're old enough to wipe yourself. You did the last time, right?"

"Mommy says I don't do a good enough job when I have flare-ups."

"And I say you can do this, bud. And you might want to mention you're allergic to cheese next time I tell you there is going to be cheese in your food."

"I need a wet wipe, not a lecture."

I glance at the ceiling. I'm officially my son's bitch. "On it." I hustle down to the kitchen and wet a wad of paper towels before hauling ass back upstairs.

I double tap the door again.

"Come in here," Dante says, unaffected by the lack of privacy.

"I'm good here."

"No way, I'm not getting up. I don't want poop juice on my new shoes."

Holding my breath, I walk in the door where Dante sits swallowed by the rim of the toilet. He's so small like I was at his age. I hand him the wet paper and step away.

"You can stay," he offers.

"I'll just wait outside."

"You need to check my butt."

I stand there as he painstakingly takes his time wiping his

ass. He doesn't want to deal with his mother's disappointment any more than I do, and I get it. That redhead is fire. "I think I've got it."

Thank Christ.

Dante gets up and turns to flush the toilet, and I jerk back in horror when I see the literal shit trailing from his ass down his legs.

"Don't move!" Gagging uncontrollably, I lift my T-shirt to cover my mouth and open the shower curtain before turning on the faucet.

"What's wrong?" Dante asks as he turns my way.

"Don't move, buddy. This is going to take some skill."

I'm still gagging, my T-shirt giving little aid due to the visual. It's everywhere. I move him onto the rug, carefully stripping everything around the literal shit sandwich he's made of himself. When his clothes are finally off, I lift him up by the arms and dispose of him in the shower, praying to God the water takes care of most of the debris.

"I didn't wipe good?"

Dante looks up at me with innocent eyes, and I can't help the tug in my chest as his lower lip quivers, but I'm gagging too much to console him.

"We'll," gag, gag, gag, dry heave, "fix it."

I thank Christ Theo is high maintenance with his need for a removable shower head. I use it to get most of the crap off him before covering him in body wash. Shrouded from head to toe in suds, I can still see the shittastic mess running down his legs.

"Okay, okay, I've been up against much bigger mountains. I scored a seventy-six-yard touchdown last week after hurdling a defensive end and a safety. I've got this."

Dante giggles, wiggling his butt as my gagging evokes another dry heave.

"Don't move means don't move!"

He frowns. "You're bossy."

"Sorry," I gag again. "Sorry."

"It's okay. You've got this," he encourages, covered from head to toe in Old Spice body wash and shit. He looks over to me with a trust very few do, and inwardly, I melt at his eagerness to please me.

"Thanks," I say as I pull my sponge from the rack and begin to scrub him down. After a few minutes, I finally have him shit free, and get him out of the shower before I start toweling him off.

Dante stands still, lifting his arms up and down to assist me, wiggling when my fingers dig into his armpits. "Ticklish, huh?"

We give twin-like smiles to each other in the mirror. His laughter fades as he takes notice of our similarities. "Heyyy! You look like me!" His statement strikes me right in the chest.

"I was here first, so maybe *you* look like *me*."

"People could think you're my daddy."

My face is the picture of control when I ask him the question I already know the answer to. "What do you know about your daddy?"

"I don't know my daddy."

"You don't know anything?"

"Nope. Are we going to play Xbox again?" He's already over the conversation, while inside, I'm fuming. He begins dressing as I pull out my phone and shoot off a text.

Troy: We need to talk.
Clarissa: Kind of in the middle of something.
Troy: I'm aware, but we need to talk. Soon.
Clarissa: Is Dante okay?

Troy: Fine. He has diarrhea, but I don't think he has much left in him.
Clarissa: Is this what we need to talk about?
Troy: Of course not. You think I would interrupt your date to talk about diarrhea?
Clarissa: Aren't you?
Troy: Jesus, no. Can you cut me a break? I'm doing you a favor.

Instantly, I know that was the wrong text to send. I'm his father. Watching him is not a favor. I just cut my own nose off to spite my face.

Troy: I didn't mean that. I'm happy about this. Spending time with him.
Troy: Clarissa?
Troy: Please don't go postal. I didn't mean that.
Clarissa: I'm on my way.

"Shi…crap," I grunt as I dial her number, and she doesn't answer.

"What's wrong?" Dante asks.

Troy: Please don't do this. I want my time with him.
Clarissa: Fine. I'll be back at 8:30.

I just lost any leverage I had in feeling angry. I'll have to choose another day to plead my case. He should know of me. What I did was wrong, but what she's doing right now isn't right, either.

Clarissa retrieves him an hour later, and as I carry a sleeping Dante home, I notice her lips are swollen from kissing, there's a bounce in her step and a light in her eyes. It's then I know she's hopeful. Hopeful that tonight was the start of something. A something she could never picture with me. For years I've watched her and feel in a way I know her, but in truth, I don't. I've had a lot of time to conjure her up in my imagination, but that's the extent of it. She could never look at me the way she did that night, and I've long since moved on from my selfish fantasies.

I lay him down in his bed and pull his covers up before lingering at his bedroom door. It's another parent thing I haven't had a chance to enjoy, and I take my time, watching him settle into position. I push down the resentment, because keeping the peace is more important for now, for *him*. Everything I do and will do from this moment forward will be for him.

"How did it go?" Clarissa asks on a whisper.

"He had an upset stomach most of the night, but pretty well." I shut his door.

"Keep it cracked."

I follow her instructions and turn to look at her. "So, I'm guessing the date went well."

Her crystalline blue eyes narrow. "None of your business."

I try and disguise the tick of my jaw. "You're right. Goodnight."

She sighs as if drawing her patience. "Okay, I'm sorry. I'm not being fair. Thank you, sincerely, for the clothes and shoes."

"Don't thank me. It's part of my job."

She nods. "Right. Well, it was a relief for me, so can I thank you for that?"

I grin. "Sure. And the date? Or are we not sharing yet?"

"It went very well. For the first time in a long time, I agreed to another."

I tap my temple. "Yeah, it's been a while, hasn't it? What was the last guy's name? He was a total douche."

She frowns. "Paul was not a douche. We just didn't have a lot in common. And it's weird you know these things."

"You refused to let me in. But you let me watch."

Her cheeks redden, and she turns and walks down the hall leading toward the front door. I can't help but study her wavy crimson hair and skin—though sun-kissed—that's pale in comparison. She's incredibly beautiful and although only a foot away, entirely out of reach. "I felt safer."

I'm distracted, but I catch her whisper.

"What?"

She turns to me when she reaches the door and lets out a breath. "I felt safer knowing you were out there. He was so small then, and the lock was flimsy."

"Really?" It's an olive branch, and I eagerly take it.

"Yeah. When I saw your truck in the parking lot, I was able to sleep better."

She looks at me, curious. "You were always reading. Had your cabin light on. What were you reading?"

"Studying, mostly."

"Ah, right." Her expression changes with my confession, and I feel some of the tension return. We reach the front door, and she gives me a look that tells me she's about to level with me. "Look, for Dante's sake, I really want to try this, at least for civility, but it's going to take me a little time to get used to it."

"I get that."

"And I can't promise friendship."

Slowly, I nod. "All right."

"So, we probably need to establish more ground rules."

"My schedule is rough. But give me a heads up, and I'll move shit around. Football is going to take up my weekends, especially on away games, and I work every available shift around that, but I'll do everything I can to be available for you both. I mean that."

She bites her lip thoughtfully, and I imagine another man kissing it. It doesn't sit well with me, and I know then I have to stop fixating on a lost cause. "Okay. If things work out, I'm probably going to want to go on more dates."

"Will you bring him around Dante?"

"I have never introduced any man to my son. You know that."

"*Our* son. And I just don't want to get him confused. I was just introduced, and my own title isn't clear yet."

She lifts her hands. "Too fast, Jenner. Just too fast. I assure you I won't interrupt what's just started, if you promise me you'll keep things the way they are for now."

"Deal."

"Goodnight." She nods toward my house.

"So, what does this new guy do?"

"He owns a real estate company. The one who rents our houses."

"Nice. Good guy?"

She drops her gaze. "I'm tired."

"Me too. So, is he?"

"He was nice in school. He seems to be now. We'll see. People change."

"You're right. They do." I lean in using her words to my advantage. Eyes locked, I get a whiff of her perfume. "They absolutely do."

She rolls her eyes. "Goodnight."

When the door shuts, I don't have to look back to know she's watching me. But I don't acknowledge it or even entertain any of the possible reasons why. I can't afford to make any more mistakes.

LAINEY'S KING RANCH CHICKEN
Finance Analyst, Omaha

Makes 8 servings
1 hour

3 lb. Chicken – Boiled & Deboned – See Note
12 Corn Tortillas – torn into chip size pieces
1 Onion – Chopped
1 Red Bell Pepper – Chopped
½ Stick Butter
1 Can Rotel Diced Tomatoes & Green Chile Peppers
2 Cans Cream of Mushroom Soup
2 Cans Cream of Chicken Soup
4 Cups Shredded, Cheddar Cheese (Mexican Blend cheese is
   also good.)

Sauté onions and pepper in butter in a large sauce pan until tender. Stir in tomatoes, soups, 1/2 of the cheese, and chicken.

Layer 1/3 of the tortilla pieces in a lightly greased 9 X 13 casserole dish. Top with 1/3 of chicken mixture and a layer of cheese. Repeat layers 2 times.

Bake at 325 degrees for 40 minutes.

Note: To save time, a rotisserie chicken will work just as well. Also, boiling boneless chicken breasts or thighs (or a mixture) in chicken broth & water will be quicker than boiling a whole chicken.

CLARISSA

P ARKER LETS DANTE OUT OF THE BOOTH, LOADING HIM WITH coins for the video games as I recite the rules.

"Stay where I can see you. No talking to adult strangers."

"Got it," Dante promises, eyes wide at the number of coins she's filling his little hands with. "Ahhh yeah!"

"You can do better than that," I scold.

"Yes, ma'am. Thank you, Auntie Parker!"

She hugs him tightly to her, and he struggles in her arms while she insists on an embarrassing hug that he would have gladly given her a year ago.

"Are you really almost six?"

"Yep," he says, wrestling her for his freedom. She kisses the crown of his head before she lets him go and joins me on the opposite side of the booth.

"Jesus. This is not a plus-size-friendly booth."

The remark pains me. Parker has always been on the heavier side, but I've never seen her the way she sees herself. She's truly beautiful, and her personality is so endearing, it's all I ever pay attention to. That is until she comments negatively about herself. Parker and I have been friends since our first year at Texas Grand. She's been the one constant in my life since my father died when we were sophomores, leaving me orphaned. My mother died when I was Dante's age. The irony is that my father had been twenty-five years older than her and was the one to die from natural causes.

"Would you stop with that? I hate it when you knock yourself." I tell her as she grimaces from my reprimand. She nods, ogling the pizza.

"Have another piece if you want it. You've only had one."

She forks a bite of salad and shoves it into her mouth. "I'll stick to this," she says, chewing around the bite, "mmm delicious." It's sarcasm at its finest, and I can't help but laugh at her candor.

"You're beautiful," I remind her. "If you want the pizza, *eat* the pizza."

"Nope." She lifts a straw full of soda and lets it go covering the rest of the pie in Coke. "Temptation destroyed. Problem solved."

"What if I wanted to eat that later?"

"You'll thank me."

"Maybe, but please stop talking about yourself that way."

"Fine, fine, okay, I've been gone for an eternity. Give me some dirt."

For the first time in what feels like a century, I have something to report.

"I have a new neighbor."

"Yeah?"

"It's Troy. He moved in next door."

She pauses with the straw halfway to her mouth. "What? When?"

"Last month."

"And you're just now telling me?!"

"You've been busy. I've been busy and in denial."

"What did you do?"

"I'm letting him be the neighbor for now. What choice do I have?"

"I'm going over there."

"Reason number three I didn't tell you."

She shifts in her seat. "I give zero shits."

"Parker, listen to me. Dante still doesn't know. And for now, we're going to keep it that way. Don't come in like a bull in a china shop. We're treading carefully here."

She narrows her eyes. "*I'm* the co-parent."

It's the truth. She is. Guilt nags at me as I think of my omission in our conversations in the last few weeks. "I'm sorry. You're right, but you were in London, and I didn't want you going postal a continent away."

Parker was on the fast track to rich and successful the minute we graduated. She stays with us between long stints overseas. When I first had Dante, she'd been my savior and was able to afford everything I couldn't, which saved our asses on multiple occasions. I don't know what I would have done without her. She's everything wrapped in one, a best friend, a co-parent, and the only family we have. Dante and I wouldn't have survived without her.

"So, is he…is he acting like a Dad?"

"He's allowed to be a friend, for now. We're testing the waters to see how this goes."

"Is he still hot?"

"Jesus. He's so beautiful." I follow Parker's gaze to see Dante playing Skee-Ball. "And I hate him."

"Yeah, me too. But hate can be amazing fuel in the bedroom."

My lips lift into a genuine smile. "I'm covered there too."

She slaps her palm on the table, her inky dark hair spilling over her shoulder as her brown eyes meet mine. "You've been holding out all over."

"This is a new development." I waggle my brows. "Brett Tompkins. We had a drink last week. And there was kissing."

"WHAT!? Oh my God, lady! Is *he* still hot?"

"Hotter."

"Than Troy?"

"We're not comparing the two."

"Well runner-up isn't bad, and he's loaded too. You know that, right?"

"Dinner is all he gets to pay for. And I like him."

Parker frowns. "You were crazy for him in college, that's not the case now?"

"I mean, it's been years since then. I'm getting to know him again. We'll see. And Troy watched Dante."

She sits back in her seat. "Let me get this straight. You've got a hot as all hell baby daddy as a baby-sitter *and* a hot as shit real estate mogul after your ass. Woman, you should be walking on a cloud!"

"I am."

"Gah. Finally. The Lord answered one of my prayers."

"Yeah, well, don't get too excited. You know my dating history."

"I would almost feel sorry for you, but I don't. Please have sex with them both and make this an epic saga so I can live vicariously through you."

"Absolutely not," I snap. "I'm never getting intimate with Troy again. Ever. Are you crazy?"

"Clarissa, he was a kid. He saw your beautiful ass and wanted it. Most guys would lie for a crack at you. You are hot, babe. He didn't know it would backfire like that. And you said a million times that you both used each other that night."

"But it did backfire. And if he hadn't lied—"

"You wouldn't have Dante."

"I know." I swallow the thought. "God, where would I be?"

"I know this. That boy makes you happy. He does. Even if his conception was an accident."

"So, you're on Troy's side?"

"No sides. Not anymore. It's time you both grew up and did what's best for your kid. Let old hurts go. Etcetera, etcetera."

"I am. I think I am. I'm trying, for Dante."

"Good." She eyes me, pushing a lock of her long dark hair off her shoulders. "This is about to get fun."

"Stop. Nothing is going to happen with Troy. He's still using his penis as a Fun Dip. I've watched him walk out two women since he's moved in. And Brett, well, he's a damned good kisser, and you know a good kiss is everything for me."

"Don't you dare hold back again, I don't give a shit if I'm in China, which I will be in November."

"Really?"

"Yep," she says with a sigh. "I'm going on another diet while I'm there." She scrunches her nose.

"Another diet?"

"Clarissa, I haven't seen my vagina in five years." A woman walking by our booth gapes at us, grabbing her son and turning him in the opposite direction.

"Sorry," Parker sputters out apologetically as laughter bursts from me. I shake my head as Parker's brown eyes come back to mine. "Oops."

"You are crazy."

"I'm serious. Our relationship is strained. I would like to

get laid again before I turn thirty. China will heal me, I know it."

I grip her hand across the table. "You're perfect to me."

"You have to say that, I know all of your dirty secrets."

"Shut up."

When the waitress delivers our ticket, Parker places her card on the table.

"No way." Most of the time, my pride speaks up and we argue about how she's wealthy and childless and can afford it, but this time, I slam a twenty on the table and end the fight. "Troy is paying."

A slow smile covers Parker's lips as she wipes fake tears from her eyes. "I'm so proud of him."

I haven't told her that he's been trying to step up, especially in the last year or so. Though she did chase him from my parking lot once, thinking it was a rare pop up on his part. When it came to Troy, I always wanted her to believe he was the bad guy, because to me, he was. But my mind is changing with his consistent efforts, the way he dotes on his son, his need to get along with me. He's kept up his part of the bargain, and that's enough for now.

"Which one are you thinking about?"

"Troy. I pray I'm not screwing up. I don't know if I want someone capable of doing such a horrible thing to raise my son. You know?"

"I understand your grudge, I do, but people change, they grow up. What he did was a bold move. A move he wouldn't make if he wasn't serious. See it for what it is, he's desperate to know Dante. And Dante's old enough to deserve a choice. This is something Dante may not forgive *you* for later."

"I know. I just hope I don't regret it."

Parker winks. "I have a good feeling."

"Last time you had a good feeling, you had me wearing assless chaps."

"And if I recall, that was a damned good night. Grand Girls stay Grand," she holds up her glass in a toast, and I clink mine.

"4 Eva."

CORRY'S QUICHE
Dog Groomer, New York

Makes 6 servings
45 minutes

1 Deep Dish Pie Shell

Line Pie Shell With:
Ham or Bacon – Cooked and Cubed
½ Cup Chopped Onion
¼ Lb. Swiss or Cheddar Cheese – Shredded

Mix and pour evenly over ham and cheese:
2 Eggs
1 Cup Light Cream (Half & Half)
Salt
Pepper
Dash of Cayenne – if desired

Bake on bottom shelf of oven at 400 degrees for 35– 40 minutes.

Cool 5 minutes before cutting to serve.

2ND QUARTER

FALL

nine

CLARISSA

"GOOD MORNING, BIRTHDAY BOY!" I STAND AT Dante's door with a tray in hand as he sits up in his bed with a budding smile on his face. Once I bring the brightly lit pancakes into the room, his smile widens.

"Oh, wow, Mommy. Thank you!"

I set the breakfast tray across his lap. "You're so welcome, Peanut. Happy Birthday. Make a wish."

Dante closes his eyes, and it's then I see his face, Troy's face. It's unreal how close they are in likeness. Anyone in the same room with them could easily draw the right conclusion, which makes me nervous. I'm not ready to uncap the truth just yet. It's only been a couple months. I've decided to wait Troy out. Though he's presenting himself in a capable and more responsible light, this is still new. He could get bored and decide family life is too mundane for him. If that's the case, he's still just a neighbor. It's the safest way to play this.

Dante blows out the six candles easily.

"Are you going to tell me your wish?"

"Nope."

"Good. I like that you're superstitious."

I smile down at him as he digs into his pancakes. "So

tonight, Auntie Parker is coming over. Are you sure you don't want to invite kids from your class to your party?"

"Nope. But can I invite Troy?"

"I've already invited him. He's coming."

He looks up at me. "You told him to come over?"

"Yeah, why not? He's a new friend."

"Is Troy your boyfriend?"

"No."

"Because you're too old?"

Blink.

Blink.

"Yes, because Mommy is old, and her skin's no longer supple."

"What's stupple mean?"

"That's supple. It means I'm a weathered old fart who has nothing on the coeds."

"What's a coed?"

"Eat your breakfast. I'll pull a towel for your shower." I kiss the crown of his head and leave him to it. He catches me on the way out.

"Mommy?"

"Yes, baby?"

"You're still pretty, even if you're old."

"Dante, I'm twenty-nine. I'm not old."

"How many times is that more than what I am?"

"Almost five."

His eyes widen. "You're five times as old as me?"

It's a good thing we don't build our self-esteem off kid compliments, I'd be under psychiatric care.

"Yes, Dante."

"Well, if you want, I'll pretend you aren't old at my party."

"I'm not old!"

"All right!"

Stomping out of his room, I open the bathroom door and rip his towel from the cabinet. "Little turd."

"I heard that."

The doorbell rings and I know it's Troy. It's the first birthday he gets to spend with his son, and I have a feeling he's going to go all out. I march my geriatric ass to the door and open it to see he's fresh-faced, looking like a million bucks, even at the early hour. Due to the natural wave in my hair, and the fact I haven't showered to tame it, I look freshly electrocuted.

"Troy," I say by way of greeting. My mood rapidly souring.

"What's with all the yelling?"

"What?"

"I heard you two going at it."

"Oh, yeah, that." Mom of the year, right here. "Dante and I were just discussing age."

"Is that Troy?" Dante calls from his room.

"Yes, eat your breakfast!" I yell back.

"Well, tell him to come back here!"

"Eat your breakfast!"

"You two need an intercom," Troy chuckles deeply, and I ignore the draw of the sound.

"He needs a muzzle. He's far too observant, and outspoken."

My son refuses to be left out of the conversation from his bedroom. "Troy, did you know Mommy is five times as old as I am today?"

Troy winces. "Ah, I can see why that didn't go over well."

"She's too old to be a suppled coed!"

Troy crosses his arms. "What exactly were you two discussing?"

"She's too old for you!" Dante supplies, humiliating me. "So, you can't be her boyfriend!"

Briefly, just briefly, I imagine using Dante's pillow to silence him.

"You told him you were too old for me?" His ridiculously blue eyes roam my face and trail down. "That's not true," he whispers before he rakes his lips with his perfect teeth. "I seem to recall—"

"Don't go there, I haven't even had my coffee." What is it about men that they are so hard-pressed to make you remember the time they had their penis inside your vagina? I assume it's just another territorial thing, or some fruit of my loins bullshit. But I'm not about to let him have his moment. "Do us both a favor and don't bring that up again."

"Fine. Are you going to let me in?" I step back as Troy steps in, he's got on snug-fitting jeans and a T-shirt, full-on man swagger in his steps.

"I'm going to take a shower."

"Need any help?"

"Just watch him, please. I need ten minutes of peace."

"Just let me know if you find any areas hard to reach. Happy to set a good example in helping the *elderly*."

"Troy, come back here! You can have my last pancake!"

Troy chuckles again, avoiding my death glare.

"No," I shout back to Dante. "Those are for you!"

Troy lifts the gift bag in his hand. "Mind if I give him one of his presents early?"

"No," I sigh, moving toward my bedroom, "go right ahead. One of us needs to do better parenting today."

"Ahhh, it's okay, Mommy." The crack of his hand on my ass fills the room and my blood boils as the fire spreads. Troy's eyes remain fixed on my burning ass as my jaw unhinges. "Look at that *bounce*. I would say that's supple."

I lean in with a hiss. "Do that again, and I'll chop off your nuts, blend them up, and serve them at his party."

He leans in, all two hundred plus pounds of him, and whispers low in my ear. "You look good, *Mommy*. Trust me."

"Troy!" Dante summons again.

"I'm coming," Troy replies, a little exasperated.

I can't help my smile.

"He's all yours, neighbor."

ten

TROY

CLARISSA SHOWERS AS I SIT WITH DANTE WHILE HE FINISHES his pancakes. He flips on his TV and begins to change the channel when an old Looney Tunes cartoon comes on.

"Hey, bud, don't discount Looney Tunes. Those are the best."

"They're old."

"Yes, but they're classic. Just watch for a few minutes. Trust me."

"K." Dante sits back, taking another bite of his pancakes as the screen pans in on a little green frog. I scan my newsfeed replaying last night's highlights while trying to ignore the fact that Clarissa is naked mere feet away from me. It's childish, but the woman is a knock-out. And her comments about being too old and not coed enough aren't jiving well with me. Why were they having that conversation in the first place? Is she curious about me? Does she ever think about that night? Does she think about me in more than a 'baby daddy' sense? If so, I hope her ass is still burning from my slap, and her other cheeks are still red from the compliment I meant. She's fucking fire. One of the hottest women I've ever laid eyes on. And she thinks she wouldn't be enough for me? Given the chance, I'd show her otherwise in a heartbeat.

Loud laughter erupts from Dante, interrupting my reverie. Chuckling at his reaction, I look up from my phone to see his mouth is parted, hysterical spittle running down his chin as he watches the frog come to life, belting out opera. He's laughing so hard I think he may choke on his pancakes. "Easy there, killer." I can't help but laugh with him at the way he's responding to the cartoon. I quickly Google the character's name and find it's Michigan J. Frog, saving it in my arsenal of things my kid loves.

Dante's still hysterical when Clarissa pops her head in, her hair wet from her shower. The smell of coconut permeates the room. My dick jolts to attention as she joins us on Dante's small mattress, all curves in tight-fitting jeans and a loose T-shirt. She looks between us, a clear face without a stitch of makeup, and I almost forget myself and push a loose strand of hair from her forehead. "What in the world is going on?"

Dante's eyes are trained on the frog who remains mute while in the presence of others before bursting into song once he's alone with his keeper. And then Dante's laughing again, his whole body shaking as Clarissa looks on, incredulous.

"I've never, *ever*, heard him laugh like this," she tells me over his shaking frame. He's hysterical.

"I told him not to count out Looney Tunes. I guess this is his first time seeing them?"

"Guess so," she says, beaming brightly as our son starts to choke. I pat Dante on the back, and he dodges my touch, so he doesn't miss any of the cartoon.

"Wow," I mouth, widening my eyes at Clarissa.

"This is definitely *something*."

The frog begins to sing again, and Dante's laugh echoes out of his bedroom, as tears pour down his face. "Oh, my God, Mommy," he exclaims, wiping his tears away. "That's the funniest thing I ever saw."

"Baby, what in the world?" Clarissa laughs with him in confusion, looking to me for answers. I'm just as clueless as he ignores us both, zeroing in on his new hero.

"You must be Parker." I stand, clad in a pointy hat that Dante insisted we all wear. I've seen her numerous times going in and out of Clarissa's apartment, but never up close. The woman is strikingly beautiful and full of piss and vinegar as she sizes me up. I can feel my balls shrinking under her withering glare.

"Does Clarissa know you're answering her door?"

I nod. "She asked me to get it." I glance back at Clarissa, who's doing shit to hide her sly smile. "And I have a good idea why."

"Uh huh. So, you're Troy."

"Yeah." She opens her mouth to spew, what I'm sure, is years' worth of pent up insults, and I raise my hands, defenseless. "And before you read me the riot act, I just want to thank you, *profusely,* for all you've done for him. I know how much you love him. So," I whisper low, "before you declare me nothing but a piece of shit sperm donor and unworthy father, just know that I've wanted for a long time to meet the other Dad in his life and I'm all ears for any tips you want to give me."

My rehearsed door speech goes over well, and I can see her eyes soften ever so slightly.

"How did you know about *me?*"

Confused, I look back to Clarissa who darts her eyes away before opening a box a candles for the cake.

"I've seen you around."

Parker guffaws. "Funny, I can only recall seeing you once when—"

"Auntie Parker!" Dante yells before he comes running into her arms. She scoops him up, the smile on her face genuine.

"Hey, Duckie, Happy Birthday."

"Thank you," he squeaks as she keeps him close while he struggles to get out of her arms.

"Just five more seconds," she snuggles him as he wiggles in an attempt to escape. She sighs, letting him go entirely.

"I got so many presents on the table," Dante exclaims proudly. "But Mommy didn't get my boats and hoes cake like I wanted."

"Because it's highly inappropriate," Clarissa chimes from the table. "And you are not to watch that movie ever again."

"I agree," Parker says, taking her ball-melting gaze from me and giving Dante her undivided attention. "So, with all those presents, I guess you don't need what I have in the trunk."

"No, I do! I do, I swear!"

"Okay then." Lifting her keys, she clicks the fob for her SUV, and the trunk opens. I stand back stupefied before damn near gasping like a girl at the number of wrapped packages, feeling my balls shrink to the size of raisins.

"Parker!" Clarissa scolds, walking past me as Dante hauls ass down the porch, his eyes wide.

"It's not much," Parker says guiltily.

Clarissa openly gapes at the truck along with me.

"Okay," Parker says, looking between the two of us, "confession, I may have taken an Ambien, and accidentally one-clicked everything on his wish list. I might have also gotten everything on mine," she brings her tone down so only we can hear, "which included six lifelike vibrators and two Womanizers," she elbows Clarissa, "and I brought one for you. I swear to God, it's the best thing ever invented."

Dante is practically screaming as he unpacks the SUV, and

I feel my enthusiasm take a nose-dive. It took me weeks to save up for the present waiting on the table. Clarissa shakes her head and pulls Parker into a hug. "I can't even be mad," she nods toward Dante, who is unknowingly dropping gifts on the lawn behind him as he brings an armful up the steps, his face lit up like Christmas. "Come in, babe."

As they hug, Parker bats her lashes my way, and I narrow my eyes and mouth, 'game on.' She mouths back, 'bring it.'

It's not much of a party. Just the four of us, but I can't help but be thankful to finally be a part of this day. When I asked Dante why he didn't invite his friends, he shied away from the question. It's something I'm determined to get to the bottom of, but today I don't want him feeling anything but elated, which he is the moment he opens my gift. It's exactly the reaction I hoped for.

"Troy! You got me a drone?"

"I did. Happy Birthday."

Though Dante had sent me dozens of amazon links, all of the gifts were less than thirty dollars. I know that conditioning. I'd done the same thing with my own mom, never asking for more than she could afford so as to not make her feel bad. That's the thing about being raised by a single parent, you tend to look at them like it's your job to take care of them as much as they do you. I'm proud of my son for being so considerate and want to reward him for it.

Both Clarissa and Parker look at me with suspicion and awe.

"Can I go play with it, Mommy, please?"

"Sure," Clarissa says, swallowing when she sees the bulk of the presents left.

Dante rushes out of the house with his gift in hand, leaving us all in the dust.

"Don't you need me to set it up for you?" I call after him, terrified to be left in the lions' den with the females.

"He's got it," Clarissa says confidently, pulling the dirty cake plates from the table. It's then I know I'm in deep shit, when I'm left with Parker with no little ears around.

"So, Troy," she turns to me, licking some icing off her finger, "let me get this straight, you impregnate her and leave her to raise your super sperm for six years without you. Why now?"

"Parker," Clarissa says in a tone I can't decipher. She's hiding something, and I know exactly what that something is. The fact that I've tried long and hard before now to be a part of his life. "Let's not brawl on his birthday. Now isn't the time."

"That's what we're talking about, timing. I think now is as good of a time as any. Don't you, Troy?"

Clarissa glances over at me, worrying her lips.

"I had a lot of growing up to do." It's the truth, and even though it pisses me off that Clarissa hasn't bothered to come to my defense nor state the facts, I still spare her. "I'm here now, and I'm hoping that counts."

"Six years?" Parker asks, unwilling to give me a break. I get it though, I would be just as cautious.

"I didn't want to cause her any more trouble than I had."

Also the truth, a muted version of it.

"Bullshit."

I sigh. "Look, I can't change what I did or how absent I've been. All I'm asking for is a chance. And whether you think so or not, I have both their best interests at heart. I don't want to take your place, just invent my own."

"How poetic."

I run a hand along my jaw and face Parker head-on. "I care about them both, very much," I meet Clarissa's eyes, and she darts hers away, so I bring my attention back to Parker. "I want to be the best father possible, and I know how much you matter to them both, so I need you to sign off on this."

Parker glances back at Clarissa, who slowly nods, but she doesn't let up.

"It's not like you asked us first. I'm just supposed to trust you?"

"It's all you can do until I prove myself."

Parker is very much an integrated part of this family, and I need her approval, nearly as much as I need Clarissa's. Sweat gathers at my temples as I sit in wait for a good minute for her verdict.

"If you don't make good with them, I'll have you know, I know people, *internationally*. I can make you disappear."

I cup my jaw to hide my smile. "And what is it you do exactly?"

"That's for me to know."

"She's a consultant," Clarissa giggles uncontrollably from where she stands at the sink.

"That's right," Parker snaps my attention back to her, slowly running a finger in a slit your throat way across her neck. "I advise clients all over the globe."

"Impressive."

"I've got your number, Troy," Parker hisses.

"Everyone does. It's twelve. Are we done with the death threats? Because if so, I'd like to spend a little time with my son before I do the yard."

Parker turns to Clarissa. "He's doing your yard too?"

Clarissa nods, unable to keep her smile to herself. It's

beautiful, and I can't help staring at her a little longer because of it. She's a vixen without knowing it and has a 'come hither' air about her. My hand is still burning from that slap I gave her this morning and itching for another go around. I knew I must have momentarily lost my damn mind touching her that way, but I couldn't help it. She thinks I'm into supple coeds, but my attraction to her has grown exponentially over the years, and she's the definition of just my fucking type. I love her fiery amber locks, her straight nose, and the shape of her lips. I love that our son's birth widened her hips giving her more contrast and curve. Her thighs are thick, and her ass is fucking heart-shaped perfection. Parker's interrogation rips me from the few seconds of appreciation I'm finally able to give without Clarissa noticing. But the pitfall is that Parker notices and I have a feeling that's not a good thing.

"So, let me get this straight," Parker says. "You're back. You're doing the yard, helping to pay the bills, and practically a live-in babysitter so she can go out on dates with her college crush?"

"He's your college crush?" I ask Clarissa, who rolls her eyes, ignoring my question.

Parker is all too happy to fill me in. "Oh, yeah, she was googly-eyed for him for years. He's a real estate mogul."

Clarissa pipes up, shaking her head. "Uh, I wouldn't go that far."

"He's got a ten-inch cock, endless bank account, and practices Ju Ju Jetsu or some shit, which means he's lethal."

"He had a green belt in Karate when he was ten," Clarissa snorts, "and I haven't seen his cock." Her bright blue eyes dart to mine at her confession, and she backtracks when she sees my smirk. "Not yet. I haven't seen it yet."

They haven't been intimate? She's been dating him at

least a month. This pleases me, though it shouldn't. I know it shouldn't. I need to stop obsessing, but I can't help my slight satisfaction with all that's been revealed today. Maybe, just maybe, there's a chance I could be more than her baby daddy. It's not much, but it's better than no chance in hell.

"Oh, he's packing," Parker assures. "Marion told me so."

Clarissa drops the dish in her hands, and it clanks loudly in the sink. "Marion slept with him?"

Parker's enthusiasm plummets as she turns to Clarissa, "Oh, crap, babe, she didn't tell you? Yeah, they dated for like ten minutes."

Clarissa looks at her pensively. "Do you know why they broke up?"

Parker turns back to me, ever the menace. "Probably because she couldn't handle all that sausage, she's a vegetarian."

"So, you think I have some gaping vagina?"

"And that's my cue to leave," I chuckle and stand. "This has been ridiculous. Parker, nice meeting you."

"Pleasure is all yours." Parker turns back to Clarissa. "No, love, you don't have an overstuffed taco. I've seen your puss, it's pretty."

"I second that," I say before two sets of eyes laser my head off.

I make my exit, chuckling as Clarissa hisses at Parker behind me, "Did you have to go that far?"

"I got a little carried away."

I shut the door and join Dante in the yard, just as the drone sets sail.

MICHELLE'S HASH BROWN CASSEROLE
Dude Ranch Housekeeper, Florida

Makes 8 servings
1 hour and 30 minutes

2 Lb. Bag Tater Tots or Hash Browns – Defrosted and
   Crumbled
1 Pint Sour Cream
1 Chopped Onion
1 Can Cream of Mushroom Soup
2 Cups Shredded Cheese
2 Tsp. Salt
1 Cup Melted Butter

Topping:
2 Cups Crushed Corn Flakes
1 Stick Melted Butter

Mix all ingredients together. Pour into 9 X 13 baking dish. Place
topping on mixture.

Bake at 350 degrees for 1 hour.

eleven

CLARISSA

"WHAT ARE YOU DOING?" I ASK PARKER AS SHE stands rapt at the window.

"Just enjoying the weather."

Dante opened the last of his presents half an hour ago and has locked himself in his room to make a video, while Parker and I soak up a little adult time with a newly uncorked bottle of Pinot.

"You've been standing there for ten minutes," I say, wiping my hand on a towel before shining the sink. I don't remember much of my mother, but do remember the way she took pride in her cleaning, always shining the faucet after she was done with the dishes. One of the few memories I have is the two of us elbow deep in suds while singing together. My mother loved soul, the classics, that much I do remember. It's what brought her and my dad together.

Dad used to tell me she was born an old soul, someone who didn't quite fit musically or fashionably in the time they existed, and that's what he loved most about her. "She had depth," he used to say, "I saw that first before I knew the color of her eyes." I have my mother's neon blue eyes, her most remarkable physical attribute, which only made his sentiment mean more.

Dad never remarried after Mom died, but had a special place in his heart for the ladies. He had lots and lots of girlfriends, who taught me a lot about a lot. Because of his eclectic tastes, I can cook a variety of dishes and have collected a ton of mixed advice about men, mostly about my own father, while his flavors of the month packed up and moved on.

Parker sips her wine. "We should have a wine day soon since you've got a good, reliable sitter."

"I'm game, I could use some adult time."

"Yeah, me too," Parker says a little breathlessly.

"You're probably freaking him out," I warn as she stands fixed at the window.

"Good, I want him afraid of me."

"Oh, I think you blew that all to hell with the horribly delivered death threats."

She gives me the stink eye. "Only because you bat them all away. I can't help that I'm a little over-protective."

"Just a little."

"He better not screw this up. I really will kill him."

"Me too."

"I can't believe you gave in that day he cornered you. So unlike you."

Swallowing a little liquid courage, I corner the sofa making my way toward her. "Parker, I haven't been completely honest about Troy."

"Meaning?"

"You know how I told you he would come around sometimes and watch us?"

"Yeah?"

"Well, the last few years, he's been coming around more and more. And…he's been sending checks."

"What?" This finally tears her eyes away from the window.

"He's been more diligent than I led on, waiting for me to give him any opportunity to meet his son."

"Bullshit. Don't give him any room on the rug, Clarissa."

"I'm not. Trust me, I don't want to, but it's the truth. It took me a while to come around, but when he noticed me notice him, he kept coming back."

Parker's mouth parts. "Why didn't you tell me?"

"Because I wanted you to hate him too. I know that makes me awful."

"It's me. We don't keep secrets." She's hurt and angry, and I don't blame her.

"Sometimes, especially in the beginning, he'd disappear for a few months, and I assumed that was the end of it. When he went missing, it was easier to ignore he'd been there. But he always came back."

"I don't understand why you didn't tell me."

"Don't you see? If I admitted it to you, then you would have forced me to give him a chance. I had to stay strong. When he truly manned up and forced himself into our lives, that's when I knew he was ready, and that's why I gave in without much of a fight. I've been fighting with my conscience for a while now. I think on some level I always knew he was coming. I needed him to be ready. He was just a kid."

"So were you."

"You know what I mean."

Parker turns back to the window. "Definitely *not* a kid anymore."

"I know."

"The ass on this guy," Parker says before glancing over her shoulder at me. "I'm pissed at you."

"Do you think I made a mistake?"

"I think you both had some growing up to do."

"Ouch."

"That's me being nice. A mistake, probably, but time will tell. He really does need to earn your trust. But this isn't about you. This is about our boy, and nothing is more important."

"Agreed. I'm sorry I lied."

"Maybe you should apologize to him."

"One day I will, when he truly deserves it."

I join Parker at the window peering through the blinds to see Troy clad in a backpack leaf blower, his jeans hanging low on his ass, his *bare* ass.

Parker's laughter erupts when I gasp at the sight of his muscular butt on full display. "I give it an eleven out of ten. Have you ever seen such a fantastic ass?"

Troy continues his task blowing the debris from a giant oak tree while clueless he has mouths frothing on half the soccer moms in the neighborhood.

"I saw a lady with a turkey neck drive right into her garage door a few minutes ago, and your neighbor on the other side of Troy has been checking her mail for about ten minutes."

Parker pours some wine into both our glasses, filling them as I try to control my laughter. "We need to tell him."

"Five more minutes?" She asks with a whine similar to Dante's.

"You're horrible."

She shrugs. "Not our fault. And payback is a bitch. Besides, how can you *not know* your ass is full-on out of your pants?"

"Kids these days," I say, clinking glasses with her before bringing my eyes back to the tightest ass in the neighborhood. "Five more minutes."

Fifteen minutes later, a breeze comes through, making Troy painfully aware of his nakedness. Parker and I both grumble in protest before tactically ducking when Troy self-consciously darts wide eyes around while adjusting his pants.

twelve

TROY

"WE'LL BE GOING OVER THIS MORE IN-DEPTH NEXT time. See you then." Our instructor flips the lights, and I remove my glasses, stand, and stretch. After practice it's lights out, and I'm looking forward to my pillow and after, some time with Dante. I'm determined to ace senior year and bring up my GPA a few points. If I don't get drafted, I want more for myself than just to settle for a different career. Though if someone told me years ago, I'd be majoring in electrical engineering and taking classes like computer science and analytic geometry, I would have laughed in their faces.

I've struggled in school my whole life. It wasn't until I declared my major that I began to seriously crack the books. With the bulk of my course load under my belt and most of my struggle over, I can concentrate on doing more than just graduating. The best things in my life have always come hard-earned. If there's anything I want to teach my son, it's that sometimes the hardest route is the best route because it's far more rewarding. Ball came naturally. And though I've done the work and put blood, sweat, and tears into the games, it's been far easier than the challenge of school.

"You're Troy Jenner, right?"

I look over to the blonde, addressing me while I'm mid-stretch. "That's me."

"Good game last week," she says, staring at the flash of abs when my shirt rides up. I extend my stretch to show her she's caught red-handed and am rewarded with her giggle.

"Thanks." Gathering my books, I size her up. She's pretty, in the girl next door kind of way, but she's got nothing on my baby mama. It strikes me then how I've subconsciously been comparing every girl to Clarissa. I need to get over it. She's got a boyfriend, and as of late, keeps our conversations more clipped than ever. Any hopes I had, have been dashed by the appearance of a BMW after she drops Dante off with me. "And you are?"

"Nora."

"Nice to meet you, Nora."

"I, uh, well, I was wondering if you needed a study partner?"

"All set for now," I say, knowing precisely what she wants a partner for. If I'm going to start dating, I'm going to have to be as selective as Clarissa. As hypocritical as it may seem, this girl seems to be the opposite of what I need. Not only that, I enjoy the chase. It's no fun if the game is already over.

"Well, if you change your mind…" She looks me over and bites her lip.

"Thanks for the offer, I'll keep it in mind," I say before we separate in the hall. Outside the building, I see another sucker dropping to his knees to propose under the Era Tree. It's a Grand tradition equivalent to an old wives' tale—if you walk alone under the tree, you walk alone forever, but if you walk with your Grand sweetheart, you'll be endlessly happy together.

Pure. Fucking. Bullshit.

I'm not at all against commitment, but for the moment, I have all I can handle. I pause to catch the girl's answer and notice a brunette with killer legs in front of me. She's a foot shorter, has on a sundress and cowgirl boots. Adorable.

"Better them than me," she mutters as the crowd roars when the girl accepts the proposal.

"Couldn't agree more," I reply just as she slams into me, and I catch her to keep her from falling. Her clean scent hits me, and my dick is instantly on high alert.

"Sorry," she sputters, "...sorry."

Our eyes finally lock, and I'm drawn in. She's beautiful, and despite her shaky demeanor, seems confident. Hazel eyes look me up and down, and I'm fully prepared to use every line in my arsenal to keep this girl talking when she darts her gaze to her booted feet.

"Nope," she says, breaking our connection before sidestepping me.

"Nope?" I ask with a chuckle.

"That arm belongs to me," she says softly, nodding toward the hand I have latched around her.

"All yours," I say, hesitantly unhanding her.

"Thanks for saving me a trip."

"Anytime."

"Good day." She crosses her boots in a ridiculous curtsey, which makes me chuckle before she skitters off.

Game on.

I catch up with her as she hauls ass toward the parking lot. "Do you mind telling me what that nope was about?"

"Just an inside joke between me, and...*me*."

"You're bruising me here, beautiful. Did that nope mean I'm not your type?"

"Exactly."

"Ouch."

"I'm sure a...ego of your size can handle it."

I'm grinning again, but she can't see it because she's practically running from me. "I'm not so sure, it's leading me in the direction away from class."

"Better switch lanes then, don't want to be late," she says breathlessly.

"What if you're wrong?" I ask, fully interested. She's gorgeous, smells amazing, and her deep twang is alluring. Interest piqued, I decide she could be just the distraction I'm looking for. I can't remember the last time I went on a real date. And from the way she's avoiding me, it's easy to tell she's been burned. She's wary of me, and for some reason that's my new catnip. Maybe this girl is the place to start.

"What if I'm right?"

Flustered, she brings her eyes to mine. Recognition, attraction, it all passes between us before she scrambles to pull her phone from her purse and takes a fake call. She's avoiding me. It's the same type of Clarissa rejection all over again.

Interesting.

"Sorry, I gotta take this," she says, her eyes drinking me in once again, and I do the same, regretfully taking her hint.

"Shame," I say before giving her freedom, for now, because after the class I'm now late for, and my nap, I have a date with my son.

I tap lightly on Clarissa's door. "Are you decent? Dante said you wanted to see me?"

"I'm dressed."

From the doorway, I poke my head in and see she's sitting at a small vanity in the corner of her bedroom.

"Nice room."

"Thanks. Come in, have a seat." I take a seat on the bed as she lines her lips in hot pink. Her dress is a deep turquoise, the front dipping low accentuating her mouth-watering cleavage while the rest of it hugs her curves.

"You look beautiful."

"Thanks." Her tone is dry, and instead of letting it deter me, I use this chance alone with her to try to bridge the gap between us. She's refusing to let me in. Her smiles are mostly forced, but she's always polite. Though I'm the last man she'd consider for a relationship, I'm determined a friendship is possible. It's what's best for all of us, but I can't seem to find an in.

"I mean that. You really are beautiful."

"I appreciate the compliment."

I shake my head. "Always so formal. Are you ever going to let me—"

"Dante has another ear infection. He's been prone to them since he was a baby. At one point, we thought we were going to have to get him tubes because he had them so often."

She reads my concern in the reflection of the mirror.

"He's fine," she says, fastening an earring. "They're less frequent now, and his hearing is perfect."

"Tell me more."

"More?" She draws her brows. "His drops—"

"I can read the directions on the medicine. Tell me more about what he was like as a baby."

"Oh, he was a living doll," she says fondly. He came out so small but got really fat when I breastfed."

"Yeah," I chuckle. "He had rolls on his rolls."

"Yeah. He was my Michelin Man-baby. Tough as tread, too. Didn't cry much when he hurt himself."

"Really?"

"Yeah. I cried more than he did. He's always been resilient."

I fight between the resentment I feel and asking more questions, and she reads my posture. You could cut the budding tension in the room with a knife.

"Sixteen hours," she says, her tone cool while she eyes me in the mirror.

"What?"

"If you want to know why I've held this grudge for so long. There's your answer. Sixteen hours. Alone, and in the worst pain of my life."

I've always been curious about his birth, but from the picture she posted, she was all smiles after, so I never considered it was that hard on her.

"I thought about messaging you just so I would have someone, *anyone*, there to hold my hand. I was two weeks early, and Parker was out of town for work. I was completely alone. My parents had both died years before, and I'm an only child. I had no one. So, I considered reaching out to you for my own selfish needs, but the more I studied your profile pic and the cocky smile you were wearing, the angrier I got."

"I'm sorry."

She turns to me, her arm resting over her chair. "Not good enough. It wasn't then, and it's not now, but I'm trying. I really am. You think I enjoy being this way? I don't. I'm not proud of the way I'm behaving. It's not as easy as just letting it go. It's not that simple."

"I get it."

"You couldn't. You couldn't possibly understand just how hard it was. During those hours, I had too much time to think about my future. The years I'd spend making decisions alone, caring for him *alone*. I wrote you off for good the second he was ripped from me. Twenty-three stitches. And Jesus, how that hurt. But it wasn't just the labor itself, it was being there, in the scariest moment of my life, without anyone I cared about to tell me it was all going to be okay. And the realization during those hours that I would be in the same position from then on out, it was all too much."

"I would've been there. I wanted to be there. If you would have just reached out, I would have been there."

"I didn't *want* you there. Despite the way you looked then, in the light of day, you were an eighteen-year-old kid. If there were any question, it would have been answered the second your name and age was printed on his birth certificate. I was hysterical, my voice went out. My labor screams were silent. I was so upset, I put my baby in distress. I assumed since so many women have done it, I could handle it, but I was so fucking wrong. The whole time I was just…sad. Sad for myself, sad for my baby who didn't have a chance at normalcy because his father told a selfish lie." Her voice is shaking, and I clench my fists, itching to pull her into my arms. She lifts her chin defiantly. "So, while you paint me the bad guy for all you've missed, and all the effort you've put in, just remember that you deprived me of what was supposed to be one of the happiest times of my life. 'I'm sorry' will never give me those moments back, will never make them less hellacious. 'I'm sorry' will never change that day."

Her confession has me reeling.

She sighs. "Troy, I don't want to be this bitch to you. I don't want to harbor this grudge anymore. For the moment, you make him happy, and that should be all that matters now. I've been holding onto this anger for six years. It's not going to disappear overnight. But I am trying."

"Tell me what to do," I don't even recognize my own voice. "What to say."

"Say you'll never leave him in that situation. Tell me you'll never ever let him feel that alone when it counts, and that's enough."

"Never, but I want to make it up to you, too."

"You can't. But you're doing what you can by him, and that's enough for me."

She stands and slides into a pair of heels. "Sometimes I wish I could go back, tell that girl that it will be hard, but he'll be worth it. Tell her just to make the best of those hours because, after that pain, she won't ever be alone again."

Words fail me as she spritzes some perfume on her wrists and walks past me and out the door. "I'll be home by eleven."

All I can do is nod.

STEPHANIE'S ANGEL FOOD CAKE WITH WHIPPED CREAM FROSTING
Baker, Oregon

Makes 8 servings

2 hours

1 Angel Food Cake Mix
1 Pint Heavy Whipping Cream
6 Tbsps. Cocoa
2/3 Cup Sugar

Make Angel Food cake according to package directions. Slightly whisk remaining ingredients together and chill in refrigerator. After cake is cooled, beat chilled mixture on high until thick and spread evenly over cake.

thirteen

CLARISSA

SHUTTING THE CAR DOOR, I WAVE AT BRETT BEFORE TURNING back to the house. We've only been on a handful of dates since he first asked me out. Not enough to tell if he's a long-term guy, but enough to know there's chemistry there. We're taking it slow, no pressure, which is fine with me. After having Dante, I gave myself the obligatory back in the saddle moment, which proved to be a fool's errand. Now I'm to the point in my life where I'm vetting in the most particular of ways. Before giving my heart and my body, I make sure that I'm capable of feeling more than chemistry. My self-worth reigns when it comes to dating, and any man who courts me will have to be as patient as I have been because I'm dating for two.

Troy has been good about watching Dante, so it's made it a lot easier for me to not worry about finding a sitter. He seems committed to Dante at this point, which makes things easy. Despite Parker's initial assessment, this is anything but a saga or a shitshow.

This could work.

Walking toward the porch, I see two lit pumpkins, the larger of the two has an intricately carved goal post with Troy's jersey number inside, the other is no doubt my son's, The Legit Life logo shining proudly due to the tea lights. The yard has been freshly mowed, the leaves bagged and brought to the curb. It's the first real house I've been able to give Dante, and I proudly stand admiring it from the yard. With Troy's help, we've had a little money for some extras. With the porch columns wrapped in colorful Halloween tinsel, and the yard lit up with a ghost and a few pumpkins Troy picked up from the home store, it feels more real to me. I'd been so worried when I took on the lease I could barely afford and now find myself thankful for Troy's weekly checks.

Turning the key, I stop halfway inside, knocked breathless by the sight of a sleeping Troy alone and shirtless on the couch in dark washed jeans and bare feet. His laptop is open on his ripped stomach, his glasses perched on the bridge of his nose. He looks entirely different to me, vulnerable, yet sexy as hell. I stop the screen door from slapping shut behind me and simply admire him from where I stand. The man is incredible to look at. Even when completely relaxed, he's perfection—broad jaw, rippling chest and abs, narrow waist, and a well-defined V that protrudes at his hips and disappears into his jeans. The sight of him so at ease on my couch is the sexiest fucking thing I've ever seen. He truly is the perfect picture of male beauty, every woman's fantasy. I hate that I'm still so attracted to him. Even after all the years of resenting him, he has the same effect on me as he did the night we met. But the sight of him this way, in Dad mode, makes me curious, and though I don't ask much about him, I'm becoming more interested in what makes him tick.

Though it's wrong, I can't help myself as I approach him and take the pad of my finger moving it along the mousepad to see what he's working on. I chalk it up to a teacher's curiosity. One day I hope to teach at a university level. Professor Arden has a nice ring to it, and the money would be a substantial change from what I'm earning now. The screen lights up his face, and I cringe when I see his nose wrinkle at the intrusive light. When I'm sure he's still asleep, I glance up to see three open Google search windows.

The best foods to feed lactose intolerant kids.

How to make the perfect frittata.

I repeatedly blink at the words. I'd mentioned just once in passing conversation how much I loved frittatas. But it's the last search that has me reeling.

Ten ways to prove yourself to your spouse.

Does he really care so much about my opinion of him?

I get no time to deal with my discovery when I sense him shift beneath me and take a step back to clear my throat, fully waking him. When his eyes open and he gives me a sleepy smile beneath his Clark Kent glasses, I damn near hit my knees. There's far too much Troy in my living room.

"Hey, how was your date?"

"Good," I squeak out as he closes his laptop and moves to sit. "Thank you for watching him."

"Don't thank me," he says in a sleep-filled voice, "it's my job."

"Right. Thanks all the same."

"No problem." He reaches for his shirt, and I fight the urge to get one last eyeful as he pulls it down over his abs. "He wasn't up too late. I think he passed out around nine."

"Oh? Good." Troy lifts a worn ball cap from the couch, and I pray he doesn't put in on backward, it's my weakness, but he does.

Bastard.

The minute he stands, crowding my space, I feel my lady bits spike to life.

"T-the pumpkins look great."

"Yeah," he glances in the direction of Dante's room, the hint of a smile on his full lips, "he did a good job."

"I'm quite sure he didn't do it alone."

"Mostly, he did. Hey, I wanted to ask you something." He takes a step toward me, and I find myself backing away. I don't miss his expression when he notices my retreat.

"What are you backing up for?"

"Nothing, it's hot in here. Did you turn the heat on?"

He shakes his head. "No. It's seventy degrees outside."

"Oh, well, I'm hot." I begin to fan my face, and his smirk widens as he trails his eyes down my body.

"Are you?"

"Hmm. So, what's your question?"

"I was hoping," he takes off his glasses and folds them in his hand, "that maybe I could go trick-or-treating with both of you next week."

"Sure. Y-yes. That would be okay."

When he hears my stutter, he smiles so big it reaches his eyes, and I grip my purse at the strap so hard I think I'll break it.

Get it together, woman. This is how you got pregnant.

Everything about him is huge, his presence, his smile—his fucking blinding white smile.

"Awesome."

"Awesome?" I ask, confused.

"Yeah, you just said I can go trick-or-treating."

"I did, didn't I?"

He draws his brows. "You okay? Are you getting sick?"

"Sick, no?" I open my mouth a mile wide to fake a yawn, but it backfires because I'm no actress. Instead of looking tired, I look like I'm ready for a bite of something from a fork he's not holding out.

"Tonsils look good," he chuckles.

"I'm clearly tired!" His eyes widen, a full-on laugh escaping him when he hears the fight or flight in my tone. I used to be a lot better at this. I used to have game, but this man single-handedly ruined it by way of a stretched-out vagina and sand dollar sized nipples.

"Thank you for taking care of the yard."

"So polite," he taunts, taking another step forward and playfully tapping my nose. "Dante has impeccable manners, just like his mother."

He smells heavenly, like man soap and fresh cologne. I gather my wits from the hit of it and remove myself from arm's reach. "Thanks."

"He's so well mannered, half the time I forget I'm talking to a kid."

"Yeah, he's got a way about him."

"So does his mother."

I ignore the compliment and head for my kitchen. "Maybe I'm not feeling well. I'll make some tea. Would you like some?"

"No, thanks, I need to get ready for work."

I look at the clock and see it's close to midnight. "Sorry, I didn't expect to be out so late."

"You know I'm good with it."

"You didn't get nearly enough sleep."

He shrugs. "I got a nap after class before I came over, and I'll grab another hour at home."

I shake my head. "I don't see how you do it."

"Years of practice," he says, gathering his bag and pulling an envelope from it before walking over and handing it to me.

"Another check? You've already given me one this week." I open the envelope and look at him over the torn edge. "Tickets?"

"I thought, maybe, for my birthday, you could bring him to one of my games before the season ends."

I nod. "I've been thinking about it. I'm sorry—"

"No apologies. It's a home game for the first of next month, and I thought maybe if you felt comfortable enough, you could bring him. There's one in there for a friend."

"That's," I swallow, "that's very considerate of you."

He nods and heads toward the door. "See you later?"

"Sure…Troy?"

"Yeah?" He turns back to me, and our eyes connect. "You… you've come a long way with him in a short time. I think it's going just fine."

He chuckles. "Just fine, huh?"

I nod. "Yes. He talks about you all the time."

This earns me another flash of teeth. "Good to know. Night, Clarissa."

"Night."

fourteen

TROY

KEVIN SQUAWKS FROM WHERE HE SITS AT THE BENCH BETWEEN lockers. "Jesus, I'm dying. I can't fucking reach my cleats. Dude, take these off me." He stretches his foot toward me, and I swat it away.

The whole locker room is grunting in a collective heap of pain. "I hope it was worth it, you mother fucker!" Someone shouts, earning whimpers of agreement.

Coach Elliot is riding us harder than ever. Someone on the team hooked up with his daughter, and he's had his nose rubbed in it. He's not sure which number sacked his own kid, so we've all been paying the price. None of us are safe. Coach hasn't let up, and from the looks of it has plans to punish all of us for the whole of the season. We've squeaked by with a few wins, but nothing behind the scenes indicates solidarity for the team. All I know is he better get his shit together because my whole future rides on this season, and we've barely managed to hang on with the wins we have.

"I don't think I can hang tonight," Kevin drawls out.

"You're not breaking my heart. I have plans anyway." I close my locker and pull on my duffle.

"To do what?"

Take my son trick-or-treating.

"None of your damned business."

"Ah, got something good on the menu?"

"It's not always about women."

"Said no man ever."

"See you later."

"What's up with you?" He rises to sit on the bench. "You haven't been hitting on much lately. You ducked out of the Hero party early. You've got something going on?"

"What's with the twenty questions? I'm all about ball and the hustle this year. What's wrong with that?"

"There's a girl."

"Nope." There's a woman, and she's made it abundantly clear I don't have a shot with her despite the mutual eye fucking. My chances crushed with every arrival of a BMW. There's more going on than a co-parent dynamic between us, but I'm not about to press it after what she told me last week in her bedroom.

Her words haunt me daily and give me no choice but to accept it's time to move on from my infatuation with her.

My shifts are more grueling due to my ball schedule, and life isn't giving me any fucking breaks financially. All my credit cards are getting close to maxed from buying stuff for Dante— things he needs, things he wants—and I can't bring myself to regret it. And then there's the fact that Clarissa is finally cashing the checks I give her to help with rent.

I asked for this responsibility, all of it, but it's getting hard to keep up with my own needs.

And through all of it, I'm frantically holding onto hope I'll get drafted. Praying for a contract that will make it so money isn't an issue for Clarissa or me ever again.

"There you go again, trapped in your own thick head. I give up. Do your thing, man, but don't tell me it's not about a girl. When a man's that far in his thoughts, it's always a woman." Kevin, though he plays an idiot, is not really as dumb as he makes himself out to be. Why any man would settle for the dunce role is beyond me, but when it comes to his friends, he's as loyal as they come, and that's the main reason I keep him around.

"I'm sorry, bro. I'll get with you soon, and we'll do our own thing."

"Whatever, I'm not a jealous girlfriend. Drop me at the library on your way home, would you?"

"Never going to give up, are you?"

"There's no story if you give up," he says as we exit the locker room.

I give Lance a nod on our way out, which he returns. Though we still don't talk much, even living in the same house, our relationship took a drastic turn once I moved in due to stumbling my way into his secrets. In a way, Lance's fate is in my hands, but he's trusted me with it. It's more of an understanding at this point than a friendship, but for us, it works.

After dropping Kevin off, I make it home to see Theo on the couch watching some reality TV show and texting with a shit-eating grin.

"Sup?"

"Hey, man," he says, not looking up from his phone.

"Got any plans tonight?"

"Nah, I'm staying in," he says, checking an incoming message before glancing up at me. "You?"

"Going to help Clarissa take Dante trick-or-treating."

He couldn't be more surprised. "Really? That's cool of you."

"Can't be too careful these days."

Theo nods. "Agreed. Have fun."

"I will. Have a good one."

Theo had been a virgin up until a month ago, and he still blames me for the massacre that occurred when he lost his virginity. Though I thought I was doing him a solid by taking him to a party and introducing him to a girl, that shit had backfired, and I can tell he still holds a grudge because I was the one who instigated it. Since we met, he's had his own wariness when it comes to me, and that stunt did not help my case. Everyone has their assumptions, and the truth is that sometimes I do fit the mold. On several occasions I've taken advantage of my status, and honestly, that type of shit never mattered to me, until recently.

I find myself caring more and more each day, and it has everything to do with a little boy, who looks like me, who I want to bear my name, and the perception of his mother. I want to be a dad, *his* Dad, not neighbor Troy, and the only way to accomplish that is by earning the respect of his mother. I don't expect Clarissa to catch wind of any rumors on campus, but she's caught me once or twice bidding farewell to a couple of girls on the way out, even though I've taken special care to get them gone before Dante wakes. Her perception is my nemesis, and it's damn near stripped me of everything important to me.

Maybe I'm asking too much, but more than anything at this point, all I want is for Clarissa to look at me, just once, like I'm worthy.

I step back from the front door, fists on my hips. When it opens, I'm met with wide eyes. I deflate as a loud laugh erupts from Clarissa's shiny lips. I study her pathetic costume and cross my arms over my chest. "I thought you said we were dressing up?"

She smiles coyly. "I meant like a mask or a *hat*." She twists so I can see the fairy wings attached to her back. It's then I notice the sparkle above her eyes that trails down her face and neck and over the rest of her exposed skin. "I didn't mean for you to go all Tim Burton."

"I wasted all my bat swagger on you," I growl, stepping inside the house.

"Taking this *neighbor* thing seriously, aren't you?" I don't miss the way she checks out my ass when I clear the doorway and lean down to whisper in her ear.

"I take plenty of things seriously, you got your fill of my ass or should I strike a pose?"

The smile leaves her as her laugh dies, and her features twist into a scowl. It only took me five seconds to piss her off this round. "He's brushing his teeth."

"For? Isn't he about to rot them with candy?"

"Exactly. Defense is the best offense."

"Uh huh."

Burning up, I shift in my suit, ready to rid myself of it, but the smile on my son's face and the awe in his eyes when he runs into the living room makes it worth it. He's worth every sacrifice I could ever make.

"BATMAN!"

"Hey, bud." When he comes into full view wearing a frog costume, carrying a top hat, I can't help my laugh. "Michigan J. Frog, I presume?"

I turn to Clarissa, who shrugs. "He insisted on changing his costume last minute. He can't stop watching the videos."

"Is it cool?" Dante looks up at me with hopeful eyes.

"The coolest thing I've ever seen."

"Really?" He squeaks, anxious for my approval, which causes a raw ache in my chest.

"Absolutely. Just don't be upset if no one gets it right away, okay?"

"That's the point. Duh."

"Go get your shoes on," Clarissa tells Dante, and he gathers them from the door and goes to sit at the kitchen table.

"He's so...cool," I say as he misses the first catch in the loop of his shoestrings and tries again.

"Yeah," Clarissa says pridefully as we both watch him tie his shoes. "He is."

I've never met any kid like him, and I can't get over the fact that I had a hand at creating him. "I can't wait to see what he comes up with next year."

She nods, surprised by my revelation that I'll be sticking around, and I face her fully, irritated by her response.

"Really?" My whisper is harsh. "Is it so hard to believe I'll be here next year?"

"What about football?"

"What about it?"

"You're going to get drafted."

"We'll cross that bridge if it happens."

"Troy, it's going to happen."

"Thanks for the vote of confidence, but I'm pretty sure football players have families as well as their careers."

"Yeah, but we're not coming with you." I swallow hard, any argument sliding down my throat. It's a daily habit when it comes to conversations with her. I can have a crowd of thousands chanting my name, but one remark from Clarissa can have me scraping my pride off the floor between us. Somehow over the years, she's gained that power over me. "Look, the draft is months away. Can we not discuss it tonight?"

She nods, and I summon my son. "Come on, buddy, candy is waiting."

Dante lights up and comes running toward me, his empty plastic jack-o-lantern in hand. Scooping him up, I hand Clarissa my phone. "Can we get a picture?" Dante wiggles in my arms, eager to get the candy gathering underway. "Hold still, So—"

Clarissa pauses with the phone halfway up, and our eyes lock at my near-fumble. "Hold still, Dante."

Eyes still trained on each other, I harden my jaw in irritation and to keep my temper in check. It's only been a few months. I have six years to make up for. Dante draws my eyes away, placing small hands on the side of my face. "What do you want a picture with me for?"

"How am I going to remember my favorite Halloween ever?" I can feel her eyes on us and wonder what she's thinking. Is she dreading me being here next year? I brave a glance her way and see her eyes shining with something like hope. My anger subsides slightly, and I'm certain I don't ever want to take that away. I'll never let her be alone again in the way she described to me. Instead of useless words assuring her of it, I'll prove that promise. And that's going to take time. The more I become integrated into their lives, the more I feel like I can do anything, everything, for them both. She's given me the chance without much of a fight these days, so why then the draft talk? Why the insistence on her stance when it comes to my leaving? And is any of her concern for my leaving for herself?

"Where did you get that costume?" She asks, eyeing it appreciatively. I'd caught her staring at me the other night and let her think I was still asleep. Attraction isn't the issue and never has been. My wonder is if she feels what I do when I look at her. Even a tenth of it?

"From my Batcave, of course," I answer her with a wink before addressing Dante. "Don't tell anyone it's me, okay?

Think I can pass for the real thing?" I'm speaking to Dante, but the words are meant for Clarissa, who I haven't looked away from.

"You look great, Troy, *really*."

"That's Bruce," I correct, "but for you two only."

"Who's Bruce?" Dante asks, darting his eyes between us.

I gape at my son. "You haven't seen Batman?"

"I don't remember," he says, wiggling out of my hold.

"Hold on, buddy, smile for Mommy." On cue, Dante turns to his mother and shows all his teeth. Clarissa and I share a laugh before I set him free and retrieve my phone.

"Ready?" She nods, and I swear I see her eyes shining with tears. "You okay?"

"Yeah, just sentimental. Who knows how many of these we'll have? He's growing up so fast."

"Nah," I say, the *we* not missed on me. She's letting me in for the moment, but I'm not about to gloat. "I trick-or-treated until I was twelve."

"You're right. This worry is premature. Let me grab my fanny pack."

Shaking my head, I can't help my smirk as she clasps the god-awful bag around her waist.

"What?" She shrugs, "they're making a comeback."

"They should have stayed where they came from."

"Oh, yeah, smartass? Where are you going to put your phone in that skin-tight suit?"

Challenge accepted, I tuck my phone into the compartment on the top of my shoulder, and she shakes her head. "Of course." Our gaze holds again, and I feel it. The same buzz from the night we met. It's subtle, but it's there, and it might as well be a gong to my chest. Her skin tints pink when she realizes she's just as caught in the moment.

"Hey, Troy," Dante squeaks from below me. "Can you be my dad, just for tonight?"

Clarissa's eyes drop. Wordless, she ushers us all outside and locks the front door before kneeling down in front of Dante and adjusting his top hat. "No one gets to know Batman's identity, baby. That's why he's Batman. Call him Batman."

"Okay," Dante agrees, nodding as my heart cracks. I'm furious, and it shows when her eyes lift to mine. Reasoning with myself, I rope that shit in. I have to be patient. Clarissa moves to whisper to me in condolence for taking a machete to my hopes, but I shake my head and grab Dante's hand, tabling it for now.

After going door to door with a mere 'ribbet' from Dante for a majority of the night, on the way home when it was just the three of us, our passive frog bursts into an impressive two-song routine, singing at the top of his little lungs. I'd been waiting for the show all night, and even though I expected it, I've never laughed so hard in my life. It was the rest of the walk home that bothered me. Two kids Dante's age passed us, pointing while calling him Weirdo McGeirdo as if it was the norm. Clarissa and Dante both had ignored them as if they hadn't heard them, but I know they had. When I opened my mouth to speak up, Clarissa shook her head at me, and I had no choice but to let it go, for the moment.

"Bruce Wayne, I get it," Dante says in a sleep-filled voice, shoveling in the last of his Kit Kat. Clarissa had replaced every piece of his candy with a stash she bought while he changed into his pajamas. She told me that you never really know what sickos were passing out, and I agreed with that. She really is an amazing mother. I couldn't ask for better, for more. But I want to, and that's the part that I have to move past. And I've been trying.

Last weekend I'd run into my country girl at the Hero party—an annual gathering the weekend before Halloween where you dress up as your hero—and I was shot down, *again*. This time she was dressed like a senior citizen, but I'd managed to pick her out of a crowd by her accent alone. There was something about her that appealed to me, and I still have no idea who she is. She'd refused to give me her name or the time of day. It's a challenge, and I was all too up for it, but my mystery girl seemed adamant about keeping me at arm's length. As of now, I'm not batting for shit, even when I'm trying to take my dating game seriously. I just keep reminding myself that all my sweetest victories have been hard-earned. Time and patience are my friends, my impulsivity problem, my worst enemy.

Dante lays tucked at my side while Clarissa sits opposite me with his feet in her lap. The itch from earlier beneath the latex comes back with a vengeance, and I become increasingly more uncomfortable in my suit, my arm draped casually around the back of the couch as I fight to keep idle and stay in the moment.

I tell myself it's an illusion of family as I glance over at Clarissa and catch her studying us both, her expression unreadable. She doesn't bother looking away when I bust her. Clarissa reaches between us as Dante's eyes start to droop, running her fingers through his fair hair. "Have fun tonight, buddy?"

"Yeah, thank you, Mommy," he says, exhausted, his eyes half-mast. He looks up at me and grips the hand I have resting on his chest. "Thank you, Troy."

"Welcome, bud."

He goes out like a light a few minutes later as the itch rears its ugly head. When Clarissa lifts him from the couch,

Dante stirs and looks up at her, "Can I sleep with you tonight, Mommy?"

"You're getting too old for that."

"Please?"

"Okay, but just for tonight."

While she deposits him in her bed, I stand like my ass is on fire. She returns a minute later, catching me as I began to rip at my suit. "Shit."

"What's wrong?" Clarissa asks, padding back into the living room.

"I don't know…s-something's wrong." It feels like my skin has caught fire. I begin to rip at the latex and struggle with the zipper as she giggles while watching me.

"Shit, don't just stand there laughing, Clarissa, help me!"

"Calm down," she says, circling me to grip the zipper, "let me at it," she instructs through residual laughter. "Stop struggling."

"It burns!" I whisper-yell. "*Hurry.*"

"Oh no, are you allergic to latex?"

"I don't think so, I don't know. Please," I plead. "Stop laughing. It's not funny, it feels like my nuts are cooking."

She's full-on laughing while I rip at the collar, not giving a shit about the integrity of the suit. "I'm serious. Please, please," I beg as she finally gets my cape off and fumbles with the zipper. Once it's down, I rip at the costume until it's at my feet.

Clarissa steps back. "Oh, my God." The look on her face paralyzes me with fear.

"Is it bad?"

"Go, g-get in a cold shower right now. You're having an allergic reaction of some sort.

"I wore this the other night for a few hours," I shriek as I haul ass down the hall. She's hot on my heels. "It's probably the heat." I shut the bathroom door behind me for a quick nut check and am relieved when I see they're angry red but still intact along with the grand commander. Upon further inspection, I notice I'm covered in tiny bumps, the boiling rash going from my neck to my groin and starting to erupt on my thighs. The upside is, I may never have to shave my balls again. "What in the *hell!?*"

A sharp knock on the door has me cracking it open.

"Here, in case it's not a heat rash," she thrusts a tiny cup at me. "Children's Benadryl, it may help some."

"It burns," I whimper, taking the cup and tossing the contents back like a shot.

She bites back a smile, retrieving the cup as she barks orders. "Get in a cold shower, use the kid soap because it's got no perfumes or dyes. Gently rub, don't scrape. I'll run next door and get you some clothes, don't put your underwear back on."

I lift a brow. "Because?"

"Because if—" She rolls her eyes. "Yep, my boy definitely has too much of your DNA. Just do what I say."

I grunt, the urge to rake my sack unbearable. "Fine."

"P-poor Batman's got a rash," she snorts before belly laughter erupts from her. Narrowing my eyes, I shut the door on her as her amusement echoes down the hall. "Guess, G-g-Gotham isn't safe tonight."

JENNY'S CREAM CHEESE AND PICANTE DIP
Intoxicologist/Bartender, Dallas

Makes 2 Cups
5 minutes

2 8 Oz. Packages Cream Cheese – softened
1 ½ Cup Picante Sauce (hot, medium or mild)
2 Tbsp. Lemon Juice – optional

Beat cream cheese and picante with hand mixer until smooth and creamy. Add lemon juice and stir well. Serve with tortilla chips or fresh vegetables.

Note: May blend in a food processor instead of using hand mixer.

fifteen

CLARISSA

T HANKFULLY THEO WAS HOME BECAUSE I FORGOT TO GRAB Troy's keys. Once I explained the situation, he led me to Troy's bedroom. Inside, I can't help but notice the view he has from his window into Dante's bedroom. I wonder how often he watches us. But in truth, I know. Troy has always been diligent with his stalking. But can it really be considered stalking when it's your own child you're watching over? I decide it can't.

I've been just as diligent in making him pay. And pay he has. It's clear with every pleading look he gives me when I retrieve Dante that he wants back into my good graces. And I'm still trying to let it happen.

Since our arrangement started and due to Troy's best behavior, guilt has been building within me for the years Dante's missed without his father. But a part of me still stands firm in my conviction that he'd committed the worst wrong of all wrongs, threatening my livelihood, all I worked for, purposefully, with his lie. And in all truth, I never once thought as a teenager, Troy would be as eager to be in his son's life as he's proven to be. It was a duplicitous lie, one that could have cost me dearly, but it didn't. And maybe I just need to take that fact at face value.

With my demand that he stay away, I gave him an out. A way of living his life carefree and without consequence. Sure, I did it out of anger and outrage, but I've never really understood why he kept coming back. Those early years, I could not, for the life of me, let it go, I couldn't let him in.

Now, I hate that Troy has me questioning myself and my decisions, but I can't imagine the last six years without Dante. Have I committed the same sin with Troy by deeming him unforgivable? I've taken years away he will never get back.

Deciding to table my struggle for the moment, I get back to business and glance around Troy's room, mildly surprised how tidy he is. Then again, I know he's been raised by his mother. He reminded me on the porch when he'd confronted me and must've forgotten some of our conversation the night we met.

"It's pretty much always been just Mom and me. She's a hardass. Doesn't let me get away with shit."

"Are you close?"

"Thick as thieves."

We've been in his truck, making out heavily for the better part of an hour.

He works his lips against my neck.

"So, you're still close with your mom?"

He pauses, his breath warm in my ear. "Let's change the subject, not really in the mood to talk about Mom."

Nerves still firing off, I stutter out more conversation as his lips glide over my skin.

"You," I sputter as his tongue traces the shell of my ear, "oh damn," I murmur, clutching him to me as his teeth sink into my flesh, "have a better subject in mind?"

"Fuck yes, I do," he inches my skirt up, his warm hands covering my thighs in a gentle caress. "This okay?"

"I never do this," I moan into his mouth.

"Uh huh, you've said. Is that a yes?"

"Yes." With permission, he begins to explore.

"Clarissa," he whispers so heatedly, my panties flood. "I need words."

I decide on action instead and bring his hand to my center. He pushes my panties to the side and circles my entrance with the pad of his finger. He groans when he feels me soaked at his fingertips, the rumble in his chest spurring me on as I buck into his touch. It's been so long. I need relief, I need to feel. I need something more than dark chocolate and my vibrator to get me through. I've been good. I've been better than good. I've been a saint since my last breakup. Looking up at Troy, I watch as he expertly plays me, his touch intoxicating, his voice pure temptation. He's golden and beautiful and the perfect way to end months of celibacy.

"Feels so good," I murmur to his lips as his eyes gleam brightly from where he hovers above me in the back of his severely mistreated Dodge. He'd offered to take me somewhere else, but I'd insisted we keep it at the bar parking lot until I was sure I could trust him. Until I was sure of what I wanted.

With his next kiss, the next deep thrust of his tongue, he slips a finger inside me, and I bow off the seat as he starts fucking me with it, adding another until I'm a puddle of 'please' beneath him.

"Troy, I need more." I breathe out, on the verge as he brushes my clit in time with the glide of his fingers. My body shudders with the tidal wave as I come while he kisses me, his tongue and fingers working me while I convulse with pleasure beneath him. When we break apart, my forehead is covered in sweat. He studies me from above, chest heaving. It's become abundantly clear what I want. Admiring him in the dim cabin, I grip his neck and pull his mouth to mine, kissing him with pure desire. He is by far the most beautiful man to ever touch me, and I don't want it to end. He pulls away, satisfaction covering his lips, his beautiful bright blue eyes hooded by alcohol and desire.

"You okay?"

"Perfect."

"Good, because I'm just getting started."

In his room, I cross my legs to stifle the throb between them and stare at his bed. His sheets rumpled from the night before. Briefly, I wonder about his type. He could have any pick of women, and from the few I've seen him escort out, it's clear that's the truth. I have to admit I expected to argue a lot more about his timeliness, about his repertoire with his son, but none of those fears have ever come to light. If he says he'll be somewhere, he's on time. If he offers to do something, he follows through. I wonder if he's still as giving in the sack. If memory serves me, he's overly generous.

Curiosity gets the best of me as I snoop through a stack of books in the corner of his room. He's well-read, which doesn't surprise me. The night we met, not only was he a feast for the eyes, he could hold a decent conversation, slipping past the superficial and putting me at ease. Searching through his underwear drawer, I pull out some briefs and see his half-empty cologne bottle. I pick it up and sniff, inhaling the heavenly scent before my phone buzzes in my fanny pack.

Troy: Are you sniffing my cologne?

Caught red-handed, I drop the bottle and turn to see him in Dante's empty bedroom, the phone to his ear, wearing a towel and nothing else.

I had no time to admire him when he was stripping, the two of us were much too frantic. The phone rings in my hand, and I see his name pop up. Even with him so far away, I can see the dare in his posture to answer it.

I'm not supposed to want to, but I do.

"I'm just grabbing a T-shirt."

"Do you think about that night?" His voice is low, gravelly, and sexy as hell. My mouth goes dry as I stand at his window, my breaths coming faster. When I don't answer, he prompts me again.

"Be honest. Do you think about it?"

"D-d-do you?" my voice is just as affected. "Do you even remember it?"

"It was the hottest fucking night of my life. Of course, I remember it. And I remember how good it felt with you stretched around me. Even after all these years."

"Troy, we can't—"

"You tasted sweet, and I loved the way you let out those moans of yours, the way your breath caught when you came. The way you kissed me back. Fuck, the way you kissed me back. You didn't hold back with me. I remember that the most."

"Troy, I can't go down this road with you."

"Why not?" He whispers hoarsely. "You could forgive me. We could start over. We could have something real this time."

Slowly I exhale, remembering the woman who drove toward his school with all the hopes in the world of starting something real.

"You can come back here and let me in. I'll start with your lips, and then drop to your ankles. Work my way up—spread you, lick you, suck you, fuck you—make you come so hard. All you have to do is just let go, Clarissa, let me try. Give us a chance. I won't touch you unless you agree."

"We are nothing alike."

"You don't know that."

"I'm with someone."

"Break it off."

"I'm happy with him."

"Are you?"

I narrow my eyes across the small expanse of yard between us.

"Maybe he's what you need, not what you want. What if I can give you both?"

"You assume too much and know nothing of my relationship."

"Can't be much of a relationship. He didn't call or text once the whole time we were together tonight."

"He's busy, and we're not exclusive. Not yet."

"You know why guys don't do exclusive at first, Clarissa? It's because they aren't at all serious about the relationship, but want all the benefits. You shouldn't play into that. That's fucking bullshit. You deserve so much better."

"Says the guy who escorts a different coed out of his house every week."

"It's not all that often, and they aren't *you*."

I snort. "You can run lines all night, Jenner, I'm well versed in bullshit. Pretty words don't work on me. Never have. If something happens, it's because *I* want it to."

"Believe it or not, I'm serious. If you were mine, I wouldn't let an hour go by without proving it. Get back here and let me show you just how good we can be."

"Troy—"

"Fine. Put the physical aside, it can wait. What if we do this right? Take our time. What if we work, what if we give Dante a real family?"

"Stop, okay, just *stop*. I'm with Brett. I'm hanging up."

I end the call and see him hang his head before he disappears from the window. Gathering some clothes, I meet him at the door of my house. He's angry, I can see it in the tick of his jaw as he takes them from me. "Thanks."

"Troy, I'm sorry. I just don't think it's a good idea."

"I get it. You don't think I'm good enough. It's fine." He drops the towel, and I can clearly see he's hard. My jaw goes slack as I drink him in. Long, thick, and fucking perfect. That's the best way to describe him. His body is a solid wall of muscle, every part of him masculine and worthy of worship, but the pissed off expression on his face is the biggest turn on of all, no matter how wrong it is. And it's because I can picture the sex with him, the grudge fucking, and it's tempting.

Following my line of sight, he glances down at his cock and smirks. "At least you know the attraction is mutual." His tone is anything but playful. I've hurt him by shooting him down. He tugs on new boxers and then pulls up his sweats before gathering his costume from the floor. Breathless, I stand in the middle of the room as he glances at me with contempt before shaking his head.

"And women wonder why I don't jump into commitment. Why I make my intentions clear. It's because of this look, it's because of these looks I get. My mother looked at my dad the same way. Either they're afraid I'll hurt them or afraid I won't ever measure up to the daydreams they have of happily fucking ever after. News flash, maybe I won't, maybe I can't. I'm not perfect, but neither are they, and neither are you. But it's expected of *me* somehow. To do the right things, say the right things." He pulls his shirt down over his taut abs and draws my eyes away with his tone. "You and I may not be going anywhere, but I'm staying put. I'm not leaving my son. And I hope you hear me." He walks over to where I stand and commands my eyes. "You keep punishing me for something you won't let me apologize for, for something you won't ever let me make up to you." He rakes his teeth across his bottom lip. "But I want to, Clarissa. Oh, how I want to."

Swallowing, I stand mute while his emotions fly around me. Emotions he's hidden well. "Fuck it," he says in a tone filled with ice. "I'm under enough pressure. Thanks for saving me from more." And with that, he shuts the door softly behind him, and I realize I'm still holding my breath.

sixteen

TROY

MY SUPERVISOR, STEVEN, NUDGES ME AND I PULL OUT MY earbuds.

"Sup?"

"You going to work through your whole break?" I look at the clock and see I've missed half of my lunch hour. "Shit. Thanks, man." I stop my place on the line and sub out.

Making my way toward the break room, I check my phone to see a text from Clarissa.

Clarissa: Okay, don't ever tell him I showed this to you.

It's four in the morning and way too late to reply, but I take a seat at the table with a sandwich in hand and click play on the video she sent.

I can clearly tell Clarissa recorded behind a crack in Dante's door while he tried his best to follow along on a Fortnite dance. A few seconds in, I damn near spit out my sandwich, watching him jerk his body while my own body tenses because I'm embarrassed for him. It's painful. My kid has absolutely no rhythm. He's got no chance of winning any female over with those dance skills.

Knowing she won't see my text due to the late hour, I respond anyway. We've pretty much been avoiding each other since I made a total ass of myself on Halloween, and I consider the text an olive branch.

Troy: OMG, that's hilarious. I feel like a dick for laughing, but the poor kid has no rhythm. Sad emoji.

To my surprise, she replies.

Clarissa: I'm just as guilty. Can you dance?
Troy: What are you doing awake?
Clarissa: I usually wake up once or twice at night, it started when he was a baby, and I've never really gotten back to a regular sleep pattern. It's a mother's curse. So, can you dance?
Troy: I'm no Fred Astaire, but I've definitely got rhythm. Especially when it's important. Winky face emoji
Clarissa: Ugh. Leave it to you to go there. Rolling eyes emoji.
Troy: My bad. Thanks for sharing the video. Our poor kid.
Clarissa: It's so sad. I hate laughing at him, but it's hysterical. Have you watched his others?
Troy: Yeah, it's crazy how outspoken he is and totally different when he's not on camera.
Clarissa: You think that's something to be concerned about?

It hits me. She's asking for advice or at least asking for my say about his well-being. It's something.

Troy: Maybe he's just more comfortable expressing himself on camera. I was shy when I was his age up until high school.

Clarissa: I can't imagine that. Like at all.

Troy: It's the truth. It might surprise you to know I had confidence issues. What about you?

Clarissa: I'm a pretty good dancer. I was on the drill team for a few years and then got bored. I had a healthy confidence growing up.

Clarissa: You there?

Troy: Trying not to picture you in tiny shorts kicking your legs up.

Clarissa: How's that going?

Troy: I'm sporting a semi in the UPS break room, and I'm not alone.

Clarissa: You're such a man.

Troy: Thank you. Want to send me a video of an old routine?

Clarissa: Goodnight.

Troy: Don't go. I'll behave.

Clarissa: I have to be up in three hours to teach American youth.

Troy: Do you like teaching?

Clarissa: Love it, but this level is hard. Hard to keep them interested.

Troy: I bet you're a fantastic teacher. If I were your student, I'd sit up front.

Clarissa: Uh huh.

Troy: I would sharpen all your pencils for you.

Clarissa: Bang my erasers too?

Troy: Yep. Bring you an apple a day.

Clarissa: I hate apples.

Troy: How un-American.
Clarissa: Deal with it.
Troy: So, do you want me to try and teach him?
Clarissa: He won't dance with me. Wouldn't hurt to try.
Troy: That's because you don't listen to anything but old shit.
Clarissa: Don't insult my tastes. I get my love for R&B and old soul from my mother.
Troy: How did she die? You never said.

When she doesn't answer for a full minute, I know I've overstepped.

Troy: You don't have to tell me.
Clarissa: Heroin overdose. I wasn't there.

I read her text twice. It's nothing I expected.

Troy: Jesus. I'm so sorry.
Clarissa: It was a long time ago.
Troy: Still, that had to suck growing up without a mom. I can't imagine life without mine.
Clarissa: That's why I'm so careful about my choices with Dante. I can't help but be overly cautious. I won't mix over the counter meds. I've never even hit a joint.
Troy: I get it.
Clarissa: Gross. Let's change the subject before I look like more of a square.
Troy: You're a square for saying square. And no one can fault you for being cautious.
Clarissa: I rarely tell anyone that's how she died. I usually say heart attack.

Troy: What did you tell Brett?

Clarissa: Heart attack. I'll be honest with him at some point, but he comes from a well-to-do family. I don't know why I lied. It wasn't my habit. I shouldn't be ashamed.

Troy: No, you shouldn't.

Clarissa: I better go to bed.

Troy: Yeah. I've still got four hours left and then school and practice.

Clarissa: You shouldn't have been Batman for Halloween. You're living more of a Superman kind of life.

Troy: From you, that's one hell of a compliment.

Clarissa: Don't run with it.

Troy: It's late, and I've caught you slipping when you're vulnerable. I won't read too much into it.

Clarissa: Don't go thinking I admire you.

Troy: I wouldn't dare. Sweet dreams.

Clarissa: Goodnight.

I can't help myself, I smile for the full four hours of the rest of my shift for two reasons, the first being my baby mama thinks I'm Superman, the other is the fact that she's not telling her boyfriend the truth about her past, but she's revealing it to me. Maybe I need to try harder for something between us. For years I've watched with longing to hold my son the way she holds him in her arms, but now, now I'm imagining holding them both in the same possessive way. I went off on her without ever giving her a chance to grasp anything I was trying to convey. How could she have taken any words I said seriously with my hard dick swinging between us? I let impulse win. It was an immature way of revealing how I feel, what I want, by trying to seduce her instead of showing her what I am truly hoping for, not another shot between her legs, but at her heart. She is exactly the type of woman I should invest myself in. I need not look any further.

LISA'S LUSCIOUS LEMON CREAM
Vet Tech, Pennsylvania

Makes 3 cups
20 minutes

2 Eggs
1 Cup Sugar
1/3 Cup Real Lemon Juice from Concentrate
1 Tbsp. Cornstarch
1/2 Cup Water
1 Tsp. Vanilla Extract
1 Cup (1/2 pint) Whipping Cream – Whipped

In bowl, beat together eggs, 1/2 cup sugar and Real Lemon. In saucepan, combine remaining sugar and cornstarch. Stir in water. Cook and stir until thickened and remove from heat. Gradually beat in egg mixture. Over low heat, cook and stir until slightly thickened. Add vanilla and cool. Fold in whipped cream. Serve with fresh fruit. Refrigerate leftovers.

Very good with pineapple, strawberries, apples, grapes, bananas, and cantaloupe.

seventeen

CLARISSA

"LOOK, MOMMY! IT'S TROY!

Troy's face graces the Jumbotron as the crowd stands on their feet, screaming their heads off, Dante and I included. It's been one hell of a football game, and mostly due to Troy's incredible plays. After being down by seven the whole second quarter, the Rangers came back kicking and screaming after halftime. Troy just scored another touchdown, one of two in the last five minutes, and this one included an impressive thirty-six-yard run that had him diving past the goal line. On the field, Troy's a force to be reckoned with, and I can see the pride in his son's eyes due to their association.

Briefly, I entertain the idea of telling Dante the truth about his father. How elated will he be when he finds out it's Troy? Will he be upset? Will he be angry with me or the both of us? I decide I could never deprive Troy of that moment. It's one he'll get to share with his son. When the time is right, and I'm confident, I'll give it to him.

Dante's still screaming along with the crowd, his little fists in the air, the look on his face priceless. I pull him to me, hugging him fiercely as he cheers for his father. It's not a moment I'd ever thought he'd have and emotions run rampant inside of me at the thought that if Troy sticks, I'll have to share him forever. For so long, it's just been the two of us, well us and Parker, and now the dynamic is changing. The selfish part of me mourns the loss, but most of me is happy for Dante. For the idea that he'll finally have two parents and all that entails. A sort of peace washes over me then. I no longer have to shoulder it all alone. Troy is invested, it's clear. I just have to believe he's going to make good on all he's promised. Seconds later, we appear on the Jumbotron, and Dante gives a thumbs up, shouting, "Go TROY!"

"Oh my God, he's so cute!" Two of the girls next to us compliment while others around us vie for their shot at the camera. It's no coincidence we're on the big screen. I know Troy set it up. I'm thankful I put on a full face tonight and curled the hair beneath my toboggan. For the last few hours, I've felt a little like my old self, back in my element at a game at my old alma mater. And I know I have Troy to thank for this as my son squeals in my arms.

Our son.

Troy's made it a point to eat breakfast with Dante every day. I don't object, loving the stability it brings in their new relationship. This morning when he was running late, I found myself looking out the window to see if he was on his way, tempted to text. It's happening, he's become a part of our routine. But this relationship is between a father and his son. And I can't for one minute let myself slip into believing we're forming more than a co-parenting relationship. I don't want to be angry anymore. I don't want Dante to see the bitter grudge I hold against his father. I'm becoming more relaxed with this new situation, but some part of me is still fearful this could blow up in my face.

"Mommy, that was so fun," Dante says in a sleepy voice from the backseat.

"You like football?"

"Yes! Troy is my favorite player."

"He would love to hear you say that. You should tell him."

"I will. You think he's coming over tonight?"

"I don't think so, buddy."

"Why?"

Because he's probably going to celebrate with a few beers and a blonde on each knee. "He's probably really tired."

"Oh, well, I'll tell him at breakfast tomorrow."

Thoughts of Troy's celebration don't sit well with me, but it's pure ignorance to feel any sort of jealousy. First, I'm in a new relationship. Secondly, he's been sleeping around since he came back into our lives, and that's more of a turnoff than anything. That alone makes it impossible for me to believe he's sincere about any sort of feelings he harbors toward me.

It's not about you.

Pushing all those thoughts away, I dial Parker's number. She answers on the second ring.

"Hey, you. I was just thinking about you."

"What time is it there?"

"It's noon."

"Ah, good. I'm glad I didn't wake you up."

"I'm drunk."

"What?"

"Yeah. I'm drunk."

"What are you drinking?"

"Huangjiu, it's like Sake but not Sake, and I just wrote another amazon review…this one is about a toilet cleaner brush."

"What in the world?" I can't help my laugh. Parker hates social media but uses product reviews to speak to strangers online about real-life issues. She claims it's therapeutic.

"Would you like to hear it?"

"Of course."

She ceremoniously clears her throat. "Here goes. Here I am in 2019 with four failed relationships, on the verge of thirty years old. I'm currently in one of the best cities in the world. It's noon, I'm drunk and bitterly alone, so I've resorted to writing a review on a toilet brush. What can I say? It's a great toilet brush. It cleans very well, getting all the marks left behind after drinking too much. The design of the brush is your typical looking brush with over 100,000 bristles and a handle large enough that you won't be covered in toilet water that looks delicious to dogs but not humans. I thought it would be larger, kinda like I thought I'd be more successful in life than I am now. So now here I am, writing metaphors while listening to Radiohead about said toilet brush—that's what I've got so far, what do you think?"

"I think you need to come home."

"Don't. I hear the worry in your voice, and I'm fine. Really. Just…"

Her voice trails off, and my eyes water.

"I'm just…lonely. I mean, I know I have you and that kid, but I want someone to spend my life with."

"You'll find him."

"Yeah." She doesn't believe me, but I refuse to believe the opposite. Parker is far too special to walk through life alone.

"Are you still happy with your job?"

"Sure," she says with a sigh. "I love it."

"Then you're exactly where you need to be. Just keep the faith."

"Okay, pity party over. What are you and the munchkin up to?"

"We don't have to change the subject."

"Yes, we do. I'm sick of me."

"I'll never be."

"Sake-to-me. What are you up to?"

"Cute. We went to Troy's game. It was incredible. It reminded me of the best of times. I felt, I don't know…nostalgic. Definitely made me miss you."

"Yeah, we were awesome, now we're all grown up and boring."

I sigh my reply, "That we are."

"So, did he play well?"

"Yes, Dante was so proud. He's passed out now."

"And what does Mommy think?"

"I think he's an incredible athlete. And nothing more."

"Girl, you're lying to yourself. Has he talked to you anymore about, *you know*, since Halloween?"

"No. And it's for the best."

"Uh huh."

"Parker, I'm serious. It's a bad idea. What if it doesn't work? How will that affect Dante? This would make an already complicated situation even worse."

"So, you're saying you want to give him a shot, but won't because of your common bond, which just so happens to be the best reason to try."

"It was so awesome seeing him in his element tonight. I'm a little dazzled, but at the end of the day, he's still the same old dog, same tricks."

"Whatever you say."

"Brett's doing well, thank you."

"Yeah? Great," she spouts dryly.

"Why don't you like him?"

"He seems to be taking his sweet assed time wooing you. That's not sitting well with me."

"It's an adult relationship. And to be honest, my first real one."

"Well, give me fireworks and passion over that bullshit any day. It sounds truly boring."

"It's not. It's comfortable."

"Whatever you say. Ganbei!" I can hear the clink of her bottle as she pours and then swallows. "One of these days you're going to have to come with me on one of these adventures."

"I will."

"Okay, I'm going to finish this bottle and see if I can turn this day into a segue for something better, maybe like in Lost in Translation, where I end up with the love of my life in a karaoke bar while we party with complete strangers."

"Do it, babe, I have all the faith."

"Yeah, and do yourself a favor and bone your neighbor, because you're missing out on the best sex of your life."

"No."

"Fine."

"Love you."

eighteen

TROY

I RIDE THE HIGH MY WHOLE DRIVE HOME, EAGER TO TRY AND CATCH Dante before he goes to sleep. I send off a last-minute text to Clarissa just before I head into our neighborhood in hopes she can keep him awake just a few minutes longer. My phone rings, and I answer without checking to see who it is, my smile already in place. She doesn't bother saying hello, but dives right in.

"Wooo weee, boy, I'm so damned proud of you. You killed it tonight."

"Thanks, Mom."

"I texted you to see if you wanted to celebrate with Luis and me. He wanted to buy you a beer."

"Sorry, I got caught up in the post-game and just wanted to shower and get home."

"So, no party tonight?"

"Plenty of them, but I'm opting out."

"Oh?"

"Yeah, I've got something better in mind." Instead of picturing Dante's reception, I see Clarissa on the Jumbotron, dressed in a Grand hoodie and matching beanie, holding our son close. She was glowing, her smile stretched across her face, and something inside of me flipped the minute I saw them.

"So, what's the big plan?"

Win her.

"Just going to take it easy."

"The news is highlighting the game now."

"No shit?"

"Yeah! They're talking about you, son! HEY, RECORD THAT!"

"On it," I hear Luis reply. "Good job, Troy," he says by way of conversation. Luis is soft-spoken and treats Mom like gold, we aren't exactly best friends, but we're friendly. As long as he treats her well, we have no issues.

"Tell him I said thanks."

"I will, and you're getting drafted," she adds proudly. "I know it."

"Let's hope so. Then I can finally buy your dream house."

"I'm happy here."

"You'll be happier on that front porch you've been dreaming about. Keep dreaming, Mom. I'm going to give it to you."

"You earned that. I wouldn't take a dime from you. I hope you know I don't expect that."

"What's the fun of becoming rich if you can't spoil the people you love?"

"You're going to make some lucky lady very happy one day."

"Hope so."

"Oh, you will."

Clarissa's scowl crosses my mind, and I can't help my chuckle.

"Yeah, well, I have a feeling she won't come easy."

"You've met her already?" Her voice lifts, hopeful. She's been hard on me growing up, especially when it comes to the ladies. I'm nowhere near ready to deal with the confrontation that's coming once I reveal the truth but decide to use her mood to start the process.

"Mom, there's something I need to tell you. Something that—"

My words are cut short when I pull into my drive and see Clarissa wrapped around her boyfriend. They're kissing and not in a friendly way. Every bit of my high evaporates when I see her grab his hand and pull him inside.

"You there? Troy?"

"Yeah, I, shit Mom, something's come up. I'll have to call you back."

"You okay?"

"Fine."

"No, you're not."

"Just keep those good thoughts coming, okay?"

I run a hand over my jaw as Clarissa's porch light clicks off.

"What happened, you were just chipper. Who pissed in your Cheerios?"

"Nothing. I'll call you later."

"Okay. Love you. Proud of you."

"Thanks, Mom."

Is she about to sleep with him? With Dante in the house? I can't say shit, I would've gladly taken a side of her bed if she'd given me the opportunity on Halloween.

Resisting the urge to shoot off another text, I white knuckle my wheel. The hardest part of wanting what you can't have is the realization it might not ever be yours. And that's where I am, swallowing the verdict after years of the same woman closing the door in my face.

Jealousy for the man who's taking what I desperately want courses through me, my eyes burn as I keep them fixed on the house I want so much to call home, the family inside to claim as my own.

The idea of what's going on behind that door is ripping at me, and there's not a fucking thing I can do about it. Her mind's been made up for years, and I'm the one who needs to face facts. I have got to let it go.

Clarissa: I've got company. See you in the morning?

The burn inside my chest worsens as I raise my phone to my ear and put my truck in reverse.

Kevin answers on the second ring.

"Sup?"

"Where are you?"

Jennifer's Sausage Dip
Biologist, Montana

Makes 10 servings
30 minutes

2 Lbs. Sausage
1 Lb. Jalapeno Velveeta
1 Lb. Velveeta
1 Envelope Garlic Dressing Mix *(May use garlic powder.)*
1 Can Evaporated Milk

Brown sausage until no longer pink. Drain. **Place all other ingredients in a saucepan. Heat on low until cheese melts. Stir sausage into cheese mixture.

Serve with tortilla chips.

**Time saver—Cheese and other ingredients can be combined in a microwave dish.

nineteen

CLARISSA

I'M TWO SIPS INTO MY MORNING COFFEE WHEN I SEE THEO ANGRILY bound down the steps of his house before throwing an instrument case in his back seat. Seconds later, Troy is in front of him, his posture deflated.

"Jesus, man. I had no idea."

"Of fucking course, you didn't," Theo says in disgust.

"I don't know what to say. I fucked up."

"Did you even talk to her? Do you ever really talk to any of them?" Troy hangs his head as Theo lays into him. "If you would have spent more than five fucking minutes luring her into your bed, you might have been able to connect the dots. Instead, you've fucked my ex!"

Eyes wide, I try to muffle the sound of my coffee going down the wrong pipe as Troy speaks up. "Tell me what to do to make this right."

"You can't do anything." Theo snaps, and briefly, I fear he may take a swing at Troy, which could be disastrous.

"That girl meant everything to me, for years, and you fuck her and treat her like she's disposable. Can't you see how wrong that is?"

Troy's voice is hoarse when he speaks. "Tell me what to do."

"How about you grow the fuck up a little?"

"It was a mistake."

"No, hell no," Theo corrects. "You don't get to claim that. That was intentional. She was *my* mistake. To you, she was just last night."

A beautiful blonde moves onto the porch, tears streaming down her face as Theo slams his car door and studies her briefly before tearing out of the driveway. Instantly I hate her for the rift she's caused. I'm not allowed to be jealous, but I am, I'm swimming in it. Did she knowingly sleep with Troy to hurt Theo? If I have to judge by the devastation on her face, it seems it was a random hookup, and the realization has taken all three of them by surprise, Troy more so as he stands there staring after his roommate seeming lost. He glances toward my house and straightens when he sees me frozen on my porch watching it unfold. I have no idea what expression I'm wearing. Troy stares at me for long seconds before walking back up to the porch and ushering the blonde inside before slamming his front door.

Is he angry with me? I'm not to blame for this damned drama. Once again, his dick got him into a mess that goes beyond a casual hookup. Will he ever learn? Minutes later, I'm on my second cup of coffee when the blonde, no longer dressed in Troy's jersey, is escorted to her car. Her face is splotchy from her tears. She didn't mean to do it. She's no victim, but what happened wasn't intentional on either of their parts. Theo couldn't see it, or maybe he could, and was too furious to care. All three of them are in this situation because of circumstance, I'm sure of it. I'm also confident that Theo and Troy's relationship won't ever be the same. I feel for Troy as he stands there staring after the girl who's pulling out of his driveway with a lot more morning after baggage than she bargained for.

"Are you okay?" I ask Troy as he turns to me, his eyes cold, distant. It stings me in a way I'm not prepared for.

"Don't you have a son to tend to? Anything else you could be doing?"

"Hey, I live here. You're the one with your drama spilling out into the street."

He stalks across the lawn, and I fight myself not to step back. He's pissed at himself, at his shitty decision making, but I'm not about to be his punching bag. I ready myself because I've never seen him so angry.

"You satisfied?"

"What?"

"Are you fucking satisfied? You got enough ammo this morning to last you some time, sweetheart. You wanted it? There you go. You were waiting for something to hold against me, to prove you're right about what a piece of shit I am. Happy?"

"Stop it. I saw what went down. You didn't mean to hurt him. I'm not going to condemn you for a mistake."

"Are you serious right now? You've been holding the same mistake over my head for six fucking years. The next time you get pissed off, I'm sure this will come up."

"I'm pissed off now."

"Nothing new."

"Hey, you know what, you ass? I was young once too. I've been there, I've dealt with drama. I'm glad those days are over for me, but don't piss on me because you made a mistake."

"Goddamn right I did," he grumbles, turning his back on me.

"What's that supposed to mean?"

"Nothing. Carry on. Nothing more to see here."

"Hey, Troy, why don't you try the adult version of dating? It's a lot easier, fewer casualties."

He turns back to me, clenching his fists.

"Yeah? Is that where your boy toy comes over at the *end* of the night and pretends what you have is real?"

"What?"

"I saw you bring him in last night. It was nearly eleven. Tell me, did he tell you where he was before he decided to come over and get some?"

"That's none of your—"

"My son is in there!"

"Keep your voice down," I choke out. "And don't make your drama mine."

"I guess I shouldn't be surprised he left before Dante woke up. He's not in it for *him*."

"Stop it. He stopped by for an hour or so and has a meeting with a client this morning. And no, I don't want Dante meeting him yet. You see, in a *mature* relationship, we take all feelings into consideration on *all sides*."

He shakes his head as if I'm clueless. "You're fooling yourself with this guy."

"Hey," I snap, all patience evaporated as I take angry steps toward him. "In an adult relationship, it's a *one at a time* process, you know, easy to remember the name of the person you're dating. Sex is gradual. There's no one and done, Troy. In the adult version, you take the time to get to know the person, make sure your goals match because you're well versed on what you do, and *do not* want. And me? Well, over the years, I've come to the conclusion that I don't want to date an adolescent who's got an agenda just to fuck me. I'll never be any man's breadcrumbs! I want to date a man worthy of my time, attention, and my son, who means more to me than any piece of ass! I put Dante *first* and make sure I don't put him in the position to question the exit of a different stranger every morning. That's the difference!

The men I date don't use women and toss them away the next day."

"At least they're aware of it, not *playing stupid.*"

My eyes water with that blow. "You bastard."

He shrugs. "Just being real, honest. That's what you want, right?"

"You want real and *honest*, how about this? This little spectacle is why I could never take you seriously! You're a child, Troy, *playing* a man, and I see right through it because I was raised by one!"

Troy visibly flinches as Dante sounds up from behind the screen door.

"Mommy?"

Our son looks fearfully between the two of us, confusion covering his features. "Why are you yelling at Troy?"

"I was bad," Troy speaks up immediately before closing his eyes and exhaling a breath. "I was really bad." Snapping my eyes to his, I see the regret cloaking him as he addresses Dante. "I let my temper get the best of me and said some things that weren't nice. Things that I shouldn't have said. I'm sorry. It won't happen again. I'm going to put myself in a timeout. I'm sorry," he says to me pointedly, and all I can do is nod.

And with that, he stalks toward his house and slams the door behind him.

twenty

TROY

I T'S BEEN A SHIT LONG WEEK. I'M EMBARRASSED I SHOWED MY ASS that way to Clarissa. She's barely met my eyes over my morning breakfast with Dante. Twice I've tried to apologize and twice she's made an excuse to leave the room. I'm a pariah in my own house as well, the tension between the walls thick. Theo's not speaking to me, which is understandable. My apologies mean shit to everyone around me. And Theo and I aren't the only brooding sacks to occupy the house.

Lance is more isolated than ever, constantly trapped in his room, waiting for the bomb to drop. Though my current situation is shit, I can't help but be grateful that I'm not in his shoes.

His expression is grim this morning as we pass each other on the stairs. "Hey man, what's good?"

"Not a fucking thing. You?"

"Same."

Last night we suffered a debilitating loss, and I feel like my future is slipping through my fingers. It's easy to see Lance feels the same.

"Fuck that asshole," Lance says, reading my mind.

"What coach in the history of fucking ever lets his personal life interfere with his career?"

"I don't know what's going on," he runs a hand down his jaw, "but there's got to be more to it."

"I can't believe he's willing to throw a season over this. We need to win."

"You and me both."

Lance is my opposite, the dark to my light, tattoo clad, more menacing in appearance. Inside he's mostly heart, and this conclusion I've come to with just the short interactions between us. I'd fumbled into discovering what makes him tick, and we aren't so different. Lance doesn't judge, and if there's one thing I know, he would keep my secrets just as safe as I have his.

He seems to weigh my expression and my stinking desperation, and I can feel the tension rolling off of him.

For the first time in six years, I'm ready to confess, in need of an outsider's perspective.

"Hey man, you want to get out of here and grab a beer?"

Lance nods. "You read my mind."

LORETTA'S DUMP CAKE
Police Officer, Army Brat, US

Makes 12 servings
1 hour

1 Large Can Crushed Pineapple – Well drained
2 Cans Cherry Pie Filling
1 Yellow Cake Mix
1/2 Cup Chopped Nuts
2 Sticks Margarine

Grease 9x13 baking dish. Add cherry pie filling and spread evenly in pan. Top with pineapple. DO NOT MIX. Sprinkle dry cake mix over fruit and top with nuts. Melt margarine and pour on top of cake mix.

Bake at 350 degrees for 45 minutes to 1 hour.

Variation:
2 cans Comstock More Fruit Apple Pie Filling may be used in place of the pineapple, cherry pie filling & nuts. Good served hot with vanilla ice cream.

twenty-one

CLARISSA

"UH, MOMMY?" DANTE SAYS THROUGH A GIGGLE.

"Yes?" I ask, pulling into our driveway.

"Why is Troy asleep on our steps?"

"What?" I turn to see Troy passed out halfway to our porch, catching flies, his hand tucked in the waistband of his sweatpants.

I look back at Dante. "Uhhhh, maybe he's sick?"

"Sick?"

"Why don't you go inside and pick out some soup while I check on him."

"Okay." He darts over to where Troy lays passed out.

"YOU SICK, TROY?" Troy jumps up from where he lays, cradling his head while Dante yells at him from where he hovers inches away. "MOMMY AND I ARE GOING TO MAKE YOU SOME SOUP!"

Troy winces with every word, cowering from the sun by placing one of his paws up to block it. It's hysterical, and I can't help my laugh as Dante puts his hand on Troy's forehead. "Mommy, he don't have a fever!"

"Doesn't have. He doesn't have a fever. Inside." I round the SUV, and Troy glances up at me from where he sits, his expression sheepish.

"I'll find you soup to make you better, Troy!" Dante bounds inside and slams the screen behind him.

When he's at a safe distance, I lift an inquisitive brow to Troy, who's now holding up both hands. "Before you decide to rip into me, I had a speech. A speech I carefully prepared and was waiting for you to come home to deliver. Seemed like a good idea at the time."

"A text would've done just fine. Come on, it's cold." I hold out my hand, and Troy takes it, staggering to his feet. I catch him, barely, before we both misstep and topple into the yard with a thud. Laughing, he rolls us to where I'm trapped beneath him. I push at his chest to no avail.

"Oh, *Cherie*," he murmurs down to me in a French accent. "I thought I would *never* get you alone."

He bats long lashes down at me.

"Get off of me, Jenner," I sputter breathlessly as his eyes rake over my face, stopping on my lips.

"You are a *girrrl*, and *I* am a *boy*, you see. Everyone has a hobby," he slides his freezing hands up my sides, and I squeal as he leans in close. "Mine is making *love*."

"Someone has been watching *way* too much Looney Tunes."

"You may call me Street Car...because of my de*sire*," he leans in and places wet kisses on my neck as I struggle beneath him. "Muah, Muah, Muah."

"Definitely drunk as a skunk. Alright, Mr. Le Pew, you've had your fun."

"Not even *close, Cherie*." He stares down at me, his eyes glazed, as my heart begins to pound.

"Get off of me, fool."

"A fool for you, *darling*, may I call you *darling*? And finally, now that I have you right where I want you, the greedy little monster we created can step aside and let me have my own way with these love tassels." He lowers his head as my eyes widen and begins blowing raspberries on my chest.

He's motorboating me in the middle of my yard in broad daylight.

"Troy!" I gasp as he continues to murmur his devotion to my tits. "Dear God, would you stop! I'm going to pee my pants. Though I'm pretty sure I wouldn't smell half as putrid as you do."

"It is the smell of love," he nuzzles my chest, and his lips drift up.

"Troy, it's the middle of the day, why have you been drinking?"

He frowns, pulling away. "Oh, it's been a horrible year for me, Cherie, but you knowww," he drawls in suggestive French. "You could cheer me right up if you wanted to."

"Troy, do you want chunky soup or stars?" Dante calls from the kitchen.

"Stars," Troy answers without taking his gaze away. "So they match those in my *eyes*."

"What?" Dante asks through a giggle.

"Stars, my good boy! All the stars!" He leans in again and smacks kisses down my chest. "Muah, muah, muah."

Aside from the liquor seeping out of his pores, he smells fantastic, his rusty platinum hair tucked under a beanie as he suggestively gazes down at me with surreal blue and glossy eyes.

"Will you be my girlfriend, *darling*?"

"Absolutely not," I snort.

"It's a little too soon for marriage, but hey, if that's what it takes. You set the date. I look fantastic in a tux."

"You're crazy."

"Crazy about you," he says before placing another full-lipped kiss to my cheek. When he pulls back, his eyes soften. "I get so jealous," he says softly. "I don't want *him* kissing you. I don't want *him* touching you. These lips," he runs a finger over my mouth. "I want them for *me*."

"Troy," I shake my head, still trapped beneath him. "We're a train wreck."

"So what? Our story is messy, unconventional. We can be messy together, that makes us perfect."

"You've got to get up, Dante will see."

"Just tell me you forgive me."

"Fine, I forgive you."

He leans down and gently takes my mouth in a soft kiss. It's all too much, his warm lips coated in whiskey, his body covering mine.

"If only you meant it," he whispers when he pulls away.

"I do. It was a nasty fight. You were upset. I know you didn't mean to hurt Theo or take it out on me."

"That's not the only thing I want forgiveness for."

"I know. I'm trying."

"I missed you this week." He's so sincere that I melt in his arms while staring at his lips, and he takes notice even in his state. "When are you going to stop fighting this?"

"It's not about *me*."

"I don't disagree. It's about us."

"Troy, there is no us."

He drops his head to my chest. "There's no story if you give up."

"What?"

"Nothing," he mumbles.

"Mommy, can I try the can opener?"

"NO!" We both answer, and Troy stumbles to his feet

before pulling me flush to him. He tips my chin with his finger.

"I'm sorry. I didn't mean any of it. I just want…"

I search his eyes. "What?"

"Something I can't have."

"Are you okay?" I manage to say around the lump forming in my throat.

"Yeah. Fine. I'll bounce back."

"Are you…" I glance toward the house.

"Sober? Not quite, but I'm good. I'll go swish with some of your mouthwash and play sick, if that's okay? I'm sorry. He shouldn't see me that way. It will never happen again."

"It's fine. I believe you."

Relief covers his features.

"Things will get better."

"Hope so." He leans in one last time and presses a kiss to my forehead. I stare after him long after the door closes behind him.

twenty-two

TROY

“**D**ante, this is Harper. She’s going to teach us all how to dance today.” Harper smiles down at Dante from where he sits in his room, fiddling with the Rubik’s Cube that Parker got him for his birthday.

“I don’t need to learn how to dance.”

“Every guy needs a little dancing skill,” I tell him, taking the toy from his hand.

“Not me. I know how.”

“I’m learning too. So is Mommy.”

“Why?”

“Because I need help,” I lean down and whisper to him. “I’m really bad at it, and I want to dance with your Mommy one day, so will you pretend for me?”

“Okay,” he says quickly as we join Clarissa in the living room. Harper is Lance’s girlfriend and a dance major, not to mention the only person I know capable of teaching my kid modern dance. When I’d asked her to help me with Dante, she’d happily agreed.

Harper connects her phone to the TV, and Frank Ocean’s “Lost” fills the room. For a solid hour, Harper shows us all the ropes, and I can’t help but get lost in the way Clarissa moves her hips, the dip, the ease in which she manipulates her body. Twice we've caught each other's gaze, our smiles syncing, the second time she mouths me a "thank you," to which I reply with a wink. I feel like a fucking fool mimicking the movements, but for my son, for her, it's worth it. The longer we practice, the more Dante gets into it, his dancing a lot less awkward than in the video. When the lesson is over, Harper bids us farewell promising Dante another hour next week as I walk her out.

"How are you doing?" I ask, knowing she and Lance are having a similar shittastic year.

"Good. Stressed but good." She pauses at the foot of the steps. "Does Lance...do you think he regrets it?"

"You mean you?"

"I'm sorry, I know I'm putting you on the spot. He's so quiet sometimes. I just worry."

"No, hell no. Not at all. We had drinks last week, and he told me he was happy."

Her smile is blinding. "Really?"

"Yeah, I promise you, he's good."

She nods several times. "I mean, he seems to be okay. It's just a lot. You know. I don't want to cause him any more stress than he's under already with his family."

"I get it, but if anything, you're making his life better, Harper. I assure you."

"I hope so. I really..." she blushes.

"Really what?"

"Really love him. So much it's scary."

"I'm pretty sure he feels the same."

"I just wish we weren't under all this bullshit. It's my fault. I hope you know this is all my fault. I'm so sorry. I lied to him."

"Don't be. And trust me, I can understand more than you

ever know how a lie can cost you. And you damn sure can't help who you fall in love with." I give myself away, sparing a glance back at Clarissa's door.

"Yeah, I noticed that," she says, looking back in the direction of the house. "It's not just you."

"Trust me, it is."

"Trust me, it's not. Give her time to come around."

"I wish it was that simple."

She shrugs. "Could be. Just be patient."

"I'm trying. Hey, thanks again, Harper."

"No problem."

"You think he has a shot at getting better?"

"Yeah. He'll be fine. And I admire you both for investing the time to make sure he's able to at least make it through a dance. A lot of parents don't worry about things like dancing."

"We just want him to be able to experience the best of everything."

"You're a good dad, Troy."

She smiles as Dante speaks up behind me. "Troy's not my Daddy, duh."

"Oh," Harper says, giving me wide eyes.

Clarissa walks outside. "Apologize right now, young man."

"Why? He's not!"

"Because duh is rude, and I never want to hear it come out of your mouth again."

"I was just bringing her sweater," Dante mumbles, holding it out to Harper.

"Thank you," she takes it as her eyes ping pong between Clarissa and me. "I'm sorry. I guess I just assumed he was your daddy." She's mortified.

"It's okay," I assure her.

"It's fine," Clarissa says softly. "Really, it's okay."

Harper mouths one last apology to Clarissa before getting into her SUV and driving away with a wave.

"She's gonna teach me to dance to "Old Town Road," and all the Fortnite dances too," Dante proclaims proudly.

Clarissa gapes down at him "Is that why you love that song so much? *Fortnite?*"

Dante opens his mouth, and Clarissa gives him the stink eye. "Say duh *one more time*. One more time."

"I wasn't going to," he huffs.

"Uh huh. Go finish your homework."

"Fine. I try to be nice and bring her sweater, and *I'm* in trouble."

"Don't you backtalk me!"

"I'm not!"

"Don't you raise your voice to me!" Clarissa says, doing the same.

"Just making sure you can hear me with your *old* ears!"

"That's it," Clarissa snaps. "No video games tonight."

"Fine!" Dante shouts. "You're old. You're old. You're *old!* You're an *old, old, Mommy!*"

"That's enough," I snap at Dante, who looks over to me in shock. "Apologize to your mother. Get inside and finish your homework with no backtalk, or you'll deal with me. Got it?"

Dante's eyes are wide as saucers having never heard that tone from me. Clarissa allows it, watching Dante expectantly. Dante's face falls as he climbs up the steps. "Sorry," he mumbles.

"Don't you dare slam that door," I bark just as he gets ready to make his dramatic exit. Clarissa raises surprised eyes to mine, her mouth parting as I keep mine trained on Dante. "Put your snack plate in the sink. And your homework better be done in thirty minutes."

"Okay," Dante mumbles.

"Nope," I correct.

"Yes, sir."

"Better. Now go."

Clarissa joins me at the foot of the steps as Dante heads to the kitchen. "Wow. Well done, neighbor."

"That's *Dad*," I say, giving her a pointed look. "Not neighbor. *Dad*."

"I know, but—"

"The longer we don't tell him, the more the omission becomes a lie. And from what I've gathered, you're not a fan of liars."

"I know, Troy, I do."

"Do you? Because you seem to be holding onto the one I told you like a lifeline, and that hasn't done any one of us any good. I'm his father, he needs to know."

"Just give it a little more time. Please. Just be patient, that's all I'm asking. It's only been a few months."

"Three. Three months, and just so you know, you're making liars out of us both," I say before heading to my own front door.

twenty-three

TROY

SITTING ON THE COUCH, I CHECK MY PHONE FOR ANY TEXT from Clarissa. Dante is having his first sleepover, and it's not sitting well with me. I could sense his nervousness this morning when we talked about it over breakfast. He's trying to be strong for his mother. He kept glancing her way, feigning excitement. I used to play strong for my own mother, so it was easy to see the truth. And the truth is he's terrified. I would give anything to be a fly on the wall at that sleepover. Trying to push it out of my mind, I glance up as Theo appears in the entryway pulling on a sports coat. We've barely spoken to each other since he blew up, despite my apologies.

"Where are you going all dressed up?"

"Rehearsal dinner."

I toss my football up in the air as he scours his appearance.

"Who's getting married?"

"A friend of a friend. What's it to you?"

I groan in frustration. "Jesus. How many times do I have to say I'm sorry?"

"You don't," he says, brushing his lapel, "I'm over it."

"You serious?" He seems just as surprised as I am that the words left his mouth.

"I mean, I don't want to hug it out with you, but yeah, I'm completely over her. I've got something much better going on."

"That so?"

"It's so. Just do me a favor and start vetting before you bring anyone else here. Not that I have any more exes. But let me make one thing clear, I don't want yours, and I don't want you ever taking a second look at mine."

"Got it. I'm not going to...see her again." I don't bother telling him I'm turning over a new leaf where the ladies are concerned. There's no point. Nobody believes shit when it comes to me. Except for the woman I can't seem to stop daydreaming about, and even then, the benefit of the doubt is hard-earned. I'm still pissed at her for holding out on Dante, but I can't fault her for being cautious.

Time and patience. Relieved I won't have to walk on eggshells anymore, I stand and pull out my wallet to hand Theo some past due rent.

"For what I owe you."

He takes the money as I grab my duffle.

"Where are you going?"

"A few guys are headed to Shreveport this weekend. I'm going to check it out. Lance left a note on the fridge that he's out until Tuesday, so the house is all yours."

"Nice."

Kevin, my old roommate, and two others from my team pull up and honk just as I reach the door. "Later."

"Later, man."

I look back at him as he straightens himself one last time. "We good?"

"Yeah, we're good."

I jog down to the SUV, dropping my duffle. I've convinced myself between the responsibilities of ball, work, school, being a parent, and Clarissa's constant rejection, I deserve a few days off to just...be. It's my senior year, and I need to take advantage of it before it's over. But nothing about leaving is sitting right with me. I glance back at Clarissa's house, anxious to see if she's heard from Dante.

"Give me two minutes."

Kevin scrolls through his phone from the front seat. "Two."

I knock and get no answer. Cracking open the door, I knock soundly again, calling her name and get no response. Walking through the living room, I see the TV muted and an empty wine glass. Apparently, Mommy has been relaxing. Chuckling, I peek my head into the bedroom to see Clarissa on her back, in nothing but a cami and skimpy purple panties, her Mac slanted on her lap. She looks so fucking sexy. I have to fight the urge to wake her up with my head between her legs. I'd lick her over the panties first. That's how I'd start it, leading with my tongue. It's when I see the Womanizer Parker gave her inches away, that I realize she's passed out post-orgasm.

Instantly I'm hard.

"Fuck," I breathe out as her perfect chest rises and falls, her mouth slightly parted. "Fuck you, life," I mumble as I situate her on the bed. Her screen lights up from the movement, and I glance at it curiously to see the contents of her spank bank. I damn near wake her up with my laugh when I see what's written on the screen.

It's a product review of her *sex toy*.

#goodconsumer90

I'm deducting a star for the name alone because nothing so pleasurable should come with such baggage. And

that's what being with a womanizer entails, baggage. So, what if this model is pretty to look at, has the build of a god and can pleasure you for hours on end? There are less glossy, lower-priced models just as capable of getting the job done without leaving you feeling like a used sack of hormones. I'm currently with the lower-priced, less risky model. And why shouldn't I be? The womanizer must be kept in check constantly, so that future models have a clear path on how to treat a woman. This is about a pleasurable epiphany, and letting go, right? A safe and effective way of reaching one's peak without any of the guilt or expectations. But how can one successfully do this if they're continually being reminded that what brings them so much pleasure is attached to a name that is SO demeaning? A woman's orgasm is 99% mental. 99%! So, what self-respecting woman wants to succumb to such demoralizing name-suck? In the end, the womanizer *will* fail as womanizers inevitably do, and it's just going to be another thing to store away—>baggage. Note to manufacturer- If you're going to make a woman's toy capable of inducing such mind-bending results, name it something else.

I can't help but read the comments beneath.

I get it. I do. I'm with you, good consumer. If you can find happiness elsewhere, why risk it?

Girl, you've got it bad. You need to rip the band-aid and get it over with. Womanizer or not, you're in deep. Do yourself a favor and see it through.

She's just trying to protect herself and her future model. Who can blame her? This model sounds like trouble.

You ain't getting any younger. Safe = sorry in my book. Take a chance.

You're right, Womanizer is a messed-up name. I'll be returning mine until the name is changed.

You can't return a sex toy lickitysplito4. Gross.

This is pathetic. You all are pathetic. You all need to get lives.

Says the troll who just got on this thread and read the whole thing to make a judgmental comment.

I was looking for honest reviews.

Yeah, for a sex toy because you're in the same "pathetic" boat.

My purchase is for a gag gift.

Sure, because spending over $200 on a gag gift makes perfect sense. At least we're honest.

This reviewer needs to be honest with herself. She's falling for the womanizer.

Staring down at her, I wrestle with the fact that she's wary of me hurting her, and I'm not ignorant as to why, she'd explained it to me the day we had it out on the lawn. Her father was a player, and she sees me in his light. But my hesitancy to commit to anyone is no longer due to my insane schedule or my son.

The truth becomes crystal-clear as I drink her in. She's the only woman I want.

And if I want any chance with her, I have a lot more to prove.

Clarissa does nothing half-assed, that includes the handling of her heart. What I do know is the less pricey model is fucking going down. I'm going to make damn sure of it. Fingers itching to touch her, I try to reel in what I'm feeling. No matter what steps I take from here on out, if I want her, I have to put *both* of them first.

Clarissa's phone buzzes next to her on the bed, and I see it's Regina Leighton, the mother of the boy hosting Dante's sleepover. Ignoring the spectacle Kevin's making outside with the horn, I swipe to answer, making a quick exit out of Clarissa's bedroom softly shutting her door.

"Hello?"

"Troy?" Dante sniffs. "Where's Mommy?"

"She's asleep."

"C-c-can you wake her up? I need her to come and get me. I don't w-want to stay here anymore."

Kevin honks again, and I quickly walk to the front door giving him the finger.

"Hurry the fuck up, man!" He shouts as the rest of the car raises hell.

I turn my back, stepping into the house.

"I'm coming to get you."

"What?"

"Can you have them text Mommy the address?"

"Okay."

"I'll be right there."

"Please hurry."

"I'm coming, bud. Don't worry." Once I'm armed with the address, I do a quick check around the house before locking Clarissa's door, knowing Dante has a key in his backpack for emergencies. Kevin meets me as I bound down the porch.

"I'm not going. Take off. I might catch up later."

His demeanor shifts. "What the hell, man? We were counting on you to help pay for the hotel."

Annoyed, I pull some twenties from my wallet and hand them to him. "There, that's enough for one night."

"You're hard up for her, aren't you?"

"Kevin, I don't have time for this shit." I pull out my keys and start toward my truck when he blocks me. "I have to go pick up Dante."

"This, this, is why you're bailing on everything? You've fallen for her?"

"I'll explain later, okay?" I move around him, and he blocks me again.

"No, not okay, we've been planning this trip for a hot minute. What the fuck is going on?"

Kevin, though clueless most of the time, has been my wingman for four years. I get why he's pissed, but Dante's cries have my heart seizing.

"Get the fuck out of my way!"

"Fuck that," he slaps my shoulder, and in a flash, we're toe to toe.

"It's not that fucking serious," I say, pushing at his chest. "But it's about to be."

"Just tell me."

"He's mine!"

"What?"

"Dante is my son."

Kevin rolls his eyes. "Dream on."

"He's mine," I repeat as Kevin swallows, his expression turning to disbelief.

"You're serious?"

"Yeah. It's a long story. But Dante needs me like *right now.*"

"Y-yeah," he says, stepping out of my way. "Yeah, you gotta go."

"Don't tell a fucking soul, Kevin. No one."

"You need me to stay back and help?" And that's Kevin, that's the kind of friend he is.

"Nope. Go. Have fun. Just tell no one, I mean it."

"Yeah. No problem. But why?"

"Kevin!"

"Got it, hold up." He jogs over to the SUV and grabs my duffle, handing it to me, along with the cash I had just given him. "Spend it on him."

"Thanks, man. You're a good friend."

"Hit me up and let me know it's all good."

"Will do."

I manage to make it to the address in minutes because it's only a neighborhood over. Pulling up, I see Dante on the front porch, his chest bouncing with his cries. My heart cracks at the sight of him dressed in the jeans and Grand hoodie I bought him. I'd even gelled his hair like mine because he'd asked me to. I should have spoken up this morning and told Clarissa my fears, but I wanted, more than anything, for him to have a good time tonight, for those fears to be unfounded and for him to find some friends. The mother approaches me, confused as Dante leaps to my side.

"Where's Clarissa?"

"She got tied up. I'm the neighbor."

She looks me up and down. "Lucky Clarissa."

I don't bother acknowledging her. "What happened?" Dante clings to my leg as she stares over at me in a way that has my stomach turning.

"Not sure, they were playing upstairs, and Dante came down not long after asking to call his mother."

"Do you know what was said?"

A little boy Dante's age and much bigger is watching behind the cracked front door with a smirk on his face.

"What did you say to him?" I ask the boy.

"Now, now, let's not go accusing anyone of any wrongdoing. Sometimes kids get scared at these things, being away from home and all."

I pull Dante closer to me. "You're raising a bully. This isn't the first time that kid has messed with Dante. Do yourself a favor and nip that crap in the bud before he permanently screws some kid up. But I can guarantee you, it won't be *this one*."

"You know, Chris wasn't even going to invite Dante. *I'm* the one who insisted on the invite."

"Yeah, well, you can see how well that worked out."

"You can go now," she says, dismissing me in a huff.

"Happy to. This is your future problem, not mine, mark my words, you're going to wish you had paid more attention." I lift Dante into my arms. His chest pumps with his cries as I run a soothing hand down his back. "It's okay, bud. It's okay." He hugs me tightly to him, his tears soaking my face, as I bend down and grab his backpack. I make sure to narrow my eyes at the little shit still staring at us before making my way back to my truck.

It's the same kid who called him a weirdo on Halloween,

and a kid with no conscience is the most dangerous thing on earth.

Safely inside the cab, I hold Dante to me until I feel his breathing even out. Once I've got him strapped in, I finally take a breath, feeling some of the tension leave my shoulders.

"What happened?"

"I was trying to show them what Harper taught me."

I physically flinch feeling Clarissa's and my efforts backfire in a big fucking way.

"You tried to teach them how to *dance?*"

Dante nods.

Fuck. Fuckity fuck!

"*You said* it was cool."

"I did, bud, for us. Most little boys don't go around teaching other boys how to dance."

"I didn't know how to play what they were playing."

"It's okay."

"I'm not like them. They make fun of my videos." His breath hitches from his crying stint, and I don't think I've ever felt anything so painful in my life. Seeing the sign, I pull into Sonic and park at the drive-in before pulling Dante out of his seat to join me up front. He looks so small, so upset, that I have to look away to keep him from seeing the emotion in my face. They hurt my kid, and I want to go back and level that fucking house.

"Does Mommy tell you to ignore them when they call you names?"

"Yes."

I can feel the cracks starting to separate me in half, terrified of his next answer. "Do they hit you?"

"No. They wouldn't let me play after I tried to show them how to dance."

"It's okay. You know that, right?" I ruffle his hair. "You were just being nice."

Dante nods. "Why are we at Sonic?"

"Slushy, then home."

"Okay." He's tired, and I can tell, but I refuse to let this wait any longer.

Once we've ordered I turn to him. "Do you like adults more than kids? Is this why you didn't invite anyone from class to your birthday party?

Dante's lip quivers. "Uh huh."

"Is that why you like Michigan J. Frog so much? Because you're just like him?"

Another nod. I wrack my brain, trying to figure out a way to make my mistake up to him when I see my packed duffle in the back seat.

"What do you think about hanging with me this weekend. Just us?"

Angela's Stuffed Bell Peppers
Lawyer, Ohio

Makes 6 servings
1 hour

6 Large Bell Peppers
2 Lbs. Hamburger Meat
1 Onion – Chopped
1 Tsp. Salt
1 Tsp. Pepper
1 Can Stewed Tomatoes
1 8 Oz. Can Tomato Sauce
1 Cup Uncooked Rice
1 Cup Water
8 Oz. Grated Cheese

Cut top off bell peppers. Scrape seeds out and rinse with water. Place peppers in large pan and completely cover with water. Boil for 5 minutes. Drain and set aside.

Brown hamburger, onion, salt, and pepper. Add stewed tomatoes, tomato sauce, rice and water. Bring to boil. Lower heat and simmer for 15 minutes. Stir in grated cheese. Stuff hamburger mixture into peppers. Top with cheese.

Bake at 350 degrees for 20 minutes.

twenty-four

CLARISSA

"MOMMY, WAKE UP, SLEEPYHEAD."

Dante's voice jerks me out of a dream. Dante?

Stunned at his sudden appearance, I pull my sheet up to my neck, darting my gaze around the bed. "W-what are you doing here?"

I feel around on the mattress for my Womanizer and begin to panic when it's not beneath the sheet where I left it.

My panic escalates when behind my son, I see a set of electric blue eyes.

Please, God, get me out of this.

But you probably shouldn't ask God for a solid when you've been caught with your hand in your pants.

"We got home last night."

"Huh?" I fumble beneath my bedspread, trying to subtly search for the evidence. "I n-need to get dressed. Some privacy, please."

"What's wrong?" Troy asks. "You look a little pale. Didn't you sleep well?" His feigned innocence has me on high alert.

"Mommy, we have something very important to ask you."

Managing to find my voice, I look over at Dante. "Why aren't you at the Leightons? Are you okay?"

"Yes. Troy came to pick me up."

"What?"

"He took me to get a slushy, made me brush my teeth, and read me a story. He slept in my room to give you some rest."

"You slept here?" I ask, sinking further into the bed, my hand still searching and coming up empty.

"Missing something?" Troy asks, his smirk now a full-on grin.

"What's wrong with your hair?" Dante asks, tilting his head.

"Ah, yeah," Troy adds, "it does look a little bunched in the back, doesn't it?" You know that moment in Forrest Gump where Forrest and little Forrest both tilt their heads while watching TV and Jenny finds it endearing? This is NOT that moment.

"Get out! Get out both of you. I'll talk to you in a minute."

"It's okay, Mommy," Troy snickers, "It's perfectly healthy to want some *me* time."

I narrow my eyes. "Go."

"But we need to ask you a question," Dante whines.

"Give me a minute, son, to p-put on some clothes." *And find my sex toy.* "Go on."

Troy ushers him out of the room but not before mouthing the words "top drawer."

I waste no time racing to my dresser and seeing that the toy was strategically hidden beneath my underwear.

He knows I used it.

He knows I used it!

Then it hits me. The review! Praying I didn't post it, I scramble to my laptop and see not only is it published, but there are seventeen comments. The last one made by an unmistakable culprit.

Pleasure-Ranger12

Did it ever occur to any of you that it's not the womanizer's fault he's got such a bad rep? That the title was slapped on him because of his performance alone and not the totality of his makeup? What if the womanizer has the best of intentions for his future model and thinks the less risky model is a douche who can't give the woman what she needs? Contrary to popular belief, not all models are made the same. Take a chance, goodconsumer90.

Covering my mouth with my hand, I read the comment over and over. Troy not only knows I masturbated, but that I then debated with trolls on the internet about my attraction to him.

I want to slice open my mattress and crawl inside.

It's worse than being picture of the week in the *People of Walmart*.

Standing in a scalding shower, I bury my face in my hands as R&B drifts through the house, and I hear the rustling of pans.

How can I face him?

And why is Dante here? The woman in me is mortified, but the mother in me overrules as I quickly towel off to see why Dante came home early.

Avoiding Troy's eyes, I pour some juice for Dante while Troy whisks some eggs.

"Okay, what happened?"

"They were mean to me, so Troy came and picked me up."

I pull him to stand in front of me, kneeling down, my heart breaking.

"They were mean to you, baby?"

"Yeah, but I don't care because I'm going to find some friends who get me. I have to find my tribe."

I look over to Troy, who smiles down at Dante.

"That's…good advice."

"Troy wants to take me someplace special and spend the night. Is that okay?"

I look over to Troy and see he's watching me carefully as he cracks another egg.

"Yes. I guess that would be fine. But after breakfast. How about pancakes?"

"Troy's making French toast."

"But your favorite is pancakes."

"Nothing wrong with French toast," Troy taunts. "Some people would say it's a better breakfast *model*."

"Pancakes are just as delicious," I argue.

"I disagree." He bites his lips as he flips a piece of toast in the pan.

"Are you really going to do this?" I ask him, standing, as Dante takes his seat.

Troy turns to me, crossing his arms over his chest. "Why don't we let Dante decide?"

"Don't bring him into this, you *weirdo*."

"Weird is good," Dante speaks up in his defense. "Weirdo means you won't *ever* be *boring*."

This he's just learned, no doubt from the man whose mouth is lifting at the stove.

"Yes, it is, I was paying your fa-" Troy's eyes widen, and his smile blinds me. I'm so flustered I've almost outed him myself.

"It was a compliment."

Dante tilts his head. "Are you okay, Mommy?"

"I'm fine, I would just prefer pancakes!"

"Not what I read," Troy mumbles.

I can feel the blush creep up my neck. I've hit my limit. "Troy, a word."

"Sorry," he holds up the spatula, "I'm mid flip, don't want to burn anything."

I nod and swallow as two sets of eyes study me.

Get it together. Get it together.

"Mommy, you need a chill pill," Dante says through a laugh.

"Where did you learn that?" I look up to Troy, who shrugs.

"Don't look at me."

"We don't take pills to chill around here, young man. You got that?!"

"Yes, ma'am."

Troy ushers me into the seat next to him. "Have a seat," he says, gently sitting me down. "I'll make you some breakfast too."

It's clear both men think I'm on the verge of snapping, so I do what I'm told as Dante places a napkin across my lap. "It's okay, Mommy, just relax."

Dante stands on his seat, grabbing the carton and pours me some orange juice. After taking a sip, I glance over at him as Troy busies himself at the stove.

"I'm sorry you had a bad time."

"It's okay. Troy made it all better."

I don't miss Troy's smile as he plates up our breakfast.

Dante crosses his silverware on his plate. "May I be excused? I'm full."

"Only one game," Troy says, "We're leaving soon."

"Yes, sir."

I sip my coffee and eye Troy. "Where will you take him?"

"Camping at the lake. That okay?"

"Sure."

With all the commotion this morning, I didn't have time to drink him in. He's dressed in a grey long john shirt that hugs his every muscle and somehow makes his eyes pop. His strawberry hair is getting longer, has more wave, and is brushed away from his face. His jaw covered in day-old stubble. He looks every part the rugged man. And I'm pretty sure I look every part the ragged woman. But none of that matters as I fight with my conscience about the events of the last twenty-four hours.

"I know what you're thinking, and you need to stop," Troy says, crumpling up his napkin and throwing it on his plate.

"I can't help it. I drink one glass of wine," I wince, "okay three, and decide to unplug, and he needed me. What if you weren't here?"

"Don't. I was here, and I'm so damned happy about that fact, so let me have my moment, okay?"

I nod, and he leans over and tips my chin, so I'm facing him.

"Promise me you won't beat yourself up about it."

"It was past eight, so I thought it was safe to relax."

"You don't have to explain it to me, Clarissa. I know you would never, ever, put him in harm's way."

"But I did. I knew those kids weren't his friends, but I wanted so much for him to fit in somewhere. I'm a fucking high school teacher, I know how cruel kids can be. What was I thinking?"

"I was thinking the same. I've noticed he doesn't invite friends over or get invited either. I was hoping for what you were. I'm just as guilty. But he's special, too sensitive for those brutes. He's got quirks, he's different, and that's okay. It's more than okay."

"How about the lining up of his toys," I grin. "How they have to be just so. And the way he gets possessive about the weirdest stuff."

"He's a neat freak for sure."

"Hey, don't you dare touch that."

We smile at each other.

"When he was just a baby, he was addicted to *Animusic*. He played those videos over and over and over again, and it took me a while to realize he was *memorizing* them. He was almost two the first time he climbed up to my PC and started using a mouse. He could barely talk in sentences then."

"He's scary smart."

"What are we going to do?"

Troy shrugs. "Let him be him. Exactly what we've been doing."

"They won't understand him," I say fearfully.

"Someone will," he says intently. "Someday, maybe sooner, maybe later, *someone* is going to stop and take notice of how special he is and stake their claim in his life. Trust me. It'll happen more than once."

I sniff. "When did you get so good at saying the perfect thing?"

"I'm a practicing father. Was that all right?"

"Better than."

A tear runs down my cheek, and he moves to sit next to me, studying it.

"What are you doing?" I ask as he leans in.

"It's beautiful, you know," he says, lifting it away with his thumb. "It's a mother's love."

We're so close. If just one of us gives, our lips will touch.

Troy lingers as I inhale his scent, his masculinity. In seconds, I get lost in his stare, the fullness of his lips, the weight and gravity of our connection. This can't happen.

"Excuse me," I say, lifting only to bang my knee on the table. Troy curses under his breath as Dante returns from the living room. "Where are you going?" He asks as I move to retreat to my bedroom.

"To get dressed." And scream in a pillow.

SARAH JANE'S SEVEN LAYER DIP
Personal Assistant, Los Angeles

Makes 12 servings
1 hour

2 8 Oz. Packages Guacamole (Add garlic powder and salt to
   taste)
1 Cup Sour Cream
1/2 Cup Mayonnaise
2 9 Oz. Cans Bean Dip
1 Bunch Green Onions – Sliced
3 Tomatoes – Chopped
1 8 Oz. Can Sliced Black Olives (Optional)
1 8 Oz. Package Sharp Cheddar Cheese – Shredded
1 Jar Picante Sauce

Combine sour cream and mayonnaise together. Spread bean
dip in 13x9 pan. Top with guacamole. Layer sour cream mixture next. Sprinkle with green onions, tomatoes, and olives.
Cover with cheese and top with Picante sauce.

Serve with tortilla chips.

twenty-five

CLARISSA

I'M SITTING AT MY VANITY AS THE BOYS GET READY TO HEAD OUT. I'm still stunned by Troy's words. They ring true. He knows his son. He's caught onto his quirks, memorized his routine, and I can't help but wonder how much of a mirror he thinks Dante is. I was an absolute mess at breakfast, ashamed and devastated, and somehow Troy managed to pull me from that place and make it...better. I decide to make it a point to thank him before they leave. And it's the leaving I'm wrestling with, though I know Troy would never let any harm come to Dante. I bat away any notion that I'm jealous as I apply my lip balm.

Am I jealous?

The truth is, Troy wouldn't take him without my permission, and I find myself at odds that he does have it, fully. I can trust him with his son.

I'm still spinning in that revelation when I see Troy in the mirror, shutting my bedroom door, his eyes trained on me as he twists the lock.

All words catch in my throat when I see the intensity in his gaze. He stalks toward me, stopping just behind me as I sit in wait.

He lifts a hand and gently runs his fingers through my

wet strands, pulling my head back slightly before gathering the hair at the nape of my neck. I draw my brows in confusion as he reaches for one of the hair ties next to my brush and secures it around his fistful of my hair. I'm just about to speak when he leans down, and his warm lips connect with the slope of my neck. His open-mouthed kiss is gentle, sensual, and I feel myself lean into it. Slowly his lips roam up and down my collarbone, up and down, covering the length of my shoulder. Mouth parted, I watch his eyes close as he begins to deepen his kiss, adding the slide of his tongue, before pulling at my sweater and exposing my shoulder.

Stunned, I watch his assault alternating between licks and bites while his warm hands wipe away the wetness of his kiss. Panting, I can do nothing but watch while he leads, his fist in my hair as his lips do all the talking. It's when he hears my moan that he begins to quicken his pace. Every touch precise, purposeful. He licks the shell of my ear before drawing the whole of my lobe into his mouth, biting, sucking as he cups my breast, lifting, molding, in worship. Nothing is off-limits as he blankets the whole of me with his touch. I'm on fire, wetness pools in my panties, my heartbeat pulsing between my thighs. I gasp as he tugs on my ponytail and my head lolls to the side as he makes quick work of covering the entirety of my neck with the same intensity of his lips. I'm moaning uncontrollably now as he encompasses me with his hands, still cupping my breasts, mouth roaming, moving to the front of my neck, tracing the divot in my throat with precise flicks of his tongue. I'm on the verge of an orgasm when he tweaks my nipple, my gasp caught by the side of his mouth as he licks playfully around my lips and pulls away, just as I lean in for more. And then he's making a slow descent down my back, his hand gliding down the front of me. My leggings are no match for his deft fingers as he presses a thick digit exactly where I need him.

Gasping, I clutch what I can, but he's still fast at work, covering me wholly in his kiss, momentum building as my chest heaves. Getting a grip on his shirt, I twist it in my hands, unable to see anything but the lust in his eyes as he pulls away, his stare piercing. I open fully for him, spreading my legs, granting him more access. He runs his finger up and down my center, massaging my clit, as my heart hammers out of control, I'm seconds away from begging for his kiss when his lips drift back up to my throat, I turn my head and we meet, open-mouthed as he thrusts his tongue in deep, kissing me to within an inch of my life.

And with one more flick of his finger, I come, and he dives while my sporadic breaths pump into his mouth. I'm thoroughly seduced, completely intoxicated as he keeps his pace, his hands working their way back up, his lips and tongue still roaming the whole of my face, chest, and neck. I've never in my life felt so worshiped, so intoxicated by a man's touch. I've never, ever, been kissed like this. When his lips finally return to mine, I grip him to me, twisting in my seat and kiss him back with everything in me. I'm rewarded with the tangle of our tongues as he thrusts so deeply, I drown. Slowly, he pulls away, staring down at me with so much heat and longing, it steals what's left of my breath.

"Just think about it."

Slowly righting my sweater, he places one more open-mouthed kiss on my neck before walking out the door.

GABBY'S SMOTHERED PORK CHOPS
Architect, New Mexico

Makes 6 servings
1 hour

1 Stick Butter
2 Cups Flour
2 Cans Cream of Mushroom Soup
½ Cup White Cooking Wine
½ Cup Water
1 Large Package Fresh Mushrooms
1-2 Large Onions
6 Pork Chops

Melt butter in skillet. Use one cup of flour to flour both sides of the pork chops. Lightly brown both sides of pork chops in butter. Mix soup, wine, water, and one cup of flour. Pour over pork chops.

twenty-six

CLARISSA

I've spent the last twenty-four hours in a daze. After an emergency call to Parker, I used the rest of my time doing things I never get a chance to do. I found myself relieved Brett was out of town. I'm not the type of woman to put her eggs in different baskets. Every time I start to feel guilty, I remember my conversation with Parker, not that it really helps.

"Hell yes! May the best man win!"

"I'm not like that. You know I hate that. I'm not my father."

"Then pick one."

"I can't. Troy is...I don't fully trust him, but Jesus, I've never felt anything like that. And Brett is a great guy. I mean that."

"It's called dating. Make both aware of the other, and there is no issue."

"This is wrong."

"It's dating. You can choose to be a monogamous dater, but that puts you in a *relationship*. Are you ready to start a relationship with either?"

"I'm not juggling two men. That's beyond my comfort zone."

"Then make it clear to Troy that he can no longer kiss you and feel you up after you apply lip balm."

"It was the best kiss of my life."

"Yeah? Then, bye-bye Brett."

"Stop it."

"Brett said you're not exclusive, right?"

"Something to that effect."

"So, you're not asking about *his* other girls."

"Who says he's seeing other women?"

"I do. Ask him. And if that's the case, you have nothing to feel guilty about. You can make out with baby daddy all you want."

"I don't do this."

"Times have changed my friend. This is the new norm. Eventually, marriage will be obsolete."

"No way. I'm traditional."

"Then stick to kissing."

"I'm not thirteen."

"Babe, you have a decision to make. Decide on one or see what happens with either."

"This is bullshit," I say, picking up the rest of Dante's toys.

"Yeah, I feel really sorry for you."

"I'm sorry. I'm being insensitive. I know you're going through a hard time."

"I'm fine. This isn't about me. This is about you finding someone suitable for our boy and for once, making yourself priority too."

"I can't risk it with Troy."

"Then you've made your decision."

"Right."

"Except you haven't."

"What?"

Parker sighs. "Look, when you find yourself unable to keep from moving forward with one, you have your answer.

Keep an open mind and heart and see where it goes. Or run a train with them both."

"I hate you."

"Make me proud. Now I have to go. I have a nooner."

"Really?"

"A meeting. Get your mind out the gutter."

"Parker, wait, what did we decide again?"

"We decided Mommy is going to have a little fun."

"I'm not sleeping with them both!"

"Konnichiwa!"

"Parker, wait!"

twenty-seven

TROY

"I can't believe we didn't catched any fish."

"That's *catch* any fish. It's getting too cold, bud. We'll try again some other time."

"Will you put the worms on the hook again?"

"Sure, but don't you want to learn to do it yourself?"

Dante's eyes bulge in my rearview. "I'm not prepared for that, Troy."

I crack up as I park in my driveway and open the back door as he unbuckles from his booster.

"Okay, remember what we talked about?"

"Yep," he squeaks as I lift him from the backseat. We're halfway across the yard when a song I don't recognize begins to drift out of the house. Eyes wide, Dante immediately starts wiggling out of my hold.

"It's me & Mommy's favorite song! Let me down!" Dante takes off like a shot as gentle drums, bass, and guitar filter through the air. "I'm coming, Mommy!" He declares, bounding up the steps.

Hot on his heels with our bags in both arms, I step inside the door behind him, seeing Clarissa standing in the middle of the living room. She looks over to me with a shy smile mouthing "hi," just as Dante leaps into her arms. Dante grabs her face with his hands stealing her attention as they begin to sing.

"Cupid, draw back your bow, and let your arrow gooo, straight to my lover's heart for *meeee*," Dante belts offkey as a smile lights up Clarissa's face and she sings along, dancing with him wrapped firmly around her as if they've been doing it for years. And it's so obvious they have. The light in his mother's eyes is unforgettable as she sings with him, swaying while he giggles with every exaggerated bounce of her hips.

And me? I'm so fucking gone, lost in the sight of them both.

It's the most beautiful thing I've ever seen, and my throat goes dry while I memorize every second of it. They're completely in sync, as they lift hands in the air at the same time, imploring Cupid while singing their hearts out. My own heart expands unbearably in my chest when they rub noses as the song drifts to a close. Clarissa's eyes catch mine over her son's shoulder, and we just…stare. I have no idea what she sees, but I'm pretty sure if it's anything like what I'm feeling, it's heavy. She beams at me before she breaks the connection, gazing down at Dante.

"Did you have fun?"

"It was the best time I've ever had!"

"Really? That's great. What did you two do?"

"I can't tell you anything, sorry, *man* stuff." Dante turns to me and winks both eyes.

I can't help my chuckle. "That's right, man stuff."

Clarissa looks between us. "Man stuff, huh? Well, all right, go unload your pack and put all your dirty clothes in the hamper.

"Yes, ma'am."

I'm thankful for the music playing in the background because the minute Dante disappears, I'm at a loss for words. All

I can do is think about the way she kissed me back. It was more than a kiss, it was a declaration on my part, and I made damn sure she knew it.

I let impulse win yesterday, unable to handle another second without touching her, tasting her, showing her just how much I want her. And I can't for one fucking second bring myself to regret it. Duffle still on my shoulder, I stuff my hands into my jeans. "So that's your favorite song, huh?"

"Yeah," she says, crossing her arms over her chest. Her hair is curled, and she's in a sweater dress, nails freshly painted, and the house is immaculate.

"You look beautiful."

"Yeah, thanks, I gave myself a little TLC."

"It shows. Smells good in here."

"I've been baking."

"Yeah?"

"I think Theo has company. You might want to wait a bit before returning home."

"Oh yeah?" I chuckle. "Good for him."

"Are you hungry?"

"Sure."

"Stay for dinner?"

"That'd be great."

She seems just as lost for the moment as I am, I decide to cut the bullshit. "Clarissa—"

She takes a tentative step toward me, keeping her voice low. "You know orgasms may be ninety-nine percent mental, but studies show that parts of a woman's brain deactivate during an orgasm, especially those involved with emotion. This explains the 'oh shit' mentality women feel after."

"You think I'm an 'oh shit?'"

"I know you were before. I'm not sure what you are now."

"Can I be a 'hot damn!' or a 'hell yes!' instead?"

We both laugh, and it dies just as quickly.

I close the space between us, leaning in to kiss her cheek. "Take your time, Clarissa. I'm not going anywhere."

"Favorite movie?" I ask, folding a pair of Dante's jeans.

"When Harry Met Sally."

Though I let impulse win yesterday, I've decided to embrace her 'adult' way of dating, using her dinner invite to my advantage to get to know her. She was nervous when we got home and dressed for me. I'm positive she's thought plenty about it and I'm not about to fumble this chance. At this point, I know everything from the age she was when she got her first kiss to her favorite color—purple. Which I could have easily guessed because the bulk of the clothes I'm folding are a varying shade of it. She tugs the thong I'm fondling from my hands, just as I hold it up.

"Behave. And it's a classic. Also, *Sweet Home Alabama.* It's about a woman who's torn between two different…" Her blush is unmistakable.

I lift a brow. "Go on."

She hides behind the shirt she holds up. "I don't think I will."

"Then let's watch it. After dinner."

"I'll pass. What about you, movies?"

"I'm more of an action movie guy. *Mission Impossible,* that kind of shit. And superhero movies."

"I see. And music?"

"Rap, rock, whatever."

She wrinkles her nose. "Just not old soul."

"I like your favorite song."

"Yeah?"

"Yeah," I say, lifting a purple bra which she snatches from my hand.

"Stop handling my delicates, Jenner."

I exhale through my teeth, shaking my head.

"Yeah," she smirks, "I know that was loaded. Look at you, growing up."

"Don't accuse me of that, you have no idea what was running through my head, Ms. A. There's a ruler involved."

She rolls her eyes, grabbing another shirt seeming lost in her thoughts before she speaks. "There's this one song. I listen for it all the time. My mother used to sing it to me while we did the dishes. I can't, for the life of me, figure out which one it is. It's haunted me for years."

"Man or woman singing?"

"Man. Like James Brown, but not James Brown. I remember in the middle of it, Mom always made me laugh. It's funny how memory works. Maybe I've heard it already, and I just don't recognize it anymore."

"I'm sure you'll know when you hear it."

"Yeah, maybe."

"And your dad?"

"He was…" she twists her lips, "well, he existed in a universe of his own where the party never ended, and champagne and women flowed like water. He was a producer out in Hollywood, where he met my mother. She was going to be his next big star before she died. And when she did, he took a job in Austin as a promotor. I think his intention was to settle down and give us a more stable life. I guess you can take the guy out of Hollywood…" she sighs. "Anyway, I moved here to attend Grand and never left."

"Did you have plans to leave after you graduated?"

She shrugs, and I can see in her eyes, our discussion is over.

Guilty, I lift a pile of Dante's laundry in question.

"Second drawer from the top of his dresser."

Walking down the hall toward his bedroom, I freeze when I hear his voice sound on the other side.

"Yo, what's up, guys. Today for the first time on Legit Life, I'm going to answer all my comments. That's right, haters, get ready."

Freezing, I stand outside his door with a handful of his clothes as Clarissa runs into my back.

"Did you hear that?" I whisper.

I glance back to see her hand over her mouth to muffle her laugh, her eyes wide. Dante speaks up again.

"Let's do this, so the first comment is from DeanBohanon700 of Rip audio. 'I'm confused on what happened to the mailman.' I know, buddy, I know. It was ridiculous. He got struck for nothing."

I turn to Clarissa. "Do you have any idea what he's saying?"

She shakes her head with a smile. "No clue. Techie stuff?"

I shrug.

Dante's voice interrupts our confusion. "Okay, there's another comment on the same video. LawrenceOppen243 says 'ye.' Uh, okay, dude. Ye, to you too."

Clarissa grips the back of my shirt, leaning in.

"This one is on my video about my new merch. Comment says, 'I ordered.' Liar, I never got email confirmation. The next comment is, 'I love Legit Life videos.' Thanks for the support, bud."

Clarissa is in hysterics at my back, her laundry dropped at my feet while I shush her.

"This next comment is for the kid who says I should use

iMovie. I don't know how many times I have to tell you, kids, I'm never going to use iMovie, not in my lifetime."

Clarissa's still muffling her laugh in my back as I try to hold in my own.

"Okay, some kid said my sniffing during my video was disgusting. Hey bro, that shirt you were wearing on your video was disgusting. Burrrrn. So, guys, if you don't like my videos get off my channel."

Clarissa hums along with her music at the stove while I chop vegetables at the table, watching Dante while he plays in the yard with his drone. It's been the perfect Sunday and more than I could have hoped for. Dante and I watched all three Spiderman movies back to back while Clarissa stretched out in her recliner grading papers. It's like nothing I've ever felt, being such a present part of their lives, and I hate the fact that I'm about to have to leave. And when I do, I'll once again be watching from afar in my bedroom when she tucks him in tonight.

But I'll take what I can get. I'll toe the line. I'll do whatever it takes.

The holidays are coming up, Thanksgiving mere days away, and it's time to talk about how that's going to go down. I lift the cutting board full of vegetables, hauling them into the kitchen ready to finally broach the subject when I hear Dante call from the porch.

"Who are you?"

"*Dante*," Clarissa groans, turning the heat down on the stove. "This kid *is* the neighborhood watch." We share a grin as she crosses the living room to get to where Dante stands at the door.

My whole body tenses when I hear the reply.

"Are you talking to me?"

"Yes, ma'am."

"Well, I'm here to see Troy."

"Troy? He's over here."

"Clarissa, wait," I say just as she steps out onto the porch.

By the time I join them, I'm too late, Pamela Jenner is eye level with her grandson.

Sally's Chicken & Dumplings
RN, North Dakota

Makes 8 servings

45 minutes

4 Boneless, Skinless Chicken Breasts
2 Tbsps Butter
2 Cans Cream of Chicken Soup
1 Box Chicken Stock or 2 Cans Chicken Broth
1 Onion – finely chopped
2 10 oz. Cans Flaky Biscuits – each cut into sixths

In a crockpot, mix together the chicken, butter, soup and onion and cover with water. Cook covered for 5 to 6 hours on low.

Once cooked, remove and shred the chicken. Return the chicken to the crockpot and stir well.

Add the biscuit pieces to the chicken and cook for an additional 30 to 45 minutes until the dough is cooked through.

This is a simple and easy dish and is great with a salad or fresh vegetables.

twenty-eight

CLARISSA

TWO THINGS ARE EVIDENT WITHIN SECONDS OF LAYING EYES on this woman. One is that genes run strong in the Jenner family. Two is that she knows without a doubt she's looking at her grandchild. Dish in her hands, she kneels down in front of Dante.

"I'm Pamela. Troy's mama. What's your name?"

"Dante."

Pamela swallows. "What's your last name?" There's a rattle in her voice, and I can feel the swell of emotions rolling off her.

"Arden. Dante Arden."

Pamela's eyes lift to meet Troy's, and I can clearly see the panic on his face.

"Mom, what are you doing here?"

"What am I doing…" she's completely baffled by his question as the casserole dish shakes in her hands, "I brought you butterscotch pudding, but you live next door. You're parked next door."

"I do," he says. "Let's head over, okay?"

She's beautiful, the years have served her well, and I make a mental note to get the name of her moisturizer at a later date, that's if she doesn't murder me on my front lawn.

Troy steps up to her in an attempt to usher her away as she looks back to Dante. She shoves the casserole into Troy's stomach as Troy whimpers out a "Mom, don't."

"How old are you?"

"You're funny," Dante says, staring at her gaping mouth. "I'm six."

"Six," she says breathlessly before she looks directly at me. "And you're his mother?" I nod, fear racing through me. I knew this day would come. I just didn't think it would be today. "I'm Clarissa. Nice to meet you, Mrs. Jenner."

"To meet me?" She looks over at her son. "I'm not sure we were supposed to meet."

"Mom," Troy pleads. "I need you to go next door, and I'll meet you there."

She lifts her chin, reading the guilt on both our faces. "I'm not going anywhere."

"Dante, go play," I order as my stomach starts to churn.

"What's wrong?" Dante looks between the three of us. "Troy, you in trouble with your Mommy?"

"It's okay, bud. Just go inside."

"Nothing's wrong, Peanut," I push gently at his shoulder. "Just go in, and we'll be in in a minute."

"I'm always sent to my room," he grumbles. "Will you be here when I come back?" Dante askes Pamela.

"I don't know." She's utterly devastated, and the guilt I feel at that moment is crippling.

I close the front door as Pamela faces off with her son.

"I would know that face anywhere," she says as tears finally surface. "He's the spitting image of you," she whispers hoarsely. "He's yours."

Troy nods slowly, the look in his eyes a mix of fear and devastation.

"Tell me, son, tell me you didn't keep this from me for six years."

"Mom, I made a huge mistake." Pamela cuts his explanation and glares over at me.

"Tell me *you* didn't know I existed."

"I'm so sorry," I say as Troy grips his mother's shoulders in an attempt to reel her back toward him.

"Mom, I lied to Clarissa. This is my fault. Put this on me. All of this is my fault."

"I have a six-year-old grandchild, and no one told me?!"

"Mom, please, keep your voice down. He doesn't know. We haven't told him yet."

Her eyes bulge. "You haven't told him in six years!"

"Damn it, Mom! Stop it!" Troy snaps. "I'm going to need you to get it together, or you need to leave. Either hear me out or go."

She looks over to Troy, furious. "You don't talk to me like that!"

"I will when it's serious. And I take this as seriously as you did. Now listen to me. I screwed up. I'm trying to be a better father. I'm trying at a relationship with him, and I can't have you bulldozing in and—"

"*Bulldozing?* I didn't even know he existed," she says just before tears spill down her cheeks. Troy's eyes close, and I can feel the crack inside him. I'm witnessing first-hand the damage I caused with my grudge. I want so much to blame Troy's lie, but this heartbreak right here, it's on me.

"Mrs. Jenner, I kept him away." She looks over to me. "Troy lied the night Dante was conceived, and I kept him away. I'm partly to blame."

"You kept my son away from his child? *Why? Why* would you do that?"

My voice is pathetic when I find it. "Because at the time, I was a new teacher, and he was a student in another school."

She turns to Troy. "You lied about being a student?"

Troy nods.

"So you could bed her?"

Biting his lips, Troy nods again. "I didn't think—"

"Jesus, Troy. No, no, you didn't think. And now I have a six-year-old baby who doesn't know his grandmother. I didn't raise you this way!"

"Mom, please stop. Please. I swear I was going to tell you."

"You've had years to tell me."

"I kept him away," I admit freely feeling the shift of her hurt shaping into fury. "I'm just as much to blame."

"And I will blame you," she says curtly, "but right now, I'm dealing with my son." She turns to him spewing anger and hurt. "How could you? How could you lie to me for so long? That baby is partly mine too, is he not? I raised his *father.*"

"Mom, I just met him three months ago."

Her eyes bulge. "How so?"

"Me," I say with lead in my voice. "That's me."

"You kept him away from his child for *six* years?"

Guilt riddles me as Troy tries to reason with her.

"Mom, look. We can't erase what's happened, but we're all doing so well now. You of all people know how hard it is to raise a child. She was just protecting him."

She glares at me. "No one needs protection from you, Troy. That's unforgivable." She takes a menacing step toward me. "And just who in the hell do you think *you* are?"

"His mother, Mrs. Jenner, but I feel ter—"

"Call me Pam, we're family after all, right?" she snaps. "I can't, I can't believe this. Why?"

When neither Troy nor I speak, she breaks down. "I'll never get that time back. You realize that, don't you?" She looks between us as her tears fall rapidly. "I'll never get that back," she cries as Troy tries to pull her into his arms. "How could you?" She says, crumbling as she pushes him away and then looks to me. "How could you?" My tears fall along with hers as Troy finally pulls her in.

All I can do is watch her cry.

TROY

My mother drives away and I look over to where Clarissa stands on her porch, a cup of coffee in hand. It's been one of the worst fucking hours of my life, and I've never seen Clarissa so upset. Enduring my mother's wrath, she went back and forth between begging for forgiveness and defending her decisions. I hate myself, I resent her, I hate the whole fucked up situation. For the first time since I came into their lives, I feel like I need some distance. We stare at each other for long moments, both spent from hammering out our mistakes. I'm unsure of what she's thinking as she looks at me and I have no idea where we stand, or if we have any footing at all.

I've just broken my mother's heart and fractured her trust.

And maybe if I'd have come clean with Mom sooner, I'd have a place in my son's life. Mom would have fought for me. That's the one thing I can't stop thinking about. I may have taken advantage that night. But did Clarissa take advantage of the fact that I was young and naïve enough to go along with her selfish declaration that I didn't get to be his father? Or was she so tainted by my lie that she genuinely believed I had no place in his world? I can feel the distance growing between us as she stands there with tears drying on her cheeks. It's then I feel the wall resurrect between us. But this time, I'm not sure who's constructing it, and instead of consoling her, I throw my sledgehammer down and walk away.

3RD QUARTER

WINTER

twenty-nine

TROY

ANTE, BALL, WORK.

Priorities.

I exhale the rest as I grip the bar in my hands and push off.

Three games left.

With any luck, we'll get to the playoffs and snag a bowl game.

I push off again, wrestling with the weight of my load.

Finish the season, get an invite to the NFL Combine, prove my worth, get drawn in the draft.

Priorities.

No more distractions. No more stalking, obsessing, day-dreaming, or fucking pining.

I can't handle any more indecision when it comes to Clarissa. Instead, I've pushed harder than ever, taken a full second off my dash time, and used the gym as my punching bag. I'm not sure what I want anymore, but I am an athlete, and that's the only thing that's getting me through.

Lance spots me as I do another set of reps.

"What's good, man? How's the BM situation?"

"Everything's coming out smooth," I grit out.

"I'm not asking about the integrity of your daily shit, Jenner."

"Keep my count, man. I don't want to talk about it."

"That bad?" He lifts the bar as I finish my set.

I down the contents of my water bottle and wipe my mouth. "Too much water under the bridge."

"She still giving you hell?"

No, she's gone quiet, and I have nothing to say. We're on opposite sides of the field, our son pulling us together on the fifty. My resentment is winning for the moment after each conversation with my mother.

"Nope, she's…whatever. It doesn't matter. I could be a fucking saint sporting a halo, and she still wouldn't have it."

Kevin takes that moment to add his two cents. "She's got a rich side piece who wears penny loafers."

I reach over to where he's pressing next to me and jab him in the sack. He damn near drops the bar on his chest, but Lance catches it.

"Fuck, man! What the hell…" Kevin sputters, cupping his sack.

I give him a pointed look, "Keep that hot air in your head."

"Easy, man," Lance chuckles, positioning himself on his back to start his lift as Kevin hovers over him.

"We aren't talking about this. I'm over it." I lift some bells to start my curls.

"Yeah, you're over it, all right. That's why you're swatting away potentials like they're flies," Kevin spits sarcastically, turning towards Lance. "He's not hitting on shit."

"I've had eight years to run that game," I say honestly. "It's getting old."

But there's more to it. The truth is that I had a glimpse of what I wanted, and that vision is disappearing by the day.

Lance and Kevin share a grin that grates on me.

219

"I'm not delusional, all right? It's just time I move on from the one and done game. I've got more going on."

"Yeah, long dark red hair, thick ass, perfect lips, and moody. Can't say that turns me off. Can I get her number?"

I glare over at Kevin as I speed up my reps.

"You hit me with those bells, dickhead, and you're getting what you give."

This makes Lance chuckle. "Ease up, man."

I look between them both, "If you two are so worried about my dick, feel free to give it a t—"

"Jenner! My office, *now*," Coach barks from the door.

Lance and I share a look, and I shrug, tossing my bells on the mat. Kevin whistles Darth Vader's theme song, and I flip him the bird before making my way to the coach's office.

"Shut the door." I do as I'm told but remain standing, a little on edge. He's a live wire, and in all my years playing with him, I've never seen him so strung out during a season. We all want an explanation, but all we can do is stand by as he continues his tirade. Plenty of coaches have bad field-side reps, but ours was never one of them, until this season. His 'fuck all' mentality seems to be his new norm, and we're stuck dealing with it.

"Have a seat," he says, motioning to the chair opposite his desk. I take a seat as he sorts through a file before snapping it shut. Seeming satisfied, he glances up at me. "I've gotten a few calls."

Instantly, my back straightens. "Yeah?"

"Do you have an agent?"

"No. I've looked into it and gotten a few calls, but I've been—"

His stare turns arctic. "What? You've been what? Is there something more pressing, Jenner?"

"No," I cup my neck. "I could use some advice."

"Here's my advice. Get an agent. And do it soon. There are thousands of athletes who would kill for an invite to the Combine. Do you think you're special?"

"Hope so." I want to swallow my fucking tongue after the look the remark gets me.

"You need that invite, Jenner."

"Understood, sir."

"And if that happens, you need to be ready. Do yourself a favor, do the research, and return the calls."

"Will do. Thanks."

He tips back in his chair, peering at me. "Don't you want to know who's interested?"

"Honestly, I'll take what I can get."

"Have it your way. We're done here."

"Thanks."

I almost make it to the door, but stop when he speaks up behind me. "Any distraction, whatever it is, let it go. Ball and ball only from here on out until your name's called. Season's almost over, but you're about to enter the hardest four months of your life. No excuses."

ERIN'S PORK CHOPS AND YUMMY RICE
Chemist, Oklahoma

Makes 6 servings
1 hour and 30 minutes

1 Stick Margarine or Butter
2 Cans Cream of Chicken Soup
1 Can Cream of Mushroom Soup
1 Can cream of Celery
2 ½ Cans Water
2 ½ Cans Minute Rice
6 Boneless Pork Chops or Boneless, Skinless Chicken Breasts

Melt butter in large baking dish. Mix soups and water together. Stir well. Add rice and stir. Pour ¾ of soup mixture into pan with butter. Lay pork chops or chicken and cover with the rest of soup mixture.

Bake at 350 degrees for 1 hour

*May need up to 15 minutes extra cooking depending on meat.

thirty

CLARISSA

"MOMMY, IT'S WIGGLING!" DANTE CALLS FROM THE bathroom from where he stands on his stool.

"Don't mess with it! You've got to let it happen naturally."

"It's hanging! Come see!"

"What did I tell you?"

"It feels funny," he giggles.

"Baby, you need to leave it alone." I worry my lip after checking my purse and debate on shooting a text. Troy's been avoiding me since our run-in with his mother, using his time with Dante at his house between his away games, school, and work. I've not put up much of a fight because I have no idea where he stands, but there is now a jarring distance between us from where we were. I saw it that day, the minute Pamela drove away, his resentment apparent with the way he looked at me—a far cry from mere hours before.

I've been iced out.

His checks are still coming weekly without fail, but his absence is noticeable. He's kept up his routine with Dante, never missing breakfast with his son. Though we stay friendly in his presence, it's all small talk, both his interest and his eyes are anywhere but on me.

This is precisely the type of thing I feared. Things got heavy, and he all but ran. We put on a united front for his mother, and for that, I owe him, but I haven't had the chance to apologize. He repeatedly tried to take the blame for all of it, and it pained me to see him so helpless.

And now, it's as if any relationship we started has evaporated into thin air. Before there was an issue of us and the blowup, things were good. Better than good. We were functioning like a family. However, between that day and Troy's new distance, I'm growing more confident that trying for anything beyond co-parenting would be a mistake. If only I could get that kiss out of my head. The longer he keeps me at arm's length, the more I try to convince myself it was just a territorial play to win me. Maybe it isn't me that Troy wanted. Maybe he just wasn't comfortable with anyone else playing house with his son.

Clarissa: Are you at work?
Troy: No, I'm off tonight.
Clarissa: How was your Thanksgiving?
Troy: It was like being dragged around a field of razor blades by my balls. Yours?
Clarissa: Far more uneventful. Do you think she'll come around?
Troy: One day, she wants to spend some time with him soon.
Clarissa: That would be fine.
Troy: I'll set it up. So, what's up?
Clarissa: Do you have any singles?
Troy: Singles?
Clarissa: Dolla dolla bills yo. (Dollar eyes emoji)
Troy: What do you have in mind? (Devil emoji.)

Clarissa: Chillout, perv. Your son's about to lose his first tooth.
Troy: Yeah, I've got a few.
Clarissa: Great. I won't have to write an IOU.
Troy: Which tooth?
Clarissa: One up front.
Troy: Shit. I hope it comes back.
Clarissa: That's usually how it works.
Troy: I mean, comes back straight. I had crooked teeth.
Clarissa: Really? Your teeth are perfect.
Troy: Yeah, after four years of braces.
Clarissa: Ha. Can't picture that. So, can I come get the money?
Troy: How about I play tooth fairy tonight?
Clarissa: How will you play it? I was thinking a stick of gum and a few dollars
Troy: That's it?
Clarissa: Yeah. He's got a mouthful to lose, and we aren't going overboard for losing teeth.
Troy: He's our kid. We can spoil him if we want.
Clarissa: Fine, Daddy Warbucks, can I run over and grab the cash or not?
Troy: You call me daddy again, and I'll make it rain.
Clarissa: Har har.
Troy: I'll bring it over later. Just let me know when he's out.
Clarissa: Okay, thanks.

The flirtatious text exchange makes me hopeful, and I can't help but spend a few minutes on myself. Troy's seen me in every imaginable state, but some part of me wants the 'what if' connection back. I let my hair down and tame it with a little beach wave spray before covering my arms with lotion. Half an hour later, I have Dante tucked in, his tooth waiting underneath his pillow for the Tooth Fairy, who pokes his head in shortly after a light knock on the door.

This particular fairy is covered in sweat, his muscular frame showcased by the long-sleeved tee clinging to him and sweatpants. His thick copper blond hair peeks out of his toboggan framing his face, outlining his square jaw. The sight of him knocks a little breath from me as I greet him.

"Hey," I say, tightening my robe. I can feel the late fall chill coming off his skin. "You've been running?"

"Yeah, that's kind of what I do."

When he finally lifts his eyes to mine, that kiss is all I think about, but in his posture, I feel the agitation he's still harboring. I don't know how to make this right, but I can sense his need to do the same.

"Troy, I wanted to tell you—"

"I was thinking—"

We share a smile, and he lifts his chin.

"You go fir—"

"What were—"

This gets a laugh from us both.

"Want some water?" I offer.

"Sure, thanks."

He follows me into the kitchen. "You smell incredible."

"Thanks."

He leans against my counter, crossing his arms. "Going anywhere?"

My phone rattles on the counter, and both our eyes drop as Brett's name lights up the screen. My eyes flick to Troy's, whose voice cools when he speaks.

"Don't not answer on my account."

"I can call him back."

"Answer it."

"I said, I'll call him back."

He shrugs, indifferent.

Maybe he regrets his declaration now that things got heavy, and a part of me hates him for it. I was doing just fine before he forced his way into my daydreams with his intoxicating kiss and words. His perfect words.

And I believed him, and for a moment, I took them seriously. And everything about his demeanor now tells me I'm a fool. But that's what words are, a fool's gold.

Pretty promises make liars out of men and suckers out of the women who believe them. It was the kiss I believed most, and now that feels like a lifetime ago.

The man in my kitchen is not the man who kissed me. He's jaded by my lack of belief in him, which I understand all too well. I'm not jaded by the first guy I kissed, or the man who took my virginity, nor the short line of boyfriends that followed.

I was raised by *the* Machiavelli.

Joseph Arden was just as handsome, just as dazzling, just as charming, equally disarming, and exploited his affect whenever it suited him.

But Dad had my devotion, and I was the only lady he couldn't leave. That was my leverage. And I'm sure as hell not going to, nor will I ever, use my son as leverage for any man, especially his own father.

Troy pulls a five-dollar bill and a printed gift card from his pocket.

"I was thinking this code, and some cash would be cool. You know so he has some game money?"

"Oh? That's perfect," I say, grabbing him a water.

"Thanks," he says, taking the bottle and standing wordlessly in the kitchen, staring at one of Dante's drawings on the fridge.

"Troy, I'm sorry. I truly am."

"It's fine," he says, eyes drifting over me before he darts them away. "Just so you know, I'm going to be working a lot, I've picked up more shifts to get Dante's Christmas presents, and I've got my games."

I cross my arms and nod. "Okay."

"So, I won't be able to watch him as often as I'd like. You might want to make other arrangements for Mr. BMW. The next few months are going to be grueling."

"It's fine. I understand. So, I was saying before that I'm sorry—"

"I heard you. You think he's out enough for me to sneak in?"

I exhale the last of my hopes to rid the tension between us.

"I would give it a few more minutes just to make sure. He still believes in this stuff for the moment. I don't want to take that away just yet."

"Cool." He leaves me in the kitchen, taking a seat in my recliner. "Mind if I watch Sports Center?"

"Uh, sure, yeah, go ahead."

After a few minutes of amiable silence, I finally speak up.

"Tell me how this works."

"What?"

"The draft."

"If I draw enough interest, I get invited to the NFL Combine. It's a four-day camp where reps from all thirty-two teams observe the potentials to see who's the best fit for their franchise."

"When will you know if you're invited?"

"By the first of January."

"That's got to be nerve-wracking."

"I have to make sure I'm ready. Push myself harder. No time for *bullshit*."

I swallow his comment. "I'm sure you will. You look," he turns to me, his lifeless stare making it hard for me to breathe. I'm not a fan of this version of Troy, and it stings me that he's become so closed off. A complete one-eighty from the man who assured me he wasn't going anywhere. It strikes me then just how much I wanted to believe him. "You look like you've been working out a lot."

"Yeah." He turns his attention back to the TV.

"And then what?"

Eyes still trained on the screen, he shrugs. "And then I may or may not get a letter to attend the draft. If I do, I'll have the choice of showing up or watching from home."

"What will you do?"

"I'll bring my mother. This is both our dream."

"That's really something. I love that you're so close to her."

"Yeah."

"I'm so sorry I caused a rift between you. I've been meaning to apologize in person, but Dante has been around and—"

"Yeah, me too." He stands, and I stop him with a hand on his chest, which he promptly removes. "Clarissa, I'm tired, okay? Too tired to fight."

I step back, feeling slapped. "It's okay, I think you've made yourself pretty clear."

He lets out a heavy exhale. "Sorry, I'm not acting the way you need me to."

"It's not that, I just thought maybe—"

"Maybe what?"

His icy demeanor contradicts his statement. This man is itching for a fight.

"Nothing, let's do this."

"I've got it." He heads toward Dante's room. Standing at the door, I look on as he tucks the money inside his pillow after retrieving the tooth. Just as he starts to step away, Dante jackknifes in the bed mumbling something about a truck. Troy jumps back as I signal him from the door not to speak. Troy glances back to where Dante sits, his eyes still closed before he falls back into his bed, none the wiser. Troy steps outside the door. "That was close."

"He does that sometimes, restless sleeper. Talks a little once in a while."

"Yeah, I got smacked in the face when we went camping. I woke up with his toe in my ear."

I chuckle. "He's growing out of it. Out of so much. He called me Mom the other day and I almost cried."

"Why?"

"Because I've always been Mommy."

"Must be nice," he mumbles before stepping past me. "Thanks for letting me have my own first."

"Troy, please, I just need you to understand. It's just been him and me for so long."

He stops in the center of my living room. "Oh, I think I've been pretty fucking understanding."

"You have. And I appreciate it so much. Just—"

"Night," he says without glancing my way.

Fed up, I call out to him from the front door as he starts to cross the lawn. "You know, you are *going somewhere* eventually, Troy. Eventually, you're leaving, and where does this situation stand? Have you thought about that?"

In his eyes, all I see is contempt. "That's *all* I think about.

And if I can earn this ticket, Clarissa, he'll never want for any-thing again. I'm making fucking sure of it. So, please, for once, stop telling me what to think, how to act, or what to feel, and stop giving me unsolicited dating advice. You want understand-ing? You got it. You want respect? All yours. You want patience? I've got some of that left for you too. You want me to think of him and *only him*, we're on the same page. Cool?"

His venom is deserved, but I'm unprepared for the hurt it causes and can barely manage my reply. "That's fine."

"Night."

thirty-one

TROY

PALMING MY FOREHEAD, I SIT ON THE BENCH, FEELING MY mapped future falling away piece by piece. We just suffered another loss. One we can't come back from. Our chances are slim to none at this point in making the playoffs. My college ball career is ending, and I'm having a tough time swallowing that I'll never have a bowl game. The locker room is eerily silent. Coach didn't mince his words with his pissing post-game rant. A few guys walk past me and give me a nod. I caught every pass, ran like my life depended on it, scored two touchdowns, but it wasn't enough.

Lance slaps me on the back as he wordlessly leaves the locker room while the rest of the guys shed their gear. There's nothing to be said, and today, even Kevin seems lost in his own thoughts.

I pull my phone from my duffle as I head out of the locker room.

Clarissa: I'm so sorry. If you need to talk, I'm here.

Talking is the last thing I want to do.

She's been nothing but apologetic since our confrontation with Mom, and I've been nothing but a prick to her. It seems like any step forward I take with her always leads to a thousand back.

I don't have much fight left in me. I'm exhausted from the expectations weighing me down. And for once, I just want to stay down.

In the past, after days like this, my first instinct would be to find a good party, a never-ending bottle, and a soft place to land, but nothing about that appeals to me.

My phone buzzes again, and I know it's Mom.

Mom: Don't give up, baby. You're the best player on that team, and you played your heart out today.

I text her back because I don't want her to worry or pop up to check on me. I just want to be alone.

Troy: I'm okay, Mom. I'll brush it off. Love you.

Grabbing my gear, I head down the hallway and out to the parking lot. I'm halfway to my truck when I hear mixed voices spewing venom.

"Happy, you little bitch?"

"P-please, please stop!"

Dropping my duffle, I head toward the crowd and tense when I hear another cry. I make my way toward the commotion, moving bodies to get through it, and then all I see is red.

thirty-two

CLARISSA

I KNOCK ON TROY'S DOOR FOR THE SECOND TIME, KNOWING HE'S home. Theo's car is gone, but Troy's King Cab is in its usual spot. When the door finally opens, it's Lance who answers.

"Hey, how are you, Lance?"

"I'm good, Clarissa. Thanks for the cookies. They were delicious."

"You're welcome. I'm so sorry about the game."

"Yeah," he says, his disappointment clear, "that was something." Lance is dangerously beautiful. When I first introduced myself to him, I was intimidated by his menacing stature. But he's as gentle as they come, the strong silent type. At least that's my impression of him now. Harper is far more outgoing. Briefly, I wonder how that dynamic plays out in their relationship.

"You played really well."

"Not well enough," I can see the sadness in his smile. "If you're looking for Troy, he's upstairs."

"Thanks," I make my way to Troy's bedroom and knock once.

"Sup?" I hear him call from behind the door, and I poke my head in to see him tense when he sees me. Shirtless, he's sprawled on his bed in sweatpants, books open and scattered all over his mattress. He catches his football mid toss. "What's wrong, where's Dante?"

"He's fine. Parker's with him."

He lifts to sit, and that's when I notice his bruised cheekbone and busted lip. "What happened?"

"Nothing. Difference of opinion with a bunch of assholes."

"Can I look at it?" I sit down next to him on the bed and palm his cheek to examine his lip. He pulls out of my grip.

"I'm okay."

"What happened?"

"I just told you. I got into a fight. It's fine."

"Not fine. You just lost a game and got into a brawl. I would say things are pretty shitty at the moment."

"I'll deal. Not the end of the world."

"And what is the end of the world?"

He draws his brows. "What?"

"What's the end of the world for Troy Jenner?"

He jerks his head back. "Are you being serious right now?"

"Yes. I would like to know."

"Any harm coming to my son. Losing another fucking game, not getting drafted, bouncing another goddamned check. Pick a nightmare, sweetheart."

"Don't be condescending."

"Right. Sorry. Thanks for stopping by, but I'm not in the mood for another lecture. As you can see, I'm busy. You can go."

"You're already kicking me out? You haven't even fucked me yet." I palm his bed and lean in with a seductive whisper. "Isn't this where the magic happens?"

His jaw goes slack, and I congratulate myself.

"Ah, a reaction. Finally. Now we're getting somewhere."

"Lady, you drive me crazy. How can I help you?" He stands and tosses his ball on the floor.

I pluck the ball from the carpet and toss it up. "First off, don't call me lady, I've seen your dick, and it makes me feel old. Two, if you're bouncing checks, Troy, I can go without one for a while until you get on your feet."

"Don't worry about it," he says, cupping his neck. "I shouldn't have said anything."

"Last time I checked, we were in this together. I'm okay. I want you to be okay too."

He exhales heavily. "Clarissa, what's this all about?"

"Because I'm worried about you. And I don't like this static going on between us. We started a friendship, and you took it away from me. And I understand why you're mad, I do, but we were trying to make it work for our son, and it *was* working. Despite the fact that you're spinning all these plates and making it look easy, I want you to know I'm aware of how hard you're working. And to let you know I care."

His eyes rake over me skeptically. "You care, huh?"

I take a seat on the corner of his bed facing him. "Of course, I do. You have my son's adoration and my respect for all you're doing, and we can both tell that you're having a hard time. Dante used his curse money yesterday to buy you this." I pull the fishing lure from my jacket pocket and hold it out to him. "He said you like the bright blue ones that look like an octopus. He took great care in picking it out."

He glances down fondly at the lure in his palm. "He loved fishing. And we didn't even get a bite."

"He misses you."

He sighs and sits next to me on his mattress, cradling the lure in his hands. "I'll do better."

"Troy, this isn't about you doing better. This is about us wanting to be there for you. Don't you get that?"

"What do I need to do?"

"Do? Nothing. Just let us be there for you. Come over. I'll make you dinner. You can spend time with your son, forget about all these burdens for a few hours and just chill. I don't want any more hard feelings between us. I want to try and make this work."

"Everything no longer going just fine?" He smirks.

"Cut the shit. You lavish all this attention, and then you just..." The air grows thick as he inches in.

"Just what?"

"Take it away." I swallow at the intensity of his gaze. I can feel the heat coming off his skin.

"Who's missing my attention, Clarissa?"

"What?"

He kneels down in front of me, tipping my chin and forcing my eyes to his. "Who's missing my attention?"

I can hear my breaths through my parted lips.

"We both miss having you around. I realize your schedule is hectic..." I reach out and run my finger over his lip, "but we've got a seven-foot tree in our house we haven't decorated yet because he wanted to wait for you."

Troy closes his eyes. "Fuck. I'm sorry."

"Troy, stop. You haven't done anything wrong. This is an invitation." I stand and offer my hand. "Come over, help him decorate his tree. I'll make you dinner. We can do this together. Okay? It's your first Christmas with him, and I don't want you to miss it. I don't want you to miss," I try to swallow my guilt, but my voice shakes anyway, "I don't want you to miss another one because of *me*."

He takes my hand, towering over me, and it's all I can do to keep from leaning in and inhaling a whiff of his cologne-scented skin. The man is temptation personified. I do my best to look unaffected, but all I want to do is release the string on his sweats. Somewhere between hating him and trying to forgive him, he's unleashed the dormant hussy that dwells inside of me.

"So, you miss me?" He teases, and I roll my eyes. "Want to demonstrate how much?"

"Don't push your luck, Jenner."

"Okay."

"Okay?"

"Yeah, okay." It's then I see some of the light I've been missing return in his eyes. "I've got a few notes to go over, and then I'll come by." I let my eyes drift down a little more before glancing at his open books.

"What's your major?"

"Electrical engineering."

I couldn't be more shocked if he'd shot me.

He chuckles. "That look you're giving me isn't insulting at all."

"Sorry," I sputter. "It's just…you failed sixth grade."

He shakes his head. "Keep underestimating me, Ms. A. I like surprising you."

"No issue there. It seems to be working in my favor."

"Nothing better than a challenge." He runs his tongue along his plump bottom lip, his eyes doing a full sweep as my pulse kicks up between my thighs.

"Easy, tiger. It's a dinner invite. And please put a shirt on, or there's a good chance Parker will lick you."

The corner of his mouth lifts. "Wouldn't want her to beat you to it."

"Dream on, stud. And stop looking at me like that."

"Thought you missed my attention?"

"Oh, shut up."

thirty-three

TROY

IT'S THE SMALLEST THINGS. THE WAY SHE WORRIES HER LIP WHEN she concentrates. The way she tucks the hair behind her ears before pushing up the sleeves on her sweater. A sweater that's way too big. No matter how hard I try, when I'm around her, I can't stop feasting. The four of us gather in the living room with mountains of decorations surrounding us. Parker hooks the ornaments handing them to Dante, who strategically places them on the tree. Clarissa bought a little electric fireplace to sit in the corner of the living room which warms the space. Soulful Christmas music is playing, the atmosphere relaxed. From behind my door to the inside of hers, it feels like a different world. And for the first time in weeks, I breathe a little easier.

It's a different home in comparison to the one I live in. Our tree is a sad ass Charlie Brown number Theo bought and decorated with exactly four Grand ornaments. It's a far cry from the lush Fraser Fir my boy is decorating. I love the light in his eyes, which I have decided are his mothers'. The minute I entered the house, and Dante greeted me with open arms, my mood shifted.

This was precisely what I needed to suck up the loss.

And the fact that Clarissa admitted she missed me, well

that's a different league of feelings. Feelings I'm not ready to act on just yet. With her, it's a curved line to walk. I could tell the other night I'd let her down. I haven't backed up a word I've said when it comes to her because of our lingering issues, but she doesn't seem to hold it against me, which is surprising.

"Hey, you, lazybones. Quit acting like you played four quarters today and open a box," she jokes, pushing a large tub my way. "We've got work to do."

"If I'm going to work, I'm going to need more of this." I lift my empty mug of eggnog, and Parker does the same.

"Me too. What's in this? It's like magic on my tongue."

"Agreed," I say, warming from the slight buzz of rum.

"It's an old recipe, y'all like it?" Clarissa beams with pride.

"Which girlfriend was this?" Parker asks.

"Girlfriend?" I ask, ping-ponging between the two of them.

Parker gives me a devilish smirk. "You didn't know about Clarissa's college phase?"

"Shut up," Clarissa rolls her eyes. "That was then."

"Awww, look at him," Parker says, studying my expression. "I think you just shot down his little elf's hopes."

"You have a little elf?" Dante asks.

"Yeah, bud. But he's hiding. He's afraid of Parker because she likes to play target practice with him."

"You want to shoot Troy's little elf? That's not nice, Auntie Parker." Dante scolds.

Parker glares at me, and I reply with a slow wink.

"Which girlfriend *means*," Clarissa says, giving us both warning looks, "that my dad was a fan of variety."

"You and your little elf know all about that, don't you, Troy?" Parker adds smartly before she hiccups.

I roll my eyes. "Parker, go choke on a reindeer—"

Dante speaks up, schooling us both. "Y'all are interrupting Mommy, and that's rude."

"Get 'em, baby," Clarissa beams with pride.

Parker stands and takes my cup. "Sorry, Troy. Allow me to get you some more."

"Sure, thanks." I turn to Clarissa. "So, the girlfriends?"

"Forget it," Clarissa says, shaking her head.

I move toward her and grab the lights she's trying to separate and nudge her shoulder. "Tell me."

She glances up at the tree as I study her exposed neck. "My dad loved a woman who knew her way around the kitchen, and when they stuck around, meaning for more than a few weeks, they'd show me how to cook. So that eggnog recipe came from Beth. She was in interior design."

"So, what are we having tonight?" I ask.

"Carol's Goulash. She was an ex-con turned church secretary from Jersey, who gave up her criminal ways for Jesus and was determined to save my father and me from eternal damnation."

"What's eternal damnation?" Dante asks.

"Parker's cooking," Clarissa jokes.

"Oh, shut it," Parker says through a hiccup.

"Sorry, it's the truth. When we lived together, you burnt broth."

"That was a ploy to get you to cook for me, sucker!"

"Goulash, huh? Never had it."

"It's *sooo* good." Dante gives me big eyes. "You will love it."

"Can't wait." I lift the lid off a new box, my chest tightening when I see it's a mix of Dante's baby ornaments. I pull them out, studying them carefully, sensing Clarissa's eyes on me.

"That was last year." She lifts an ornament, unwrapping it from the tissue. "And this one was his first."

We both chuckle as I hold it up.

"Jesus, that breast milk did him good."

"And now he's so small," she whispers.

"I'm not small!" Dante yells, offended. "I'm bigger."

"Don't worry, I was small too, bud."

"How did you get big?"

I chuckle. "Big boy breast milk."

"Mommy, can I have some of that?"

"In twenty years," Parker answers.

"I'm going to tear your little elf off," Clarissa grumbles as I open another box, and she moves to take it from me. "Not that one."

"No way," I slap her hand. When I open it, I see the contents of what I know is Clarissa's childhood.

Parker passes me my refreshed cup of eggnog while I sort through pictures. In the one I hold, Clarissa's smiling, toothless, and wearing an NSYNC T-shirt.

"Awesome," I say, chuckling as she rips it from my hand, trying to steal the box back. I swat her hand again.

"Ouch," she says, withdrawing.

"Then leave me alone."

"You two play nice," Dante scolds, hanging a wreath ornament. "Santa is watching."

"Yes, sir," I say, studying the pictures. I flip through them, stilling on one of Clarissa and a beautiful woman, who is, without a doubt, her mother. They're doing dishes.

"That's the only one I have of the two of us."

I flip it over and read the scribbling on the back.

My baby & me, AG 5

She lifts another picture from the box.

"This was her headshot. She's like Julia Roberts beautiful, right?"

"Yeah," I agree readily. "So are you. You look just like her."

"Aww, well damn, now I feel guilty," Parker says as I lift my mug. "Uh, Troy, I may or may not have slipped an Ambien into your eggnog. The buzz choice is up to you from here on, my friend."

"Parker!"

"Sorry. You said he never gets any sleep. I was just trying to be helpful."

"You worry about my sleep too?" I ask Clarissa, who casts her eyes down, grabbing the box from my hands.

"I just don't see how you do it."

I lean in with a "Hey," and she finally looks up at me through her lashes. "Don't worry about me, pretty woman."

"You're pushing so hard."

"I've got this," I say softly. "And thanks for having my back. You too, Parker, but I think I'll toss this out."

"Good thinking." Clarissa glares at Parker over her shoulder. "Not cool."

"Sorry, babe. I thought it would be funny to watch him faceplant in your goulash." She sheepishly flashes all her teeth. "Are we not in revenge mode anymore? I must have missed the memo."

Dante speaks up next. "What's a memo?"

"Do you want to read his Christmas story tonight?" Clarissa asks as I shovel in my third bowl of goulash.

"Sure."

"I'll get it," Dante says, pushing away from the table. "Mommy, which day is it?"

"Day eight."

"Okay!" He shouts before running toward his room.

"Will you text me the next time you make this?" I ask around a mouthful of macaroni. Clarissa laughs as she retrieves my bowl, and I stop her, spooning the last of the goulash in my mouth. "That's not an answer," I say, poking her side as she stacks our bowls in her hands.

"Okay, okay," she says, jerking away from my fingers, "I p-p-promise."

"I forgot you are ticklish." I begin to work her sides as Parker chimes in.

"This is so…" she rests her chin in her hand with a sigh, her eyes hooded as she looks between the two of us. "It's like watching a Hallmark movie, but I can read the *bow chicka wow wow* going on in your filthy minds, which makes it *so much better.*"

Clarissa knocks Parker's arm from beneath her. "Would you stop making things weird?" She hauls the dishes to the sink, and I stand, gathering the glasses.

"I'll help."

Clarissa shakes her head. "You sit."

"I wasn't raised that way."

"Yeah, well," she says, snagging the glasses from my hands, "no one else in this house today ran a thirty-five-yard touchdown and slam dunked a ball through the goal post."

"You saw that, huh?"

She smiles. "So did Dante. Pretty awesome."

"Did you tell your good neighbor you dumped Mr. Tighty Whities?" Parker bellows from the table just as Clarissa snatches her mug away.

"No more eggnog for you."

Clarissa nervously darts her gaze away from the question

in my eyes as Dante comes running back to the table with his book.

"*I'll* read it to Troy, Mommy!"

"Oh, yeah," she taps his nose. "I forgot you can read."

"*Duh.*" Dante slaps his forehead. "Oh, poop. I'm sorry. I know I'm not supposed to say that no more."

"Anymore. You aren't supposed to say that *anymore.* I'll let it slide this once," Clarissa says breezily, and I know it has everything to do with the help of Captain Morgan and the carb coma we're all succumbing to. Sink filling, she pushes up her sleeves, glancing over at me while I study the book. "It's a set I got him last year. One book for every day before Christmas. He's doing great with his vocabulary and comprehension, but we're working on his—"

"Tenses, I know."

We share a smile just as Parker's starts sputtering out porn music.

"Parker!" Clarissa hisses as I scoop up Dante and hang him over my shoulder.

"Let's go, bud, before things turn ugly in here." Dante giggles as he's forced to give them both dangling kisses goodnight.

"Good night, Auntie Parker."

"Night, Duckie."

"Make sure you brush your teeth," Clarissa calls after us, and I give her a wink.

"I've got this."

She gives me a shy smile. "I know you do."

CAROL'S GOULASH
Church Secretary, New Jersey

Makes 8–10 servings
1 hour

2 Lbs. Hamburger
1 Large Onion – Chopped
Garlic Powder – To taste
Salt – To Taste
Pepper – To Taste
2 Cans Rotel
7 8 Oz. Cans Tomato Sauce
7 8 Oz. Cans Water
1 Large Can Corn
3 Cups Macaroni

Brown hamburger meat, onion, salt, pepper, and garlic powder. Drain. Add Rotel, tomato sauce, water, and corn. Bring to boil. Add macaroni. Cook 12 to 15 minutes or until macaroni is tender.

thirty-four

CLARISSA

TROY RETURNS TO THE LIVING ROOM AS I LIGHT THE LAST candle.

"Wow, it looks amazing in here."

"Nothing better than having a real tree in your house." I stand back as he admires it with me.

"It's awesome."

"Yeah," I turn to him and look him over. I can see the fatigue in his posture. "You okay?"

"I'm good," he says. "I didn't realize how much I needed this. Just being with him makes me feel better. Thank you."

"Of course."

"Where's Parker?"

"Her Ambien kicked in. She's snoring it off in my bed."

"I guess I'll go."

"Are you tired?"

"Not too much, why?"

"Because I have something for you."

One side of his mouth lifts. "Do you?"

"Yeah, an early Christmas present." I take a seat on the couch and pat the cushion next to me. He takes his place as I cue up my phone, hitting the mirror option before throwing the first video on my TV. In seconds, a six-month-old Dante is on-screen wiggling on the floor in an attempt to crawl. Troy's face lights up in recognition. "So, he wasn't exactly a crawler, he more or less dragged himself around by his arms."

Troy chuckles. "I see."

"He, uh, well, he might have had a hard time crawling, but when it was time to walk, it was like chasing lightning. I'm thinking he got that from his father."

Pride fills his eyes as he watches rapt, a smile gracing his lips. When the video ends, he looks over to me.

"Got any more?"

"Hundreds."

"Let's see them."

Troy tosses a piece of popcorn in his mouth and damn near chokes on it watching Dante's first attempt at jailbreak.

"Oh, my God," he chuckles. "How old was he here?"

"Thirteen months. Can you believe that?" I watch as Dante stacks his blanket and his animals so he has just enough room to pull himself up and over.

"Rewind that, would you?"

I nod and play it again.

"Oh, this is fucking epic," he says, grinning from ear to ear.

"He was so damned cute."

"Yeah, he was. What was that baseball outfit you dressed him in all the time?"

"You saw that?"

Troy nods. "Yeah, it was cool. Even if it was the wrong sport."

"Hmm, I still have it somewhere. It says 'Mommy's Little

Slugger' on the front. I saved a few of my favorites to have a quilt made one day."

"That's cool," Troy says, his eyes still on the screen. We watch one video after another. He's completely smitten with Dante, and it's so easy to see from the expression he's wearing. I'm drawn into a video when Troy cups my chin turning me to face him. "Thank you for this. I can't tell you how much it means to me."

I fight the quiver in my lip as I try and find the right words. Pausing the video, I turn to face him fully. "I'm so sorry. I know it will never be enough. But I am. You should've been there. You should have had the chance to be there. I had no right to take this away from you. I hope one day you will forgive me. I hope," a tear I can't hold spills over and slides down my cheek. "I hope one day I can forgive myself."

Softly, he runs his knuckles down my face. "I could've fought harder. I could have tried to talk to you instead of being such a fucking creeper."

"I was scary."

"So fucking scary," he chuckles, catching another tear with the stroke of his fingers. "We both did unforgivable shit. It's time to let it go."

"Do you mean that?" I hear the shake in my voice when he nods.

"Yeah. I'm sorry I've been such a dick lately."

"I can't stop thinking about the look on your mother's face. I'm...I feel terrible."

"It's time to move on."

"I would love that," I place my hand over his where it rests on my face. "Are we okay?"

"We're okay," he murmurs, sliding his hand down to push the hair off my shoulders.

"He was a gift. You know? I never saw more for my life than being a teacher. I had no fancy plans other than that. I'm living my dream, Troy. It might not seem like much of one, but I've wanted to teach since I was a little girl and having our son, I think it made me a better pupil, and hopefully a better teacher. You deserve to live your dream too," I say as he traces my jaw with a finger. "You're so insanely talented. You'll make it, I know you will."

"Now, I've got an even better reason to make it happen." He runs a hand down my arm, and I visibly shiver. His brow lifts.

"Like that, did you?"

"Maybe."

He moves his hand back up before gently brushing his fingertips along my collar bone, and I shiver again.

"Fuck," he murmurs, watching me intently. "You're so responsive."

"I remember that night," I blurt. "When you asked me if I ever thought about it, I was embarrassed to tell you just how often I did. I still do."

"Me too."

"I think in a way, I hurt myself the day I showed up to your school. I built it up in my mind, the idea of you and me. I'd hoped that maybe you would be happy about the baby. About seeing me and…"

"It didn't go down like that at all."

"Not at all. But I do remember, Troy. And that night was…"

"Fucking amazing," his voice drops as he cups the back of my head, and we both draw closer.

"Back then, we were a news at eleven headline waiting to happen."

"But we aren't now."

"Not now, no," I say breathlessly.

We're close. My nipples draw tight beneath my sweater as his eyes rake over my face. "No more Brett?"

I bite my lip and turn my head back and forth.

"Why?"

"He wasn't for me."

"Any particular reason?" We're a breath apart, my body completely alive, wired, the pull too much to ignore.

Parker's voice has us both jumping back.

"Sausages. I bought them." The condiments clink together as she jerks open the fridge. "I bought Summer Sausage. Who ate it?" A second later, Parker enters the living room in nothing but slippers and a long T-shirt, her phone in her hand. "Why is it so dark in here? Are y'all watching Love Island?"

"Oh, Lord. It's an Ambien sleepwalk." I hang my head and stand before I make my way toward her. "Come on, babe, let's get you back to bed."

Parker turns to me speaking as if she's not in a prescription-induced coma. "Do you smell pickles? Ohhhh, let's go to Target."

Troy chuckles, and I meet his eyes over her shoulder while turning her back in the direction of my bedroom. "I better go strap her into bed."

The looks we exchange are filled with need. And in his eyes, I see the promise of something more.

"I'll see myself out. Night, pretty woman."

"Night, neighbor."

Kim's NO-BAKE Billionaire Pie
Psychologist, Wisconsin

Makes 8 servings
20 minutes

2 Cups Powdered Sugar
1 Stick Butter
1 Large Egg
1/4 Tsp. Salt
2 8-Inch Pie Crusts
1/4 Tsp. Vanilla
2 Packages Dream Whip
1/2 Cup Pecans
1 Cup Pineapple – drained

Cream butter, sugar, egg, salt, and vanilla. Fill pie crusts with mixture. Follow directions on box and whip Dream Whip. Add pineapple and nuts to Dream Whip. Spoon into pies. Chill.

thirty-five

CLARISSA

"It's supposed to snow tonight," I say folding some wrapping paper against a box.

"That's cool."

"It will be Dante's first White Christmas."

"I wish I would have known. I would have ordered a sled."

"I've got cookie sheets that'll work just fine, Mr. Engineer."

He grins. "That'll work too."

Troy glances down at the directions before grabbing a training wheel and adding it to the bike he's been constructing for the last fifteen minutes. I secure the last piece of tape on one of Santa's gifts before arranging it beneath the tree.

"Need any help?" I slide over to where he sits in the middle of the living room.

"Sure," he says absently. "Hand me that snap driver."

"Got it," I say, sorting through his toolbox. The toolbox he bought when he decided I needed a few repairs around the house. Since our night of home movies weeks ago, his season ended with only one more win killing all hopes of Texas Grand making the playoffs. And because he's on winter break from school, he's been pushing himself harder than ever. He's restless, nervous about the invite to the NFL Combine, and no amount of assurance on my part seems to help. His whole future rides on the next few months, and so he's been spending endless hours at the gym during the day before working the extra shifts he's picked up at night. He's bulked up, and it shows. His clothes cling to him, perfectly accentuating his insane build. He's in a cream sweater and dark jeans and looks fucking mouthwatering. We've barely had any time alone since our almost kiss, and I can't stop thinking about what might have happened if Parker hadn't interrupted the moment. Since then, it's been lingering looks, and too brief kisses goodnight once he's tucked Dante in. Tonight, I decided to pull out all the big guns, wearing a set of red silk pajamas and only a red thong beneath.

I'm waxed, spritzed, and buffed, in hopes of something other than a PG kiss goodnight. I have no idea where we stand, but I'm teetering on the brink of madness at this point.

"You know what a snap driver is, don't you?" Troy prompts from where he sits as I sort through the endless box of tools giving him a clear shot of cleavage through my silky top.

"Of course, I do." I have absolutely no idea what the hell a snap driver is. But I damn sure won't tell him that as I take my time, glancing between him and the toolbox. He doesn't so much as look my way as I scrutinize every tool.

"Then you are aware it's a figment of my imagination." He chuckles as I look up and see his movie star grin before narrowing my eyes.

"You dick."

"Sorry, couldn't resist. So, I guess having me around has come in handy?"

"Don't go fishing for compliments after insulting a woman's intelligence."

"You're the smartest woman I know," he says easily as he

tests the wheels on the bike before flipping it over and unlatching the kickstand.

"What?"

He studies the bike after weighing my expression. "It's good, I swear, and I got the dorky ass helmet you demanded and knee pads."

"Thank you."

"Don't thank me. I'm his—"

"I mean for that compliment."

"Oh," he waves his hand. "Well, you are."

"It's nice of you to say."

"Well, I mean it."

I yawn, and he stands.

"Tired, huh?" He looks at the clock. "This is normally the time I get ready for work."

"How can you stand it?"

"Sometimes, I can't. I'll be happy when I have one job, even if it looks like it's going to be UPS."

"Troy, you'll get drafted. There's so much talk, and you had a spectacular season despite the way it ended."

He shakes his head, his disappointment evident. "Let's not go there tonight, okay?"

I nod. "Okay." I perk up for his sake. "Hey, you want some eggnog?"

"Nah, I'm good."

"Coffee?"

Tea? Me?

I'm doting on him like a lovesick teenager, but I can't seem to help myself.

"I'm good," he repeats, grabbing another box and pulling out the contents. "This is fun," he says, opening another set of directions.

"Never has been for me. I'm thankful you're here. I used to have a hell of a time doing this alone. Parker would sometimes help when she was home, but she usually just dictated while I pulled my hair out. And the irony is Dante is so good at this kind of stuff. Now I see where he gets it. I'm glad you're here."

"You said that," he looks over to me as he rips open the plastic, and for that brief moment, I swear I see a flash of heat in his eyes. However, just as quickly as it appears, it's gone.

"What?" He asks without looking my way.

"I'm just wondering if you're missing something tonight."

"Missing something?" He opens a bag of screws.

"You know, a party, booze," I hold out my hands from my chest. "Big breasted elves."

"Clarissa, I'm not into that anymore."

"Hmm," I say, pulling the trash from the carpet.

He grabs my free hand and commands my eyes. "I'm exactly where I want to be. Okay?"

He slides his thumb over the back of my hand, and I melt into that touch as my skin heats.

It's ridiculous. I'm ridiculous. I'm a horny, needy woman. Maybe that's why I haven't been on the receiving end of more of his attention because I'm reeking of desperation. I feel like a fool as I gather the rest of the trash.

"He's going to love this," Troy says. "I can't wait to see his face."

"I was thinking. If you want to spend the night on the couch, you're welcome to, so you can be here when he wakes up."

"Yeah. That will be cool."

"Okay. I'll be right back."

He nods, intent on his task.

I crack Dante's door for a quick check and see he's hanging

off the bed. I right him beneath the covers before closing his door and setting a decorative ring of bells on the handle to ensure we can hear him coming.

Armed with blankets and a pillow, I pad into the living room to see Troy standing and stretching.

"You're done already?"

I bend over to inspect Dante's new desk and light stands. "This is awesome. What a good idea. He's going to love making his videos with this."

"Jesus Christ," I hear uttered in annoyance and glance over my shoulder to see Troy scrubbing his face with his palm.

"What's wrong?"

"Nothing," he says hoarsely.

I frown and take a step forward. "Troy, what's going on? I thought we were okay."

He stares down at me, pushing the hair away from my shoulder. "We are."

"Why are you acting so weird?"

"It's nothing," he says, "I just have a lot on my mind. I'm going to head home. I'll probably be up anyway when he wakes up."

"You're not going to stay?"

"No. I've got some stuff to do."

"It's one in the morning," I hear the whine in my own voice and inwardly cringe.

Shut up! Shut up! Shut up!

But I can't stop the thoughts racing through my mind. Jealousy burns through me at the idea that it might not be stuff, but a who he needs to do.

He leans down and kisses my cheek. "Merry Christmas. See you in the morning."

"Do you want me to text you when—" The door shuts

behind him, and I stand there staring blankly at it, wondering where I went wrong.

Just weeks ago, he couldn't keep his hands off me. Unable to handle another second of his hot and cold, I stalk after him.

"Troy." He's halfway across the yard when I catch up with him, freezing in nothing but my pajamas. "What in the *hell* is your problem? I thought we were okay?"

He lets out a slow exhale. "I don't want to fight."

"Why are you angry?"

"I'm not angry."

"Oh, really? Is that why you won't even look at me?"

"I'll see you in the morning. We're good, I promise."

"Fine, whatever, better go get to doing *whomever* you need to do."

He turns on a dime and grabs my wrist, and before I know what's happening, I'm flush to him as he places my palm over his erection. I gasp at the feel of the bulge in his jeans as he leans in close.

"In an adult relationship, sex is gradual," he grits out. "There's no one and done." Heat rolls off him as he runs my hand back and forth along the length of his cock. "You take the time to get to know the person, make sure your goals match because you're well versed on what you do, and *do not* want."

Realization dawns that my own words have come back to bite me in the ass.

"I want to be what you need. I want to be that man for you. And I'm fucking trying." Mouth parted, he growls, yanking me closer. "It's not anyone but *you,* and right now, I'm not in the mood for conversation. It's taking everything I have not to rip those fucking pajamas off your body, spread your legs and eat that beautiful pussy and ass you so painstakingly keep waving in my face."

In the next second, I'm covered in nothing but Troy, his warm hands, lips, and tongue as he plunges it into my mouth. I kiss him back in a fever, wrapping around him and tugging at his hair. He grips my ass fully while I climb him like a monkey before grinding on him like a stripper.

"Jesus Christ, I swear you're trying to kill me," he rasps out between kisses as I grip his sweater, pulling in for more. Enveloped in his hold, he deepens the kiss as I hook my ankles around his waist. It's freezing, but we're an inferno in between our two yards, the neighborhood eerily silent. Only the sound of our kiss and mingling fast breaths between us.

He rips himself away. "Fuck, I can't take this."

My lips are too busy for a reply as I suck on his neck, inhaling his cologne, my body lit. And then we're moving, my lips locked on his neck as he opens the door to his house.

This has me pulling back.

"Theo's in Houston, Lance went home." That's all he manages to get out as he whisks me up the stairs and sets me down on the edge of his bed. We both turn to see Dante sleeping soundly feet away. And then we're kissing again while he slowly unbuttons the top of my pajamas, moving the material just enough to expose one of my breasts before pulling it into his mouth.

I moan, my head falling back as he alternates between licks and sucks.

"Tell me what you want," he murmurs, gliding a warm hand up my neck before threading his fingers through my hair.

"Troy," I say, whimpering as my pulse pounds between my legs.

"I love that answer," he says, rimming a finger along the waistband of my pajamas.

"Touch me, please."

"You're sure?"

I nod.

"I need words, Clarissa."

"Yes, touch me, please. I'm so fucking wet."

He groans in reply, drawing the string on my bottoms, giving them just enough of a push so they slide to the floor. His perfect lips part when he sees my thong.

"I have to have a taste," he says, turning me to face his bed before pinning my hands on the mattress. And then he's exploring, covering me with calloused hands. "Jesus, Clarissa, you thought I could want someone else? Can't you feel how much I want *you*?" He presses his cock against me, making me gasp. "I've been losing my fucking mind, trying to hold back." He runs his hands along my thighs before massaging my ass with his palms.

"Every time I stroke my cock, every time I come, it's with your name on my lips," he murmurs before his tongue darts out, covering the material gathered at my soaked slit. My back bows at the feel of him as he continues to taunt me without enough contact. Fire trails from my head to my toes as he ravages me with mouth and hands, my erratic breaths, and his groans the only sounds in the room.

"I'm trying to give you what you want," he says, between licks pulling at the material with his teeth and nudging my legs further apart with his nose.

"Troy, please," I plead as he lifts the string and runs the flat part of his tongue in a complete sweep down my core. I damn near collapse on my hands as he fucks me with his tongue. I'm already on the verge, the friction of my nipples on his comforter causing another spike of pleasure as my moans grow louder.

"So sexy." Palming my ass, he spreads me as his tongue

darts out, the material becoming the bane of my existence, his flick rhythmic as he drives me to the brink.

"Take them off," I beg as he plunges deeper before lowering to suck my clit through the silk.

"Jesus, Troy, please. Please!"

I lift to remove my thong and get rewarded with a slap on the ass.

"Don't you fucking dare. I've been dreaming about this for years."

"Please, Troy, I need you."

"No," he says, kissing down the length of my back, his hand snaking around my waist. His fingers dip inside my panties, sliding between my lips to massage my clit. "I need *you*. You're all I can think about anymore. No one else. No one," he says, running his tongue along the shell of my ear. "I haven't touched another woman since that day we fought on that lawn, and I don't want to." I turn my head and meet his lips as he brings me into his kiss. Moth and flame, our mouths collide over and over, our hunger consuming us both. He carries me with him, turning me over, his eyes roaming the whole of me. He's still fully dressed as I lay helplessly bare, breasts exposed, in a soaked thong.

"Everything I kiss, everything I touch tonight, now belongs to me. You hear me?"

I nod.

"Words, Clarissa."

"Yes, I want that too. Troy, please," I reach for him, and he shakes his head, using a finger to tug one side of my thong just past my hip, his eyes intent on mine.

"Did you break up with him for me?"

I moan, frenzied, as he continues the working of his fingers.

"Clarissa," he growls, demanding an answer.

"Yes," I rasp out. "Are we really doing this?"

"Yes, and we're doing it right," he murmurs before running a trail of kisses down to my navel. I grip his head as he begins to inch down toward the other side of my thong.

When his lips finally drift back to mine, we're tangled tongues inhaling each other's moans. He pulls away, running a finger up my slit before hooking the center of my panties and sliding them down. Kneeling between my thighs, his eyes intent, he darts his tongue out in a double tap on my swollen clit.

"This what you want?"

"Yes!"

He licks me smoothly before thrusting his tongue inside me fully.

"*Troy.*" I lift his name, my voice hoarse, the ache consuming me.

"Perfect," he whispers before hooking his arms around my thighs and opening me wider. Dire need courses through me just as he lowers his head and pulls in my clit between his lips and sucks. Hand over my mouth, I do my best to muffle my scream as he drinks me, his tongue vibrating as he hums on my pussy. Drunk on his licks, I crest on the wave of my orgasm just as he pushes his fingers inside me, twisting them in beckoning. His palm pins me flat to the bed while he relentlessly eats me until I'm gasping his name over and over. The shockwaves steal my voice as I convulse on his tongue, and he laps it up hungrily. The aftershock is so intense, I shake uncontrollably as he continues with the thrash of his tongue until I'm fighting for reprieve, too sensitive for more. I push at his head in an attempt to close my legs as he keeps me hostage, fucking me with his fingers, sucking my clit as I cry out to him over and over. When I'm spent again, he pulls away, satisfied, the lusty gleam in his eyes all I can see as he wipes his mouth. Lifting to hover above me, he studies me as my breathing evens, stroking my face, my hair, before leaning in to take my lips and kissing me deeply. Reaching between us, I start to unbutton his jeans, and he stops my movement.

"Not yet. The next time I push inside of you, there won't be a doubt in your mind about me. Because I want all of it." He presses warm lips to my chest, where my heart pounds and again to the side of my temple, erasing all doubts of where we stand, ending our discussion.

"Troy, let me touch you," I whisper, palming his girth. He pulls my hand from between us and kisses it with the shake of his head before easily hauling us to sit where we have a clear view of Dante. He's still sleeping soundly as I lay in Troy's arms just as snow begins to fall.

"We'll do it right this time," he murmurs again, pressing another kiss to my temple. "For *us*, and for him."

Ruth's Beef Brisket
Bank teller, South Carolina

Makes 8 servings
2 hours and 30 minutes

3 Lb. Boneless Beef Brisket – Well Trimmed
¼ Cup Liquid Smoke
1 Tsp. Onion Salt
1 Tsp. Garlic Salt
Salt to Taste

Smoky Sauce (combine all ingredients and simmer 5 minutes):
1 Tbsp. Liquid Smoke
½ Cup Ketchup
1 ½ Tbsp. Brown Sugar
1½ Tsp. Dry Mustard
¼ Cup Water
3 Tbsp. Melted Butter
1 Tsp. Celery Seeds
Dash of Pepper
2 Tbsp. Worcestershire Sauce

Sprinkle brisket with regular salt and place on a large piece of aluminum foil. Set in a shallow pan and pour liquid smoke over meat. Seal foil and refrigerate overnight. Remove brisket from refrigerator. Sprinkle with onion salt and garlic salt. Reseal foil.

Bake at 300 degrees for 2 hours. Slice thin. Serve with Smoky Sauce.

thirty-six

CLARISSA

"MOMMY WAKE UP! IT SNOWED, AND WE HAVE TO SEE if Santa came!" Dante exclaims jumping into my bed in the Michigan J. Frog pajamas and matching slippers Troy bought him to wear last night. I groan as he bounces around me with boundless energy. Eyeing the clock, I see I've only had a mere hour of sleep.

For me, Santa most definitely came, *and* delivered. Troy and I spent the rest of the night on my couch, making out like a couple of teenagers, and even with the lack of sleep, I feel as if I'm floating on air, my feet haven't touched the ground since he lifted me from the freezing lawn. Dante jumps into my bed, ready with his demands.

"Hurry up! Hurry up!"

I pull him to me from where I lay and squeeze. "Merry Christmas, Peanut. Just let me brush my teeth."

"Gah, hurry, please!"

"Morning, bud," Troy pokes his head into my bedroom and Dante turns to interrogate him.

"Did you see? Did Santa come?"

"I think he might have."

"Hurry, Mommy!"

Troy's eyes rake over me with heated appreciation.

"Morning good neighbor."

He gives me a breathtaking smile, his own eyes red-rimmed from lack of sleep. "Morning."

I rip my eyes away and still Dante's bounce on my stomach. "Why don't you let Troy take you to see what Santa brought?"

"You sure?" Troy asks.

"Of course, I'll be right out."

"Come on!" Dante springs from my bed and grabs Troy's hand ushering him out of my room.

After wrangling with my sexed-up hair and making myself somewhat presentable, I join my men in the living room as Dante gushes over his new desk.

"I didn't know I wanted this!"

"Santa knew," I say, giving Troy the compliment. Pride shines in his father's eyes as he shows Dante the ins and outs of his new desk and the lighting equipment.

"I love it!"

"Did you like your bike?"

"Yep. Troy's going to teach me how to ride it."

Troy. Not Mommy. I curl my lip at him, and he chuckles.

Dante rips through his presents while Troy and I sit back, sipping coffee, sharing heated looks. It's when Dante reads the tag on a large package that he grabs Troy's attention.

"This says from Troy, and it's *big*," Dante says, moving to sit in his lap. Troy wraps around him as if they've been doing it for years, which warms my heart. I look on, just as curious about the contents. Dante's eyes bulge when Troy helps to open the taped box.

"IT'S ALL MY MERCH! Mommy, LOOK!" Dante lifts up the contents consisting of T-shirts, hoodies, coffee mugs, posters, and more, all brandishing The Legit Life Logo which Dante had designed himself. He's beside himself with excitement as he sorts through it. It's hundreds of dollars of merchandise that I haven't been able to afford, and I'm blown away by Troy's gesture. "You got me all of it! TROY! This is *awesome!*"

"I thought we could design your set, and you could wear it when you make your videos."

Dante turns in Troy's lap and throws himself at him, hugging him tightly. "Thank you *soooo* much!"

"Welcome, bud,"

"You're my best friend," Dante says easily, which stuns us both. Eyes locked after his confession, Dante moves from his lap and digs into the rest of his presents. Troy clears his throat, but I don't miss the emotion shining in his eyes.

thirty-seven

TROY

Troy: You look beautiful this morning, Ms. A. Did you do something new to your hair?

Clarissa's phone buzzes on the table, her smile growing while she reads my message. Our eyes meet over Dante's head as he finishes his cereal.

Clarissa: It's called afterglow. Something new was done to me. I had a very wicked man sneak into my bedroom last night to have his way with me.
Troy: That so?
Clarissa: Oh, it's so. He must have borrowed my house key from his son. If he keeps it up, he might earn his own key. He's got a very persuasive tongue.

"Troy," Dante grips my face with his hands. "Are you listening?"

"Sorry, bud. What were you saying?"

"I said that Carly wants me to be her boyfriend."

This has Clarissa snapping her head up. "What?"

"I told her no. But I didn't tell her cause she was ugly. Don't worry, Mommy."

"So, you don't like her?" I ask as he slurps the almond milk from the side of his bowl like I taught him. A trick his mother isn't fond of.

"No way. She's always putting heart stickers on my hand. Gross."

"Be nice to her," Clarissa warns. "One day, you might think differently about her."

"I'm not marrying anyone," Dante says with the shake of his head. "Ever. Never."

I chuckle. "The right girl will change your mind one day," I say as Clarissa grins at me. "And drive you crazy." Her smile morphs into a scowl. "But in a good way."

Troy: We need a date.

Clarissa: Our sitter just left for India for three weeks.

Just as I'm about to type my reply, a notification pops up in my email, and I tense.

"Troy! Did you hear me!?"

I look over to Clarissa, and immediately, she sees it.

"Dante, go, go get dressed. Your clothes are on your bed."

Clarissa's already standing next to me as I scan the email.

"Is that it? Did you get the invite to the Combine?"

"I'm in," I say, shaking my head. "I'm in."

She leans down and wraps her arms around me. "Troy, this is awesome."

She glances toward the hallway and turns back to me, stealing a kiss. "I'm so proud of you."

"I can't believe it."

"I can't believe you're shocked. You had to know."

I can't help my smile. "Holy shit. I'm going." She runs her hands through my hair.

"I know just how to celebrate. Dinner tonight and after…" She waggles her brows.

"Sounds perfect," I say before glancing up at her, some of the high I'm feeling dispersing. "But we need to talk."

"About?" She asks, alarm covering her face. Since Christmas, we've spent every spare moment together through the New Year. I've taken advantage of her couch when Theo texts to let me know he needs the house. Things are getting serious for him and his girlfriend, and he's made it abundantly clear he wants me nowhere near that.

Lance has been a fucking wreck up until he left to go back to his family's ranch for winter break. Harper broke up with him a few games before the season ended. Despite our budding friendship, he refuses to tell me what happened, but I have my suspicions.

No one, not even Theo, suspects a damn thing about the fact that my truck's always parked next door while my bedroom is unoccupied. Everyone a house over is too wrapped up in their own lives, all of us moving in different directions once we snatch our diplomas. And I'm about to find myself moving away from the only place in years that's felt like home.

Clarissa takes the chair next to me. "Okay, you're making me nervous. I don't think I can wait until dinner."

I grab her hand and kiss the back of it before threading our fingers.

"I didn't bring it up before because I wasn't sure…"

"Tell me."

"There's this camp—"

"I'm ready," Dante says, racing into the room with his backpack.

"You forgot your folder," Clarissa says, glancing inside.

"Oh, duh," he freezes, darting his eyes at Clarissa, "duh,

do, da, le, do," Dante sing songs with a giggle, and we can't help our laugh.

"Good save, baby," she says, shaking her head.

She squeezes my hand as soon as he's out of earshot.

"Okay, so there's a camp?"

"Yeah. It's a prep camp for the Combine. And it's expensive. Like *really* fucking expensive. I reserved a spot months ago in the off chance I'd be invited, but if I go—" I run a hand down my face.

"You wouldn't be able to help out for a while."

I nod. "It would be like taking out a student loan I may never be able to pay back."

"That expensive?"

"Yeah."

"Okay, so do it. Bet on yourself. I am."

"Fuck, you're incredible," I whisper.

"How long will you be gone?"

This is the part I dread most. "Six weeks. And I would need to leave tomorrow."

"Tomorrow?"

"I wasn't about to spend the money without the invite, but if I want in, I have to report within the next few days to keep my spot, and it's a long drive."

"What about school?"

"I'll miss a little, but I'll make it up."

"You have to go," she whispers.

"I know. I have to do whatever it takes. Whatever it takes."

She nods. "You've got this."

I can tell she's being strong for me, but what we have is new, and I don't want to gamble with it.

"I'm not going anywhere." She repeats my words back to me, seeing the apprehension in my face. In this second, I'd move mountains just to fucking pull her to me and kiss her fears away. The secrets we're hiding from our son are piling up, but I can't in good judgment say the timing is right. Just as the thought drifts through my head to broach the subject of when, Dante busts us.

"Mommy? Why are you holding Troy's hand?"

Clarissa squeezes it and lets go. "Because Troy just got really good news. He's going to camp."

"Clarissa," I say softly.

"You're going. We'll make it work," she whispers, "we will." I want so bad to hold her and hate the fact I can't.

"What camp?"

"Football camp."

"For how long?"

"I would leave tomorrow, bud, and I won't be back for a long time."

"How many sleeps?"

"Forty-four."

"Yeah, no," he shakes his head as if it's final. "No, you don't need to go. You're already good at football. They can have camp without you."

Clarissa speaks up, saving me once again. "Dante, he needs to go so he can get into shape."

Dante frowns. "You're already strong. You can lift me over your head!"

"They'll make me stronger, bud. Faster."

"How much stronger?"

"Like the Hulk," I say, tossing him up and carrying him toward the door at my side. His whines bouncing out with each of my steps. "But, who, will, play, Xbox, with, me?"

"Theo will."

"I don't want Theo."

"I'll call you every day."

"I can come see you. Right, Mommy? We'll go too?"

"No, baby, we can't come to this camp," she says, locking up the house and taking the key off the chain before handing it to me. I glance down to where it sits in my palm and close it in my fist. She leans in with a whisper. "So you don't forget where home is."

She ushers Dante down the steps. "Come on, we can't be late for school."

"I'm sorry," I whisper as we make our way to her SUV.

"No way, this is happening," she gives me a serene smile, and I see all her strength in it. "And you need to be smiling about it right now. We've got your back. See you tonight?"

"Tonight," I say, walking down the steps before shooting off a text.

Troy: I'm kissing the hell out of you right now.

Amy's Sausage Snack Wraps
Chiropractor, Chicago IL

Makes 48 snacks
30 minutes

2 8 Ounce Cans Pillsbury Refrigerated Crescent Dinner Rolls
48 Cocktail-Sized Smoked Link Sausages

Unroll both cans of dough and separate into 16 triangles. Cut each triangle lengthwise into thirds. Place sausage on shortest side of each triangle. Starting at shortest side, roll up to opposite point. Place on ungreased cookie sheet.

Bake at 375 degrees for 12 to 15 minutes or until golden brown.

Serve warm. If desired, serve with ketchup or mustard.

thirty-eight

CLARISSA

I T'S BEEN LESS THAN TWO DAYS SINCE TROY PACKED UP HIS TRUCK, and I've been walking in a nightmare. Work has been a living hell, hormones, and testosterone flying at me from all sides. I drove through a construction site this morning and got two flat tires, started my period, and was alerted to that fact by one of my students. That was just from seven to lunch. Dante had a rare meltdown in the grocery store after I picked him up, and we've been fighting ever since.

All I want is a bath and a little FaceTime with Troy.

Walking my laundry into my bedroom, I glance over at my vanity, picturing Troy behind me, his eyes lit with lust as his lips cover my skin. That fantasy gets me through as I fold a week's worth of laundry. They say love is a drug, and while I've had an inkling of it, I'm positive I've never been so doped up on endorphins in my life. I've never felt a rush the way I do when he touches me. His voice alone sets me off. Just the rumble of his laugh activates me. His smile, the way his eyes light up when he walks through my door.

I can see the appeal of the overload, but this high is natural. This high I'll allow myself.

I already miss him. Forty-two sleeps to go.

My phone lights up with the number of Brett's office, and I hesitate but decide to answer.

"Hello?"

"Ms. Arden?"

"Yes."

"Hi, this is Marissa with Brett Tompkins' office."

"We've met Marissa, how can I help you?"

"Well, I'm sorry to be the bearer of bad news, but it appears your check for rent this month has been returned."

"I'm sorry?" Mortified, I rush to my open laptop and click into my bank account to see that I am, in fact, in the negative by nearly seven hundred dollars.

"I'm so sorry. I'll bring a cashier's check by tomorrow, if that's all right."

"There's a two-hundred-dollar late fee after the sixth."

"That's today. Can it possibly be waived?"

I wrack my brain on how I might have mismanaged my money.

"I can ask Mr. Tompkins."

"No. NO! Please don't do that. I'll bring it by today before five."

"That's fine. See you then."

"FUCK FUCK FUCK FUCK FUCK FUCK FUCK FUCK!"

I toss my cell on the bed and jump when I see Dante's reflection in the vanity mirror, his eyes wide. "You owe me sooo much money. The F word is four dollars each."

"Dante. I'm telling you right now. Get out of here and find something to do for thirty minutes. I need thirty minutes."

"Mommy, I added it up, and that's," he starts ticking off his fingers.

"You have no idea because you can't multiply! OUT!"

"FINE!" He makes his way out of the bedroom as I sit on my bed with my laptop.

Within a matter of minutes, I know exactly why I'm poor.

My education. My deferred student loan payments. After half an hour on the phone, I'm no closer to a solution.

"SHIT!"

"Two more dollars, Mommy!" Dante calls from where his sonic ears pick up signals from space. It's a miracle Troy and I have gotten away with our bickering so far.

"Dante, we no longer give curse money in this house."

"Nuh-uh." Deciding not to fight with my six-year-old, I busy myself with my laundry, trying my best not to freak out. I've been through worse. I'll get through this. Opening my dresser drawer, I see Troy's cream sweater sitting on top of my T-shirts. I pull it out to see a note attached to the breast. I slip the sweater on and bring the V of the neck to my nose, inhaling deeply. I blame the tears that spring to my eyes on my hormones.

Wear this when you need me, pretty woman, and I hope you wear it a lot.

Yours,
Troy

Walking up the sidewalk into Brett's office, I cringe when I see his BMW in the parking lot. The man is rarely there during business hours, why does he have to be in today? Cashier's check in hand and emergency savings drained, I walk into the reception area, thankful to see his door closed. Envelope ready, I hand it to the receptionist.

"222 Ohara drive. You called this morning."

"Yes, hold on a minute." She picks up her phone and presses an extension. "Mr. Tompkins." I wince as she looks up at me with a plastic smile. "Ms. Arden is here." I'm still cringing when he opens his door and lifts brown eyes to mine.

"Hey, you," he says, ushering me toward his office.

"Hey, Brett, I can't stay, I have to pick up Dante from the neighbors."

He slides his hands in his slacks. This man was my college dream. He'd been a slight obsession for me for multiple semesters. He's beautiful in the polished suit sense, a take control kind of man, ambitious. All the things I found attractive. But after just a few short months of dating him, all my curiosity was quenched and swapped out for disappointment. But I can't help but to be thankful for the trade-off as I take another whiff of the cologne from my sweater.

"Come on," he tilts his head toward his office, "you've got a few minutes."

"Just a few," I say, walking into his office. He closes the door behind him as my phone buzzes.

Troy: How many sleeps left?

I press my lips together to hide my smile and glance up at Brett, who's taking a seat behind his desk.

Clarissa: I can't talk right now. I'm in the middle of a love affair with a cream sweater. Which I will need every day.
Troy: (Smiley face emoji) Call you later, baby, I need to check-in.

My heart warms at the sentiment.

Clarissa: It's a date. (Kissing face emoji)

Brett clears his throat. "How've you been?"

"Fine. Just stopped by to pay rent."

"Yeah. I saw that. Everything okay?"

"This is embarrassing. But yes. Everything is fine."

Visions of bitch-slapping receptionists dancing in my head, I give him a polite smile. That witch knew we were dating because I've met him at his office more than once. I'm sure she wants nothing more than to bone her boss, if she hasn't already. It occurs to me now just how often he called to tell me he'd be working late at the office.

I'm willing to bet she pranced in his office today with his morning coffee, twirling her hair with a 'guess whose check bounced?' ready on her tongue.

"Shit happens, right?"

"Yes, it certainly does. But I'm sure you have no clue what this is like. Ever bounced a check, Brett?"

"No, but I'm not ignorant to the issues of the working class."

I can't believe I dated this asshat.

"How very philanthropic of you." I'd chosen my clothes and words carefully while with him trying to fit some idealistic mold. It was exhausting, and I despised that I felt I had to put on such airs to try and impress him. As much of a gentleman as he was, we didn't mesh, not in the real sense.

It strikes me now just how much Troy and I have in common. We were both raised by single parents, both of us hustlers doing whatever we have to, to reach our goals, to take care of our family. We even fold our towels the same way. I love that.

And then there's our little boy, who brings us so much joy, living proof of just how well we fit. It's while sitting in my ex-boyfriend's office on one of the shittiest of days I've had in years that I realize I'm falling for him.

I'm falling for Troy.

I smile as Brett cringes. "That did sound horrible. I didn't bring you in here to belittle you. It's the last thing I want to do."

"You're doing a fantastic job."

He barks out a laugh. "God, you don't mince words. I love that about you. I'm sorry. I'm really not trying to be a dick."

"Just stop saying you've played on my field when you're in a different ballpark, and we're good."

"Fair enough," he straightens his tie. "So, how are you, really?"

"Good."

"Dante?"

"He's wonderful."

"Good to hear," he leans in, his fingers splayed on his desk. "If you need me to cut you a break on rent, just let me know. It's not a problem."

"That's not necessary, but thank you."

"Look, if I'm in the position to help, let me."

"You'll always be in the position to help. I appreciate it. But I'm a big girl. It was a bank error."

"Okay. So, how's the school year going?"

"Good, almost over."

"And Roy?"

"You know damned well his name is Troy."

"Right. Clarissa—"

I stand. "I really need to get going. I don't want to keep Dante waiting."

He sighs. "Okay. Please tell Parker I said hello."

"I will."

He rounds the desk and pulls me in for a hug. When he

pulls away, he keeps his hands on my hips. "If you ever change your mind, *for any reason*, call me."

I pull away, giving him back his hands. "Thanks, Brett. I will."

Just as I reach his door, he stops me. "I really fucked up with you. I should have taken us more seriously."

"No," I say, glancing back at him. "Don't be sorry. It worked out the way it was supposed to."

"I like your cologne." I can hear a hint of jealousy in his voice.

"Thanks, it's a new one."

"Oh yeah, what's it called?"

"Take notes."

I can't help my strut as I walk out.

thirty-nine

Troy: I can't feel shit.

Clarissa: Wish I was there to kiss it and make it better.

Troy: I can't believe I'm paying for this.

Clarissa: It will be worth it when they call your name.

Troy: It will. But this is seriously hell on earth.

Clarissa: Stop whining, Jenner. Think of Dante in class sporting his father's NFL jersey.

Troy: Now that's good motivation.

Clarissa: Need more?

Troy: Bring it, baby.

Clarissa: Think of Dante's mother sporting your NFL jersey with her lips wrapped around your cock.

Troy: Jesus, yes please. Give me more.

Clarissa: Sorry, I have to go shape young minds.

Troy: You're cruel and filthy.

Clarissa: FaceTime tonight?

Troy: It's a date.

JAMEY'S CROCKPOT POTATO SOUP
Restaurant Manager, Beaver Falls, PA

Makes 6 servings
6 hours

1 30 Oz. Bag Southern Style Hash Brown potatoes
2 14 Oz Cans Chicken Broth
1 Can Cream of Chicken Soup
1/2 Cup Onion – chopped
1/3 Tsp. Pepper
1 8 Oz. Cream Cheese – softened

Optional Toppings:
Green Onion – chopped
Bacon Bits
Shredded Cheese

Combine broth, soup, onion and pepper in slow cooker and stir well. Add potatoes. Cover and cook on low for 5 hours.

Stir in cream cheese and continue to cook for 30 minutes stirring occasionally until cheese is melted.

Garnish with optional toppings as desired.

forty

CLARISSA

"**C**OME ON, BABY, PLEASE."

I blow in my hands, rubbing them together before trying the ignition again.

"It's not going to start, Mommy. You've tried a hundred times."

"Shit!" I bang my hands against the wheel as Dante opens his mouth to claim his reward. "Not a word, son."

I glance over to where Theo's car sits in the driveway and debate on asking for a favor. I turn it one last time and get nothing but a mechanic light in the dash.

"Maybe I can fix it?" Dante pipes from the back seat.

"It's okay, Peanut, I'll get it fixed." I chew on my lip and decide I don't have a choice. "Come on, we're going to ask Theo for a ride." I gather Dante, pulling his hood up as I walk across the yard and knock on the door. Theo answers after a beat with a sleepy smile.

"Hey, Clarissa, good morning, Dante."

"Hey, bud."

I can't help my laugh. "Theo, I'm so sorry to bother you, but my car isn't starting, and I was wondering if you could give us a ride to school?"

"Sure. Just let me grab my coat."

The ride to school is filled with updates, mostly about Troy.

"Theo, did you know Troy is at camp?"

"Yeah, pretty cool."

"He's going to be in the Enful."

"That's NFL, baby," I correct. "The National Football League."

"I knewed that."

"You knew that."

"That's what I said."

"Sorry," I say, glancing at Theo. "I know it's early."

"It's fine. Happy to give you a lift. Will you need a ride home?"

"No, I'll figure it out. Thank you."

"Troy is going to be as big as the Hulk," Dante supplies.

"Someone's got a new hero," Theo says with a smirk.

"He's definitely a fan. How about you? You've been busy yourself."

"Yeah," he glances over at me. "It's been a good year."

"What's she like?"

"Loud, beautiful, crazy, *everything*."

"That good?"

"Better." Theo glances in the rearview. "Dante, how was your Christmas?"

"Santa brought me a desk and a new bike. And all my Legit Life Merch. I'm wearing my hoodie now, see?"

"He's driving, sweetheart."

"You should get a hoodie, Theo. I'll make five bucks."

"Dante, that's rude."

"Sorry. But it's soft. You should get one, Theo. It's Legit."

Theo chuckles. "I believe you. I think I may be able to order one."

"Okay, I'll send you the link when I get home."

"They're sixty dollars," I whisper to Theo.

"It's cool," he says.

"You really don't have to."

"I'll look for your confirmation email," Dante practically shouts, appearing between our seats, making us both jump as we pull up to his school.

"Thank Theo for the ride, Dante. And if he doesn't want to buy a hoodie, he doesn't have to."

"Thanks, Theo, bye Mommy," a teacher who is clearly freezing her ass off waves to the two of us before leading Dante into school.

"He's something else," Theo chuckles.

"Yeah, a natural salesman. Seriously, don't worry about the hoodie."

"It's not a problem."

Since when is sixty dollars not a problem for a college kid? Sixty dollars is a fortune to me some days. Apparently, Theo's in better financial shape than I am because I have no clue how I'm going to repair my car.

"Do you know what's wrong?"

"Wrong?"

"With your SUV?"

"Oh, uh, it's like eleven years old. It's gasping for air at this point."

"I know a guy at Honda if you're looking for something new."

"Thanks, I need something. I was going to try to wait until next month, but the universe decided to take a shit on me."

"Well, let me know."

"I will."

The rest of the way to school, I wrack my brain, trying to think of a way to arrange and rearrange. I could barely afford to pay rent this month with the shortage of Troy's checks. He had to quit his job at UPS because they wouldn't give him leave. He's officially unemployed and spending a fortune on a bet that may or may not pay off. Like a fool, I'd started to count on that money, and now we're both gambling on his ticket. I have no business doing that.

None.

I've always been self-reliant. Always. And now I've grown used to the help.

Troy needs me to be strong and get him through this time, and I'll be the same support to him as he's been to me in the last five months. As I thank Theo and shoulder my bag, I decide I'll take on Troy's mindset.

I'll do whatever it takes.

forty-one

TROY

"**H**ey, little man," I say when Dante answers Clarissa's phone.

"Hey, Troy!"

"What are you doing?"

"Helping Mommy cook dinner."

"Whose recipe tonight?"

Suddenly I'm staring at the ceiling.

"Dante?"

"Sorry, I had to wash my hands. We're having Terri's Roast. She was a legal scretary from Virginia."

"That's secretary," I hear Clarissa correct. "And for dessert," Clarissa adds, coming into view, wiping her hands on a towel. My chest tightens at the sight of her. "We have Joanne's Mud Pie."

"Mommy says she was Canadan. It's got gummy worms in it!"

"Oh, yeah?"

"That's Canadian," Clarissa corrects.

"Mommy says Joanne said *aboot*," Dante giggles. "It's about but it sou—"

I chuckle. "I get it, bud."

"How are you?" Clarissa asks, eyes full of concern.

"Hanging in," I wink.

"Why are you putting your finger on the screen?" Dante asks, tilting his head. I realize that I'm outlining Clarissa's face with my finger like a fucking douche. Jesus. I want to take my own man card.

"There was a gnat on my screen."

"Eww. You should clean your phone. Mommy says there's more acteria on a phone than a piece of poop."

"Is that so?"

"That's bacteria, baby," Clarissa chimes in.

"That's what I said, *gah*."

"Uh huh," she replies. I can hear the smile in her voice.

"Troy, when are you coming back?" Dante asks pulling the phone and conversation from Clarissa's reach. "How many sleeps?"

"Thirty, little man."

"That's too many!" He whines.

"Okay, go set the table," Clarissa says, taking the phone.

"K. Bye, Troy!"

"Night, bud."

Clarissa watches his retreat before turning back to face me. "We've got about a minute."

"I miss the hell out of you."

"That'll teach you not to be such a badass. What's the housing like?"

"Lifeless, shitty. I want some of that pot roast."

"I'll make some when you get home."

"Yeah?"

"Of course."

"Talked to Mom, said she's watching Dante tomorrow night."

"Yeah," her eyes dart away. "I've got a parent-teacher conference. Is that okay?"

"Do they still have parent-teacher conferences in high school?"

"They do if their kid writes, 'Ms. Arden has DSL's on the chalkboard.'"

"DSL's?"

She leans in on a whisper. "Dick sucking lips."

I throw my head back with a laugh.

"Har, har, laugh it up."

"Yeah, well, just remember those lips belong to—"

"*And* he's back," Clarissa warns.

"Blocked by my own sperm," I mutter.

"What's sperm?"

I show all my teeth as Clarissa gives me wide eyes. "Thanks, Troy. Really."

"Sorry." 'I miss you,' I mouth.

"Me too."

"Call me after lights out?"

"If you're lucky."

I kick back on my couch. "I'm feeling pretty damned lucky."

"That's two dollars you owe me, Troy!"

Joanne's Mud Pie
Transportation Manager, Canada

Makes 6–8 servings
20 minutes

1 Package Oreos – Crushed
2 Large Packages Instant Chocolate Pudding
6 Cups Milk
1 Large Container Cool Whip
Gummy Worms

Make pudding as directed on package. Stir half of Cool Whip into pudding. Set aside enough Oreos to use for a topping. Stir the rest of the Oreos into the pudding mixture. Pour pudding mixture into bowl or individual serving dishes. Sprinkle remaining Oreos on top of pudding. Place gummy worms on top. Chill for at least 1 hour. Top with remaining Cool Whip when serving.

forty-two

CLARISSA

"Hey, you two," I walk in exhausted, aching for a hot bath. Pamela looks up from where she cradles a sleeping Dante on our couch. "Shoot, I was hoping to be home in time to tuck him in."

She reads my posture. "You okay?"

"Yeah. Long day. Thanks so much for watching him."

"No problem, anytime."

I lift Dante from her arms. "I'm just going to put him down. Do you mind staying for a second so we can talk?"

"Sure."

Things are still a bit awkward between us though we're both trying to find our groove. It's obvious she still harbors resentment toward me, but I'm determined to try and mend this fence. Once I have Dante in bed, I walk out to see Pamela looking at the freshly hung photos I have on the wall.

"I have copies of all of them that you're welcome to."

She looks over at me and I damn near flinch at the hurt in her eyes.

"I know I've apologized—"

She raises a hand. "I think we've beaten this horse to death. I'm still trying to work my way around it with my own son."

"I caused that, and I'm sorry."

"He didn't have many friends growing up," she says, scanning the pictures before glancing back at me. "He was the sweetest, most considerate child. I see a lot of Troy in Dante. And I know it has a lot to do with how you're raising him. But that baby is most definitely my grandson." She smiles. "Just as shy in public, but observant, he watches everyone like a hawk."

"Troy was shy?"

"So shy. I was worried for so long he would never snap out of it. But then puberty hit, and then came football, and dear God, it was like whiplash. I don't think he ever really knew how to handle it."

"That's so different from the guy I know."

"Look closer, darlin'."

"I'm sorry?"

She shakes her head. "You wanted to talk to me?"

"I know I have no right to ask you for anything, but I need a favor."

"Shoot."

forty-three

TROY

Parker: Hey, spermenator. Do you know where our girl is?

Troy: Always nice to hear from you, Parker. And no, I haven't talked to her since this morning.

Parker: She's not texting back.

Troy: Probably because it's after eleven. And you've always had your wine and Ambien after eleven.

Parker: She told you she avoids my calls after eleven?

Troy: No.

Parker: LIAR! Women. You think you know them, then some penis comes along, and it's no more titties before testes.

Troy: Titties before testes? That's a thing?

Parker: I just made it a thing.

Troy: Will there be anything else?

Parker: Yes. What are your intentions with my BFF?

Troy: How about none of your damned business.

Parker: EHHH. Wrong answer.

Troy: Jesus. Even your texts are annoying.

Parker: Secretly, you adore me.

Troy: Rub your fingers together, and you'll get an inkling of how much.

Parker: Well, you bought me a Christmas gift.

Troy: You STOLE my Grand hoodie. That wasn't a gift.

Parker: I'm wearing it now, and it's amazing.

Troy: Make sure you wash it before you return it.

Parker: If you want it back so much, It's in India. Come and get it. (Devil emoji)

Troy: Nah, keep it. But make sure to write a review. (Devil emoji)

Parker: I'm going to kill your baby mama. (Cursing emoji)

Troy: Will there be anything else?

Parker: Yes. Please don't hurt her.

I tense at the idea that Clarissa voiced that fear to Parker, and that doesn't sit well with me.

Troy: Hey, baby, you up?

Minutes later, and without a reply from Clarissa, I get an Amazon link from Parker.

GrandGirl#08 Reviewer Ranking 1,037

Men's XL Texas Grand Hoodie-Garnet

I got this hoodie gently used. Well, the hoodie, I can't say much for the previous owner, but I have my suspicions this hoodie has seen more floors on the Grand campus than thongs on an adult film set. Anyhoo, it's nice and comfortable and seems to be doing its job for the moment. But, if at any point in time, it starts to show any wear and tear, I will reduce it to an unrecognizable

pile of muscled material...slowly, oh so slowly, and thread by thread.

So far, this hoodie has shown no signs of distress— in fact, I'm rooting for this hoodie to bring years of comfort and happiness—despite the lineup of new and capable hoodies waiting on the sidelines.

Note to the previous owner – If I find any signs of irreparable damage, I will be asking for a FULL refund via pound of flesh.

Grand girls stay Grand. Grand guys better damn well measure up.

Sharpens scissors.

"Hey, Troy," Dante answers, as I settle into bed.

"Hey, bud, what are you doing?"

"Nonny is teaching me how to play checkers."

"Who's Nonny?"

"*I'm Nonny*," my mother replies, coming into view.

"What are you two doing?"

"Trying to teach this kid there's more to life than the internet."

"Yet, I see you're wearing his merch."

She rolls her eyes. "I've never in my life paid twenty-seven dollars for a T-shirt."

"You got suckered."

"It's Legit," Dante pipes in, offended.

"How much did you make off her?"

Dante whispers into the phone. "Two dollars."

I can't help my laugh. My son is a hustler. "How many more sleeps?"

"Too many. Where is Mommy?"

"She left with a work friend."

"Girl's night," my mom says. "She should be home soon."

"It's nice of you to watch him."

"It's not a favor, son. Dante, I'll be in the kitchen. Don't make a move without me." I hear him agree as she moves into the other room.

"How is camp?"

"It's good. My forty is the best it's ever been. It's grueling though."

"Worth the money?"

"Let's hope so."

"You still going to graduate in May?"

"Yes. It's going to be a bitch to catch up, but I should be good."

"That's my boy. You know your dad called not too long ago."

"Yeah, he on the 'what if my son becomes a millionaire' train?"

"Probably."

"Won't that be a kick in the teeth."

"God, I know I'm not supposed to rejoice, but I love that you feel that way."

"I've got nothing for him," I say honestly. "Let's not talk about this now." I lift my chin, and she nods in understanding.

"Right. Little ears."

"So, will you tell Clarissa to call me when she gets in? She's been hard to reach lately. Everything okay?"

"She's got a job and a child."

"I know."

"Don't give her a hard time for it," she says in her business tone.

"Well, well, well, look who's tap-dancing over enemy lines. You two seem to be getting along." I can't help my smile. I was worried it might not happen, but I should have known.

"She's a good woman. I'm having a hard time staying pissed off."

"Now you see how I feel."

This gets her attention. "How do you feel?"

"Like I want to be sitting where you are."

Mom smiles. "I like her. I really do. I like her for you. She's got a good head on her shoulders, she's beautiful, and makes beautiful babies."

"That she does."

"I can't wait for the next one."

"Cart before the horse, Mom."

"You two little shits started it that way."

"You owe me two more bucks, Nonny," Dante says. "I got your checkers too."

"That ought to teach you," I say.

She sighs. "Love you, son. I'm going to go put this little light out."

"Love you, Mom."

"Love you, Troy!" Dante shouts just as she ends the call, and my heart flips in my chest.

LAUREN'S EGGS BENEDICT
Commercial Specialist, New Jersey

Makes 6 servings
20 minutes

Hollandaise Sauce
2 Egg yolks
1 stick of butter
1 tbsp real lemon juice

3 English muffins
Margarine
**6 Thin Slices Fully Cooked Canadian-style Bacon or Smoked
    Ham**
1 Tsp. Butter
6 Poached Eggs

To prepare Hollandaise Sauce; slightly beat egg yolks, add one
half stick of butter and lemon juice, stir over low flame until
butter melts. Add the rest of the butter and stir until it thick-
ens. * increase the amount of lemon juice to suit your taste.
Keep warm. Split English muffins and toast. Spread each muffin half with margarine and keep warm. Cook Canadian-style
bacon in 1 teaspoon margarine over medium heat until light
brown. Prepare poached eggs. Place 1 slice bacon on split side
of each muffin half and top with poached egg. Spoon warm
sauce over eggs

forty-four

CLARISSA

"Y OU LOOK TIRED," TROY SAYS AS I SETTLE INTO BED.

"Thanks."

"That's not the way I meant it."

"I know. I am tired. You spoiled me when you were here, and I guess I got used to it."

"I'll be home soon."

"I know."

"It's been hard to get ahold of you."

"I'm sorry. I meant to call you back last night and fell asleep when I put Dante to bed."

"It's cool. Everything okay?"

"Yeah, fine. Why?"

"Parker's been trying to get ahold of you too."

"Yeah, I spoke to her, thanks for ratting me out."

He winces. "My bad."

"Yeah, you're going to pay for that."

"I'll make it up to you."

"I'm going to hold you to it. It feels like forever since I've seen you." My eyes water and I curse my stupid hormones.

His expression grows serious. "What's wrong?"

I sniffle and do my best to get it together. "I just miss you. It's stupid, right? You'll be back in a couple weeks."

"It's been a long fucking month. The longest of my life, if I'm honest. Too much time away, from Dante, from you. I don't know how I'm going to feel when I'm on the road."

"You'll be playing, not training. Doing what you love. Right now, you're jumping through hoops to make it happen. It'll all work out in your favor."

His beautiful blue eyes penetrate me through the screen as he lays on a pillow, his hand behind his head, bicep bulging. "Fuck, I wish I was there."

"Me too, I would lick the shit out of that bicep."

"You like that?"

"*Uh huh.*"

His mouth lifts. "Will you like me when I'm old, fat, and have saggy man butt?"

I smirk. "Doubt it."

"Damn, that's cruel."

I shrug. "Just being honest. Mind tipping that camera down a bit?"

He slowly moves the phone down his torso to his happy trail. He's always been muscular, but now he's got the build of a gladiator. My fantasies kick into overdrive as I soak him in.

"A little further."

"Nope," he says through perfect lips. "Skin for skin."

"I'm already naked."

"Really?"

"No. I have on a grumpy cat T-shirt with a strawberry oatmeal stain. You're dating a single mom, dude. Wise up."

"Not single anymore."

"Sorry," I wince. "Force of habit."

"Yeah, well sexiest mom I've ever seen."

I drop the phone to my T-shirt and zero in on the stain. "Like that? That doing it for you?"

"Fuck, yes, that's hot," he chuckles.

"Oh, wait, here's some toothpaste, freshly sprayed."

"Damn, let me get one-handed real quick."

We laugh together as I pull the camera back up.

"Do you want more?" He asks.

"More toothpaste? I'm all set."

He rolls his eyes. "You know what I'm asking."

"Kids? Sure…probably."

"How many?"

I can't stop staring. He's glowing, literally glowing on the screen. For just a second, I revel in the fact that he's mine. "I don't know."

"How about five?"

"I'm so sorry this had to end. It was awesome knowing you," I say, lifting my finger to end the call.

"Don't you dare," he warns. "I'm serious."

"Why five?"

"Because I've always pictured myself with a big family one day. I don't know. I love the idea of a houseful of kids."

"Well then, *you* can push them out of your *penis*. Let them suck the marrow out of your breasts and bones and scream in your ear for the first five years."

He shrugs. "We can negotiate. You know, seeing how this is an adult relationship."

"Smartass. Are you always going to use that against me?"

"Probably."

My curiosity gets the best of me. "Have you ever been serious with a girl?"

"Yes," he says easily.

I feel my hackles rise, but I asked. "Tell me about her."

"Gorgeous blonde. Shaggy hair, perfect teeth, doe eyes. I was so in love. Never been in love like that and never will again."

"Really?" I ask, swallowing. "So, what was her name?"

"Maura." I hate that name. I hate her.

"What happened?"

"We had to put her to sleep."

"You ass, you were talking about a dog!"

"God, you're sexy when you're jealous."

"I don't get jealous."

"Liar. You so do. Your nostrils flare. Dead giveaway."

"Eat poop, Jenner."

"What about you?" He asks.

"I had the typical high school love story that ended out of boredom, and then I had the great honor of dumping the guy who didn't give a damn about my affections in college."

He snorts. "Sweet revenge."

"Exactly."

"I love that you dumped him for me."

"It was because he was not for me…and because I wanted to keep making out with you. I'm a classy bitch."

"So classy and beautiful."

"So, you've really never been in love?"

"I have. October 5th, 2012, was the first time I fell."

"I love that he's the love of your life. He's mine too."

"He told me he loved me the other day on the phone while I was talking with my mom."

"He did?"

"Yeah. I'm glad I was alone after."

"Why? Did you get emotional?"

"Little bit."

"Such a softie."

"You're making me this way."

"Am I?"

"Yeah." He bites his lip. "Between you and that kid, I'm so screwed."

"Listen to your pillow talk, who knew you were so romantic?"

"I finally found the right girl. Maura may have to take second."

"Troy," I murmur.

"Oatmeal stain or not, if I were in the bed with you right now, I wouldn't take my lips off you all night."

"Trust me, *all* of me misses you."

"Miss my lips?"

"Yes," I sink into the bed.

"Show me where," he whispers hoarsely.

"No way."

"Come on. I'll show you what's missing you."

"Troy—"

"Nope, if you tell me there's no sexting in adult relationships, I'm calling bullshit."

"I was just going to say, let me lock the door."

"Oh, well then, carry on."

"Give me a second."

I drop the phone and lock my door while running my fingers through my hair and slipping off my T-shirt. Getting comfortable in bed, I fan my hair out on my pillow and lift my phone.

"Are you naked now?"

"Panties."

"Which ones? Tell me the ones with the black lace and purple bows."

I slip the phone beneath the sheets and hear his groan. "Hell, yes." I pull the phone back up, face hot with embarrassment.

"So, what are you kissing first?" I ask.

"Sucking, I'm sucking on your lips."

"Okay," I giggle. "Troy, this is—" I shake my head. "I don't know if I can do this."

He rakes his bottom lip with his teeth, a habit I now love, his voice coated in heat. "Trust me?"

"Yes."

"I miss you," his voice is gravelly, and instantly he's with me in the room. I can practically feel his whisper in my ear.

"I miss you too."

"You're so beautiful, from those lips to that neck to those nipples. Show me what I'm missing, show me how you touch yourself," he murmurs.

"Tell me what to touch," I whisper back, hypnotized by the heat of his voice and the neon blue eyes gazing back at me.

"Start from the top."

I lift the phone, angling it down and uncover one of my nipples, circling it with my finger. His eyes close briefly before he opens them, setting me on fire. He's turned on, and there's nothing funny about it.

"You're so perfect, lick those lips for me," he whispers, and I can see his hand descending as I dart my tongue along my lips.

"Let me see." The phone drifts down his ripped torso, and I nearly gasp when he pulls out his rock-hard cock. My mouth waters at the sight of it.

This is really happening.

I imagine what I'd do if he were in front of me.

"Brush your thumb over the tip," I order, and he does before giving his cock a long pull.

"Good, but I would have licked that pre-cum off first."

His eyes close as he slowly strokes his length. "Jesus, Clarissa."

"I'm swirling my tongue over the head, waiting for you to buck your hips so I can take you to the back of my throat."

"Fuck, yes," he's working his cock now in full view as I slip my hand in my panties.

"Uh uh," he says, watching me intently. "Let me see."

"I'll give you a partial view," I say, shying away from his demands.

"No. Fucking. Way. Let me see that beautiful pussy," he's working his hand faster, and I use my free hand to slip my panties off.

"Naked?" He drawls out, slowing his pace.

"Yes."

"Show me."

I lower my phone and spread for him using my middle finger to rub my swollen clit. I tilt the camera, so I'm able to get a partial view and am surprised at how turned on I am by the sight of us both touching ourselves so intimately.

"I need you here," I whimper, "I don't want to do this without you."

"I'm there," he says, pumping his cock, his breaths coming fast.

"I'm with you," I bow a little off my mattress, the sight of him enough to have me working my fingers, massaging my clit in circles. I'm soaked, and I can feel the onslaught coming.

"Look at me," he orders as his body tenses, his strong jaw locking as his cock spills over, and he pumps his orgasm out. It's so fucking filthy on the screen, and all it does is turn me on more.

"Show me," he groans as I work my fingers flicking my clit, over and over until finally I tip and spill, gasping out his name more frustrated than sated. I need him too much. I want him too much. I miss him too fucking much for not having had him long enough.

"I need more," I say softly.

"I'll give you everything," he promises, his voice sincere, "everything."

"Hurry up and come home."

"Soon."

forty-five

CLARISSA

"GOLDING WROTE *THE LORD OF THE FLIES,* PENNING one of the best representations of the end of innocence."

"Funny, I witnessed the end of innocence in my back seat last week."

The whole class bursts into laughter. Inwardly I cringe before turning to face *him,* the one cocky student who thinks it's fun to goad me until I lose my cool. Every classroom has one.

I narrow my eyes at the little bastard who's wearing a satisfied grin. "How fantastic for you, Mr. Timmons. I'm sure she too was enlightened as well on how experience really does make the man."

"Trust me, I'm good," he snickers, and every student in the room looks on at me with expectation. I refuse to give in.

"I'll just have to take your word for it."

"No need," he kicks back in his seat, lifting his chin in suggestion. "I'm free tonight."

"Watch it," I snap in warning, which does nothing to wipe the smile off his face. Gathering myself together, I glance at the clock. Four more minutes until I'm free of this adolescent prison. "So, what do you think Golding's ideals were regarding government?"

I perch on the side of my desk, imploring thirty students to raise their hands. It's been one of the toughest years of my career. The longer I teach, the less relevant I feel. Or maybe it's this particular day that has me bummed. I search the crowd of students and am relieved when a hand pops up in the back. It's the face and body attached to the hand that has me reeling.

"Sir, mind telling me what you're doing in my classroom?" I'm elated to see him looking sexy as the devil in a hoodie and jeans and of course, his signature Cheshire smile.

"Rumor has it, it's your birthday."

"Happy Birthday, Ms. Arden," one of the girls squeaks, her eyes glued to Troy. It's all I can do to keep from rolling my own eyes.

Troy's remain trained on me, an infuriating smirk on his lips. "And I'd like to answer the question, if I may."

"This question is for my students."

"Technically, I am a student."

Commotion erupts in the back, and I can hear the faint whispers of a few of the football team. "That's Troy Jenner, man."

"No shit?"

"He's going pro. Did you see his highlight reel? *Sick*."

I cross my arms. "Okay, Mr. Jenner. Let's hear it."

"While anarchy was the basis of the book, they still formed a set of rules which, in essence, *is* government. I think he was trying more or less to highlight the corruption of those governing. Oh, yeah, and it's a really bad idea to leave a bunch of sadistic kids unsupervised on an island."

I nod. "I don't disagree."

"There's a first."

"To a point." I scowl at him, where he sits dwarfing a desk that's far too incompetent for his frame. He raises his hand again, and I have to bite back my smile.

"More to add?"

"Yes, I'd very much like to take you to dinner."

"I don't date students. That's highly inappropriate, Mr. Jenner."

"One can only hope." The bell rings, and the laughter fades as my students gather their books.

"I would do more than read the Cliffs Notes," I call after them as they pass my desk. "You will not pass this test without reading the novel, I assure you."

"Happy Birthday, Ms. A," a few of them say on their way out.

"Thank you."

The students scatter quickly due to the weekend itch while Troy remains at the back of the class, his smile appearing between the warm bodies crossing his path. When we're alone, I sit on the edge of my desk.

"When did you get back?" It's taking all my strength not to fly down the aisle and launch myself in his arms.

"An hour ago, and I had to come straight to you. You make tweed slacks fucking sexy. I knew I wouldn't be the only teenage boy who fantasized about you."

"Thanks for encouraging inappropriate behavior in my classroom, Mr. Jenner. Way to set an example."

"Sorry, couldn't help myself, Ms. A." He stands and begins sauntering down the aisle toward me. "You know he's got a thing for you. I'm willing to bet most of them do. Half of them were probably half-mast looking at you in those pants."

I look down at my outfit. "I dress like a nun here."

His eyes rake me in, and I do the same. He's absolutely perfect, and every day I pinch myself that he's mine. And not just because of the way he looks, but because of what lies beneath. While he was away and when our schedules permitted, we fell asleep together after hours of talking on FaceTime, no subject off-limits. But nothing beats having him here, seeing him in the flesh, being able to touch him. He's definitely the rainbow after more than forty days and nights without land. His presence a promise of something new.

And the fact that I'm comparing him to a biblical story only proves how deep I'm in.

"No, not at all a nun," he murmurs as he finally reaches me. "You're every man's dream. *This* man's dream."

Fingers itching to touch him, I hear myself whimper. He smells so damned good. "I would give anything to kiss you right now, Clarissa."

"Same."

"Then get your things, sexy, I have the rest of the day planned."

"What about Dante?"

"Parker's doing us a solid."

"You two finally call a truce?"

He shrugs. "She hasn't poisoned my food lately."

"Don't get cocky, you've been absent."

"I'm here now, and you've got seconds before I snap. Hurry up, baby, I'm fucking dying."

I gather my books as he darts his eyes toward the door and then leans in.

"No, Troy, we can't. Not here."

"Then hurry up," he grits out, his voice molten. "Fuck, what I wouldn't give for ten minutes alone with you in this room."

I gather my bag and toss it over my shoulder, not giving a damn about what I might've missed. "How did you even get in here?" I ask, unable to hide my elation as we both walk down the hall at a manic pace.

"Sweet talk."

"Poor girl."

He sighs. "Wasn't a girl."

"Damn," I laugh, "you went *there,* huh?"

He pushes the door open and ushers me out. "There's very little I wouldn't do for you, Ms. A."

In Troy's truck, I study him as he drives. He's so fucking handsome, so masculine, and yet I find myself completely floored with how different his personality is in comparison to all his perfection. He's the first to admit when he's wrong. The first one to take others into consideration. Sure, he's cocky but only to a point. He's never played indifferent to the feelings of others, especially his son's. Troy isn't the reason women stereotype, he's the exception. You don't have to dig deep to see his layers. He'll gladly lift his armor to show you what lays beneath, you need only ask.

The most dangerous people are the ones you let get close, only to reveal their Gemini side once you've confessed or given them a lot more of yourself than you should've. Troy's the opposite of that type, giving you only enough to draw your conclusions before subtly blowing you away with his depth, the beauty of his strength, the inner workings of his heart. I've seen his anger, his temper, I've seen his lows, the good and the bad, and none of it has changed my opinion of him.

"What are you thinking?"

"That I'm lucky," I say without hesitation. "That I'm so lucky you're mine." He turns to me, his eyes filling with emotion as I tell him my truth. "You've surprised me, Troy. In the best way." He stares at me for long seconds and then pulls his truck over at a bustling car wash. "What's going on here?"

"Quick stop. I want to give you something."

He plucks his phone from the console before jumping out of his truck, cornering his hood, opening my door, and hauling me into his arms. We hold each other for long seconds while he strokes my back, running his fingers through my hair before pulling away to smile down at me.

"Welcome home."

"Home looks so beautiful."

I look up at him through my lashes. "What are we doing?"

He leans past me, turning up the volume in his truck.

"Putting our dance lessons to good use."

"Here? Are you crazy?"

"Shhh…" he says, tapping play on his phone before pulling me back in his hold, just as Ray LaMontagne starts to croon "Hold You in My Arms."

"This isn't embarrassing at all," I nervously giggle as a few people tirelessly scrubbing their cars glance over at us like the love-crazed weirdos we've become.

"I'm up here," he says softly while tilting my chin up with his finger.

"So, the car wash, huh? Does this often work with the ladies?"

"You're my first."

"Your first what?"

"You're all my firsts. Relax," he whispers, kissing my cheek before nuzzling my neck.

"Who knew you would be such a romantic."

His eyes fill with pride. "Isn't that a good thing?"

"It's a great thing. By the way, my sweater is almost out of cologne."

He chuckles. "On it." As we dance, I sink into his hold, the words hitting hard, resonating deep. The wind kicks up, but I stay comfortable in the warmth emanating from him.

When the next song starts to play, Troy grips my ass, pulling me close, thighs nestled between mine, our dancing bordering indecent as he moves us to the beat of the bass. I shake my head, still feeling the eyes on our backs but give into him, dancing along.

It's when the man begins to sing that all my bells go off and my heart does a somersault. "Oh, my God!"

Troy continues to rock with me in his arms as I bang on his biceps.

"Troy! Oh, my God! It's the SONG! TROY! It's the song!"

Tears flood my eyes, and as I begin to move back and forth with him, emotions running rampant, I'm a hysterical mix of laughter and tears as we sway to the music.

"This is it!" I shout happily through my tears as he cups the back of my head and peers down at me with a blinding smile.

"I hoped it was...listen," he lifts a finger, "right...here... Ahhhhh, *baby!*" He sings to me as I burst into laughter due to his animation.

"You found it," I say, shaking my head. And then we're dancing, in the freezing cold, in a car wash off the side of a Texas highway. I couldn't care less who's watching as I cling to him, swaying my hips, a mess of emotion. Troy pulls me closer, kissing the cold tears from my face. When the song ends, I shake my head repeatedly, more tears spilling over. I'm sure I'm a spectacle, but I can't stop the shake in my voice.

"How, *how* did you figure it out?" I ask, my heart beating a mile a minute.

"The picture."

"The picture?"

"The one of you and your mom you showed me. On the back, it said: My baby & me, AG 5."

"I always thought it meant age five."

"No," he says, pushing the hair off my shoulders, "It's called "Tired of Being Alone," by Al Green."

"Wow. I'm just…Troy, this is everything."

"I can't take all the credit. Theo is a maestro, and he helped me figure it out. It was a long shot, but I listened to his greatest hits and could only find one song that would make me crack a smile in the middle. You said there was that one part that always made you laugh."

"I can't believe you remembered that."

He stops his movements, cupping my face. "I've memorized *you,* Clarissa, the shape of your lips, the lilt of your voice, your every smile, every mood, your everything. I used to think it was because I've grown so used to watching because of Dante," he wipes another tear from my cheek, "but it's not just our son, baby, it's *you.* He wasn't the only one I was falling for."

I shake my head incredulous, my heart exploding with his sentiment. "This is…I can't believe it. It's the best gift I've ever gotten. You, you gave me a piece of my childhood back. Thank you," I kiss his jaw, his nose, his neck over and over as he holds me close. "You have no idea what this means to me." I kiss him again and again, my heart soaring. "I'm so thankful. You have no idea how much."

"I think I'm getting a good idea," he manages through the rain of affection as I run my kisses along his jaw.

I look up to him, and he searches my eyes, his alight with raw happiness at my reaction. I can feel the shake in his limbs as my heart speeds up. Troy's lips seal over my mouth before he deepens our kiss. Clinging to each other, his tongue strokes mine, seeking, exploring, while I melt in his embrace. This kiss just as powerful as our last and the kiss before, but behind it, I feel more than I imagined possible. My body sinks into him, and he grips the back of my head, plunging his tongue over and over until we're breathless.

"Take me home and ravage me, superstar."

"No can do, baby, I've got a promise to keep."

"I don't think I can take much more of this adult dating."

"All in good time. Happy Birthday, pretty woman."

"I love thirty."

"You should. It looks fucking amazing on you."

"No, no, that's you."

I reach up and tug at the back of his neck, bringing him closer until I'm kissing him with all I feel, and he kisses me back just as fevered. Horns of passersby sound around us, and I couldn't care less, because for the first time since we met, we're no longer a secret, and I don't care who sees that I've fallen for Troy Jenner.

4TH QUARTER

SPRING

forty-six

CLARISSA

TROY NESTLES HIMSELF BETWEEN MY PARTED LEGS, WHERE I sit on the dryer sweeping his tongue across my lips. Opening for him, he deepens our kiss while tugging the neck of my T-shirt beneath my breasts. It's a trick he does often, cradling them together before he feasts. My nipples draw tight in anticipation, the pulse between my thighs beats heavy from the hunger in his eyes. The stroke of his thumbs over the lace covering my pebbled flesh has me on the verge as he grinds his rock-hard length just where I need him. He silences my whimper with his tongue just as Dante calls to him from the living room.

"Troy, can we play football?"

Reluctantly he pulls his lips away, eyes full of lust while he caresses the swell of my cleavage with his palm. "Sure, bud, but only for a few minutes. We have to head to the airport soon."

Slowly, he lifts my aching flesh from the lace of my bra before sucking my nipple into his mouth.

Yes, we're horrible parents.

It's been ten days of utter bliss. Since Troy's been home, we've been doing a hell of a lot of 'laundry.' Ever the hustler, he's been working odd jobs with Kevin in construction to try and catch up on his bills. When he's not working out for endless hours to keep up his time and stamina, we spend every spare adult second exploring each other's bodies. He's given me exactly what I asked for, what I hoped for, a real courting, and I'm loving every minute of it.

"I can't find it. Where is it?" Dante asks.

"In my truck," Troy calls, before placing a tongue-filled kiss on my shoulder. "Keys are on the table."

"K!"

Warm hands cover me while his lips travel, and I entertain getting down on my knees for a second time.

"Fuck, baby, I'm about to explode," he rasps out against my skin as I clutch him to me.

"Me too," I murmur, ripping at his hair. "If you would stop being so stingy with the penis, maybe we wouldn't be so sexually frustrated."

"That's 'Grand Commander,'" he says pointedly through the worship of his lips, "and I have a point to prove," he murmurs, running his knuckles down my cheek.

"Fine, fine, you've proved it, you're now the poster boy of courting and commitment, happy?"

"Hell yes, I am," he says softly, his eyes lifting to mine, the sentiment blanketing me in warmth, resonating deep.

I beam up at him, sliding my fingers through his thick mane. "Me too."

"How many sleeps?" he groans. After the Combine, he's set to meet up and sign with an agent. They've been talking for the past three weeks, and he's kept me in the loop. The closer the draft gets, the more he's scrutinized by different camps. His performance in the next few days is key, and I can't believe how relaxed he is with the pressure he's under.

"Six sleeps. You'll make it."

"No, I won't," he groans, rubbing his erection against me.

"You've got this. I'm so excited for you. You're going to kill it. And we'll be cheering you on from here."

"Troy! I got the football and your medicine!"

"Okay, bud," Troy nuzzles my neck and steals another kiss before pulling away, drawing his brows. "Wait. My what?"

"What's he talking about?"

"Medicine? No clue," he says, his eyes dropping to my love tassels to which he gives separate parting kisses. "See you in six days," he murmurs to them as I giggle.

"Come on." Righting my shirt, I push at his chest, and he unlocks the door, sauntering down the hall. Our fingers separate just before he reaches the living room and comes to a jarring halt.

Stopped short, I peek around Troy to see what's got him tensing and see Dante standing in the middle of the living room, holding up a needle. My heart seizes, the whoosh of blood pulsing in my ears, all life and breath knocked out of me by the sight.

"Is this your shots?" Dante asks Troy, wrinkling his nose. "I hate shots."

Immobilized by fear, Dante and I jump with the boom of Troy's voice. "Dante, NO! DROP IT!"

Troy's within reach in seconds, ripping the syringe away from his hand. Dante's so stunned by Troy's reaction that he begins to cry. I'm still standing in the hallway in shock while Troy inspects the needle before turning to Dante.

"Where did you find this?!" Troy roars. Hysterical, Dante screams out his reply.

"I didn't open it! Troy, I *promise!*" Dante's terrified voice lifts in defense as his eyes shoot to mine in appeal. "Mommy, I didn't open it!"

Fear like I've never known thrums through me as I race to

where Dante stands and jerk him into my arms. I don't recognize the sound of my own voice as I sit with Dante on my lap and begin to search him.

"What is it?!" I shriek frantically, inspecting Dante. "Troy," I look up to where he stands, "what is it?!"

He looks over to me, his face ashen. "Steroids. It's empty, and the cap is still on. He didn't open it."

I run my palms over Dante's arms before turning his hands over and over.

"Dante, please tell Mommy, did you open it? Did you stick yourself on accident?"

"No, no, I promise. I didn't! Troy tooked it! I wasn't playing with it!" His chest pumps with his cries, his voice, and lips quivering.

"You won't be in trouble, I promise. Please, baby, tell me the truth!"

From above me, Troy speaks, but he might as well be on another planet. "Clarissa, he didn't open it."

I examine Dante from head to foot. "Accidents happen. I won't be mad at all," I'm trying to stay calm, but I'm getting hysterical myself. "I don't know what to do!" I cry as I grip Dante to me, and he sobs in my neck. "I have to take him to the hospital! Troy, we have to take him in!" Dante clings to me, my cries further fueling his. Troy stops me when I stand, pulling us both into his arms.

"He didn't open it. I watched him," Troy says hoarsely. "He's okay. It didn't touch him, Clarissa. I snatched it as soon as he pulled it from the bag."

I'm shaking so hard I feel like I'm going to implode.

"He's okay," Troy assures before I jerk us out of his hold as rage rolls through me.

I lift my murderous gaze to his. "Why was that in your truck, Troy?"

He swallows, shaking his head.

"Why was that in your truck?!"

"I don't know. I don't know where it came from. It's not mine."

"Then, who does it belong to?"

"I don't know."

"You don't know?"

"I swear to God, I don't know. It could've bee—"

"This could have…" I shake my head, unable to say the words.

"He's okay. Look at him. He's okay."

I tear my eyes away from Troy. "You need to leave."

"Clarissa, it's not mine."

I try to control the heat of my voice as Dante shakes in my arms. "Troy, you need to go home."

"He's okay. Look at him, Clarissa, he's okay." He moves toward us, and I jerk my head, livid.

"Go."

"Don't. Please don't do this. It's not mine."

I grip Dante to me, smoothing his hair as he sobs into my chest. "Just go." Emotion fills his eyes, his features twisting as he studies his son, who's wrapped around me, breath hitching, and body shaking from his cries.

"Dante, I'm sorry I scared you," Troy whispers hoarsely. "I'm so sorry, bud."

Unable to handle all that I'm feeling, I burst into tears, turning my back on Troy before I make my way into the bedroom and shut the door.

forty-seven

TROY

Troy: Please talk to me. It's not mine. I would never be that reckless.
Clarissa: Whatever it takes. Isn't that what you told me?
Troy: That's not me, and you know it. I'm coming over.
Clarissa: Don't. I mean it, Troy. Don't make a scene. I just got him calm. How am I supposed to explain this to him?
Troy: I will, if you let me.
Clarissa: I can't handle this right now. I don't know what to think.
Troy: You know me. This isn't me. I don't want to leave things like this. Please talk to me.

I dial her number and get voicemail.

"Jesus, fuck!" I hurl my phone at the wall and rip at my hair.

Her reaction was knee-jerk. I know it. I can't for one second tell her she's overreacting, because I get it. I felt every ounce of her fear. I felt the same terror when I saw him holding that needle. But this woman knows me, she knows my heart, she knows *me*. I have to believe that when her anger subsides, she won't think the worst. But I'm out of time.

"FUCK!"

Lance knocks on my door. "Hey, man, you good?"

"Do I fucking look good?"

"What's going on?"

"Dante found some juice and a needle in my truck, and Clarissa thinks it's mine."

"You don't juice."

"I know that, but she's too pissed off to see the light of day. I need to leave, like now, for Combine. She won't even talk to me. It's all fucked."

Lance crosses his arms. "She's just freaking out. She'll calm down."

"You don't get it. Her mom went out with a needle. This is a deal-breaker for her."

"All you can do is plead your case."

"That's all I seem to fucking do with this woman." I'm busting from the inside out. "The cap was on. It didn't touch him. He's fine."

"You're sure?"

"Yeah. If I weren't, we wouldn't be having this conversation. I saw him pull it out of the bag, and then it was in my hand."

"Then go. You'll sort this shit when you get back."

"What the hell am I going to do?"

"Go to camp, man, it's all you can do."

"I can't leave it like this!"

"You've got no choice. This is what the league will be like. The game doesn't give a shit about your personal life. This is your chance, man, don't blow it."

"I don't know," I scrub my jaw. "You should have seen her. I think she believes it was mine. Fuck, she was supposed to drop me at the airport."

"I've got you." He pulls up his phone and shoots off a text.

"She'll come around. You need to go."

"I don't know if I can."

"You're going. Your boy is alright. I'll go and check on them both in a bit. I swear to you. I've got this handled. Go."

"Fuck, Lance, if I lose her..." I grab my duffle and head downstairs as an Uber pulls up. The driver, who looks a hell of a lot like a bald Carrot Top, introduces himself as Dave and takes my luggage as I scan Clarissa's house. A house that encases the whole of my fucking heart.

"I've got this," Lance assures me from where he stands on the porch. "This is just as much for them now as it is for you. You'll work it out when you get back."

"Right," I linger at the open door of a Taurus. "Please, baby," I whisper as I stare at her front door, praying for a glimpse of her. All my hopes evaporate when the house stays lifeless.

"You gotta go, man," Lance calls out as I linger.

"Text me?"

"Go."

Nodding as my heart cracks, I climb into the back seat and shut the door before the car speeds away from the curb.

SHARON'S BROCCOLI RICE CASSEROLE
PE Teacher, Louisiana

Makes 10-12 servings
1 hour

1 Stick Butter – Melted
½ Cup Chopped Onion
1 Can Cream of Mushroom Soup
1 10 oz. Package Frozen Chopped Broccoli
3 Cups Cooked Rice (2 cups uncooked plus 2 cups water)
1 16 oz. Jar Cheese Whiz
1 8 oz. Package Shredded Cheese

Cook broccoli according to package directions. Drain and set aside.

Sauté onion in butter until soft but not brown. Add soup and heat.

Mix broccoli, rice, soup mixture and Cheese Whiz together.

Pour into a buttered 9x13 casserole pan.

Top with shredded cheese.

Bake at 350 degrees for 30 minutes.

forty-eight

CLARISSA

"**M**OMMY, HE'S WEARING MY LEGIT LIFE SHIRT!" Dante exclaims, watching the highlights of the first day of the Combine.

"That's so awesome," Parker says, nudging me. "Isn't it, Mommy?"

"Yeah, it's great, baby."

Dante prances around the living room. "I'm going to be famous like Troy! Oh! I'll make a video of Troy wearing my merch! I bet I get some orders!"

"Great idea, Duckie," Parker says as Dante races off to his bedroom.

Parker turns to me as soon as he's out of earshot. "Hey, enough is enough. It was a freak incident. You need to snap out of it. He's okay."

"I'm fine," I lie.

"Bullshit. You don't believe him?"

"Would you?"

She sips her wine. "I mean, yeah, I think you should give him the benefit of the doubt. He deserves that much. He's taken great strides to prove himself."

"You're right."

"But you're still not convinced."

"I can't get the image out of my head." I rub my forehead with my palm, my eyes stinging with fresh tears. "I've always wondered how he does it all. You know? School, work, practice, running on little to no sleep. But it's just not…I don't for one second want to believe it."

"Then don't."

"It's not that simple."

"Has he ever shown aggression? You know, 'roid rage?"

"No. I mean, he has a temper, but nothing outlandish. He's never once been aggressive toward Dante."

"Then, there you go. I think if it's his, it's old and he's too afraid to admit it because he knows he'd lose you over it. Or it's not his, and he's being honest, and you're punishing him for nothing. Either way, something tells me he's not the type to use. And it wasn't heroin in that needle, babe."

"I know. But when I saw Dante with that needle, Parker… God, I'll never be able to explain how scared I was. I couldn't move. I've never, ever felt fear like that."

She squeezes my hand. "I can only imagine. But don't you think you're overreacting? He was probably terrified too. You haven't replied to any of his texts."

"My son was standing in the middle of my living room with certain death in his hands."

"You know what I mean."

"I can't bring myself to feel guilty about Troy right now. That kid is my whole life."

"And he's Troy's whole life, and you and Dante are his world. He needs you right now, and you've all but shut him out."

"I just can't pretend like I'm okay when I'm not."

"I get it, but you can fake it."

"How? Talking to him will only lead to an argument.

He needs to concentrate, and I don't think I can just breeze through a 'we'll work it out' conversation. He'll see right through me."

Parker picks up my phone. "His whole future is riding on the next few days. He needs your support, and he's got to be on top of his game. Just text him, *right now* and say something supportive. You can hash it out when he gets back."

"You're right."

I lift my phone and hit reply, my fingers hovering over the keys, but the image of Dante holding that needle is all I see, and I can't manage to find a single reassuring thing to say. I'm still furious. Troy's needle or not, we could have lost our son. That's all I can think of. All I can feel. Anger. Outrage. The constant replay of my worst fucking fear.

Parker watches me, reading my hesitation. "Clarissa, his whole life is in your hands right now."

"Now who's being dramatic?" I sigh, handing her my phone. "I'm still too angry. His drugs or not. I'm angry. You do it."

"Are you serious? Clarissa, this is selfish."

"What if he is using? It will change *everything*. Not only will we be over, but I don't know if I'll be able to trust him with Dante."

"I'm pretty sure they drug test in the NFL."

"You think they can't find ways around that?"

"Clarissa, the man has been nothing short of perfect the last few months and doesn't have a manipulative bone in his body."

"Have you forgotten how our son was conceived?"

"Stop it. You're sabotaging your relationship, your happiness. Don't use this as an excuse to push him away, or you'll be fucking up."

"I'm trying."

"You're not trying, you're running. You're in love with that man, and you're terrified of the other shoe dropping."

"This isn't a shoe, Parker. This is a kick in the head."

"It's not his. I know it isn't."

"I hope you're right," I stand and shake my head. "I have to get to work. Text him for me. Okay? I just can't do it right now."

"Fine." She takes my phone and starts typing.

"Wait, what are you going to say?"

"That you're sorry you overreacted, and you're proud of him. Oh, and that you're studying at all hours of the day for your realtor's license as a side gig because you don't want to count on his future millions. And that you've secretly been working nights to make ends meet while he chases his dreams."

"Don't you dare."

"Fine. I'll leave that part out, but I don't know why you haven't told him."

"Because he's under enough pressure and I don't want him feeling guilty. I have to explain this to him myself, or he won't understand."

"Yet you don't mind freezing him out when it's most crucial." Parker raises a loaded brow over the top of my phone. "There, sent."

Dante comes running into the living room with his phone in his hand. "I knewed it. I got two orders already! Can we call Troy?"

"He's busy, baby," I say, running my fingers through his hair. "Why don't you make a video to thank him and text it? He'll love it."

"K!"

"He's replying," Parker says, lifting the phone to me.

I shake my head. "I can't, not right now."

She rolls her eyes reading his response before replying. "I'll figure out an excuse for you until you get your shit together."

"Thanks," I say, shouldering my purse and calling out to Dante. "I'm leaving, Peanut. I'll be home late, so be good for Parker."

"K, Mommy!"

forty-nine

TROY

Troy: Morning, baby.

Clarissa: How's it going?

Troy: I murdered my dash yesterday, thanks to you.

Clarissa: Awesome. We're so proud of you. Hey, Parker is taking me to the spa for a few days as a late birthday present, because she's the best friend that ever lived. Your mom is watching Dante so you can reach him there. Kick that ass! I'll text you when I get back.

Troy: I've got a half-hour before I check-in. Can you FaceTime?

Clarissa: We're boarding.

Troy: Boarding?

Clarissa: The spa is in Arizona. Cell phone use is limited. It's a cleansing thing, which I need because I'm way too uptight.

Troy: No, you're not. You had a bad scare. And I'm so fucking sorry. I'll get down to the bottom of it when I get home.

Clarissa: Okay.

Troy: You believe me, right?

Clarissa: I believe in you. Make us proud.

Troy: I'm working on it. Just keep the home fires burning.
Clarissa: I'll do my part if you do yours. (Winky face emoji)

Happy and relieved, I toss my napkin down on the room service tray and reach under the covers to give the grand commander a pep talk. Seconds later, I shoot off a text.

Troy: How's that for my part? (Devil emoji)
Clarissa: Oh, wow. You sent a picture of your dick.

I chuckle.

Troy: What my baby wants my baby gets. I'm so fucking glad we're okay. Enjoy yourself. You deserve it. Miss you.
Troy: Baby, you there?
Clarissa: Of course. Just enjoying the view. Now, go kick some ass.
Troy: Enjoy your trip.
Clarissa: Taking off. (Kiss face emoji)

"Hey, bud," I greet Dante as my mother's face pops up on the screen behind him.

"Hey, baby, well, if you aren't the toast of the town. They were talking about you on Sports Center last night!"

"I saw. I just signed with my agent. Hey, have you heard from Clarissa? Is she back from Arizona?"

"When was Clarissa in Arizona?"

"She's not in Arizona," Dante says, popping a strawberry in his mouth.

"She's back?"

"She didn't go to Arizona," Dante supplies. "Auntie Parker lied to you."

"What?"

"I heard them talking 'cause Mommy didn't want to text you."

Mom's brows lift higher and higher with each word. "What's this about?"

"I found Troy's medicine, and Mommy got really, really mad, and cried *forever*."

Mind racing, I scrub my jaw, emotions running rampant while facing off with my mother.

"What medicine, son?"

"Mom, give me a second. Dante, are you sure you heard that?"

"Uh huh."

"What else did she say?"

Dante speaks around a mouthful, evident worry on his face. "Are you going to be mad at her?"

"No. Just tell me."

"She said you wouldn't know how hard she's working to make you guilty. Auntie Parker doesn't like her work friend."

"What work friend?"

"The man."

"Okay," Mom says, interrupting my interrogation. "Dante, go into Nonny's closet and grab the new puzzle."

"Okay, Nonny. Bye, Troy, Love you!"

"You too, bud."

With Dante occupied, Mom walks out onto her porch, shutting the door behind her.

"Troy, what in the hell is going on?"

"I wish I knew."

"What medicine is he talking about?"

"Right before I left, Dante found a needle and a used bottle of steroids in my truck."

"Not yours." It's not a question, it's what she thinks, if only Clarissa could believe the same.

"That's what I told her, but it's obvious she's having a hard time believing me. But Mom, it was fucking horrible. Scared the shit out of us both. Clarissa freaked out—"

"Because of her mother," she nods. "I can only imagine what she was feeling. So, she's been avoiding you since, and Parker has been texting you instead?"

"I'm guessing that's the truth of it." I scrub my face again, angry and irritated. "Fuck."

"I'll talk to her," Mom offers.

"No, Mom, stay out of it. I mean it. She needs to be able to take *my word* for it. This is between us."

"And Parker too I guess."

"Jesus. Do you know what he's talking about work friends?"

Mom winces, her expression guilty. "Mom? Are you serious? You've been covering for her?"

"Yes, but only because I agree with her reasoning. She's been picking up shifts at night, waitressing."

"What?" Sinking where I stand in my hotel room, I stare out of the window as the pieces fall into place.

"Don't give her hell for it. Money got tight when you went to camp, and she just didn't want you feeling guilty."

"Who's the man?"

"I'll let her explain that. God, you two are total idiots."

"Thanks, Mom."

"Hey, at this point in my life, I think anyone under forty is an idiot. Best be getting your ass on the next plane home."

Alyssa's Angel Hair Pasta with Chicken
Social Studies Teacher- Minneapolis, MN

Makes 6-8 servings
45 hour

1 Cup Prepared Hidden Valley Ranch Original Ranch Salad dressing **tastes best if you buy the spice packet and make it from scratch.
1/3 Cup Dijon style Mustard
4 Boneless, skinless, chicken breast
½ Cup butter
1/3 Cup Dry White Wine
10oz Angel Hair Pasta Cooked and Drained
1oz Parsley

In a small bowl, whisk together salad dressing and mustard, then set aside to thicken—can be prepared a day ahead and refrigerated until ready to use.

In medium skillet, sauté chicken in butter until browned; transfer to dish to keep warm.

Pour wine into skillet and cook over medium-high heat, scraping up any browned bits from the skillet, for about five minutes. Whisk in dressing mixture, blend well. Serve chicken and sauce over pasta. Sprinkle with parsley if desired.

fifty

CLARISSA

THE DOOR CLOSES BEHIND TROY, AND HE GLOWERS AT ME from where he stands. Parker and I jerk to attention, mouths gaping, from where we sit on the couch. We've spent the day in my living room, being total slobs watching chick flicks while eating copious amounts of carbs. We were halfway into some Netflix Original when we heard the screen sound, and the door was unlocked a second before Troy appeared, knocking the wind out of me.

"You came home early," is all I can say as his furious eyes rake over me.

"Where's Dante?"

He's livid, looking gorgeous in black track pants and a matching jacket, his hair slightly mussed from a day of travel.

"He's in his room."

Troy drops his duffle and pulls his wallet from it. "Parker, could you do me a favor and take Dante for a slushy?"

"What?" I ask, hearing the fear in my voice. I've never seen him so angry.

"Holy hell," Parker whispers before standing. "Keep your money, good sir, it's my treat. Duckie! Troy's home and we're going to get a slushy."

I tuck my hair behind my ears, knowing I look like hell as he

hostilely peruses me. He knows. What? I'm not sure. How much?
I have no clue, but if the contempt in his stare is any indication
of his discoveries, I'm in for one hell of a fight.

Dante comes running, and Troy scoops him into his arms,
barely able to mask the anger in his tone. "Hey, bud."

"I got twelve merch orders because you wored my shirt."

"I wore your shirt. And that's awesome."

"Are you getting drafted now?"

"Hope so. Hey, I really need to talk to Mommy, so Aunt
Parker is going to take you to Sonic for a bit, okay?"

"Ahhh man, you just got here!"

"We'll spend the day together tomorrow, okay? Promise."

"All day?" Dante prompts.

"All day. I'll take you fishing."

I clear my throat. "He's got school tomorrow."

"He can miss a day," Troy says, his voice full of disdain.
Parker's eyes fly to mine, and I swallow.

Troy sets Dante down. "Go get your shoes on."

"K." Dante grabs his shoes from the entry as Parker twists her
hands in front of her. The tension in the room becomes unbearably thick as dread cloaks me. Parker lifts worried eyes to Troy.

"Uh. Can I just say—"

"Nope," Troy cuts her off, eyes still trained on me.

Parker puckers her lips out and nods. "Dante, forget the
shoes, we're good."

"I can't go without shoes! Don't be silly, Auntie. I'm almost
ready."

Parker walks over to where I sit, her eyes wide. "Uh, text me?"

All I can do is nod.

"Ready," Dante says as Troy catches him once more, kneeling
to hug him. "See you tomorrow."

"K."

"Love you," Troy says, ruffling his hair.

"Love you," Dante replies, as Parker ushers him out.

When the door closes behind them, Troy crosses his arms.

"How was the spa?"

"I'm sorry."

"Jesus Christ, Clarissa."

"I'm not proud of myself."

"But you're proud of me, right?" His voice is ice. "Did you send a single one of those texts?"

I close my eyes briefly, both ashamed and terrified of the truth. "No."

He fists his hands at his sides. "You don't believe me."

"I panicked."

"Because I've given you every reason to doubt me, right?"

"That's not it at all."

"Then what!? What is it!?"

"It's a culmination of everything. That needle, us, the future."

"The future?"

"Troy, you don't know what's going to happen, and you don't know how you'll feel about me six months from now."

"I think that's a question you need to ask yourself."

"Meaning?"

"Meaning less than a week ago, I was sure about how you felt. Now I'm not sure about anything anymore when it comes to you."

"Don't say that."

"Why, why can't I? What exactly have we been doing here? I thought we were building something."

"We were, we are. It just scared me."

"It scared the shit out of me too!"

"I know. I'm sorry. I just couldn't pretend I was fine when

I wasn't. It was a reality check. Things are getting serious between us."

"That was the whole point!"

"I'm not pointing a loaded gun at our son's chest!"

"Is that what I am now? A goddamn loaded gun?"

"That's what this relationship has the potential to be. I freaked. It was wrong, and I'm sorry. I am truly sorry, I should've talked it through with you. But Dante—"

"Stop hiding behind our son! This is about you and *your* shit. *Your* trust issues. *Your fucking baggage.* It has nothing to do with him! This *is about us*! Our relationship outside of our son."

"That's where you're wrong. There is no relationship outside of him! There never will be. Every word we say, every decision we make, all of it affects him."

"There's an us in there too, Clarissa, but you wouldn't even give me a fucking chance to defend myself because you've deemed yourself judge, jury and executioner, always ready to pass a fucking sentence when I've been nothing but transparent with you."

"It was wrong to shut down like I did, but Troy, that was my worst fear come to life. It shook me to my core. And I did doubt you, and I was terrified to admit it because of how well things were going, but I haven't just been sitting here picking you apart in my mind. I've been working too—"

"Yeah, working hard, been busy *lying* to me."

"Who told you I was lying?"

"Our son. Why don't you want me feeling guilty?"

"What?" I'm visibly shaking, and he sees it.

"Who's your work friend?"

"When you left for camp, I ran into some financial trouble. I didn't want to put any more pressure on you, so I took a job waiting tables for quick cash and decided to aim for something a little more long-term, more lucrative. I've been studying to get my realtor's license, and Brett let me intern—"

"Brett, as in your ex-boyfriend? You called your ex-boyfriend for help?"

"It's not like that. I've been working with one of his top realtors while studying for the exam."

"And you didn't think this was something you should let me in on?"

"Absolutely, but not when you were under so much pressure. The week you left for camp; I got two flat tires, my car broke down, my rent check bounced, and then the fridge went out. I spent my whole tax return fixing it all. Things got tight. I was terrified. It was a wake-up call. I had to do something!"

"So, you call on another fucking man!?"

"I did whatever it took to make sure our son had a roof over his head! You inspired me, so I stepped up. This isn't about Brett! This is about me not depending on—"

"Me! Not depending on me! Because you still don't fucking trust me!"

"You weren't here! I had to make shit happen. Relying on someone else is not something I'm used to. It's been that way my whole life! I had to do something! I had to—"

"You had to trust me. That's all you had to do," he says, scooping up his duffle.

"Troy, I'm sorry. I overreacted. I am sorry. You deserved better. I was planning on talking to you when you got home."

"You weren't there for me when I needed you most. Just for once, couldn't you put my feelings, my needs before yours?"

"That's all I've been doing!"

"The answer is no. You couldn't. And so, I sent a dick pic to your best friend."

"What?"

"Did you two laugh it up?" He spits in utter disgust.

"Jesus, no. Of course not, I had no idea. I'm going to kill her. Troy—"

"Here," He pulls a folded piece of paper from the mesh of his duffle and hands it to me.

"What's this?"

I scan the paper. It's a lab report with his name on the top. Results from a drug test at Combine the day after Dante found the syringe. Negative for all substances. "It's your fucking proof."

"Troy, I believed you—"

"No, you didn't, and you'll never fully trust me. Not the way I need you to."

He walks over to where I stand and places his key in my palm. "In your eyes, I'll always be the teenager who lied and got you pregnant, not the man you rely on."

I feel myself rip in half as I search his eyes. "Troy, this has gotten way out of hand."

He steps back. "I agree."

I take one forward, and he shakes his head. "Don't."

"Don't?" I swallow. "Don't now or don't ever? What are you saying?"

The decision in his eyes terrifies me. "I'm saying this isn't going to work out." He retrieves his duffle and shakes his head. "I'm saying it's over."

"Troy," I cry as he opens the door and turns back, eyes watering, his resignation clear.

"You don't mean it. You're angry with me. Don't do this. We've overcome so much to be together. I was upset. I had a right to be, but I was always planning on talking to you, hashing it out with you. I just had to calm down, get my bearings. Dante—"

"Yes, let's talk about Dante. It's been seven fucking months. Do you ever plan on telling him I'm his father?"

"Of course, I was just waiting—"

"For what? What in the hell are you waiting for?"

"For us to—"

"There is *no us*. Not anymore and not without him, so you better keep that shit in mind."

Reeling, I feel my hackles rise. "What in the hell is that supposed to mean?"

"It means don't even dream of keeping me from my son because of this."

"Troy, I would never—"

"Oh, but you have, haven't you?"

I have no defense. None.

"Just a heads up, those checks you cashed are a paper trail, proof of child support."

"What?" I place my hand on my stomach, feeling kicked as bile climbs my throat.

"I don't want things to get ugly, but Dante is all that's between us now, and I refuse to let you hold that over my head anymore."

I begin to shake uncontrollably. "Y-you d-don't mean that."

"Do yourself a favor and play fair, and I will too. I don't want to hurt you."

Blistering pain rolls through me as I try and grasp the events of the last few minutes. I'm face to face with Troy's Gemini, and the hardest part is that I know I'm the one who is responsible for bringing it out of him.

"You would try and take him from me?"

"Never. But you're no longer the only parent who gets to make decisions. Get used to it."

I shake my head. "You're not saying this to me."

He shrugs as if he hasn't just stabbed me in the heart. "I guess deep down, I was protecting myself too. How's that for a one-eighty? In the last twenty-four hours, I've realized I. Can't. Fucking. Trust. *You.*"

"You've made your point." My voice cracks, as my heart shatters. "Go."

"I'll pick up Dante in the morning," and with that, he shuts the door.

fifty-one

TROY

"HEY, MAN, GOOD TO HAVE YOU BACK," KEVIN SAYS, clapping me on the shoulder.

"Good to be back," I lie, scanning the party. Nothing about being here appeals to me. Everything feels fucked personally and everything seems to be going right for me professionally.

Inside I'm a shell. Outside I'm still the man I've always been, a free agent in every sense of the word. Business as usual.

And I hate every fucking minute of it.

She's with him.

The same thought eats me from the inside out and has been for hours as I sip my beer to try and numb up. But I'm deluding myself. Nothing is working. Nothing.

Dante senses the separation between his mother and me, but he's none the wiser about our relationship or lack thereof. We were right to keep it hidden. It's been weeks since I handed back her key. The consistent stab I feel every time I open my eyes in the morning is enough to end me. The ache worsens when I turn over in my bed to see Clarissa readying Dante for another day, another day without me.

Aside from being close to my son, I hate my living situation and can't wait until the semester is over. I want no part of existing in this house the way things are. Theo's head is in the fucking clouds, hence why he agreed to let me throw this get together, and Lance already has one foot out the door.

I'm about to get drafted, graduate with my degree, and live my dream.

Inside this full circle, I'm empty.

And it's pure fucking torture.

She's with him.

Finishing school and snatching my diploma feels like a sentence, much like loving a woman who can't give me the whole of herself. But I refuse to pay any more for crimes I didn't commit. And every day, I battle with the guilt of just how much I hurt her with my threats and the way I left things.

When I confronted her, I was unreasonably angry and rightfully so.

It was all take and no give with her, and I'd hit my fucking limit.

And the feeling of seeing her now is both dose and withdrawal, either side of a prison I can't seem to escape.

This unrequited love shit is for the birds.

But wasn't it love we had? What we felt?

Wanting this woman is torture. Loving this woman is fucking humiliating.

This shit has to end, but lately, I can't seem to breathe without the air scraping the rawness in my chest. The hurt only fuels my anger. I'm drowning in resentment, teetering on the brink of love and hate for her. All of that effort, everything I did to earn my family, was for nothing.

Because she's with him.

And right now, I'd give anything, *do anything,* to make this ache in my chest cease.

We haven't spoken. No words, just texts, and all of them

about Dante. She's working her ass off. I know that much by the absence of her SUV in the late hours of the night. She hasn't once looked my way when we've crossed paths, and I know it has everything to do with my threats. It's as if I took the knife from my own heart and drove it straight into her back. I went *there*, to a place she's not likely to forgive me for. And I did it purposefully, eradicating our chances because, without trust, we have nothing. And with that decision, that's exactly what we are, nothing. But today she threw the dagger back the second she got into that BMW. The proverbial nail in our coffin.

With the work done and the start of my future mere weeks away, I can't seem to take a step forward or in any direction.

I need something other than the constant need I battle with daily, to be close, to reclaim my family, my place. But it's no longer mine, so instead, I reach for my next beer.

And that's when I see *her*, my mystery girl, sauntering up to my party. Her sudden appearance jars me, and I take it as a sign. And this time, I won't take no for an answer.

DIANE'S PASTA SALAD
Sales Rep-Rhode Island

Makes 8 servings
30 minutes

Tri-Color Pasta (or pasta of your choice)
Zesty Italian Dressing (Preferably Kraft or Wal-Mart brand)
Mozzarella Cheese – cut into cubes
Broccoli Florets
Cauliflower Florets
Sliced Olives
Cherry Tomatoes – Halved (or diced tomatoes)
Purple Onion – Chopped
Ham or Salami – cubed

The amount of each ingredient depends on number of people to be served. One package of pasta makes enough for a family.

Mix all ingredients adding Italian Dressing to taste.

Chill for a few hours before serving.

fifty-two

CLARISSA

Parker: You need to come home. Now. Some shit just went down next door. Something's wrong.

"Where are you tonight?" Brett says, sipping his coffee.

I close my laptop, satisfied with my progress. "Brett, I need to get home. Something's come up. I'm sorry. I'm going to have to cut this short."

"Sure." Ever the gentleman, he helps me slip on my coat and opens my car door. Once inside, he glances over at me as he starts the drive toward my house.

"There's a spring carnival coming up. What do you think about us going together? Maybe bringing Dante?"

"I don't think that's a good idea."

"It's him, isn't it?"

"Yes."

He sighs, pulling up to a stoplight. "I figured as much."

"I'm sorry."

"Are you in love with him?"

"Yes. Very much so. But you should know when you and I started dating, I had the same intentions you did."

"It's fine," he glances over at me. "I waited too long and it cost me."

"Please tell me we can be friends. You did me a huge favor tonight and I'm thankful for all your help."

"Of course, and don't worry, you're ready. You'll do great."

"Thank you. I'm nervous."

"Don't be. And as soon as you pass, we'll get you situated somewhere."

"I can't take a job at your agency, Brett."

"Are you sure?"

"Yes. I'm sorry. I just wouldn't feel comfortable. I hope you understand."

"Okay, I've got a few contacts I can send your way."

"I would appreciate that."

Minutes later, I'm sifting through my notes on my phone when Brett pulls up to my house, stopping at the curb. I turn to him.

"Clarissa, I would hate myself if I didn't at least try—"

I shake my head, cutting him off. "Brett, I'm sorry. I just want to focus on getting my license and on Dante right now. I'm nowhere near ready for anything else."

"Okay, but I hoped," he leans over, giving me a chaste kiss, and I let him but the truth of the matter is, I'll never want for another man's kiss the way I do Troy's. I'm irrevocably in love with him. Something I realized far too late.

"I swore there was something there."

"There was, I just…I'm sorry."

"Yeah, me too." He nods toward the porch. "Looks like I'm not the only one who's sorry."

I look over, my heart sinking when I see Troy sitting there with a clear view into the car. Unfastening my seat belt, I glance over at Brett, "You kissed me knowing he was watching?"

Brett shrugs. "Am I supposed to feel guilty? I'm pretty sure he stepped over the same line when we dated."

"You don't know anything about him. About us. That was a dick move."

He shrugs. "Made me feel better."

"Way to make me not regret my decision, asshole."

"I have a feeling you'll be doing that on your own," he spouts smugly before straightening in his seat.

"Do me a favor and lose my number."

I slam his car door, and Brett takes off. Walking toward Troy, I spot a Honda I don't recognize in my driveway. Confused, I approach the porch where Troy sits flipping keys in his hand.

"Are you going to introduce him to Dante?"

"It's not like that. And the answer is no. He's an asshole, and when I'm done with a man, I'm done."

"You don't say? Not the impression I just got."

"Have you been drinking?"

"Yes, I'm a college senior. Isn't that what we're supposed to do?"

He's drunk. Or very close to it. "I want to talk to you, I do, but I don't think we should have this conversation tonight."

"If you think he's a good guy, I guess, introduce him. Fuck," he says, standing and holding out the keys.

"Troy," I sigh. "That man will never meet our son. And what's this?"

"Your new SUV," he says, clicking the FOB. "I sold my truck."

"You what?"

"It's paid for. The title is in your glove compartment."

"You sold your truck?"

He shrugs. "You needed something reliable."

"But you loved that truck."

"Theo got me a good deal," he says, ignoring my protest. "There was a mix up at the dealership, and it was supposed to be delivered yesterday, but it was dropped off tonight."

I hold the keys out to him. "Just another thing to add to your paper trail, huh? No, thanks. I don't want it."

"Clarissa, I didn't mean that. I'm sorry."

"Yeah, me too. You'll never know how much, but I'm not about to give you another reason to—"

His hand shoots out gripping mine before pressing the keys into it. "You *will* take it. Your SUV is shot."

"I'm not giving you more ammunition against me."

"I didn't mean it," he says hoarsely. "You know I didn't. I would never hurt you that way. I was pissed...just...please take it. I don't want you driving around in that piece of shit anymore. Trust me, it's more for me than for you."

Tears fill my eyes. "I don't know which move damns me with you."

"Take it," he says, shoving his hands in his jeans. "It would be a weight off my shoulders."

"Okay...t-thank you." The wind kicks up, and his scent hits me. It's comforting, while at the same time tearing me apart.

"It's used. I'll get you something better when I sign a contract."

"I don't want your fucking money," I sniff, batting a tear away.

"Trust me," he says in a cool tone. "I know."

"Damn it, Troy. What I did, it was never about you, it was about me and my peace of mind. About my own ability to support myself and our son, no matter what relationship I'm in."

"Let's not do this," he says. "Let's just *not*."

"Fine." I look him over, the ache to touch him unbearable as he stands looking gorgeous in a thin blue V-neck and dark jeans.

"What about you?"

"I'm fine. I'll find something."

"Good to hear, but that's not what I was asking."

He toes the loose board on my porch. "I got my letter today. An official invite to the draft."

"That's incredible," I sniff, the sight of him so close and so distant my undoing. I miss him in a way I never imagined possible. Every day is a struggle. Even with his threats, I can't bring myself to stay angry at him.

"So, I threw a little party at the house."

"Well," I swallow. "You have every reason to celebrate."

"Do I?"

"Of course, it's all you've been working for."

"I must look so fucking pathetic to you."

I shake my head. "Not at all. It wasn't that long ago I was doing the same thing. You're just trying to have a good time, get the most out of your year."

"And what a year it's been." He looks over at me, his eyes glistening. "A banner fucking year for Troy Jenner."

"Parker said she heard a commotion a while ago. Did something happen?"

"Yeah, what always happens. I fucked up."

"How?"

"I thought I saw something in someone else, just for once, I thought, maybe if I could convince her I wasn't the man *you* see…" I feel the stab of his admission everywhere.

Her. There's a her.

"I wanted it to happen because it would mean I could stop thinking about you for five goddamn minutes."

"Troy, I can't hear this. Okay? I can't. I took the keys. I will never keep you from your son. I don't ever want him to be without you. I've given you what you've asked for, but I can't hear this."

"I watched him kiss you," he grits out. "There's a whole lot I can handle, but that's not it."

"What you saw was a lie. I did *not* kiss him back—"

"Do you hate me?" He asks, his eyes shining with regret.

"Do you hate me?" I rasp out, unable to keep the tears from falling.

He shakes his head, fisting his eyes. "You're the best thing that's ever happened to me. And I seem to be the worst thing that's ever happened to you."

"I don't think that way at all."

His voice is distant, he's not hearing me. Every part of me is helplessly flailing with the knowledge I pushed him away to the point he's entertaining the idea of other women.

"I keep coming back here because this is where I want to be. I don't want to be anywhere else. But I'm not the man for you."

"You're the *only* man for me," I sniffle again, ducking my head to catch his gaze. "You are the *only* man for me. I'm in love with you, Troy. I *love* you."

His eyes search mine for endless seconds, and for the first time since our conversation started, I feel his need to believe me. My hopes fall away when his blue gaze drops to the porch between us.

"I tell you I hit on another woman, and you tell me you love me." He shakes his head, his eyes incredulous. "Can't you see how fucked up we are?"

"Messy. That's what we are, but messy together makes us perfect. You said that. I guess you forgot that part."

"I don't want to."

He rakes a hand through his hair as I study him. I've never seen him so distraught.

"Troy, what happened tonight?"

"I did what I always do, I screwed things up by thinking I could mean more."

"You mean a lot to plenty of people, including your son *and me*."

He brings watery eyes to mine. "Hope so."

"Please, you're scaring the hell out of me. Tell me what—"

"I have to leave," he says, his voice cracking as he wipes at his eyes furiously with the back of his hand. "I'm going to have to b-break a promise to Dante. I'm supposed to take him fishing tomorrow, but I have shit to figure out."

"What do you mean, leave?"

"I've been kicked out."

"Theo kicked you out?"

He nods. "I deserved it. Trust me."

"What did you do?"

"It was his girlfriend."

"What?"

"I hit on his girlfriend." He shakes his head. "It was a misunderstanding, but no one will believe that. He sure as hell didn't. To him, it's just me being me, right? It should come as no surprise to anyone that this entitled *jock* tried to take what didn't belong to him. Just Troy being Troy."

"That's not who you are at all."

His eyes snap to mine. "You're the only one who's seen me, in years. You're the *only one* who's seen me, and you"—tears glide down his face—"you still couldn't believe me. You're the one person in the fucking world I needed to believe me."

"Tell me what to say." My heart is chipping away piece by

piece, and I'm helpless to stop it. "Tell me what to say, what to do."

He swallows. "I can't do this anymore with you," another tear glides down his cheek. "I can't be here anymore. Just... don't let my son think I left him. Promise me. I'll apologize to him myself when I can do it without feeling like *this*." He buries his face in his hands, his chest pumping with his silent cries. I'm ashes standing next to him, the unbearable ache to pull him into me making it impossible to breathe. "I just need to get myself t-together," he cries hoarsely, his body shuddering. "I'm trying, Clarissa. I'm trying so f-f-fucking hard."

"I know you are. Troy, I know," unable to take another second, I move to embrace him, and he jerks his head, staring down at me with red-rimmed eyes.

"I love you so fucking much it hurts," he says softly, "but that's all it seems to do to me. You keep breaking my heart." And that's when my own heart stops. He grabs my hand, pulling my palm flat to his chest. "I would've given it all up for you. Everything, *ball, everything*, if you would have just given me all of you."

Openly crying, we stare at the other, our hearts raw. I've never in my life loathed myself so much. It's agony, the sight of him so openly broken, my doing and undoing.

"I hate myself for letting you down. I hate the mess I've made. Please don't go. Stay here with us. We can fix this." I cling to him, feeling him slip away by the second. Just as he tears himself from my grasp, lifting accusing eyes to mine.

"You know, it was Kevin's needle," he says, anger lacing his words as my jaw goes slack. "Apparently, he was experimenting and decided not to make a habit of it. Don't worry, we had a fist to mouth conversation about it tonight after Theo made sure everyone at that party knew what a piece of shit I am." He lets out a self-deprecating chuckle before his face turns solemn. "I don't know if I can forgive him." He drops his head. "Jesus, I feel like I've lost everyone."

"You haven't, Troy, please don't go. Stay. We can fix this." Clutching my chest, I try to breathe through the pain.

"I can't," he drops his stare to the ground as he speaks. "And I can't have anything real with anyone else until I get over you. And I can't do that if I see you every damned day."

"Troy, please hear me, I love you, I trust you. I'm so sorry I was so selfish, so fucking blind. Please don't go. I'll do anything."

The shake of his head says it all. It's too late.

"I can't. I'm sorry, I can't. I need to step back, okay?"

I nod as tears slide down my cheeks. "If that's what you really want."

"I'm exhausted. I'm so fucking exhausted." He shoves his hands in his pockets and makes his way down the steps as a white Taurus pulls up. Halfway to the car, he turns back to me, his eyes pleading. "Just don't let him think less of me, okay? I will get it together, Clarissa, I swear. I will."

"I know you will."

"Please just tell him I'm coming back. Promise me you'll tell him I'm coming back."

"I promise," I manage to get out before he climbs into the back of the car, and the driver pulls away. Just inside the door, I collapse into Parker's waiting arms.

ALTA'S CHICKEN ENCHILADAS
Cheerleader, Texas

Makes 10 servings
1 hour and 30 minutes

6–8 Chicken Breasts **Time saver—use 2 cooked rotisserie chickens
10 Flour Tortillas
1 Medium Onion – Chopped
12 Oz. Grated Cheddar Cheese
4 Cans Cream of Chicken Soup
4 Oz. Can Chopped Green Chilies
1/2 Cup Water

Boil chicken for about 45 minutes after water starts to boil.

Remove meat and cut into bite size pieces.

Heat soup, green chilies, and water in saucepan.

*TIP-Spread a large spoonful of soup mixture into the bottom of the pan to keep the enchiladas from sticking.

Place chicken, onion, cheese, and a spoonful of sauce in a tortilla and roll up. Put rolled up tortilla in baking dish. Repeat until the desired number of enchiladas are made.

Pour remaining sauce over enchiladas. Sprinkle any remaining cheese over top.

Bake at 350 degrees for 20-25 minutes.

These are very good served with sour cream and a dash of hot sauce.

fifty-three

CLARISSA

THE NEXT MORNING, I MADE AN EXCUSE FOR TROY AT breakfast and Dante sulked for the rest of the day and through the night. It's only been a few days, the house eerily empty despite the racket Dante makes, but I know it's the ache I'm battling inside.

I lost him.

I've lost him and ruined any chance of the future we'd been dreaming up together. Parker had to leave early this morning for a short trip, and I only managed to go through the motions, every movement a chore, while trying to remind myself to breathe. I broke my own heart because of my inability to trust what I knew to be the truth. My biggest mistake is that I wanted concrete answers, conviction. But love is not concrete, it's fragile, unforgivingly so. I wanted to love Troy without the risk, but in the end, I realized the only way I could have proved my love was by taking one.

And I failed.

I'm a coward.

A fucking fool.

I self-sabotaged because of my issues.

Dante knows something's amiss. Every morning when I exit my bedroom, I do my best to put on a brave face, assuring him Troy will be back soon. Days are bearable due to my work-load, but the nights are too much to take. All I do is replay every second of our time together, of what we had—every kiss, every look, every touch, every word. His smile, his laugh, the way he loved me, doted on me. The way he fathered his son with the utmost care. The things he noticed that I didn't.

Every night after putting Dante down, I gaze over at Troy's empty bedroom, thinking of how much time I wasted with my hesitance.

I spoon more green beans on Dante's plate, and he pushes it away.

"I don't need anymore."

"Okay, then brownies?"

"No. I'm full. I don't want to eat my feelings."

"What? Where did you learn that?"

"I'm not supposed to tell."

Parker.

Instantly, I'm on alert. When she's down, sometimes she's way down. Have I missed something? She seemed fine when she called to check on me.

"Did you hear someone having an adult conversation?"

"No."

"Don't lie to me, son."

"I'm not! I'm not supposed to tell!"

He walks into his bathroom in an attempt to evade me, and I follow as he grabs his toothbrush.

"Dante. I want you to tell me where you heard that."

"It's a secret."

"Dante," I warn.

"He'll be mad at me."

"Who?"

"Troy."

"Dante, tell me this instant."

"Fine," he squeezes paste on his brush and shoves it in his mouth.

"Wheb Trub was little, his dabydy…"

"Son," I warn, taking the toothbrush out of his hands.

He huffs, spitting out a mouthful of paste. "When Troy was little, his daddy left him all alone with his mommy, and he ate his feelings and got *really* fat. All the boys in school were mean to him, 'cause he was a weirdo."

"What?" It's like a punch to the stomach.

"But it's okay, Mommy, because he started running real, real, fast."

"Really fast," I correct with my heart beating in my throat.

"He ran until he wasn't fat, but he was still a weirdo." Dante points to his chest. "Inside. Like me. Then he found us, so he's sticking to us."

I turn away and grab a hand towel, trying to gather myself together. "He said that?" I hand him his toothbrush back.

"He said he knows we're the only ones that know he's Bruce Wayne."

Not Batman, or badass, or any other part of the persona that he's been fighting against that's genuinely *not* him. And it doesn't matter how many times he tells the world otherwise, or what actions he takes, because of the way he looks, because of his ability to carry a football, he's placed on a pedestal. A pedestal, he can't stand.

It's all I can do to keep from crumpling as his spitting image turns to me.

"Can I pick a story now?"

The next morning, I pour Dante's cereal at a loss for another excuse when my phone lights up with Troy's name. It's like a knife to the chest.

I slide to answer my heartbeat in my throat. "Hey."

"Hey, can I talk to him?"

"Of course. Can I just ask if you're okay?"

"Fine. I don't have much time."

"Okay." I feel the shake in my voice as I call Dante. "Baby. Troy's on the phone."

Dante runs in, grabbing my cell from my hand.

"Hey, Troy. I saved you some cereal." Dante rearranges a few magnets on the fridge as Troy speaks. "Sorry. Mommy says I can't have my phone on until after school." It's apparent he didn't even want to call my number. He doesn't want to have a thing to do with me. I grip the chair at the kitchen table as I try to absorb that blow.

"You coming over? Oh," his voice dips in disappointment as does my heart. "Tomorrow then, *maybe?*" Another pause before Dante glances up at me. "Let me ask. Mommy, can I go with Troy and Nonny tomorrow after school? Please?"

"Sure."

"She says yes. Uh huh. Okay. Okay. Love you. Bye."

Dante hands the phone back to me. "Hey."

He's already gone.

fifty-four

TROY

"THANKS, MOM," I TELL HER AS SHE PILES THE EGGS ON
my plate. Fresh off the clock, I was about to
crash when Mom dragged me into the kitchen.
I'd managed to get a few shifts back part-time at UPS after I
quit working with Kevin. I've been avoiding his calls, along with
anyone else that doesn't have to do with my immediate future.
Kevin texted last night asking to meet up, but I didn't reply. I'm
sure part of it was to reach out again and apologize. But I know
another part is because the librarian finally crushed his hopes.

I'm still too pissed to talk it out with him. I could have lost
my son because of his stupid fucking experiment with something he had no business messing with. I could blame it on the
coach and his unrealistic demands, but the simple truth is, he
fucked up, like many of us do. And I know more than anyone
how lousy timing and shitty circumstances can ruin a person.
Ruin lives.

When I cool off, I know I'll eventually reach out. Kevin
would never intentionally or unintentionally hurt Dante. And
he deserved a fair shake with that girl, but that's not real life. In
real life, there's a million other Kevins out there suffering from
the same type of unreturned affection. Another first-hand experience I can relate to.

I feel for him, but I can't handle anything more. At this point, it's too much. After leaving the house on Ohara, there was no way to get my head straight staying with friends, so I played it safe, burying my head in the books and work after taking my mother up on her offer to use her spare bedroom. The upside is I've gotten to know Luis, and he seems to be a great guy.

"Morning," Luis walks into the kitchen, kissing my mother soundly before clapping a hand on my back. "I guess it's good night to you?"

"Yeah," I say as he grabs the lunch my mom's just readied for him.

"Thanks, baby. See y'all later."

She sends him off with another kiss, and I can't help but feel happy for her and take note of the light in her eyes as they follow him out the front door.

"I like him, Mom. I mean that. You deserve to be happy."

"Thanks, baby. He is pretty amazing, isn't he?"

"Yeah, he's cool."

I shovel more eggs in, thankful it's a Saturday, and I'll be able to sleep in a little longer.

Mom hovers next to me, and it's then I know the offer for breakfast was a ruse.

I look up to where she stands, arms crossed.

"Come on, Mom. I'm exhausted."

"It's been weeks. Don't you think it's time?"

I sigh, bracing myself. Mom isn't the type to make the hard parts easier. She's the type to deal with shit as it comes, and it's one of the things I've always respected her for most, while it still remains one of my biggest weaknesses. I much prefer to think my way around my issues.

And right now, I'm in the midst of full-blown avoidance.

Case in point, after I pick Dante up, Clarissa meets Mom at the door when she comes for him. As immature as it is, I don't want to see her, which has done shit to ease the sting of missing her.

A part of me is embarrassed for being so vulnerable in front of her, the other is glad I finally stood up for my mangled fucking heart where she is concerned.

Though, no part of this is making my decision and new reality any less shitty. Dante remains confused as to why we aren't speaking. In hindsight, I realize now why Clarissa was so hesitant to start a relationship. It's because of our current predicament. Constant excuses as to why things have so drastically changed.

Lately, he's been reading into every conversation we have, looking for clues, asking questions that I don't have answers to. At one point, he had some semblance of a family, and with our rift, we've ripped it away.

The fucked-up part is with the damage done, the damage she so painstakingly tried to avoid, we never got a real shot at making us work. I could blame it on her selfishness. I could blame myself because I'd shot her down even when she was ready to admit her mistake and begged me not to let go.

The irony is, though I've tried in every way imaginable, I haven't. I just refuse to admit it. I love her wholly and completely. Even with all the hurt we've caused to the other. But I can't, for the life of me, find the strength to go another round with her. Not now, maybe not ever. Because of the power she holds over me, the carelessness she's used with my heart, I fear I may never come back the same man.

"I'll go back soon. When I'm ready."

"You have to face her, son. Dante is not okay. Yesterday, he asked me if I knew why everybody was so sad. I lied to my grandson. Don't put me in that position again."

Suddenly, the eggs aren't so appetizing and feel like rubber in my mouth.

"Fuck," I push the plate away and run a hand through my hair. "Sorry, Mom. And I'm sorry you're having to deal with this. I'm signing soon. I'll get a place as soon as I get a check."

"Hey, that's not it," she says, taking a seat next to me. "First of all, Luis is happy about having you here. And we have plenty of room."

"I don't want to inconvenience you."

"Don't be ridiculous. You're my son. There's no such thing."

I glance over as she pours me more juice. "I love you."

"Love you too. And I hate that she broke your heart. But you have to talk to her. You've got to push your feelings aside. Dante is scared."

"I will. Soon. I just need a little more time."

"Okay." She shovels more eggs onto my plate.

"Mom, I'm done."

"The hell you are. Eat."

"Yes, ma'am."

She looks me over carefully, weighing her words. Her hair is already up, her makeup done. The woman has self-respect in abundance, has always taken care of herself, no matter the circumstances. It's another habit of hers I find admirable. She's the definition of a backbone. I feel like hell. I haven't been sleeping at all, even after upping my workouts to try and pass out.

"You look beautiful."

"You look like shit."

"Thanks."

"Are you sure you're making the right decision?"

I nod. "I can't be with someone who doesn't have my back and won't trust me to have hers."

"Then I pray she does the work because you two were beautiful together. Your family is beautiful. And even if your relationship isn't where you want it, make no mistake, son, that is your family."

I swallow the truth of it. "I know."

"Good. Glad you know it all. So, when are you going over there?"

"Soon."

"How soon?"

"Mom," I say exasperated, pushing my plate away. "Enough."

"Just remember when you were working your ass off to get drafted, she was working *her* ass off to keep your son warm. So, stop punishing her for keeping the secrets she kept out of love, *for you*, so you could do what you needed to do."

"Doesn't change the fact we don't trust each other."

"I think you know that's not true."

"I've done everything I can to prove myself to her, and it's not good enough."

"No, you haven't."

"What?" I gape at her. "You're kidding me, right? Mom—"

"You keep convincing yourself that everything is so cut and dried. If you want a *real* family, it comes with the good and bad—cuts, bruises, and bumps, and there is no end date for that. You two will fight and often. You're so much alike it's scary. Pig-headed, stubborn…"

"Great talk, Mom."

"Sit your ass down, right now."

I blow out a breath resuming my seat at the table.

"You're also both loving—selfless and a little selfish— but you both love that little boy with all your heart and soul. You're amazing parents, but clueless with relationships.

Having the real thing means good months and bad months, maybe a bad *year or two*, rinse and repeat. You two have yet to figure out how to get past a bad day, and that's okay, it comes with time. You want to call it quits with her, fine. But you're going to have a hell of a time keeping *any* relationship, unless you leave the scoreboard on the field where it belongs. Right or wrong, who did what to whom—who gives a shit? Your son is suffering, and here you are, still in love with her. If you were so damned determined to outshine any other man in her life, why didn't you do the one thing you *had* to do that no other man has managed?"

Swallowing, I stare at my plate. "Stay."

"I'll get your keys."

Pulling up the driveway, I see Theo on the porch with Dante and am instantly on edge. I'm already dreading facing Clarissa and don't want to deal with the aftermath of my falling out with Theo. He deserves an apology, but I'm over his assumptions about me, over defending myself, and I can see the clear accusation in his eyes when Dante greets me on the steps.

"Hey, little man, where's your mom?"

Dante shakes his head. "She's inside, but she's crying."

I spare a glance at Theo, who's already armored up.

"Tell me you didn't. Jesus Christ, Jenner."

Dante looks between us, confused. "What did he do?"

"Nothing to worry about, bud," I say, giving Theo a warning look before turning back to my son. "Hey, Dante, do you mind letting me talk to Theo a minute?"

"Mama got that cereal you like," he supplies as I grip his

shoulder, trying to hide my flinch at his words as I walk him toward the door.

"Yeah, maybe I'll have some after I do the grass. Go on inside for a second, okay?"

"If this is man talk, I'm cool. *I'm* the man of this house."

Another blow and I do the best I can to hide my reaction. "Go on," I say, ushering him inside.

"Fine," Dante huffs. "Later, Theo."

I hang my head when the door closes. "I don't expect you to understand."

"Please don't confuse me for someone who cares enough about you to want to understand. It's *them* I care about."

This pisses me off. "You think I don't?"

"I don't think you care about anyone above yourself."

"Well, you're fucking wrong. Look, you hate me, and that's fine, but there's something you need to know about Laney."

"Save your breath."

"She wasn't lying. She never once gave me any reason to go after her. She wouldn't even tell me her name. Every bit of that cat and mouse was *me*. It was *all* me. She'd already told me to fuck off *twice* before you came outside and at every turn before that. I'm the one who ran up on her. I'm the one who tried to force it. I was in a fucked-up place."

He glares at me from where he stands, not backing off an inch.

"I just thought you should know."

"She already told me this herself."

"Yeah, but I'm guessing you didn't believe her." I can see the grudge he's held for years for wrongs done to him that have shit to do with me. His hang-ups have to do with his own insecurities. Just like Clarissa, he rode me hard, waiting for the day for me to fuck up with a pre-prepared 'I knew it' on his tongue.

"And I should believe you?"

"Yeah, you should because when she looked at me, she saw me the same way you do, and I think that's what attracted me to her. I wanted to prove you both wrong." I glance at Clarissa's door. "But I was trying to prove myself to the wrong people." I glare over at Theo. "You assume so much about me, just like everyone else, and I just never bothered to correct you."

"Troy! Mommy won't come outside!" Dante pokes his head out of the door, and I kneel down and pull him close. "Listen, bud. You know better. I'm in a serious conversation. Give me a minute."

I don't miss the connection Theo makes when he finally sees it, and I don't bother trying to hide it. Those days are over for me.

"He's yours."

I nod.

"And you haven't told him?"

The nerve on this guy. I take a step forward. "This is messier than you could ever imagine and fuck the look on your face, Houseman. Do you think I answered your ad because I couldn't find anywhere else to live closer to campus? Half my friends wouldn't even charge me to live at their spots. Your address was my chance to be closer to *him* and look out for them both. She," I wipe a hand down my face, "she doesn't want anything to do with me." He's the wrong person to air my grievances to, but I can't help myself.

"You think I wanted to pay rent late every month? Contrary to what you think, I wasn't getting my dick waxed every time I had a late night, I was working my fucking ass off to pay the rent for *three*. Between that and ball—" I shake my head disgusted with the fact that once again, I'm explaining my actions to a lost cause. "You know what? I could fill a fucking book with

what you *don't* know. You got the only explanation I owe you."
I walk inside and slam the door. Dante's head pops up, and he
pauses his game.

"I got in trouble at school today. Mommy's mad. I put myself in timeout, but she doesn't care. Are you mad at me too?"

I hate the fear in his voice. I hate that things are so fucked
up between his mother and me. We're both guilty. I let my
crushed heart and anger toward her get in the way of what
matters most. What should always come first. But I won't lie
to him.

"I'm not mad at you. It's not good to get in trouble, but
I'm not mad."

"You and Theo not friends anymore? Is that why you
moved?"

I nod. "We're just having a difference of opinion."

He thinks I'm a piece of shit, and I'm having a hard time
proving myself differently. It ends here. I'll be the father Dante's
come to trust. I walk over to where he sits and run my knuckles
through his hair.

"Grown-up stuff gets confusing sometimes. Hang in there
with me, okay?"

"K."

"Trust me?"

"Yep."

"Good. Play your game. I'm going to talk to your mom.
And we'll talk about why you got in trouble in a little while,
okay?"

"K." I start to make my way toward her room. "Troy?"

"Yeah, bud?"

"Are you going to spank me?"

"Spank you?" I bite my lips to hide my grin. "No."

"K, 'cause that would hurt real bad."

"Really bad. And I would never hurt you. You know that, right?

"Uh huh."

Unable to help it, I walk over and pull him into me. He hugs me back tightly, without reservation, something we both clearly need. Placing a kiss at the top of his head, I pull away.

"No matter what, I'm proud of you. You know that?"

"Yeah."

I tip his chin up. "Saw your video last night. Did you edit that new intro yourself?"

"Yeah! You watched it?"

"I watch them all."

"Really?"

His happiness means everything to me. As does the woman just a room away.

"Let me go talk to her, and maybe you and I can get lunch after. Just the two of us."

"K. Is she sad 'cause you don't kiss her in the laundry room anymore?"

Gaping, I stare down at him at a loss for words. My mother is right. We're idiots. While we were falling in love, our son was watching. It doesn't matter what we did behind closed doors, he was witness to it all, which is why he felt our split as much as we did.

"Dante, that's private *adult* stuff."

"K. Can we have tacos?"

That was way too easy. But relieved, I answer with a bribe. "Anything you want."

"I'm in trouble. Mommy might not let me go."

"I'll talk to her."

"K."

"Don't interrupt us unless it's an emergency."

"Yes, sir."

Making my way toward her room, I rope in all my apprehension and knock on her door.

"Hey," I hear her say when I poke my head in. She's sitting on the side of her bed, crumbling a tissue in her hand and blotting her eyes.

I kneel down in front of her and grab her hands holding them between mine. "I'm sorry."

"It's fine. I'm fine."

"It's not fine. Everything's fucked."

"I know," she says, a tear cresting on her cheek before falling, "we got too messy."

"I don't want to live like this anymore."

"Me neither." She slides a hand down my jaw. "I'm so sorry I hurt you. You did everything right. From the minute you stepped up to my door. You're right. I gave you hell and not enough of what you deserved. But I do respect you, Troy, and I trust you, for whatever it's worth."

"It's worth a lot," I say, trying my best to keep my shit together.

"He knows we're not okay. He asks me every day what's going on, and I don't know what to tell him."

"He knows about us."

"I know," she says softly. "I just keep avoiding his questions."

"It's time to stop. We'll tell him together that sometimes grown-ups fight and don't always know how to fix it. But if they're family, they find a way to work it out. And we will."

She nods, looking more forlorn than she did when I walked into the room.

"Troy, I don't ever want him to lose you because of me."

"He won't. I just needed to step back, for me."

She worries her bottom lip and nods.

"We apologize and move on. If we're okay, he's okay."

"Right." She nods. "You're right."

"It just feels shitty now because we got knocked out of sorts. We'll fix it."

"Okay," she straightens, and exhales a stressed breath.

"Okay."

I stand and look down at her, and she tugs at my hand, sliding her fingers between mine. "I've always credited myself with having it together, having it under control." Her face crumbles. "I'm not feeling so together anymore."

"You and me both. It's just a rough time. It'll pass. Let's just concentrate on him for the moment, okay?" I pull my hand away from hers and see the sting in her eyes. Touching her right now means playing with more fire and I refuse to let my son burn again. He's suffered enough. And not just now. He's paid for years of our back and forth, our mistakes.

"Yes. Of course."

"Okay. He got in trouble today at school?"

She nods and I resist the urge to brush the hair from her shoulder. "Let me take this one. Why don't you call Parker, go out, and get some TLC? Have some wine. I've got him."

"Yeah, that sounds...I could use that. You sure?"

"Positive."

"Thank you. I'll, I'm...God, I'm a mess."

"You're beautiful," I whisper, unable to help myself as I push a dark red lock away from her shoulder. Imploring blue eyes stare up at me before I make a quick exit out of her room, fists clenching. It's then I know, it doesn't matter that my mind is determined to quit her, my heart will never catch up.

KAYLA'S SOUTHERN STYLE POTATO SALAD
Property Manager, Texas

Makes 8 servings
45 minutes

4 Lbs. Red Potatoes – scrubbed & cut into bite-size pieces
4 Large Eggs
1 ¼ Cups Mayonnaise
½ Cup Finely Chopped Green Onion Tops
1 3/4 Tsp. Salt
½ Tsp. Celery Seeds

Boil potatoes with skin on until tender but not too soft. Drain and set aside to cool.

Boil eggs for 12 minutes after water comes to a boil. Peel and let cool. Cut into bite-size pieces.

In a large bowl, mix mayonnaise, salt, celery seeds and onion until thoroughly mixed. Add potatoes and eggs. Mix gently until blended.

Serve at room temperature for up to 2 hours after making. Refrigerate leftovers.

It tastes best when served at room temperature but is delicious cold, too.

fifty-five

CLARISSA

P ARKER AND I SPEND THE DAY GETTING OUR NAILS DONE AND
opening a few bottles of wine. Parker simply listens and
nods. The best type of friend can linger in the dark with
you awhile without trying to shed light. So, instead of trying to
point out an upside or spout off some words of encouragement,
she simply held my hand and dwelled there with me. And I felt
better for it. Nothing resolved, but with a polished set of nails
and slight wine buzz, I walk through my front door to see the
living room empty.

It's a little after eight. I assume Dante's halfway through his
book with Troy and make my way toward his bedroom. Just as
I'm about to open his door, I'm stopped short by the conversation on the other side.

"—Sometimes, women need men to be strong, so they ar-
en't so scared themselves. But if you find one you really care
about, you can tell them what you're afraid of, and they'll have
your back too."

"Do you have Mommy's back?"

"Yep and yours until I take my last breath. That's a promise."

"Then Mommy and me have your back, Troy. We promise
too."

"Good to know, bud."

"Hey, Troy?"

"Yeah?"

"Are you going away like you said?"

"Probably."

"K."

"Don't worry. I'll never leave you long."

"A week, two tops," Dante squeaks as if they've had this conversation before.

"Right."

"And you'll call me every day," Dante reminds.

"That's right. Every day."

"'Cause I'm your sun, and you're my moon, and where I go, you're right behind me."

"Right."

"'Cause you love me."

He pauses before giving a hoarse reply. "So much, bud."

"Don't be sad, Troy. One week, two tops."

"Right."

"I love you."

"Love you too. Goodnight."

Hand over my mouth, I race to the bathroom and turn the fan and shower on. I'm still crying uncontrollably a minute later when Troy knocks on the door. I can't bring myself to open it.

"Hey," I say, a clear rattle in my voice.

"Hey, when did you get in?"

I stifle my cries in my hand, knowing I'm taking too damn long to reply.

"J-j-just a minute ago…I wanted to take a quick shower before I tucked him in," my voice cracks and I wince hoping he didn't hear it. He pauses outside the door, and I know I've given myself away. He's still punishing me, and for him, I'll endure it, in hopes one day he'll forgive me. In hopes that one day, he'll look at me the way he did just weeks before. Parker told me today that he waited over six years for me to see him for who he really is. It's now my loyalty in question and my own redemption I'm after.

"I have a shift later. I'm going to head out."

"Okay, goodnight."

"Night."

fifty-six

TROY

THE PHONE RINGS JUST AS I GET OUT OF CLASS, AND I SEE Clarissa's name and stop in the middle of the hall. She never calls anymore.

"Hey, everything okay?"

Silence on the other end of the line, followed by a sniffle, has me on high alert. "Clarissa?"

"Troy." This cry is unlike anything I've ever heard. I make a beeline for my mom's truck.

"I'm on my way. What happened?"

"I happened. I…j-just, I'm sorry."

"What for?"

"Can…can you come over?"

"I'm coming. Is Dante okay?"

"Oh, he's fine. I'm sorry if I worried you. I'm fine," another sob. "I just…I'm sorry. I'm sorry…for so much."

"Clarissa, you're scaring me. Tell me what's wrong."

"You're on your way?"

"Yes, I'll be there in ten."

"O-kay." She sobs again, and my heart plummets as I speed toward her house.

Racing down the road, I wrack my brain for anything that could have happened, the panic inside me building. She keeps apologizing, but I can't imagine what for, and it's killing me inside. After an agonizing drive, I rush to her front door, feeling Theo's eyes on my back as I knock sharply and then let myself inside. I find Clarissa at her kitchen table, a piece of paper in her hand. She looks over to me, her face soaked with tears before she sets the letter down on the table and turns to me, twisting her hands in front of her.

"Where's Dante?"

"With your mother. They'll be back in an hour or so."

I reach her in two strides and pull her to me, wrapping my arms around her.

"What is it? What's wrong?"

"I just…Troy, I'm so sorry. I'm so sorry for locking you out of his life. I've been admitting it to myself for months, but it's time I admit it to you." I keep her close, encircling her in my arms as she looks up at me with tears streaming down her cheeks. "I was wrong, *so wrong* to keep you away from him. I was so angry and terrified, but that's no excuse. It was a huge mistake, and I'll never be able to make it up to you."

I shake my head. "No more apologies. I understand why you did it. I'm not saying it was right, but maybe it wasn't wrong either. We've been back and forth over this. Why are you so upset?"

She turns back to the table and lifts the paper. "I was going through his folder, and I found this and…here."

Hesitantly, I let her go and take the letter, my eyes burning when I see Dante's handwriting and the first sentence.

I don have a daddy. But I have my naybor Troy. And he better than having a daddy. Becaus he my very best frend. He watches my videos. He plays XBox with me. He weres my merch. He give me choclates Mommy says I cant have. If I could have a Daddy I would pick Troy. But I don need one no more.

"This is," I look up to Clarissa, whose eyes search mine as she nods and nods.

"He chose you." A tear I can't help slides down my face as she palms my cheeks. "He chose you no matter what his DNA is. He chooses you."

"This is…thank you."

"Keep it. It's yours. He's yours, no matter how much I've screwed it up. He'll always be yours." She sniffles again, and I pull her to me and wipe her tears away with my thumbs. "It's okay, Clarissa. I'm not mad anymore. I'm not anything anymore. I just want us to be good."

"Troy, it's time."

"Time?" My heart begins to pound.

"Past time to tell him. Just another thing to be sorry for." She worries her lip. "I hope he forgives me."

"He won't even hold a grudge."

"He's half mine," she grimaces through fear-filled eyes. "There's a good chance he's good at holding a grudge."

I'm smiling like an idiot. "We really doing this?"

"Yes," she wraps her arms around me and leans in and whispers in my ear. "I'm so glad it was you, Troy. I know I've led you to believe otherwise in the past, but I'm so glad it was you. You're an amazing father."

I pull her to me, the scent of her shampoo making breathing harder, but I ignore it and let the feel of her in. It's been so long since I've had her this close. I ignore the bells going off and simply hold her, leaning in. "And I couldn't want a better mother for my son." When we separate, she's smiling. "Can I be there when you tell him?"

"Yeah, of course. We should do this together."

"This is special. I want this to be about the two of you."

"I want you there. I'm nervous."

"There's no reason to be. He's going to be over the moon."

"Do you trust me to say the right thing?"

"Yeah, yeah, I do. I trust you, Troy. I really do."

I sigh a breath of relief. "Thank you. What do you think I should say?"

She wipes beneath her eyes. "Whatever is in your heart."

"Dante, can you put that down for a minute so I can talk to you?"

"Man to man?" He asks, and I can't help my grin.

"Of course."

"Let's go to my office." He heads toward the porch eyeing his mother. He knows something's up. My son is no dummy.

"Why is Mommy crying?"

"She's happy."

"I don't cry when I'm happy."

"You will one day."

"Have you?"

I have a feeling I'm close.

"Sure, I have. Come on, bud." Dante steps outside just as the breeze picks up. He turns to me expectantly, and I kneel down in front of him where he stands. "So, I know you've been wondering about your daddy."

"Uh huh."

"I wanted to be the one to tell you…I'm your daddy."

"Funny," he says with a nervous giggle. "You're not my daddy."

"I am your daddy. I promise. That's why I moved next door, so I could be closer to you."

"You're playing."

"No, I'm not. I'm your daddy." I tell him in a serious tone, and from the look on his face, he believes me. His smile disappears as he glances past my shoulder at Clarissa and then back to me. I can feel his confusion, the nervous rattle coming from his frame as his world tilts on its axis.

"Why didn't you tell me before?" His lip quivers as he looks through the screen where his mother stands. "Mommy?"

"It's true," she says tearfully. "Troy is your daddy."

"You didn't tell me till now?"

"I wanted you to know me first before I told you. We both did."

Dante looks lost and again looks to his mother as fat tears spill down his cheeks. He's so incredibly raw, so vulnerable, my heart drops when his tone turns accusatory. "Mommy, did you know before?"

"Yes, baby."

"How long?"

"As long as you've been alive."

He draws his brows. "How?"

"That's another talk we'll have one day," I say, unable to help the upward tilt to my lips, which disappears the minute I hear Dante's voice crack.

"You both didn't tell me!"

"Look at me, Dante," I say, shooting Clarissa a reassuring look before facing him. Dante finally gives me his undivided attention, and I see the hurt, along with a little wonder that sparks some hope inside me. "There's a play in football called fourth and inches. And what that means is that it's your last chance to reach the goal line. You have to make your very best play to reach it, or the chance is gone. When you get to this point, you're so close that you can taste it, touch it, feel it, but you have a way to get to the goal. You have to work *really, really* hard to get there. Do your absolute best. And that's what I've been doing since the day you were born."

His voice shakes with his question. "I'm the goal?"

"You're the goal."

His face crumbles, and relief washes over me as he collides with my chest and cries into my shirt. I run a soothing hand down his back as his little body shakes. Surprised by his response, a little sob erupts out of Clarissa from where she stands. "It's okay, buddy, I'm here, and I'm not going anywhere. I'm your daddy from today on, okay?"

He nods into my shirt, his unexpected emotion causing my eyes to well. Clarissa wipes her eyes as ours connect over his shoulder, and she gives me a teary smile. Dante cries for a few minutes as I continue to tell him how I love him, of how bad I want to be his daddy. Of how I've always loved him. Of how I couldn't wait to tell him. "You're the best thing I've ever done. And if you'll let me have this job, I'll be so happy."

"You make me happy," he sniffs as he pulls away and looks at his mom. "That's okay, right, Mommy?"

"Of course," she says, clearing her face with her palms.

Dante looks back to me with apprehension on his features.

"You can still be the man of the house."

"I know."

Clarissa and I chuckle as his face crumbles again. I've never seen him so emotional, and I wonder if Clarissa has either.

"So, what's wrong then? Whatcha thinking?"

"It's just…" He puts a consoling hand on my shoulder. "I'm sorry, Troy."

"For what? You have nothing to be sorry for."

"You must be really *bad* at football."

I draw my brows. "Why do you say that?"

"I'm six!" His eyes widen. "You took a long, looong time to get to the goal. That's not good. You are really, really, *bad* at football."

I throw my head back and laugh, and Clarissa joins us both on the porch, laughter bursting out of her. "I'm serious. This is serious," Dante squeaks as we collectively gather him into our arms.

CINDY'S CHOCOLATE ICE BOX CAKE
Administrative Assistant, Boston, MA

Makes 8 servings
1 hour

2 Packages German Chocolate
4 Tbsp. Water
4 Eggs – Separated
1 Tsp. Vanilla
1 Dozen Lady Fingers – Plain
1/2 Pint Whipping Cream
3/4 Cup Sugar

Dissolve chocolate in double broiler. Add water and stir well. Fold in slightly beaten egg yolks. Add vanilla. Cool Mixture. Beat egg whites until stiff. Fold cooled chocolate mixture into egg whites. Line narrow bowl or mold with Lady Fingers, brown side out. Pour 1/2 chocolate mixture over Lady Fingers. Add another layer of Lady Fingers. Add the rest of the chocolate mixture. Chill in the refrigerator until set (about 2 hours). Whip whipped cream and sugar until stiff. Top chocolate with whipped cream and chocolate sprinkles.

fifty-seven

CLARISSA

IT'S BEEN THE LONGEST WEEK OF MY LIFE. WITH FINALS OUT OF the way, the school days drag by. I'm merely going through the motions at this point. Passing my real estate exam brought me little joy, and for the last few nights, I've been updating my résumé to send to realtors, in hopes of finding the right fit. With the end of the school year just around the corner, I'm thankful for the distraction of working this summer. With the job comes flexible hours, which I'll need to get to spend my time with Dante. I'm hoping with the extra income, I'll be able to afford our first real vacation.

Troy graduates soon, and I have every intention of watching him walk the stage with or without an invite, but I've been holding my breath in hopes for one. Whether he thinks so or not, he's still punishing me. Keeping me at arm's length. We're back to the place of doing things together as a family, and while I'm all smiles while we're together, inside my heart withers with every goodbye. Soon he'll be gone for weeks at a time.

It's taken all my strength not to ask any questions about us, but as far as I can tell, he meant what he said. Dante may be our only tie.

Laptop open, I sit in my chair, staring up at the ceiling berating myself for what I had, and the chance I lost. Men like

Troy don't come around often. I'm furious with myself for ever thinking differently. For taking advantage of his patience. For not waking up sooner. I just keep remembering the inhuman amount of patience he displayed when it came to me, and that's all that keeps me going.

A part of me wonders if he hasn't started the process of moving on. The thought of him touching another woman eats me alive.

I don't think I'll be able to bear it when another claims his heart.

Gathering myself from my recliner, I begin to turn out the lights when a light knock sounds at the door. My heart leaps into a gallop when I see Troy on the other side. His hands stuffed in his jeans.

"Hey," he says softly, peeking past my shoulder. "Sorry, I know it's late."

"He's asleep," I say, opening the door and ushering him inside.

"I know. I just want to check in on him."

I glance past to see a new King Cab in the driveway. "You got your truck back?"

"This one's new. Well, it's an older model but new to me."

"It's really nice."

"Thanks. So, can I see him?"

"Sure, okay." I gesture toward Dante's room.

"Thank you." He pads through the house and twists the knob, peeking in where Dante lays asleep on his side, hair still damp from his shower. Troy studies him for a long minute, exhaling fully when he sees he's safe and asleep.

"I've never felt a love like this," he says softly. "And I know I never will. Kids aren't harmless, they're terrifying. I love him so much," he says with an ache in his voice that gives me a sinking feeling. "I can't imagine any harm coming to him. I can't imagine how that would feel." I touch his arm and lean in on a whisper of my own.

"Troy, is everything okay?"

He looks over at me, the picture of beauty, the love in his eyes hypnotic. I know the look. I've seen it dozens of times, for myself, and it never fails to take my breath away. This man, the way he loves, everything about him moves me.

I'm too wrapped up in all I feel to speak and thankful when Troy is the first to break the silence. "You know, I was his age when my parents split up. When Dad left, I played okay with it because I knew they made each other miserable. But it killed me. I suffered in silence. I understood why he left her, but I couldn't understand why he left me too. After a while, I came around, and I was okay with it. She was tough, fair, but so loving. But she worked her fingers to the bone. That's what I hold against my dad now. Not the fact that he left me, but that he left *her* alone in the struggle. I couldn't have been easy. Hell, I know I wasn't. But she loved me, cared for me so well, I never suffered." He turns to me and palms my cheek. "I don't want you to suffer. I don't want him to ever see you suffer. I don't want him to want for anything. I'll spend my whole life making sure he's cared for, both of you. This, I swear, Clarissa."

The sincerity in his eyes, his voice, is my unraveling. "And maybe if I would have told you how important that was to me before, you would have understood just how badly I wanted to be the one you leaned on."

"I'm so sorry that I made you feel like I didn't trust you to do that."

He slowly shakes his head before his lips upturn. "Are we going to spend the rest of our lives apologizing to each other?"

I shrug, returning his smile. "It's a step up from fighting?"

"You know, I loved some of those fights."

I nod. "Me too." Apprehension covers his features. "Is everything okay?"

"It is now." He softly shuts the door. "He's my strength, Clarissa. He's my reserve. All I have to do is lay eyes on him, and I'm whole."

"You know, Dante means strength," I say softly. "Well technically, it means endurance. The minute I found out he was coming, I knew I was going to need it in abundance. I'm not trying to guilt you," I say, placing my hands on his jaw. "I'm saying you're exactly right. As much as he needs us to guide him, we need him too. He's got a quiet strength, a kid's resilience we need to see, need to be reminded of. He's got a lot of it because he's your son."

He pulls away from my hands and lets out a breath before looking back at me. "Thank you."

Ignoring the pain from his rejection, I focus on him. I've been selfish enough. His phone rattles in his hand and he glances down and frowns.

"Troy, what's wrong."

"It's Theo, says he needs me to come over, says he needs my help."

"Are you two doing okay?"

"This is the first I've heard from him."

"Are you gonna go?"

"Yeah, I owe him an apology."

"Hopefully you two can work it out?"

"Yeah, maybe."

"So, what's wrong then? Are you nervous about the draft?"

"Yes and no. I'm pretty sure I know where I'm going."

"Where?"

"The Giants."

"New York?"

"Yeah."

"Congratulations," I say, hiding my devastation. New York. He's leaving us. And it's not a short drive. I suck up my own feelings and try to put on a brave face. "That's amazing."

I can sense the tension building in him as he fists his hands at his sides. "Yeah."

"Why don't I get the feeling you're excited?"

"I don't want to leave him."

"You won't."

He scans my pajamas with a smirk. "Grand girls—"

"Stay Grand, and don't you forget it," I finish, returning his smile.

"I don't want to leave *you*," he says softly.

"*We'll* be here cheering you on. We'll make it work. I promise."

"From here," he says, his tone somber. "That's what's killing me."

"Troy, it's pro ball. It's a dream come true. It's what you've been working your ass off for. You know, since your *teaching career* didn't work out."

We share a smile.

"Finally," I laugh. "I can make a joke."

His expression again turns sullen.

"We'll come up," I offer, "you can come down, and we'll—"

His next words strike me right in the chest. "I want you to come with me."

"What?" I damn near stumble into the wall as he takes my hand and leads me into the living room. He sits me down on the couch and begins to pace.

"Hear me out, okay?"

I nod and watch him as he runs a pattern on my rug, cupping his neck.

"I'll set you up. We can get him in a private school if it makes you feel safer. You can teach anywhere, right?"

"Yes, but Troy, New York?"

"Yeah. There's a ton of places outside the city that are more ideal for raising a family. I sent you an email when I pulled up tonight. There's a house and—"

"That's a lot to ask."

He blows out a breath and hangs his head. "I know." He lifts his eyes meeting mine. "But I'm asking. If there were something keeping you here, I wouldn't. But you aren't buying this place, right? You hate the owner."

"Cute."

"Just, do me a favor and look at the email."

"Now?"

He nods.

"Okay."

I pull my laptop from my chair and see that he did send an email a few minutes before he knocked on the door. I click on the listing, and my eyes bulge.

"Troy, that's entirely *too much* house."

"But it's beautiful, right? Look, it has a blue door. Dr. Seuss blue, but we can paint it purple."

"Troy, I don't expect you to take care of me."

"I want to. Whatever amount I get, I know damn well I can afford this house. As of next week, I'm a rich man. I want this for Dante and for you. Please," he kneels down before me. "Just tell me you'll consider it. I'll get something close."

And with that statement, I feel he's closed the door on us. I try to hide the hurt as I look over at him.

"Can I think about it?"

"Of course." He lifts one side of his mouth. "It's crazy, I worked for it for years and years, but I never thought the day would come. I hoped and prayed, but I never thought it would actually happen. Pro ball, Clarissa. It's insane."

"You made it happen. You're an amazing player."

He shakes his head as I linger on the fact that he's no longer mine.

"Troy, what about your...personal life? Don't you eventually want to start a family?"

He leans down and presses his lips to my temple before pulling away, his eyes penetrating mine. "I started my family seven years ago. Goodnight."

fifty-eight

CLARISSA

ANTE EXITS THE RIDE ALL SMILES AS HE RUNS TOWARD ME with Troy on his heels. "That one wasn't scary at all."

"You did good," I say as they join Parker and me where we wait by the ticket booth.

"I'm ready for that," Dante points to the mile-high cage ride that flips twenty times within a minute, and Troy, Parker, and I all shake our heads in agreement. We've been at it for a few hours and covered most of the carnival. After our resounding no to his request to ride adult rides, he's dragging us all to the dollar games.

Troy picked the three of us up earlier this morning, and it's been all smiles and niceties. I've been caught staring at him a few times today, making me feel like a damned love-sick fool. Parker's elbowed me twice to keep me from completely humiliating myself.

Feeling this way is slowly killing me inside. As soon as Dante's bedroom light is off, Troy leaves, leaving me alone in the house to miss him. Ever present, he's kept things painfully platonic. This man, who invaded my life nine months ago with promises I was completely unsure he would keep, promises I hoped with all my heart he would, for my son, and now admittedly, for me, is ruling my heart and mind. I can't push myself past the new normal. I can't for the life of me accept it. I'm losing my mind trying to find a way not to feel so much, not to want him the way I do. I'm so deep, I'll never be able to find my way out.

I can't unlove Troy Jenner. He's made it impossible.

"Plans for this summer?" Parker looks between us as Dante tries his hand at the ring toss.

"I just got a call back at one of the real estate firms I applied for," I say as Troy's eyes flick to mine in surprise. "You passed?"

"Yes. I took it last week."

"That's awesome. Why didn't you tell me?"

"I just..." I trail off. Didn't think you cared? Because it's one of the reasons why you're still pissed at me? Instead of voicing those thoughts, I remain mute as he studies me.

"Can I try again?" Dante asks as Troy and Parker both pull out the cash.

I roll my eyes as Parker smirks with victory, giving Dante a twenty. "Fill her up."

Troy gives her the win turning back to me. "So, you took the job?"

"I applied for it before..." I trail off again as Parker perks up.

"Before what?" She looks between us, and I widen my eyes at Troy in warning. I don't want Parker blowing a gasket in the middle of a carnival about the possibility of us moving. She'll give every temperamental three-year-old in a one-mile radius a run for their money.

"Vacation," I say, saving both our asses. "I can't take a new job and then ask for vacation. We were thinking right after Troy's graduation."

"Oh, yeah?" Parker says. "Where?"

Dante looks up to me. "Yeah, where?"

"I thought I would let Daddy decide."

Troy's eyes, still on me, soften considerably, and I shrug. "I mean, if you have time."

"I'll make time."

Parker's eyes ping pong between us.

"We've never been anywhere," I say, ruffling Dante's hair.

"Stop that, Mommy, I have gel in."

"Not for my lack of trying," Parker gripes indignant. "I've been trying to get us on vacation for years."

"You'll be coming with us," Troy says, without missing a beat.

Parker turns to him. "Ah, will you buy me a pony too, rich athlete?"

"I would like a pony too," Dante says seriously.

"No ponies," he says, his eyes trailing over me in a look that's anything but platonic. I shiver, and Troy's lips lift in recognition before he pulls his son away from the money pit and hauls him on his shoulders. "Where should we go?"

"Disney?" Dante suggests.

"Maybe," Troy says, absently glancing over at me. "When will you know if you're taking the job?"

"Soon," I promise as we exchange another look. I'm seriously considering the move despite the state of our relationship. I don't want either one of them suffering without the other. Also, I don't want the distance away from Troy.

"Oh, it's the blue kind!" Dante says, pointing to a nearby concession stand. "Can I have one?"

"You just had a pushup, bud."

"It's the fair," Parker scolds. "He should have one of *everything*."

"True," Troy says, looking over to me, seeking permission.

"Up to you."

"Come on," Parker insists, forever the doting 'yes' aunt.

A minute later, and after twenty questions, Dante stands on the table as a man guides his arm to catch the sweet fluffy cotton. Dante's smile is breathtaking. He's still somewhere between a baby and a boy, and it both hurts my heart and fills me with pride.

"Hey, man, there's a line back here," a guy grumbles from behind us.

Dante looks over to where the man stands, his smile fading slightly. Troy is the first to speak, turning back.

"You'll get your turn. He's almost got the hang of it. Chill out."

"Seriously? He's not getting the hang of it. Sometime today, guy."

Troy glares back at the man, nothing but warning in his eyes.

"Troy, don't," I whisper.

Parker speaks up. "Are you really going to be that jerk that deprives a kid of a good time?"

The guy scours Parker's appearance, a smug smirk on his face. He looks to be in his mid-twenties and straight off the set of a rerun of *Jersey Shore*. "I see you talking, but all I hear is moo, moo, moo, moo, moo. I mean, are you really one to talk about deprivation? It looks like you haven't deprived yourself of a meal *ever*."

My breath catches in my throat as Troy's fist slams into his face, and he goes down in a wordless heap.

Gasps sound around us as Troy throws a twenty on the table, grabs a bag of ready cotton candy, lifts his son from where he stands motionless, and calmly walks away. Stunned, Parker and I silently follow him out of the carnival and into the parking lot.

"Sorry, bud," Troy says to Dante, securing him into his seat.

"Can you teach me how to punch?" Dante askes, his eyes still wide, his face stained with the blue cotton candy.

Troy sighs. "I shouldn't have done that. You know that, right? It's not okay to hit."

"I'm glad you punched him. He was mean to Auntie Parker."

"That's not what you do," Troy says, clicking his seatbelt. He hands him a bottled water from the cooler he'd made, full of Dante's favorite snacks. Too shocked to speak, I pile into the truck next to him while Parker, just as speechless, climbs in next to Dante.

"I'm sorry we had to leave," Troy offers to everyone in the truck before turning the ignition.

"It's okay, Daddy. You're not the bad guy," Dante says, assuring his father of the truth as I try not to lose my shit sitting next to him.

The ride home is filled with Dante's musings on the situation. Troy patiently answers all of his questions as I reach back, holding out my hand for Parker, who I know, is quietly crying behind me, humiliated.

She squeezes my hand and lets go as I sit helpless, wanting to talk to her, to tell her she's beautiful. To tell her misery loves company, and that bastard saw happiness and confidence, not her weight. It was her light he wanted to dim.

But I can't because I'll only embarrass her further. The tension is palpable as Troy pulls in the driveway and turns back to address Parker after throwing his truck into park. His beautiful blue eyes sincere as he speaks.

"The first thing I thought when I looked at you, aside from fear you would rip me to shreds, was that you have the most beautiful eyes I've ever seen and the face to match. That's the first thing I thought about you, Parker. It's the truth. You're beautiful. Truly. So please don't let that asshole make you feel differently." And with that, he gets out of the truck, collects his son, and makes his way toward the house.

Mouth gaping, I turn back to see Parker smiling through her tears. "And this is the man you didn't want raising your son?" She looks back the way Troy retreated and then turns to me. "You think I have a shot with him?"

Tears gather in my eyes. "I'm so in love with him."

"Well, that definitely puts a kink in my plans."

"Do you think I still have a chance?"

"I saw the way he looked at you today. That's not infatuation, Clarissa."

"Parker, would you—"

"On it."

She hops out of the truck and makes a beeline for Troy, taking Dante from his arms before kissing Troy's cheek and walking Dante to her car. Troy stares on in disbelief turning back to me, his posture deflated, he walks into the house, the screen door slapping behind him. I follow on his heels, as he stands in the living room, his back to me, fuming, no doubt doing a mental count to ten, before he turns to me, arms crossed.

"Was that really necessary? I apologized. I know that wasn't the right thing to—what are you doing?"

I drop my purse and slowly lift my T-shirt before unfastening my bra.

Troy watches on, the confusion in his eyes turning into heated curiosity.

"You once told me it's not a story if you give up." Unsure

if this is seduction or idiocy, I exhale my fears and slowly let one side of my bra fall down my shoulder, then the other, before pulling the tie from my hair.

"Clarissa, don't." I can hear the pain in his voice, his conflict, as I slowly start to unbuckle my jeans. "I'm going out of my mind. I want us back. And I've been a fool, but I can't handle this anymore. I want this story. I want our story, this life with you so much it's killing me. I'm not afraid to bare myself to you. You once said you would give me everything if I gave you all of me. I'm hoping that's still the truth. Because this is all of me. My body, my heart, my life. It's—"

"Clarissa, stop!"

Undeterred by the bite of his rejection, I seize the moment. It's my time to prove I will fight for him, as he has for me. It's time to show him that words aren't a fool's gold when spoken from the right heart.

I love him. I believe in him. I believe in us, and I'll do whatever it takes to make him see what I do, a future, together.

Love requires a little bit of idiocy and a hell of a lot of bravery, and I'll be the fool for him.

"No, Troy, I'm not afraid anymore," I shake my head pushing my jeans over my hips just as he charges me, and a sharp knock sounds on the door behind me.

"UPS!"

"Jesus Christ!" I shriek as I turn to see the man look up from his screen and into the living room with a clear view of my thong clad ass and bare love tassels. Troy's already in front of me, blocking the man's view before slamming the door in his face.

Troy hangs his head, shaking it with a light chuckle. "What are the fucking odds?"

On the other side of the door, we hear, "Troy, uh, hey man, I'm going to need a signature before I can leave this here."

Troy sighs, glancing back at me, cowering on the couch, blanket covering me to my neck before he opens the door and signs for the package. "How you doing, George?"

"Not nearly as good as you."

"Do me a favor, and don't mention this."

George replies breezily. "Never saw a thing."

"Thanks, man."

"Better not keep her waiting," George says with a chuckle as I melt between the couch cushions.

Troy shuts the door and turns to me with a million-dollar smile as I shrink under my throw. "That did not go as planned."

"And when have plans ever been in our favor?"

"We just can't win, huh?"

He kneels down in front of me. "You were saying?"

I cover my face with my hands, too embarrassed to look up. "I'm such an idiot."

"Yes, we are," he says softly before scooping me in his arms. "Mom says we'll grow out of it by the time we're forty."

"Good to know."

I look up at him, his scent hitting me as he slowly carries me toward my bedroom. "I love you. It's that simple and that complicated. I want to fight with you, and make up with you, and go to sleep with you, and wake up with you, and raise kids with you. And *only* with you. I miss you so much." I press my lips against the hollow of his throat. "You think we'll ever get our shit together?"

"Probably not."

"We're hopeless."

"Perfect fucking mess," he says softly, setting me in front of my bed, brushing my hair back from my shoulders.

"Forgive me, Troy. *Please.*"

"I already have."

I slide my panties down my legs and stand completely nude in the bright light of day, my heart beating wildly as I stare at the man who spent months capturing my son's heart and wholly taking mine in the process.

"You've bared yourself to me in a hundred ways since you came into my life. I've fallen for every side of you, good and bad, I want it all. I don't deserve you. I know I don't. But I do respect you, Troy, more than you'll ever know. I've never been more certain about any man. I trust you completely, and I'll earn your trust back. I'll earn you. I'm begging you not to give up. If you still want—"

"One question."

"Anything." I rasp out eagerly.

"What took you so long?" he says gruffly before he crushes our mouths together.

Our tongues duel hungrily as he grips my ass in his hands and squeezes so hard, I gasp into his mouth. He closes our kiss and pulls away, his arms pinning me to him. "I've missed you too, so fucking much," he whispers before pressing a gentle kiss to my lips, "you're all I see, all I can feel. I tried so hard to get over you, but I couldn't, I never will. I'll fight with you, I'll make up with you, go to sleep and wake up with you, Dr. Seuss," he chuckles, as my cheeks heat, my tears spilling over, "I'll give you five babies," he grunts, as I pull at his shorts before gripping his thick dick in my hands.

"Two," I protest.

"Three."

"Negotiations are now open," he beams down at me.

"You were hard-earned and well-worth it, I wanted to earn this, to earn you." He slides his hands up my sides, caressing me, covering me with his muscular touch. "But I needed you in the same place. We had to be in the same place."

I press my forehead to his and nod. "I love you."

"God, I must have dreamed this a thousand times," he murmurs, taking bites of my neck, my chest, soothing the sting with his lips before bringing his hungry mouth back to mine.

I pump him in my hand as he kisses me with a surety we both share.

Some things have to be learned over time, but the only thing I know for sure is, this man and I belong together. All I can do is be thankful at this point for every trial that led us back to each other. Though our timing was horribly off, fate made us so in the form of a little boy, the spitting image of his father, and our guiding light.

The minute my back touches the mattress, he uses the movement to thrust against me, our collective gasps filling the room. Eyes locked, he rears back, before lining himself up and slowly pushing inside me. I grip his shoulders, widening my legs as he fills me slowly, inch by inch.

"Fucking worth it," he murmurs. "Every fight, every struggle, the wait, the pain, the ache, loving you, needing you, wanting you, missing you—all of it—worth it to get us to this point, right here."

Rearing back, he keeps us connected, eyes and lips, before filling me fully. My back bows off the mattress as he draws back, and thrusts in again so deep he steals my breath. We're somewhere between fucking and making love, and all I can do is moan out his name.

His eyes devour me, leaving nothing untouched until he again pulls back, his stare fixed on where we connect.

We've deprived ourselves of each other for so long, in more ways than one, and this is an act of completion on the same level. There's no turning back. I don't want to know what life is like without Troy Jenner, ever again.

"Troy," I whimper as he pins my hands and thrusts into me, the headboard thumping against the wall.

"Look at us," he growls as he drives in again. I revel in the feel, in the filthy and beautiful sight of us connecting. It's then we go feral, tongues tasting, hands exploring, skin slapping, slick while he fucks me wildly, and I match his thrusts. After a few deep drives, he pulls back and places one hand on my stomach the other beneath my ass and flips me so easily a giggle comes out of me, until he steals it away by driving in deep as I lay on my stomach. He pins me to the mattress, his hands on my hips as he rolls into me, so deep all I can do is cry out his name.

"Goddamn," he grunts out as I bask in the feel of his weight on my back, soaking up each second beneath him. Lips latched to my neck, he buries himself, thrusting up as my orgasm hits me like a tidal wave. I come so hard, my voice fails me mid-cry as the shudders run through me.

"Fuck, baby, I'm going to lose it," he draws out, turning me back over, cupping my heaving chest. "Beautiful," he says watching my reaction to him before lifting my leg to his hip and pushing back in, tilting his pelvis for precision. "This time I watch you come," he beckons, pumping in and out, in and out, massaging my breasts, tweaking my nipples, covering my stomach in a warm caress. His eyes convey so much as he keeps his thrusts deep, pinpointing where I need him before licking the pad of his finger and pressing it against my clit. I crest on the verge as he rolls into his fucking before I detonate. Bliss ripples through me as my toes curl. His eyes flare when he feels me tightening around him again, coming apart.

His thrusts pick up until he empties inside me, his body convulsing as he exhales a loud groan. I circle his neck with my arm, stroking the sweaty hair at his temple as we both try and catch our breath.

"Worth it," I murmur as he caresses my shoulder with his thumb.

"So worth it," he whispers back. "You and Dante, you've redefined my dreams. My everything is yours."

I smile so wide, I know I'll feel it tomorrow, and a new and brilliant smile lifts his lips. "Are we going to tell Dante?" He pulls back to weigh my expression. "That we're together?"

"Yes."

Relief covers him, and he smiles before resuming his position on my chest. "Thank you." His lips do the rest of his thanking as he positions himself between my thighs.

"Already?"

He rakes his bottom lip. "How much time do we have left?"

"Forever?"

"I can work with that," he says, positioning himself and slowly pushing into me while we both watch.

Four hours later...

I scramble toward the headboard until I'm dragged to the end of the bed by my ankles. I'm covered in sweat from head to foot even after two showers. I've never in my life been so exhausted.

"Troy, I can't. I *cannot* possibly have more sex. Please," I giggle as he flips me to face him. "I can no longer negotiate."

"Then I win by default. Shortest argument we've ever had. And now, finally," he says, giving me a devilish grin, "we get to have *make up* sex."

Two hours later...

"No. No. I beg of you. Please, Troy. Please. I love you, but I can't, Oh, God!"

One hour later...

"Troy, please, your...sex drive is... inhuman. Haven't...ah... you had...right enou—right there, right fucking there!"

Thirty minutes later...

His voice rumbles at my neck. "Baby, you can't fake sleep, you're ticklish."

"S-s-s-stahp. That better be your elbow. Oh, God. How? How, how, *how* are you hard *again*? How?"

One week later...

"To announce the New York Giants' selection, two-time bowl winner Roy Hall."

Parker and I sit on the couch, our hearts beating in our throats as Roy walks toward the stage.

"Thank you. For the sixty-ninth selection in the 2019

NFL Draft, The New York Giants select Troy Jenner, wide receiver, Texas Grand University."

Parker and I jump from the couch, screaming bloody murder as the camera pans in on Troy, who's already hugging Pamela, tears shining in both their eyes while Dante jumps at their sides, his fists held high in the air. Troy whispers to Pam, who's bawling, before he scoops Dante up in his arms. I hated that I couldn't attend, but I have a school year to finish. I also have a house to pack and very little time to do it. Not to mention Parker is leaving tomorrow for two months. I need to get in as much time with her as I can because we're family and both our lives are about to change, drastically.

Troy whispers into Dante's ear, and I can see him mouth, "Love you, Mommy!" When Troy winks at the camera and taps his watch, I know it's for me. He's telling me it's time for us. Once we've fulfilled our obligations in Texas, our future begins. It's amazing what can happen in a year, in a day, in a moment. And this moment helped to map our future.

We had plans either way, because…I'm a planner. And no matter what happened with the draft, we had backup. But as long as we were together, it didn't matter which plan we followed because I stayed confident knowing we would be fine either way. Troy gave me that. That peace of mind. It's a gift that I don't think he'll ever fully understand.

All our plans consisted of starting our family, it was the *where* that was up in the air. And the family addition negotiations are still ongoing. *Nightly.*

Parker is still blubbering as the draft coverage goes to commercial. "God, that was awesome."

"Yeah," I run my fingers underneath my eyes and nod. "He did it."

"He so did it," she beams.

I toss a couch pillow at her. "Lady, from the minute you met him you were team Troy, even when you tried to pull that tough guy bullshit."

"Fine, I admit I love him, *now*. He gives me hope." She sighs. "And I can't believe you're moving to New York. Shit," her voice cracks and then she's crying again as I pull her to me.

"How often do you fly through La Guardia?"

"Like every three weeks."

"So, I'll see you *every* month."

"Yes." She nods into my shoulder.

"And I'll have your room ready."

"Okay."

"No more crying. I, for one, am done crying in 2019."

"Okay."

"Damn it, Parker, stop it," I say, getting misty-eyed as the doorbell rings.

It's UPS, and I can't for the life of me meet the eyes of the delivery man. I sign for the package, opening it to pull out a Giant's jersey. I hold it up and inhale. Troy's doused it with his cologne.

"Oh, my God," Parker says, her eyes tearing up. "He had that delivered at the exact right moment."

"Well, to quote my son, 'duh.' He is their employee. Sweet, isn't it?"

Parker nods, tears still running down her face as I sniff the jersey.

"I love this cologne. I need to find out the name of it. I would bathe in it."

"That's all you have to say?"

"Uh, I like the jersey?"

"Uh huh, and?"

"Go, Giants?" I raise my fist for a little extra enthusiasm.

"Babe," Parker swallows. "Look again."

I turn the Jersey back and forth and shake my head. "What?! Out with it already!"

"One more time," Parker insists, her eyes as wide as her smile.

I turn the jersey over again when it finally hits me.

MRS. JENNER

epilogue

"**D**AD! SOMEONE'S AT THE DOOR!" I HEAR DANTE CALL as I sink into my freshly-filled tub.

"Then go get it, son!"

"I'm filming!"

"Where's your mom?"

I roll my eyes. "I'm in the tub! Can you two stop yelling and get the door?"

"Dad!"

"Get the door, Dante! I've got Toby with me."

I tense up. "You don't know who it is, don't send him to the door!"

"I'm setting up the intercom, so we don't sound like the damned Costanzas anymore!"

"Who's the Costanzas?" Dante asks.

"Google it."

"I'm filming!"

"Jesus," I say, grabbing my towel. "Shut up, shut up, you two or you're going to wake the baby. I've got it!"

I can hear the nervousness in my husband's voice when he hears the irritation in mine. "I've got it, baby. Stay in the tub."

"I've got it, Mom!"

I sigh, covered in suds with one foot out of the tub. "Somebody, please just get the door!"

And that's when Zoe, our three-month-old, decides to speak up and our one-year-old joins in, doing his own impression of a Costanza.

"I used my key!" Parker calls out from the entryway. "Merry Christmas, Jenners!"

"Mom," Dante calls, "You woke Zoe up."

"This is ridiculous. You sure this is what you want?" Troy says behind the door.

"Hell, yes, stop whining and just get your sexy ass in here."

"This probably isn't safe. Where did you come up with this twisted fantasy?"

"Uh, nowhere in particular."

"You're a sick woman. This is your Christmas present?"

"Yes. Troy, the candles are lit. The sex police are asleep, and Auntie Parker is on watch. Your mom and Luis will be here in seven hours. Need I say more?"

"I'm coming."

"What's taking so long?"

"I feel like an idiot."

"It'll pay off. I assure you."

"Baby, I've done some shit in my days, but this…"

"Days I don't need to know about."

He pauses behind the door. "Good point. Let's never have that talk."

"Stop stalling and get your butt out here."

"Is this about the new gardener? Is he putting the moves on you? Cause I'll kick his ass."

"He's like…sixty years old."

"You and I know age ain't nothing but a number." Just as he says it, the bathroom door bursts open, and my man stands at the threshold wearing nothing but a leaf blower, his fists on his hips, his head cocked to the side.

Laughter bursts from me as he points the hose in my direction. "I knew it. This is payback for something."

"Not at all," I manage to say as he stalks toward me. I lift my hand to stop him and circle my pointer in demand. He narrows his eyes but slowly turns, giving me full view of his perfect ass before turning back to give me the better view.

"I really would have preferred a cape."

"No, this is much better, even better than my fantasies."

"Yeah? You like this, *weirdo*?" He turns again as I nod repeatedly. "This is what turns my wife on?" I nod and nod as he models my present. Yes, I bought a leaf blower and had my husband open it in front of my children and best friend—the only other person who would understand my fantasy. Sue me.

"So, this really is more for you than me, huh?" He's smiling, and it steals my breath. He would do anything for me, even wear a power tool buck naked on Christmas Eve.

"I love you so much," I murmur before lifting on all fours, moving toward him on the prowl. He meets me on the edge of the bed and grips my face in his hands.

"I don't think I'll ever fully understand you, and I love it."

"Weirdo means I'll never be boring, right?"

"Never that," he murmurs as I drink him in. He's the picture of innocence as he gazes down at me curiously while completely vulnerable, just the way I like him. My mouth waters as he hardens due to my needy stare. For the last week, I've put him through the wringer, making him service me at my every whim. I've gotten little complaint, until tonight.

"You're insatiable and getting scarier. I don't even know what to think," he says, as I grip his delicious length in my hand.

"Don't think, baby, just let me do this."

I wrap my lips around him and hear a low groan from above before I take him to the back of my throat. Enthusiastically, I bob, digging my nails into his ass, pulling him closer to swallow the whole of him.

"Fuck, if you'll suck me like this, I'll strap a fucking dishwasher on my back."

I giggle around his cock, and it jumps in my mouth.

"Shiiiitttt," he manages to get out through his clenched jaw as I suck him like he's my last supper.

"Damn, baby," he says, his eyes glittering down on me as I work him with my mouth. "I'm," bob, "making," suck, "a list," lick, "right now of all the power tools I can g-g-get on my back. The list is long," he grits out. "Take your time down there."

"I want you so bad right now," I murmur to him through my mouthful. He looks down at me with so much love, so much adoration, I feel complete. Blissfully, I suck him, acting out my fantasy from years ago. I love that I married the man I fantasize about. I love that he humors all my childish whims, but most of all, I love the way he looks at me the same way he did the crazy year we fell in love. Thinks of me the same, treats me the same, touches me the same. He never lied to me again after the night we met and has yet to break a single promise. And my love for him has only grown.

There's nothing between us now but our messy love, trust, and respect, along with the three little reminders that we made the right decision with each other.

We could have so easily given up. At one point, we had every reason to. We did everything backward and went through the hard years to get to the honeymoon.

We grew up together. And that's a feat, in and of itself.

We could be living completely different lives if we hadn't woken up, and that would have been the real tragedy. And what a honeymoon it's been.

"Clarissa," he grunts, running his fingers through my hair, his gentle caress spurring me on, "baby, I need to touch you."

"Just a few more minutes," I murmur gazing up at him while pumping him in my hand.

"No way," he says, his eyes pooling with desire while I alternate my licks between his shaft and crown. "I'm not going to last long if you keep that up."

"I'm so…mmmm," I mumble around him before letting him go with a pop. "I haven't been this horny since I got pregnant with Zoe."

All activity ceases, especially mine, as I try and recall my last period, and Troy's eyes widen.

"No," I whisper yell, "no way. I'm on the pill *and* the foam, *and* I've been putting in the diaphragm."

"You're pregnant," he murmurs, running a hand along my jaw, his eyes welling with emotion before he shakes his head with a chuckle. "Birth control doesn't exist for us."

"No," I say, shaking my head. "Negotiations closed. Please, no."

"Yes."

"But I just lost a little of the baby weight! I can't do that again so soon!"

"Baby," he says, letting the power tool off his back and pulling me to him.

"No, no!" I say, backing away from him as he comes toward me, his smile beaming.

"Yes. Yes!"

"Troy," I push at his chest, furious with myself, furious

with him. No matter what we do, what measures we take, we can't seem to stop procreating. "Wait…" I look up and nod. "I just had my period."

"No, you didn't."

"I'm not pregnant," I say defiantly. "So, you can wipe that damned smile off your face!"

He tugs at my ankles, drawing me to the end of the bed and climbs on top of me, pinning my wrists next to my face. All I see in his eyes is love and awe. "Merry Christmas to me. I fucking love you so much."

"Troy," I whine weakly as he kisses me from head to toe, the smile never leaving his eyes. "It's too soon."

"It's not."

"I'm like a Gremlin, one drop of your sperm, and I multiply, babies flying out everywhere."

"I'll make it up to you," he promises.

"How, with another baby? I just had another baby three months ago!"

"And she's a perfect little temperamental redhead, just like her mother." He leans in, eyes sparkling, and kisses me deeply, his tongue making it impossible to protest, my body sighing in welcome as I open for him. It's useless, I'm entirely defenseless against my husband's charms and super penis.

Utterly soaked and ready, he watches my reaction as he presses into me.

I moan when he hits my spot, the length of his cock setting me off as he rolls his hips and hits me, *there*, again and again until I throw my head back convulsing, praising his name. It's sheer bliss, ecstasy, and he delivers every single time. *Every. Single. Time.*

"I love you," I say, sinking into his rhythm as I wrap around him, and he sinks in deeper, in our perfect fit. He takes his time, setting me off repeatedly before he picks up the pace. Hearts pounding, I trace the planes of his chest, his arms, meeting his hips with the buck of mine, watching his eyes flare. His jaw goes slack before he pours himself into me. It's when he's resting on my chest that I murmur words that I know to be true.

"You're the best thing that's ever happened to me," I say softly, stroking the damp hair on his forehead. "You once told me you thought you were the worst, but it's simply not true. I'll take any baby you give me, Troy Jenner, because of the man you are."

I caress his biceps while he searches my face.

"I mean it. You are the best man I've ever known."

Voice clogged with emotion, his eyes shine. "Only because you made me this way. You made damned sure I deserved you."

"Thank you for not giving up."

"Never, Mrs. Jenner."

One hour later…

I lightly rake my nails down my husband's chest as he sleeps next to me flipping another page on my kindle. The house is completely silent as snow falls outside our bedroom window. Troy has gifted us a house I could only dream of, and every single day, I'm thankful for the chance we took on each other. For his persistence in winning me, for the faith he kept for the both of us. No longer a struggling single mother but a wife, a professor, a realtor and part of a bigger picture I never saw for myself. Mostly due to the belief and unrelenting love of the man sleeping next to me. Feeling sentimental in remembrance of our first white Christmas, I close my book and stare down at Troy. Just as I'm reaching for the light to settle in and cuddle up with my better half, Troy jackknives in the bed, scaring the hell out of me. I jump back as his head turns my way, Exorcist-style, while ice-blue flames shoot from his eyes.

"You saw me assed out that day and didn't say a word."

GrandGirl#08 Reviewer Ranking 1,015

Metropolis-Fur Shag Rug-Shag Away!

Here I am on Christmas Eve, listening to my best friend and her god-shaped husband bang it out a few doors down, and I'm not bitter. Not at all. In fact, I'm happy for them, because no doubt I'm going to get another niece or nephew to spoil because birth control for them is pointless. But that's not why I'm no longer bitter. You see, I've finally met someone, and while he's not the sophisticated millionaire with a British accent and mile-long dong I always hoped for, he's perfect for _me_. He's a simple working man, an Uber driver, and the greatest guy a girl could ask for. He sees past the superficial; is kind, intelligent, considerate, well-spoken, and surprisingly an animal in the sack—or shall I say _rug_—which is why I'm writing this review. I have to say, this rug served its purpose, and despite the mild burn, I've ordered two more because one can never be sure when and where the mood will strike. I hate to say it, guys, but those

looking for my reviews might be hard-pressed to find them in the future, because my schedule is looking pretty busy. It's all thanks to a flat tire and the owner of the chariot that saved this damsel from another year of lonely rants. Merry Christmas, internet void. Here's hoping you find your own Dave.

Konnichiwa!

Before you go:
Download *The Underdog Mom's cookbook* here for FREE with newsletter signup
dl.bookfunnel.com/k62frfdvs7

Listen to *The Guy on the Left* playlist on Spotify-

THE END

Read Lance's story *The Guy in the Middle*, now

about the author

USA Today bestselling author and Texas native, Kate Stewart, lives in North Carolina with her husband, Nick. Nestled within the Blue Ridge Mountains, Kate pens messy, sexy, angst-filled contemporary romance, as well as romantic comedy and erotic suspense.

Kate's title, *Drive*, was named one of the best romances of 2017 by The New York Daily News and Huffington Post. *Drive* was also a finalist in the Goodreads Choice awards for best contemporary romance of 2017. The Ravenhood Trilogy, consisting of *Flock, Exodus,* and *The Finish Line*, has become an international bestseller and reader favorite. Her holiday release, *The Plight Before Christmas*, ranked #6 on Amazon's Top 100. Kate's works have been featured in *USA TODAY, BuzzFeed, The New York Daily News, Huffington Post* and translated into a dozen languages.

Kate is a lover of all things '80s and '90s, especially John Hughes films and rap. She dabbles a little in photography, can knit a simple stitch scarf for necessity, and on occasion, does very well at whiskey.

Other titles available now by Kate

Romantic Suspense

The Ravenhood Series
Flock
Exodus
The Finish Line

Lust & Lies Series
Sexual Awakenings
Excess
Predator and Prey
The Lust & Lies Box set: Sexual Awakenings, Excess, Predator and Prey

Contemporary Romance

In Reading Order

Room 212
Never Me (Companion to Room 212 and The Reluctant Romantic Series)
The Reluctant Romantics Series
The Fall
The Mind
The Heart
The Reluctant Romantics Box Set: The Fall, The Heart, The Mind
Loving the White Liar

The Bittersweet Symphony
Drive
Reverse

The Real
Someone Else's Ocean
Heartbreak Warfare
Method

Romantic Dramedy

Balls in Play Series
Anything but Minor
Major Love
Sweeping the Series Novella
Balls in play Box Set: Anything but Minor, Major Love, Sweeping the Series, The Golden Sombrero

The Underdogs Series
The Guy on the Right
The Guy on the Left
The Guy in the Middle
The Underdogs Box Set: The Guy on The Right, The Guy on the Left, The Guy in the Middle

The Plight Before Christmas

Let's stay in touch!

Email
authorkatestewart@gmail.com

Facebook
www.facebook.com/authorkatestewart

Website
www.katestewartwrites.com

Instagram
www.instagram.com/authorkatestewart/?hl=en

Book Group
www.facebook.com/groups/793483714004942

Spotify
open.spotify.com/user/authorkatestewart

Sign up for the newsletter now and get a free
eBook from Kate's Library!

Newsletter signup
www.katestewartwrites.com/contact-me.html

thank you

I have many to thank, but first, a little story. Our family has this cookbook, which happens to be my most prized possession. I know we're not supposed to love THINGS, but this isn't just a thing, this is a history. Between the pages of this book is a holiday, or a birthday, in essence, it's a combination of memories. Like most families, mine always centered around the kitchen, the hub of our get-togethers. And like many others, this cookbook is full of recipes handed down from one generation to the next.

We've always taken great care to keep our family recipes a secret, but with the go ahead of my stepmother, the Matriarch of the family, I was allowed to share some of ours with you.

Not all of these we can take credit for. I'm sure some of us picked these up from others along the way with varied ingredients in one way or another to suit our tastes, but this collection belongs to the Scotts, so thank you, Alta Scott, for being a rock, a best friend, and for the gift of your spatula and mother's love. I will treasure this book as I treasure our relationship, always.

I need to thank my team, Autumn, Donna, Bex, Christy, and Grey. Without you, I would not have made it through this or any other book. But this one was especially hard, and I could not have done it without your dedication, friendship, and support. Grey, thank you so much for that night, and every day after. You'll never know what that meant to me. Donna, I tell you every day, but DAMN, you are the most incredible friend, patience and endurance personified. Christy, you uplift me so often, just by being yourself. I adore you. Autumn, what a friendship we have. Big or small, you're the problem solver, a guiding light, and so dear to me. Thank you for all you do. Bex-a-million, you're worth a trillion. Thank you for laughing when it's not funny, so I can laugh with you. Because of you, I look a lot more together and you're the reason and glue. I'm so proud to know and love every single one of you.

Thank you to my beta team-Christy, Kathy, Rhonda, Maria, Maiween, Stacy, and Alta. Thank you for making the process bearable, for showing up, for being honest, and being friends. This job is impossible without you.

Thank you to my proofers-Joy, Marissa, and Bethany, for taking on such a tremendous task last minute and coming through. You are the bees knees—pun intended, Bethany. Wink emoji.

Thank you to my ASSKICKING group, for your endless friendship and support. I can't do this job without you.

A huge thank you to my sisters, Kristan and Angela, who make up a huge part of my backbone and keep me grounded when this job makes me crazy.

Thank you to all my author homies who continue to be a huge support and for this book especially—Jewel E. Ann, Emma Scott, and Kennedy Ryan who set down their coffee and took the time to just listen. Love y'all.

Thank you to my cover designer, Amy Queau, who continues to show up and kick ass, sometimes mine, while staying a dear friend.

Thank you, Stacey Ryan Blake of Champagne Formats, for being you, because you, my friend, are amazing.

Thank you to my husband, Nick, who continues to put socks on my feet and coffee in my hands when I'm barely aware of my own existence. In the words of the great Salt-N-Pepa "Whatta man, whatta man, whatta man, whatta mighty good man!"

Last, but not least, thank you, dear reader for continuing to support my dream by reading my love stories. I've got much more to come. And I'm so very thankful for every word/step you take on this journey with me.

XO,
Kate

Made in United States
Orlando, FL
23 September 2024

51844708R00235